Bumper Book of

Adventure Stories

Bumper Book of

Adventure Stories

The Secret of Moon Castle
The Treasure Hunters
Smuggler Ben

This edition produced exclusively for Bookmart by
Armada, an imprint of HarperCollins Children's Books,
part of HarperCollins Publishers Ltd 1990

The Enid Blyton signature is a trademark of Darrell
Waters Ltd

All rights reserved

Printed and bound in Great Britain by HarperCollins
Manufacturing Ltd, Glasgow

Contents

The Secret of Moon Castle

The Secret of Moon Castle was first published
in a single volume in the U.K. in hardback in 1953 by
Basil Blackwell Ltd, and in paperback in 1965 in
Armada.

Copyright © Enid Blyton 1953

Home From School

Two girls were standing at their front gate one sunny afternoon in July.

"The car ought to be here by now," said Nora. "I hope it hasn't had a puncture or anything. I'm longing to see Mike – and Jack too, of course."

"So am I," said Peggy, her sister. "I wonder if Paul will be with them? Is he going to spend his holidays with us – or go back to Baronia? I wonder."

Paul was the little Prince of Baronia, a great friend of Nora, Peggy, Mike and Jack. He went to the same school as the boys, and had had plenty of adventures with them.

"I expect he'll spend a few days with us first," said Nora, swinging on the gate. "He usually does, doesn't he? Then he'll have to go back to Baronia to see his parents – and all his many brothers and sisters!"

"It's a silly idea, our school breaking up two whole days before the boys'," said Peggy. "We go back earlier too – that's even more of a nuisance!"

"Here's a car – and it's bringing the boys!" said Nora, suddenly. "They've come in Paul's car – the big blue and silver one. I wonder if Ranni is driving it?"

Ranni was Paul's man, who had vowed to look after Paul from the moment when he was put into his arms on the day he was born. He was devoted to the little Prince, and had shared many adventures with him. And now here he was, driving the great Baronian blue and silver car, bringing the three boys home in state!

The girls swung the big gates open as the car came near. They yelled as the car swept in. "Mike! Jack! Paul! Hurrah! Welcome back!"

The car stopped with a squeal of brakes, and Ranni, who was at the wheel, smiled at them through his fiery red beard. Three heads were poked out of the nearest window.

"Hallo, girls! Jump in. We thought you'd be looking for us!" called Mike. The door was swung open, and the girls squeezed in at the back with the three boys making room for them.

Nora gave Mike a hug. He was her twin, and the two were very fond of each other. Except that Nora was smaller than Mike, they were very much alike, with black, curly hair and bright, merry eyes. Golden-haired Peggy was a year older, but Mike was as tall as she was.

"Hallo!" said Jack, giving each of the girls a friendly punch. "What do you mean by breaking up sooner than we did!"

Jack was not their brother. He had no parents, and the Arnolds had adopted him as a big brother for Mike, Nora and Peggy. He thought the world of them all, and grinned around happily, his blue eyes shining in his brown face.

Prince Paul never punched the girls in the friendly way that the other boys did. Baronian manners did not allow that! He bowed politely to each of the girls, smiling happily – but they hadn't the beautiful manners of Baronia, and fell on him like a couple of puppies.

"Is he still ticklish? Yes, he is! Paul, are you going to stay with us for the holidays – or just for a few days – or what?"

"Stop tickling me," said Paul, trying to push them off. "Hey, Ranni, Ranni! Stop the car and turn them out!"

The car swept up to the front door, and Ranni leapt out, grinning. He went to the back to get the school trunks piled there on top of one another.

The door flew open and Mrs Arnold stood there smiling. "Welcome back, boys!" she said. Mike ran to hug his mother. "We're home!" he shouted. "Good old home!"

Jack kissed Mrs Arnold, and then Paul followed his usual custom, bent over her hand with a deep bow, and kissed it politely. The others used to laugh at Paul's grand manners, but they had got so used to them by now that they didn't really notice them.

"Come along in," said Mrs Arnold. "We'd better get out of Ranni's way. He's bringing the trunks in. Ranni, how *can* you manage two trunks at once!"

Ranni grinned. He was big, and enormously strong. Two trunks were nothing to him! He went up the stairs with them easily.

"Mother! What a lovely smell!" said Mike, sniffing. "Buttered toast – and hot scones!"

"Quite right," said his mother. "You've probably forgotten that you asked me to have them for tea as soon as you got home these holidays – though why you took it into your head to ask for such things on a hot July day I don't know."

Jack put his head in at the dining-room door. Tea was already laid there. "My word!" he said. "Home-made éclairs too – and the biggest chocolate sponge sandwich I ever saw! When do we have tea?"

"As soon as you've washed your hands," said Mrs Arnold. "I'll get the toast and scones brought in now, so don't be long."

They weren't long. All five of them tore upstairs, laughing and shouting, glad to be together again. Prince Paul was pleased too – he loved this English family, with its friendliness and generosity.

When they came down, someone else was with Mrs Arnold. The three boys smiled at the small, grey-eyed woman sitting beside Mrs Arnold.

"Dimmy!" they said, and went to shake hands. Paul, as usual, bowed from his waist, and then unexpectedly gave the little woman a hug.

Dimmy's real name was Miss Dimity, and she often came to help Mrs Arnold, especially when the children were home. They all liked her, and teased her – and although she

11

looked so gentle and timid, she could be very firm indeed, as they had found out many a time.

"Good old Dimmy!" said Mike, and looked as if he was going to try to lift her up. She pushed him off.

"No, no, Mike – I know you're almost as big as I am now – but I'm really not going to be tossed about like a bag of potatoes! Sit down before the toast gets cold."

For a little while there was silence as the five children helped themselves from the full plates on the table. Paul gave a loud sigh.

"Now this is what I call *real* food – almost as good as Baronia. Mrs Arnold, I have been half-starved all the term!"

"Don't you believe it!" said Jack. "You should just see the whopping great parcels he gets from Baronia every week!"

"I can guess what they are like,' said Mrs Arnold. "Paul's mother often sends me one too – full of the most delicious things. I had a letter from the Queen, your mother, this morning, Paul. She sends you her love and is looking forward to seeing you."

"Oh – is Paul going to Baronia very soon?" asked Nora, in a disappointed voice. "Peggy and I haven't seen him for a whole term. Can't he stay with us for a bit?"

"Well, I have rather a surprise for you," said her mother, smiling round. "Paul's father and mother have an idea that they would like to come over here for a month or two, and get to know us all better. They want to bring two of Paul's brothers, as well, so that they may know a little of England before they come over here to school."

"Oh *Mother*! How super!" cried Peggy. "But there won't be room here for the King and Queen and servants – they're sure to bring servants, aren't they, Paul? They never travel anywhere without heaps of guards and menservants and maids. Surely they're not coming *here*?"

"No, dear – of course not," said her mother. "Don't be

12

silly! There's hardly room for you five to spread yourselves in the holidays. No – Paul's father wants us to look out for a really big place, where he can bring his wife, two boys, and about twenty servants."

"Gosh!" said Mike. "He'll want a castle!"

"That's just what he suggests," said Mrs Arnold, handing a plate of very buttery scones round.

"I say! Does he really?" said Nora. "Paul, did you know about this?"

Paul shook his dark head. His mouth was too full to speak! His eyes shone, and he tried to swallow down his mouthful too quickly, and began to choke.

There was a lot of banging on the back at this, and Paul went purple in the face.

"Do leave him alone," said Mrs Arnold. "You're making him much worse. Drink some tea, Paul."

"A castle! I say – what fun to ring up the estate agents, and say, 'Please will you send me particulars of a dozen or so castles'," said Mike.

"Mother, do they know what castle they're going to yet?" asked Nora. "Is it anywhere near here? Can we go and see it?"

"Idiot! You know there's no castle near here," said Mike.

"Let Mother answer my questions," said Nora. "Mother, what castle are they going to?"

"My dear child, I told you I only got the letter this morning," said her mother. "Paul's mother has only just thought of the idea. She has asked me to find out what I can, and perhaps go and see over any suitable place – not that I would know in the least whether a castle would be suitable to live in or not!"

"Well, I suppose they only want to rent one, not buy one," said Mike. "You'd better take Paul with you, Mother, and let him poke round a few old castles. He'll know what his mother will fancy! Anyone want this last scone? If so, say the word."

Nobody did, so Mike took it. Everyone began to talk

13

excitedly about the news Mrs Arnold had just given. Paul, recovered from his choking fit, talked more loudly than anyone. He was really thrilled.

"You will all be able to come and stay with me," he announced. "We will share this castle together. You shall know my two brothers. You shall . . ."

"Your mother may not want us," said Mike.

"She certainly won't want you for very long," said Mrs Arnold, with a smile. "A noisy crowd like you! Actually, she says in her letter that she hopes we will *all* go and stay for a little while, so it should be great fun."

"If only we can find a really *good* castle!" said Nora.

"What do you mean – a *good* castle?" said Mike. "You don't suppose we're going to look for half-ruined ones, do you? Mother, have you heard of any yet?"

"Mike – I only got the letter *today*," said his mother. "Now, finish your tea for goodness sake. We'll have any amount of castles to see by next week."

"Castle-hunting – I shall like that!" said Jack. "I wonder which we'll choose – a really exciting one, I hope!"

Choosing A Castle

The next few days were very exciting in more ways than one. For one thing it was great fun to be at home again – no lessons – no bells clanging – no prep in the evenings. For another thing it was most exciting to read through the particulars of various castles that could be rented.

There were not very many. Mrs Arnold looked through the papers that came, and quickly decided which offers were no good. Big mansions were offered as well, and it really seemed to Mrs Arnold that it might almost be better to take one of those for Paul's family. The castles seemed in such remote places, or had been empty for some time, with just a caretaker in.

"Oh *no*, Mother – do let's have a castle," said Mike. "A big house wouldn't be nearly such fun."

"I'm not thinking about how much fun I can provide for you children," said his mother. "I'm thinking about the difficulties Paul's mother will have, in a big, bare castle, with very old-fashioned ways of lighting and heating."

"But Baronia isn't modern, either," said Mike. "Paul's own castle hasn't got a lot of things that a big hotel in England would have, for instance. Mother, do find a castle. It sounds so much more exciting than a big house."

"Look through these," said his mother. "Take the papers with you, and pore over them with the others. They are all ones I think are no good. You will see what I mean when you read through the particulars."

Mike carried away the papers, feeling rather thrilled. What fun to try to choose a castle. He called the other four, and they took the papers out into the garden.

"Here you are – have one or two each," said Mike. "We'll all read through them, and see what we think. Mother's turned all these down."

They read solemnly through the particulars. "Castle and fifty thousand acres," said Jack. "Whew! Do people rent fifty thousand acres as well? Oh – *this* castle's no good. It's only got twelve rooms furnished – goodness knows how many your parents will want, Paul. It must be maddening to be a King and Queen and have to have such enormous places to live in."

"I like our castle in Baronia," said Paul. "But I would rather be an ordinary boy and live the life you do, Jack."

"I don't wonder Mother turned these down," said Mike, putting down his papers. "They're no good at all. Either the owners want to live in one wing of the castle too – or they want Paul's people to rent it for a whole year – or the place

15

isn't furnished. It's a lot more difficult than I thought it would be, to get a castle for a month or two!"

"There's one here," said Peggy, suddenly. "It sounds rather thrilling. I don't quite know why Mother turned it down. Listen."

The others turned to her. They were all lying on the grass, the papers spread around them. Peggy told them about the particulars she held in her hand.

"It's called Moon Castle," she said. "That's a lovely name, isn't it? Moon Castle! And it's big, but not too big – just about right for Paul's family. It's got caretakers in, so it should be in fairly good order. It can be had immediately, because the owners don't live in it. It's high on a hill with 'wonderful panoramic views over a countryside of moorland, wood and waterways'."

"It sounds good," said Mike, sitting up. "Go on – anything else?"

"It's very old," said Peggy. "It says here, 'a castle full of myth and legend', whatever that means. And it says, 'What stories its old walls could tell – tales of violence and mystery, hate and greed'. Goodness, it's just as well that old walls don't suddenly begin to talk, if that's the kind of thing they say!"

"It really does sound rather good," said Nora. "Why did Mother turn it down, I wonder?"

"There she is!" said Mike, as his mother came out into the garden, with a basket and a pair of scissors for picking flowers. "Mother! Hey, Mother! Why did you turn down Moon Castle? It sounds super."

"Moon Castle? Well, really because it sounds so very cut off from everywhere," said Mrs Arnold. "It isn't near any town – and the only village anywhere near is an old ruined one which has the queer name of Moon. I suppose that's how the castle got its name."

"But would it matter, being cut off from everywhere?" asked Peggy.

"It's called Moon Castle."

17

"Yes, I think so," said her mother. "For a big household such as Paul's mother would bring, you would need good shops at least *fairly* near – but the nearest shops are about twenty miles away, it seems to me. It sounded such a lonely, desolate place – it really gave me the creeps!"

"Oh *Mother*! But that's the sort of castle we'd all love," said Nora. "And Paul's mother would bring plenty of cars –wouldn't she, Paul? So that shopping would be easy."

"Well – not *plenty*," said Paul, laughing. "But enough."

"Another drawback is that there wouldn't be any people to make friends with," said Mrs Arnold. "No neighbours, for instance. What the poor, wretched caretakers do with themselves I really cannot imagine!"

"They probably get in a month's stores at once!" said Jack. He turned to the others, "I say, do you remember when we ran away to the Secret Island – where there were no shops – no neighbours except the rabbits and the birds – and everything was lonely and desolate? But what a wonderful time we had!"

"Yes. We did," agreed the others. Mike turned to his mother. "Mother, do let's see what this Moon Castle is really like. Can't we just go and *see* it? Paul, what do *you* think? Would your mother mind its being so far from everywhere – and having 'old walls that could tell tales of mystery and violence' and all the rest of it?"

Paul laughed. "No. Mother wouldn't mind a bit. I expect the walls of our own castle at home are far older than the walls of Moon Castle – and could tell just as fiercesome tales. Mrs Arnold, is the castle too far away for us to go and have a look at it?"

Mike glanced down at the papers in Peggy's hands. "It's nearest station is Bolingblow," he said. "I've never heard of it! Bolingblow – where is it?"

"It's about one hundred miles away," said his mother. She took the papers from Peggy and looked at them again. "Of course, I don't know how much of the castle is furnished

– it says 'partly furnished' – that might mean only two or three rooms. And we don't even know whether the furnishings are in good repair or not – they might be mouldering away!"

"Well, Mother, let's go and *see*,' said Mike, half-impatiently. "It will save such a lot of writing to and fro if we go and have a look. I must say I like the sound of it. It sounds sort of – sort of mysterious – and lost – it belongs to the past and not to nowadays. It . . ."

"Mike's going all romantic," said Nora, with a laugh. "Mike, you'll expect King Arthur's knights to go riding out of·the castle, won't you?"

"Don't be an ass," said Mike. "Mother, can't we just go and *look*? Can't you telephone and say we're coming?"

"There's no telephone," said his mother. "That is another reason why I turned it down. The Queen of Baronia will not expect a castle without a telephone!"

"Oh," said Mike, thinking that his mother was quite right there. Then Miss Dimity unexpectedly put in a word. She had come up to listen to the conversation.

"I must say that *I* thought Moon Castle would have done very well for Paul's family," she said. "Except for being twenty miles away from shops, and no telephone, it sounded ideal to me. After all, Paul's mother will have powerful cars to send for any goods she wants – or to take messages. It might be worth seeing. We've got to hurry up and find one, because the family want to come almost immediately!"

"Let's go today," said Mike. "Nothing like doing things at once. Mother, ask Ranni to bring the car round. Let's go today!"

"Yes, do let's," said Paul. "I know what my parents are like! They will change their minds about a castle and a holiday here, if they don't get news of one very soon!"

"Oh dear – you do *rush* me so!" said Mrs Arnold, laughing. "Well – I suppose we'd better make up our minds and go and see this place at once. Paul, find Ranni and tell him. We will be ready in a quarter of an hour. We won't take a picnic lunch – though I should like to – but it would take too long to get ready. Mike, find the right maps, will you – we must look out the best way to go."

After that there was an enormous amount of rushing about, shouting and excitement. It was a very hot day, so the girls put on clean, cool cotton frocks. The boys put on coloured cotton shirts and shorts, except for Jack who considered himself too big and wore grey trousers.

Dimmy was not going. Even without her it would be a tremendous squash in the big blue and silver car belonging to Prince Paul. She waved them off.

"See you some time tonight," she said. "I hope you won't give the caretakers too big a shock, arriving so suddenly out of the blue! I shall be longing to hear all about the castle when you come back."

They went off excitedly. Paul and Mike were in front with Ranni. Mrs Arnold and the girls and Jack were behind. Mike had the map in front, and was poring over it, ready to tell Ranni the roads to take.

They were soon out in the country, speeding along between hedges, with fields of yellowing corn each side. The poppies gleamed in it here and there, and blue chicory flowers shone by the wayside.

"This way now," said Mike, as they came to a corner. "Then east for a good bit till we come to a bridge. Then to the town of Sarchester – then north towards Bolingblow. After that there are only minor roads shown on the map. I hope they will be good enough for a magnificent car like this!"

"Where do we have lunch?" asked Peggy.

"I *thought* somebody would ask that in a minute or two," said Mrs Arnold. "We'll have it at one o'clock, if we are near or in a town."

"We should be at Bolingblow by then," said Mike,

reckoning up quickly. "This car goes at such a speed, it simply *eats* up the miles."

"We should perhaps ask a few questions at Bolingblow about the castle," said Mrs Arnold.

"Yes, we could," said Peggy, and broke into a funny little song that made the others laugh.

> *"O Castle of the Moon,*
> *We're coming to you soon,*
> *This very afternoon,*
> *O Castle of the Moon!"*

The others picked up the words, and the car rushed on with everyone singing the silly little song:

> *"We're coming soon,*
> *O Castle of the Moon!"*

Moon Castle

Ranni drove the car into the town of Bolingblow at just after one o'clock. It was a pretty town with wide streets, and a market-place in the centre.

Mrs Arnold approved of it. "There are good shops here," she said. "And this hotel that Ranni has brought us to looks very nice. Old and picturesque and spotlessly clean."

They were all very hungry, and delighted to find a very good lunch being served. "Iced melon – good!" said Mike. "What's to follow? Cold chicken and ham and salad. Couldn't be better. All I shall want after that is an ice- cream or two."

The little waitress smiled at the hungry children, and took

21

their orders quickly. Soon they were all tucking in, too busy to talk.

When the bill was being paid Mrs Arnold asked the waitress one or two questions.

"Is the road to Moon Castle good, do you know? And about how long will it take us to get there in a car?"

"Moon Castle!" said the waitress, in surprise. "You can't go there. It's not open to the public, you know. No one is allowed to see over it."

"I hear it may be rented this summer," said Mrs Arnold. "I want to go and see it."

"Rented!" said the waitress. "Well, I would never have thought anyone would want to take an old, desolate place like that. It's such a way to the nearest town. Good gracious, nobody's lived there for years and years."

"Oh dear – then I don't expect it's in very good condition," said Mrs Arnold, feeling that her journey would probably be wasted. "There are caretakers, I believe."

"I don't know," said the waitress. "I did hear that once a month somebody comes over in a car to take back goods – food and oil and so on – so I suppose caretakers *are* there. My word! I wouldn't live in that lonely old place for anything. I've heard that queer things go on there – very queer."

"Ooooh! What? asked Nora at once.

"I don't know," said the little waitress. "All I know is that some brainy fellow went there once to ask to see some old books in the big library there – and he was frightened out of his wits! Said the books leapt out of the shelves at him, or something."

Everyone laughed. "That's good!" said Mike. "I'd love to live in a castle where books leapt out of bookshelves. I'd say, 'Hey there – is there a good mystery story waiting for me? Well, jump out, please, and I'll catch you!'"

The waitress didn't like being laughed at. She tossed her head. "Oh well – it's a queer old place that nobody knows

22

much about nowadays. I wouldn't go near it if you paid me."

The children went off to find the car, smiling at the waitress's indignant face. They got into the car and Ranni looked round inquiringly at Mrs Arnold.

"The Castle, madam?" he asked. She nodded, and Mike looked at the map.

"Not such good roads now," he said. "Turn right at the end of the town, Ranni."

"I must say that I don't like what I hear about Moon Castle," said Mrs Arnold, as they drove off. "If nobody has lived there for so long – except the caretakers – the place must be in a very poor condition."

"Yes – it doesn't sound too good," said Mike. "How queer people are – owning a castle and never bothering about it at all! Gosh – what a road this is!"

Ranni had to slow down because the road became very bad just there, and continued bad all the rest of the way. It was full of ruts, and was uneven and in places very stony. The car went carefully.

"We should come to a fork in the road here," said Mike. "Yes, look – there it is. We take the left-hand fork, Ranni."

"That is a good thing," said Ranni. "We could not have taken the other fork! There is hardly any road to be seen!"

It was quite true. The right-hand fork was not really a road – just a fifth-rate cart-track, unused now, and overgrown. Peggy pointed to something in the distance, about half a mile up the track.

"Look," she said. "Houses of some sort. Mother, do you suppose that's all that is left of the ruined village of Moon. Why is it ruined, do you suppose?"

"Peggy, dear, how *should* I know?" said her mother. "The people probably found it too lonely and just left it."

"I can see a few of the roofs," said Peggy. "They look all tumble-down. It might be fun to go and explore a ruined village."

"Well, everyone to his taste," said her mother. "I can think of a lot of better things to do than wander through smelly old villages with not a soul there!"

"Why should it be smelly?" Peggy wanted to know, but just then the car wheels went into such a series of ruts that Mrs Arnold was half-afraid the springs would be broken. But Ranni assured her that they were very, very strong.

"Baronian cars are built for country like this," he said. "All bumps and jumps and humps. The springs cannot break, Madam Arnold. Soon we should see the castle. There is a hill over yonder. It must be there."

They all looked eagerly at the hill coming into view. It was very steep indeed, covered with trees on the slope. Jack gave a sudden exclamation.

"There's the castle – there, right at the top – well, almost at the top! It backs into the hill for protection from the

"There's the castle – there, right at the top!"

24

wind, I suppose. Look at that one great tower! It soars up higher than the hill. Just one tower. How queer!"

"Still, it *looks* like a castle, even if it's only got one tower," said Nora. "I think it's grand. It's got all sorts of turrets and bits and pieces sticking up round it. What a wonderful view it must have over the countryside. All the same – it *would* be lonely to live there always!"

"It certainly looks grand enough for your father and mother, Paul," said Jack. "I mean – it's a *proper* castle – strong and big and *commanding*-looking, if you know what I mean."

Paul did. He was rather taken with it, from the outside. It was such typical English countryside around too – and how his mother would love the little town of Bolingblow, the market-place, the corn-fields, and the countryfolk themselves.

"Well, commanding-looking or not, I can't believe that the inside will be worth seeing as far as furnishing is concerned," said Mrs Arnold. "I expect it has been allowed to fall to pieces! However, we shall soon see. We are nearly there now."

They were going up the steep hill now. Ranni had put the car into bottom gear, and it growled up slowly, the hill-road just as bad as the road they had left. The road wound to right and left in order to make the climbing of the hill easier.

The castle seemed even bigger and more overpowering as they came nearer. "It's watching us!" said Nora, suddenly. "It's saying: 'What is this horrible noisy thing coming to disturb my dreaming?' I'm sure it's watching us:"

"Don't be silly," said Peggy, uneasily. "You do say such stupid things, Nora. My word – what a grand place it is! Towering up into the sky – its one great tower soaring up high. I like it! It belongs to the days of the old knights and their ladies, not to our days."

They came to a great gateway. The gates were shut. Jack

jumped out to open them. Ranni was afraid they might be locked, but they were not. Jack managed to open them, though they creaked and groaned as if they hated to be touched.

The car went through, and up a weed-covered drive that swept round to a great entrance. A flight of wide steps went up to a great door studded with iron nails.

"Well – here we are," said Mrs Arnold, in the sort of voice that meant she wished they weren't! She got out of the car, helped politely by Prince Paul. Ranni leapt up the steps to ring or knock – or whatever one did at a castle like this.

There was a great chain hanging down, with a wrought-iron handle on the end. "Is that the bell?" said Mike, doubtfully. "There's no knocker. Mother, look – there are cobwebs all over the door – even down the opening-crack. It looks as if the door hasn't been opened for years!"

"It does," said Mrs Arnold, beginning to wonder what they would find inside the castle – if they ever got there!

"Shall I pull this chain-thing and hope a bell rings?" said Mike. "Right – well, here goes!"

He gave the chain a big heave. Nothing happened. No sound came, no jingle, no clanging. Mike pulled again. Still nothing happened.

Then Ranni pulled it – and he gave it such a tug that the chain came off and dropped round his shoulders! He threw it down in disgust.

"So old that the rust has eaten into the chain!" he said. "I will hammer on the door."

He hammered with his great fists, and then shouted so that the echoes suddenly swept round them and made them jump.

Nobody came. The door remained fast shut. "Well," said Mrs Arnold, "this is most disappointing. I suppose we must just give it up."

"Oh *no*, Mother! We can't just tamely go back home

26

after actually getting to the front door!" said Mike, quite shocked. "Let's walk round a bit and see if we can see another door – a back door perhaps. Or don't castles have back doors? Has *your* castle got a back door, Paul?"

"Plenty," said Paul, grinning. "Look – we will go this way. There seems a kind of path."

They followed Paul, Mrs Arnold not at all liking the idea of trying to find another way in. She had quite given up the idea of taking the castle for Paul's parents, but she knew what an outcry the children would make if she insisted on their going back to the car at once.

The overgrown way led round the walls of the castle. They came to a small door set in the wall, but that had no bell, knocker or handle. They went on again and suddenly saw a little clearing, set within a small wall of its own.

"Look," said Peggy, and stopped. "Washing hanging out on a line! There *must* be somebody here, then! Yes, see – there's a fairly big door set in the wall there, that leads into that yard – or drying-ground, whatever it is – where the washing is. This must be the kitchen quarters. If we yell, somebody might hear us now."

Mike obligingly yelled, and made them all jump, for he had a most stentorian voice when he liked.

"HEY! IS ANYONE ABOUT?" he yelled.

Nobody answered. A few hens scuttled across the yard and disappeared under some bushes. A tabby cat streaked across and disappeared, too.

"HEY!" began Mike again, and stopped. Somebody had come cautiously out of the big door nearby – the one that led into the yard.

It was a little plump woman with grey hair. She was followed by two others, remarkably like her in face, but both tall and thin. All three stared at the visitors in surprise.

"What do you want?" said the plump woman, in a frightened voice. "Who are you? Why have you come here? No one's allowed here, you know."

Inside The Castle

Mrs Arnold stepped forward, with the estate agent's letter in her hand. "We have come to see over the castle," she said. "Is it convenient to do so now? We couldn't telephone you, of course, because the castle is not on the phone."

"But – but no one is allowed to see over the castle," said the little woman, and her two tall companions nodded their heads vigorously in agreement.

"We are not sightseers," said Mrs Arnold. "We got the particulars of the castle from the agents, who said that the castle could be viewed at any time, if we took with us this letter. It came with the particulars. It is possible that it might suit a friend of mine, who wants to rent a big place for a month or two."

"Well – my son isn't in," said the woman, looking very taken aback. "He told me nobody was to come in. He said nobody would ever want this place. Nobody has ever come to see it, to buy it, or rent it before. Nobody. I really don't know if I can let you in."

"But we have come all this way to see it!" protested Mrs Arnold. "This is ridiculous! I'm afraid you will get into serious trouble with the owners if you refuse to allow people to see over their castle with a view to renting it. You could be making them lose a great deal of money. Can't you see that? Your son has nothing to do with it!"

"Well, he said we weren't to let anyone in," said the woman, and she turned to her tall companions, not knowing what to do. They held a hurried conference in whispers. The children and Mrs Arnold waited impatiently. How unhelpful these women were!

The little plump woman turned round at last. "Well – I

don't know what my son will say," she said again, "but I suppose I must let you in! I and my two sisters are the caretakers."

"Yes – I'm afraid you *must* let us in and also take us round," said Mrs Arnold, firmly. "What does your son do here? Is he a caretaker too?"

"Oh no. My son is very, very clever," said the little woman, proudly. "He is a scientist. I can't tell you the number of exams he has passed."

"Why does he bury himself here then?" said Mrs Arnold, thinking that this mysterious son must be a spoilt and lazy fellow, living in luxury in the castle, waited on by the three women!

"He has work to do," said the little woman, speaking proudly again. "Important work that needs quiet and peace. I don't know *what* he'll say if people come to live in the castle."

"It really doesn't matter in the least what he says about it," said Mrs Arnold, getting annoyed. "The castle doesn't belong to him. If he makes this kind of trouble every time anyone comes to view it, he will certainly lose you your job! Now please don't say any more about your son, but just take us round at once."

"Yes, madam," said the little woman, looking scared. The other two remained quite silent, but followed behind the party, looking grim.

"What is your name?" asked Mrs Arnold, as they went down a passage.

"I'm Mrs Brimming, and my sisters are Miss Edie Lots and Miss Hannah Lots," said the little woman. "Er – would the person who wants the castle need the whole place?"

"Certainly," said Mrs Arnold. "Except your own quarters, of course. Why?"

Mrs Brimming said nothing in answer to that, but flashed a quick look at her two long-faced sisters. The children, finding Mrs Brimming too slow in her showing-round, went on in front, down the corridor, eager to see the castle.

They came out into a great hall, hung with magnificent brocade curtains. Suits of armour stood all round, gleaming brightly. Paul slapped one and it gave out a hollow noise. "I'd like to wear one of these!" he said. "I'd like to pull the vizor down over my face and peer through it."

"You'd be too small to wear a suit of armour," said Jack. "I could get into one, nicely though!"

Mrs Arnold caught a look of alarm on Mrs Brimming's face. "It's all right!" she said, with a laugh. "They won't really walk about in these suits of armour! What a lovely hall this is!"

"Yes," said the woman, and led them to a big door. She swung it open. Inside was a really beautiful room, with graceful furniture upholstered in a royal blue, dimmed with the years. A carpet stretched the whole length of the room, its colours dimmed too, in a lovely soft pattern of blues, reds and creams. The children's feet sank into it as they trod over it.

"My mother would like this," said Paul, at once. "Oh, look at that clock!"

A great clock hung on the wall. It had been made in the shape of a church with a spire. As the children looked at it, a bell inside the church began to toll the hour. It was three o'clock.

"Look! There's an angel coming out of that door in the clock – at the bottom there!" cried Peggy. "A little angel with wings and a trumpet!"

The angel stood there with his trumpet, and then went slowly back again, and the door shut.

"I've never seen a clock like *that* before!" said Nora, in delight.

"There are many curious things here," said Mrs Brimming. "Lord Moon – the one who lived at the beginning of last century, collected many strange marvels from all over the world. There is a musical-box that plays a hundred different tunes, and—"

It gave out a hollow noise.

"Oh! Where is it?" cried Peggy, in delight.

But Mrs Arnold, glancing at her watch, saw that there was only time to look over the castle itself, certainly not to listen to musical-boxes playing a hundred tunes!

"You'll have time to set the musical-box going if we come here," she said. "We must hurry up. Will you show us all the rooms there are, except, of course, your own quarters, Mrs Brimming? My friend, who is the Queen of Baronia, will bring her own servants, and they will, of course, want the use of the kitchen."

"I see," said Mrs Brimming, looking as if she was about to remark that she really didn't know what her son would say to that! "Well, the kitchens are big enough. We use only a corner of them. I'll take you to the other rooms and then upstairs."

All the rooms were beautiful. Upstairs the bedrooms were just the same – magnificently furnished, with wonderful pictures, strange but beautiful ornaments, unusual and most extravagant curtains. Some of them made Peggy think of "cloth of gold", they shone and shimmered so.

Nothing was mouldering, ragged, cobwebby or dirty. Everything was beautifully kept, and Mrs Arnold could not see a speck of dust anywhere. Queer as these three caretakers were, they had certainly tended the castle with the most loving and thorough care.

Upstairs there was a great room whose walls were lined with books from floor to ceiling. The children gazed in amazement. Except in the big public libraries they had never in their lives seen so many books together!

"How wonderful!" said Mike, staring. "I say – what a room for a rainy day! We could never, never get to the end of all these books!"

"They're old," said Jack. "I bet they wouldn't be very interesting. What a waste – to have thousands and thousands of books – and not a soul to read them!"

"My son reads them," said Mrs Brimming, proudly. Nobody said anything. Everybody was tired of Mrs Brimming's son!

On the third storey were great attics – rooms in which were stored enormous chests, old furniture and curious junk of all kinds.

"I don't think my friend would want the attics," said Mrs Arnold, who had been counting up the rooms as they went through them. "The first and second storeys would be enough. How beautifully the whole place is kept! Do you and your sisters keep it like this – does no one else help you?"

"No one," said Mrs Brimming, proudly, and the Misses Edie and Hannah Lots shook their heads too. They led the way downstairs again, to one of the rooms there. "We have been here by ourselves for years. We love this old castle. Our family has always been here, doing some kind of work – yes, our great-great-great-grandmother was here, when the present Lord's great-great-great-grandfather was lord. That's his picture over there."

The children looked at a great portrait that hung over the fireplace of the room they were in. It showed a grim-faced man with a lock of black hair falling over his forehead, his eyes looking quite fiercely at them.

"He doesn't seem to like us much," said Peggy. "I wish he wouldn't look quite so fierce. I shan't be in *this* room much, if we come here – I should never feel comfortable with great-great-great Lord Moon glaring at me!"

The others laughed. Then Mike suddenly thought of something. "We haven't been up the tower – the one, tall tower! We *must* see that!"

There was silence. Mrs Brimming looked at her sisters, and they looked back. Nobody said anything.

"Well – what about the tower?" said Mike again, surprised at the silence. "Can't we see it? I bet your mother will like the tower, Paul! She'll sit up at the top and gaze out

33

"He doesn't seem to like us much," said Peggy.

over the countryside. What a view there must be from the top. Let's go and explore it."

"Well, I'll just stay here and discuss a few things with the caretakers," said Mrs Arnold, who did not particularly want to climb hundreds of stone steps up to the top of the tall tower. "You can wander round. I suppose the tower is in good order too, Mrs Brimming?"

"Yes, madam," said Mrs Brimming, after a little pause. "There's nothing to see there, though. Nothing. I am sure your friend will not want to use the tower – so many steps up, you know – and only small, stone-walled rooms and tiny windows – no use at all."

"It's locked," said one of the Miss Lots, unexpectedly. "Fast–locked."

"Where's the key then?" said Mike at once. He wasn't going to miss going to the top of the tower!

There was another pause. "It's lost," said the other Miss Lots.

"Lost for years," added the first one. "But there's nothing there to see."

"There's a view, surely!" said Mike, puzzled. He didn't believe all this about locked doors and lost keys. Why didn't the caretakers want them to see the tower? Had they neglected it?

"Well, you must find the key before my friend comes," said Mrs Arnold. "She will certainly like to see the view from the top of the tower. Now – I must just ask a few questions about such things as food and so on. You go off for twenty minutes, children, but keep out of mischief, please!"

"Of course!" said Peggy, indignantly. "Come on, Mike." She dropped her voice to a whisper. "Let's go and find the tower!"

An Unpleasant Fellow

They went out of the room, followed by the eyes of all three caretakers. They shut the door behind them. They were in the great hall, and the suits of armour gleamed all around. Peggy gave a little shiver.

"Now I feel as if these suits of armour are watching me!" she said. "Those two Miss Lots give me the creeps. What a peculiar family."

"The son sounds the most peculiar of the lot," said Mike. "I don't feel as if I'm going to like him somehow. But I say – what a castle! Paul, do you like it?"

"Yes, I do, very much," said the little Prince, his eyes shining. "And my mother will love it. So will my two brothers. There will be plenty of room here for all of us, you too! We shall have a grand time!"

"Now – where would the entrance to the tower be?" wondered Jack. "It's on the east side of the castle. So it must be in this direction – down this passage. Come on."

They all followed Jack. He took them down a dark passage hung with what seemed like tapestry, though it was difficult to tell in the dark.

"I wish I'd got a torch," said Mike. "We'd better bring our torches and plenty of batteries, because there only seem to be a few lights in this place, and I bet they don't switch them all on each night!"

They came to the end of the passage, and found themselves in a small square room, whose walls were lined with old chests. Mike lifted up a lid and looked inside. A strong smell of mothballs at once floated out. Nora sneezed.

"Rugs, I think – or curtains or something," said Mike, letting the lid shut with a bang. "I must say those three old caretakers really *do* take care of everything! Now – what about this tower?"

"There doesn't seem to be any entrance to it from here," said Jack, looking all round. He went to a hanging of tapestry that fell from the ceiling of the room to the floor, covering a space left between the many chests. He lifted up the tapestry and gave an exclamation.

"Here's the door to the tower – at least, I should think it leads to the tower."

The others crowded over to look. It was a tall, narrow door, black with age, and looked very strong. There was a handle made of a black iron ring, and an enormous keyhole.

Mike turned the handle to and fro. He could hear a latch clicking, but however hard he pushed at the door it would not open.

"Locked," he said, in disappointment. "And no key. Do you suppose it really *is* lost, Jack?"

"No," said Jack. "I'm sure they didn't want us to use the tower. I bet their awful son uses it – locks himself away from the three old ladies!"

"To do his wonderful scientific work, I suppose," said Mike, with a grin. "Or to laze the days away without anyone knowing. I wonder what he's like. He won't like having to keep in his place when your mother comes, Paul. He'll have to clear out of the tower, if he does use it – we'll have the view to ourselves then!"

Jack took hold of the iron handle and gave the door another shake, a very violent one. Just as he was doing this, footsteps sounded in the long corridor that led to the little square room where they stood.

The children swung round to see who was coming. Jack still had his hand on the iron ring of the tower door.

A man came into the room. He stopped short at once when he saw the children, and gazed at them, astounded. He was short, burly and very dark. His eyes seemed almost black, and his big nose and thin-lipped mouth made him very ugly.

He shouted loudly. "What are you doing here? How dare you? Clear out at once, the lot of you! Take your hand off that iron ring, boy. The door's locked, and you've no business to be snooping round my castle."

The children gasped. *His* castle! Whatever did he mean?

"It's Lord Moon's castle," said Jack, who was the only one who felt able to answer the angry man. "Are you Lord Moon?"

"It doesn't matter who I am!" said the man, taken aback at Jack's words. "I've told you to clear out. How did you get in? Nobody is allowed here, nobody!"

"My mother, the Queen of Baronia, is going to rent this castle from Lord Moon," said Prince Paul, suddenly finding his tongue, and speaking in the imperious way that often made the children laugh. But they didn't laugh now. They were glad of Paul's sudden imperiousness!

37

The man stared at Paul as if he couldn't believe his ears. His shaggy eyebrows came down low over his eyes so that they seemed to be only slits.

"What fairy-tale is this?" he demanded, suddenly. "The Queen of Baronia! I never heard of her! You clear out, I say – and if you ever come round here again I'll take the lot of you up to the top of the tower and throw you out!"

Jack tried again. "But it's true!" he cried. "We're all coming to stay here and we want to look at the tower rooms so that our friend can describe them to his mother. She will be sure to want to know what they are like. You seem to be able to get into the tower, so will you please unlock it for us?"

The man exploded into fury. He stuttered something, raised his hands and came towards them, looking so fierce that they backed away. The girls fled down the corridor. The boys stood their ground a moment, and then they too took to their heels! The man was strong and could have knocked all three of them down easily. He raced after them.

The five children ran down the passage, into the hall, and then flung open the door of the room where they had left Mrs Arnold and the three sister caretakers.

"Good gracious!" began Mrs Arnold, annoyed at this sudden entry, "I must say—"

After the children came the man, muttering fiercely. He stopped in surprise in the doorway. Then he marched in and addressed his mother.

"What's all this? I caught these children snooping round the castle. Who's this woman too?"

"Guy, calm yourself," said Mrs Brimming, in a shaky voice. "This is someone with a letter from the estate agents. She – she thinks her friend, the Queen of Baronia, would like to rent Moon Castle. She has come to see it – these children belong to her. And this small boy is the son of the Queen of Baronia – Prince Paul. It's – it's quite all right. They have every right to be here."

"Didn't I tell you nobody was allowed in?" said her son,

38

fiercely. "What's all this about renting? I don't believe a word of it."

Mrs Arnold began to feel alarmed. What an extraordinary man! She beckoned to Mike. "Go and fetch Ranni," she said. Mike sped off into the hall and went to the great front door. They had left Ranni and the car outside the flight of steps that led up to it from the drive. How Mike hoped he would be there, waiting!

The front door was well and truly bolted, and had two great keys in the locks. Mike dragged back the bolts, and turned the keys with difficulty. The door came open with a terrible groan, as if it resented being awakened from its long, long sleep.

Ranni was down in the drive, standing patiently beside the car. He saw Mike at once, and sprang up the steps, quick to note the urgency in the boy's face.

"Mother wants you," said Mike, and ran back down the hall to the room where he had left everyone. Big Ranni followed, his boots making a great noise on the stone floor.

Guy, the son of the scared Mrs Brimming, was now examining the letter, which he had almost snatched out of Mrs Arnold's hand when she had offered it to him to prove the truth of her words. His face was as black as thunder.

"Why didn't you write to make an appointment?" he demanded. "No one is allowed in without an appointment! And I must tell you that no one has rented this castle for years – not for years! I cannot—"

"You sent for me, madam?" interrupted Ranni's deep voice. Guy looked up at once, and was astounded to see the enormous Baronian standing beside Mrs Arnold.

"Yes, Ranni," said Mrs Arnold. "I have been over this castle, and I think your master, the King of Baronia, will find it to his liking. This man here – the son of one of the caretakers – does not appear to like our coming. Do you think your master will allow him to stay here when he brings his own servants?"

Ranni knew perfectly well what Mrs Arnold wanted him to say. He looked at Guy with much dislike. Then he bowed to Mrs Arnold and spoke loudly.

"Madam, you know my master's wishes. His Majesty will certainly not allow anyone here except the caretakers. I will get His Majesty's orders and convey them to this man. He will certainly have no right to be here or to object to anything."

The children looked at Guy triumphantly. Good old Ranni! Mrs Brimming gave a little cry. "But he's only my son. He always lives here. He didn't mean to be rude. It's only that . . ."

"I don't think we need to talk about it any more," said Mrs Arnold. "Your son will have to leave the castle while my friends are renting it. He appears to think the castle belongs to him!"

Guy had gone purple in the face. He took a step forward and opened his mouth – but nobody knew what he wanted to say because Ranni also took a step forward. That was enough! One glance at the big Ranni, with his flaming red beard and steady eyes, made Guy change his mind quickly. He muttered something under his breath, swung round and went out of the room.

"I think we'll go now," said Mrs Arnold, picking up the letter that Guy had flung down on a table. "I will tell the estate agents to contact Lord Moon and arrange everything quickly. My friends would like to come in ten days' time, as I told you – earlier if possible, if it can be arranged. I shall tell them how beautifully kept the castle is – and you may be sure that the Queen's servants will keep everything just as well."

"Madam – please don't tell Lord Moon that my son – that my son – behaved rudely," begged Mrs Brimming, looking suddenly tearful. "He – well, he helps to look after the castle too, you see – and he didn't know anyone was coming to see it – or rent it."

40

"That doesn't excuse his behaviour," said Mrs Arnold. "But I assure you I shall make no trouble for him or for you, if he makes none either. But he must certainly leave the castle while my friend's family is here. We expect *you* to remain here, of course – but not your son or any other relations or friends. We shall make that clear to Lord Moon."

Mrs Arnold said good day and walked to the front door, followed by the children and Ranni. The caretakers did not follow them. They remained behind, gloomy and upset.

But from an upstairs window two angry eyes watched the great blue and silver car set off down the drive. Nobody saw them but Ranni – and he said nothing!

Plans

When the five children got back home again, they found Captain Arnold there. He had been away on business, and was very glad to see them. He swung Peggy and Nora up in his arms, one after the other.

The boys clustered round him, glad to see him. "Where in the world have you been?" he demanded. "I came home expecting to find a loving wife and five excited children to greet me – and nobody was here except Dimmy!"

"I did my best to give him a good welcome," Dimmy said to Mrs Arnold. "But don't fret – he's only been in ten minutes! He hasn't had to wait long."

It was eight o'clock, and everyone was very hungry. "We'll tell you our news when we've washed and are sitting down to supper," said Mrs Arnold. "We've really had a most exciting day!"

So they told Captain Arnold all about how they had been

to visit Moon Castle – its magnificence, its grandeur, its loneliness – how beautifully it was kept by the three caretaker-sisters, and all about the angry son.

"Ha! He's been frightening people away, I expect!" said Captain Arnold. "Likes to think he's King of the Castle – probably brings his own friends there and impresses them very much. If I were Lord Moon I'd make a few enquiries as to why the castle hasn't been let before – and I'd find out how many friends of that son have been staying at the castle – living there for months, I expect! He sounds a bad lot."

"He soon came to his senses when Ranni appeared, though," said Mike, with a grin. "He hardly said a word after that."

"It's a most lovely place," said Mrs Arnold. "I shall ring up the agents first thing tomorrow, and tell them to get in touch with Paul's father. The place is quite ready to go into immediately. I could order all the food and other goods that will be needed. I made enquiries about what shops to go to when I was in Bolingblow."

"Do you think we'll be there next week?" said Paul, hopefully.

"I don't see why not," said Mrs Arnold. "I imagine your people will all fly over, Paul. If only we have a good summer! It's such lovely country round about the castle – real English countryside. Your mother will love it."

"Shall we go and stay with you as soon as your family come?" asked Nora, eagerly, turning to Paul.

"No, no," said her mother, answering for Paul. "Of course not. Only Paul will go to join them at first. We must give them time to settle in a little! But we will certainly join them later."

"Paul will be able to go up the tower before we do," said Peggy, enviously. "Paul, write and tell us about everything, won't you – the tower – and if the key is produced – and if that horrid man Mr Brimming has gone, and . . ."

"Of course he'll be gone," said her mother. "I certainly

will not have him hanging round the place. He seemed to me to be a little mad. The caretakers will have to keep out of the way too, and not interfere with the Queen's servants at all. I think they will be quite sensible – especially if that man isn't around. He seemed to have them under his thumb."

"I'll explore everything and take you everywhere when you come," promised Paul.

Dimmy was very interested to hear about it all. She was not going to the castle when the others did, but Paul said that she really must come just for the day. He was very fond of Dimmy. He turned to Captain Arnold, a thought suddenly striking him.

"Sir – will you be able to come too? Are you on leave for a time?"

"I hope so," said Captain Arnold, helping himself to a large plateful of trifle. "It's not certain, though. I might be off on a very interesting job."

"What job?" asked everyone, but he shook his head. "I shan't tell you till I know," he said. "I hope it will be after we come back from Moon Castle."

Nora yawned hugely, patting her hand over her mouth. "Oh dear – sorry, everyone, but I do feel so sleepy. I even feel too sleepy to have another helping of trifle, which is an awful pity!"

"It isn't," said Paul. "It means I can have it instead!"

Mike and Paul scrabbled for the last helping and made a mess on the table. "I knew that would happen," said Dimmy. "Never mind! It's nice to see every single dish finished up – so much easier to wash! Now there's Peggy yawning and Paul too."

"Get to bed, everyone," said Mrs Arnold. "I'd like a little peace with my husband! I haven't seen him for a very long time!"

The five children went up to bed, everyone yawning now. Mike wanted to talk about Moon Castle, but as both

Jack and Paul were sound asleep as soon as their heads were on the pillow, he had to lie and think instead.

Moon Castle! Fancy there being a castle like that – so very, very old – so beautifully kept – with such strange things in it. He remembered the church-shaped clock and the angel appearing at the church door. And he must remember to look for the musical-box that played a hundred tunes – and could he *possibly* try on a suit of armour? And – and . . .

But Mike was now as fast asleep as the others. Mrs Arnold sat downstairs and talked quietly with her much-travelled husband. He was one of the finest pilots in the world. How many times had he flown round the world? He had lost count! Mrs Arnold, too, was a fine pilot, and had gone on many record flights with her husband. She knew almost as much about aeroplanes as he did.

"This new job you spoke of?" she said. "Is it important? Can you tell me?"

"Yes, I'll tell you," said her husband. "It is to fly a new plane – a queer one, but a beauty! It's a wonderplane. It can rise straight up in the air at a great speed, for one thing, and it gains height in a most remarkable manner."

"Amazing!" said Mrs Arnold. "Will you be on a test flight with it, then? When will it be ready? Do you know?"

"I don't," said her husband. "Yes, it's a test flight, all right. I shall put it through a few hair-raising tests, you may be sure! The speed it goes! I've got to wear special clothes, and some queer apparatus over my head because of the enormous speed – faster than sound again, you know!"

"I want to come and see you take off," said Mrs Arnold. "I always bring you luck, don't I? The only time I couldn't come and watch, you had an accident. I must come and see you this very special, important time, my dear!"

"Yes – you must," said Captain Arnold, knocking out his pipe. "I only hope it doesn't come at a time when you want to go to Moon Castle with the Queen and her family. You'd enjoy that so much!"

"Well, if the times clash, I shall come with *you*, dear – and the children can go off to the castle with Dimmy," said his wife. "I *must* come with you and bring you luck when you fly this new plane."

They went off to bed, and soon everyone in the house was sleeping. How many dreamt about Moon Castle? Certainly all the five children did.

It was their first thought in the morning too. They pestered Mrs Arnold after breakfast to telephone the agents at once. She protested. "I *must* telephone Paul's mother first! It takes a little time to get a clear line to telephone Baronia."

But at last all the telephoning was done. The Queen approved heartily. She spoke to Paul too, and the boy was excited to hear his mother's voice coming so clearly over so many miles.

"Dear Paul!" said his mother, in the Baronian language. "I shall see you soon. And your brothers are so excited to be coming to England – such a wonderful country! Mrs Arnold will arrange everything as quickly as possible."

The agents were pleased to hear that Lord Moon's castle had been let. "It's the first time for years," they told Mrs Arnold. "We've had such difficulty in letting it. We've sent a few people there to see it – but they came back with queer stories – either they couldn't get in – or things were made difficult for them. I don't really know what happened. We do hope the Queen of Baronia will like her stay there. I am glad, too, to hear that the place is in such beautiful order. Perhaps we shall have better luck with it now."

Mrs Arnold thought that Mr Guy Brimming must have been the one who had made things difficult! She did not say so, but determined that she would make things very hard for that unpleasant fellow if he did not take himself off and remain away!

"Well, we don't even need to get into touch with Lord Moon," she told the children. "Apparently if the agents are

45

"I have arranged to take the castle for your mother, Paul."

satisfied, they are the judges as to whether the new tenants may go in, and when. So I arranged to take the castle for your mother, Paul, this day week!"

"Oh *good*!" said Paul, delighted. "Only seven days to wait! Well, I suppose Mother will let those three old ladies know what she wants in the way of food and so on – or are you going to do all that Mrs Arnold?"

"Oh, I shall do that," said Mrs Arnold. "What a shock for the three old things when loads of goods arrive day after day! They will hardly know where to put them!"

"Does it cost a lot to rent a castle?" said Mike, thinking that he might like to rent one himself some day.

"Good gracious, yes!" said his mother. "Why, are you thinking of renting one, dear? Just save up a few thousand pounds then!"

"Goodness!" said Mike, abandoning his ideas of castles at once. "Mother, you will be able to come too, won't you? I did hear you say something to Dimmy this morning that you might not be able to."

"Well – there's a chance that your father might like to have me with him when he goes to his new job," said his mother. "But I shall join you afterwards – and Dimmy can go with you, if it happens at an awkward time. But Daddy will soon know, and I'll tell you immediately! I promise!"

Captain Arnold came home that night with the news they wanted. "It's all right!" he said. "I'm to go next week – and as the job will probably only take a week, your mother and I will be home in time to join Paul and his people at Moon Castle in a fortnight's time – probably on the very day we have been asked!"

"Oh good!" said Mike. "Paul will have to go next week, of course, when his family come over – and then we can all go together the week after, when they are settled in."

"Better enjoy this week here while you're all

together," said Dimmy. "You'll be all alone with me next week!"

"Can't we go and watch the new tests too, Daddy?" asked Peggy. "Why can't we?"

"Oh, they're very hush-hush!" said her father. "No sightseers allowed. Cheer up – all our plans are going well these holidays! Nothing will go wrong, I'm sure!"

But he wasn't right about that – something *did* go wrong before the week was up!

Things Go A Little Wrong

The first inkling that things were going wrong came in three days' time, when Mrs Arnold got a letter from Paul's mother, the Queen.

"Any news from my mother?" asked Paul, eagerly. "What a long letter, Mrs Arnold!"

"Yes – it is," said Mrs Arnold. "Oh dear – one of your brothers is ill, Paul dear. It's Boris, who was coming to Moon Castle with your mother in a few days' time!"

"Oh," said Paul, dolefully. "What's the matter with him? He's not *very* ill, is he?"

"No. But they are afraid it is measles," said Mrs Arnold. "Oh, what a pity! Your other brother hasn't had measles, she says – so he will be in quarantine, if Boris has it, as they've been together, of course."

"Oh, Mrs Arnold – it won't mean that my mother can't come, will it?" said Paul, full of dismay. "What about Moon Castle? What about—"

"Well, we won't begin to worry till we know for certain Boris *has* got measles," said Mrs Arnold. "Your mother says it may not be. Perhaps she will come and bring some of

48

the other children, and leave Boris and his brother behind, if they have measles. Don't worry about it."

But Paul did worry, of course. Their lovely, lovely plans! Bother Boris! He was always getting things. Now perhaps they wouldn't be able to go to Moon Castle – and it was going to be such an adventure!

Mike and the others were very disappointed too, because if the trip to England was cancelled they wouldn't have the fun of going to Moon Castle either!

"The only person who will be pleased about this is that horrid man Mr Brimming," said Mike, gloomily. "He'll rejoice like anything!"

Two more days passed. "Any news from my mother?" Paul asked at every post-time. "Mrs Arnold, we're supposed to have the castle the day after tomorrow, aren't we? What will happen if Mother decides not to come? Do you just tell the caretakers, or what?"

"Now don't keep worrying your head about it," said Mrs Arnold. "Your mother is going to telephone today after lunch. We shall know then."

"R-r-r-r-r-ing!" went the telephone bell after lunch, and the children rushed into the hall. Mrs Arnold pushed them firmly away. She took up the receiver. A voice came to her ear.

"A personal call from Baronia, please, for Mrs Arnold."

"I am Mrs Arnold," was the answer, and then came a lot of clicking noises and far-off voices.

The children stood round breathlessly, trying to hear what was said to Mrs Arnold. She listened carefully, nodding, and saying "Yes. Yes, I see. Yes, a very good idea. Yes. Yes. No, of course not. Yes, I agree."

The children, who could make nothing at all of all this, went nearly mad with impatience. Paul stood as close to Mrs Arnold as he could, hoping to catch a word or two from his mother's long talk. But he couldn't.

At last Mrs Arnold said good-bye, and put back the

receiver with a click. Paul gave a wail. "Why didn't you let me speak to her? Why didn't you?"

"Because it was a personal call, and because that wasn't your mother!" said Mrs Arnold, laughing at the little Prince's fierce expression. "Now listen and I'll tell you what was being said. It's not so bad as we feared."

"Why? Tell us – quick, Mother!" said Mike.

"That was your mother's secretary," said Mrs Arnold to Paul. "Boris *has* got measles – and Gregor, your brother, developed it two days ago. But it's only very slight indeed, and they'll be up and about in no time."

"What's going to happen then? Is Mother going to leave them and come over here?" demanded Paul.

"No. She doesn't want to leave them. But she is sure she will be able to come in about ten days' time, and bring them too," said Mrs Arnold. "So what she proposes is this – as she has rented the castle from the day after tomorrow, she thinks it would be a good idea for us all to go there and settle in till they come!"

"Oh how super!" cried Peggy and Nora together. Then Nora looked solemn. "But Mother," she said, "what about you and Daddy? You're going off with Daddy soon, aren't you, to those new tests? Shall you let him go alone after all, and come with us?"

"Well, dear, I think I *must* go with Daddy," said her mother. "I do bring him luck, you know. But Dimmy will go with you – won't you, Dimmy? And you'll have Ranni as well. And it will only be for a short time – a week or so. It will be nice for your mother to find you well settled in, Paul, and Dimmy able to show the servants the rooms, and where everything is to go."

"Yes. I'd be pleased to do that," said Dimmy, who had been listening to everything with interest. "I've not seen this wonderful castle – and now I shall! But when will the servants come? I don't feel that I can manage hordes of Baronian servants, all speaking a language I don't know! Not even with Ranni's help!"

50

"The servants will not come until the day before the Queen arrives," said Mrs Arnold. "The children can easily look after themselves, with your help. There will be any amount of food arriving, because I can't very well cancel that. I'll give you the lists, and you will know what is there. Well – what do you say, children?"

"Lovely! Super! Smashing!" said everyone at once. Peggy gave her mother a hug. "I wish you were coming too, though," she said. "Still – you'll come and join us when the Queen arrives, won't you? The plane tests will be over by then."

"I'll do my very best," said her mother. "Now – we'll have to get busy! There are your clothes to see to – the agents to ring up – and I must write a letter to the three caretakers to tell them that our plans are altered, and only you children are coming for the time being."

"I'll see to their clothes," said Dimmy. "They won't want to take a great deal this warm weather. Now, you children, if you want to take any special books or games you'd better look them out and let me have them to pack. And please, Mike, don't imagine that means you can take your whole railway set or anything like that!"

"How many books can we each take?" said Jack. Then he remembered the big library at the castle. "Wait, though – we'll have all those books to read we saw in the bookcases that covered the walls in the library at Moon Castle. We shan't mind a rainy day one bit!"

"Well, *I'm* taking a few books of my own," said Mike. "Those old books in the library might be too dull to read. I'm taking my favourite adventure books."

"We really ought to have a book written about *our* adventures," said Nora, going upstairs with Peggy. "They would make most exciting books."

"And everyone would wish they knew us and could share our adventures!" said Paul. "I bet most children would like to visit our Secret Island – the one we escaped to the first time I knew you – do you remember?"

"Come along, chatterboxes," said Miss Dimmy, pushing the children up the stairs. "Let me look at the clothes in your chests of drawers, and see exactly how much washing and ironing and mending I've got to do. You'll have to help, Peggy and Nora, if there's too much."

"Oh we will," they promised, feeling so happy at the thought of going off to Moon Castle that even the thought of mending clothes didn't depress them.

Captain Arnold was told the news when he got home that night. "Well, it's a mercy the boys have only got a slight attack of measles," he said. "It would have been maddening to cancel the visit to Moon Castle altogether. Anyway, the children will be all right with Dimmy."

Those two days were very full. Mrs Arnold rushed here and there, looking for this and that. Dimmy washed and ironed and mended without stopping. The boys began packing books and games at the bottom of the two big cases. Peggy and Nora began singing the silly little Moon song again!

"O Castle of the Moon,
We'll see you very soon!"

Mike added to it, after a great deal of thought:

"And many a happy hour
We'll spend up in the tower!"

"I wonder if that man will have gone," said Jack, suddenly. He called to Mrs Arnold. "I say, Mrs Arnold! Did you write to the caretakers? You haven't heard from them, I suppose?"

"There hasn't been time to hear from them," said Mrs Arnold. "Yes, I wrote, of course. I wrote to Mrs Brimming. Why?"

"I was just wondering about that man called Guy," said Jack. "I was hoping he would have gone."

"Oh yes, of course he will have gone," said Mrs Arnold. "I

told the agents that unless he went we would not rent the castle. You needn't worry about him. You won't see much of the old ladies either. I don't suppose – unless they do any dusting or cleaning till the Queen's servants arrive."

"Who's doing the cooking?" asked Peggy. "Dimmy? Will those three old women let her use the kitchen stove?"

"I don't know," said Mrs Arnold. "When I wrote I said they could choose what they would prefer to do – cook for you and be paid for it – or allow Dimmy to cook in the kitchen. I've no doubt they would rather do the cooking and earn a little extra money. I hope so, because it will be easier for Dimmy."

"I wish tomorrow would hurry up and come," said Nora, appearing with an armful of ironed clothes.

"Can't you think of anything else to say?" said Mike. "I've heard you say that about twelve times already. What's the time? Nearly tea-time. Well, this time tomorrow we'll be in the castle of the Moon!"

At last everything was packed and ready. The suitcases were shut. Dimmy went round to make sure that everything necessary had been packed and nothing left out. Mrs Arnold and her husband were also leaving on the day following. The children had not been told their address, as the tests were not to be made known – in fact even Captain Arnold was not sure exactly where he was to go the next day.

"I vote we all go to bed early," he said at supper-time. "I want to be absolutely fresh tomorow – and you look tired out already, my dear," he said, turning to his wife. "So does Dimmy."

"*We're* not tired," said Mike. "But we'll go to bed early and make tomorrow come all the quicker! What time is Ranni coming for us in the car?"

"About half-past ten," said his mother. You can have your lunch at that hotel in Bolingblow again, if you like. And I suppose I need hardly warn you to take great care of

53

At last everything was packed and ready.

all that beautiful furniture at the castle during your stay – and . . ."

"Mother, we'll behave like Princes and Princesses!" said Mike, laughing. "Come on, everyone – let's go to bed. Hurrah for tomorrow – and the Castle of the Moon!"

The Castle Again

Everyone was in a great rush the next morning. The house was to be left empty for the time being. Mrs Hunt, the woman who cooked and helped in the house, was to go home, and to come in daily only to dust and open the windows. She would come and feed the hens too.

Captain Arnold had his bag ready, and Mrs Arnold had packed a small one for herself. Mike wanted to open one of the suitcases, and put in two books he suddenly longed to take at the last moment.

"You can't open them," said Dimmy. "You've done that twice already and messed everything up inside. Now I've locked the case and I've got the key safe!"

"Blow!" said Mike, and went to see if he could open Paul's school trunk, which he was taking with him. But Dimmy had artfully locked that too.

Ranni came round with the shining car at exactly half-past ten. He grinned at the excited children. "So we go back to the castle!" he said. "The poor car – she will bump herself to death!"

"Baronian cars don't mind bumps," said Paul. "You said so yourself! Anyway, I rather like them. Goodbye, Captain Arnold, and the very best of luck with your new tests."

"Thank you," said Captain Arnold. "If you hear something that sounds like a big sneeze, and it's gone almost before it's come, it'll be me in the new plane!"

Everyone laughed. Nora hugged her father. "Be careful, Daddy, won't you?" she said. "And good luck!"

Soon all the good-byes had been said and the car set off, with Captain and Mrs Arnold waving from the doorstep. They were off!

It was rather a squash in the big car again, but nobody minded except Dimmy, who said that Nora was the most fidgety person to sit next to that she had ever known in her life. But when Peggy took Nora's place Miss Dimmy changed her mind, and said that she thought Peggy was worse than Nora. Certainly none of the five children stopped talking or leaning out of windows, or stretching across one another for the whole journey.

They had lunch at Bolingblow again, and the same little waitress served them.

"We went to the castle," said Peggy. "It's WONDERFUL!"

"And we're going again now – to stay!" said Nora.

The waitress laughed. She didn't believe Nora. "No one stays there," she said. "So don't you try to pull my leg. It's got a bad name, Moon Castle has."

"Why has it?" asked Mike at once.

"Well – people say Things Happen there," said the waitress, mysteriously. "I told you before about the fellow who went to see some old books in the library there!"

"Oh yes – and they jumped out of the shelves at him!" said Peggy, with a giggle. "We do hope that will happen when *we're* there! But do please believe us – we really *are* going there to stay."

The waitress stared at them, still finding this difficult to believe. "I did hear say that any amount of goods have been ordered and sent to the castle," she said. "Any amount – food and stuff. Would that be for you?"

"Well, partly," said Peggy. "Do you know any more tales about the castle?"

"Noises!" said the waitress, lowering her voice as if she was half-afraid to speak. "Noises! I did hear there were very strange noises."

"What sort?" asked Mike, in great interest.

"I don't know. Nobody knows," said the girl. "Just noises. Don't you go to that castle. You go home while there's time!"

She went off with their plates. Peggy laughed. "This is very thrilling. Isn't it queer how all old places have strange stories about them? I wouldn't be a bit surprised if that man Guy put out these tales, just to keep the castle to himself and prevent people going there. I bet there aren't any Noises or Things that Happen!"

"I agree with you," said Mike. "It's just tales. Well – we'll soon find out. Personally I'd like something to happen."

"Not Noises," said Nora. "I don't like noises – queer noises, I mean – when you don't know what makes them."

"Like the wicker chair in our bedroom," said Peggy. "At night it suddenly gives a creak *exactly* as if somebody had sat down in it. But when I put my light on there's nobody there."

"Of course there isn't," said Dimmy. "It's merely the wickerwork relaxing after having to bear your big lump of a weight, Peggy!"

They were now on to ice-creams. They were so nice that Miss Dimmy ordered a second round. Nora patted her arm affectionately.

"I do like some of your habits, Dimmy," she said. "Like ordering another lot of ice-creams – and looking the other way when one of us orders a third lot."

"There'll be *no* third lot," said Dimmy. "I'm calling for the bill!"

The children grinned. They didn't really want a third ice-cream, but it was always fun to pull Dimmy's leg. The waitress came up with the bill.

"I've been talking to my friend over there about Moon Castle," she said in a low voice. "She's the niece of the grocer who sent up some of the goods. And she says the driver of the van was so scared when he got to the castle that he just dumped all the things in the drive, shouted 'Here they are!' jumped back into the van, and went down the hill as if a hundred dogs were after him."

"But why was he so scared?" said Nora, puzzled. "There's absolutely nothing frightening about the front door! The driver must be crazy!"

"I tell you, it's a scary place," said the waitress, who seemed quite determined to make the most of what little she knew. "Well – you come in here and see me when you've been there a day or two. I guess you'll have some queer tales to tell!"

The children laughed. "There are only three harmless old caretakers up there now," said Mike. "They would be more scared than anyone else if Things Happened, like you said."

"Ah – caretakers! Three of them – *that's* queer!" said the waitress.

"Why? Do they fly about on broomsticks at night?" asked Jack with a grin.

The waitress was cross. She piled the plates together loudly and walked off.

"Come on," said Mike. "Off to the castle of the Moon, we'll be there very soon – no, I've got it wrong. Anyway, come on, everyone!"

They went back to the car. Ranni was already in the driving-seat, waiting patiently. It was somehow rather comforting to see him there, big and burly and confident, after hearing the waitress's tales. They all got into the car, feeling very well-fed indeed. Now for the castle!

Ranni drove off. They followed the same road as before, bumpy and full of ruts. Ranni drove carefully. Nora and Peggy looked out for the fork that led to the ruined village.

58

"I meant to have asked the waitress if she knew anything about that," said Nora, regretfully. "But I forgot. I'm sure she would have had a wonderful story about it."

"Look – there's the fork to it," said Peggy. "I vote we go and explore it one day. It's only about a mile from here. I'd like to explore a ruined village."

They passed the fork and the children once more caught a glimpse of tumble-down roofs and a desolate group of houses huddled together.

And then they were on the steep road to the castle. They wound to and fro on the slope, their engine sounding loudly as they went. Not even the powerful Baronian car could go up in top gear!

The entrance gates were again shut and Mike hopped out to open them. Up the drive they went and swept round to the front door. That too was shut.

"Well – here we are," said Mike, looking up at the towering castle. "It seems awfully big when we're as near as this. Now, what happens? Do we ring the bell again? On no – you broke the chain, Ranni! I hope we don't have to go all round the back, like we did before."

"The chain is mended," said Ranni, and the children, looking towards the door, saw that he was right. "We can get in at the front this time!"

Jack leapt up the wide flight of steps and took hold of the iron handle at the end of the chain. He pulled it downwards.

This time a bell rang! A loud jangle sounded somewhere back in the castle, a cracked, harsh noise, as if the bell was big, but broken.

Ranni heaved the cases and Paul's trunk up the steps. Everyone stood patiently waiting for the door to open. Jack got impatient and rang the bell again. Then he jumped. The door was opening slowly and quietly in front of him.

But no one was there! The children stood there, expecting one of the old caretakers to appear. But no one came. Was someone behind the door?

The door was opening slowly and quietly in front of him.

Jack ran in to see. No – the hall was empty. "How queer!" said Dimmy. "Somebody *must* have opened the door in answer to the bell – but why should they disappear at once?"

"One of the Queer Things that Happen!" said Mike, with a chuckle. "Oh well – I expect one of the sisters did open it, but got so scared of Ranni and his red beard that she fled at once. It's so dark in the hall that we wouldn't notice anyone scuttling away. Shall I give you a hand, Ranni?"

Ranni wanted no help. "You go and find someone and ask if everything is ready for us," he said, standing inside the hall. Jack looked at Dimmy.

"Shall I go and get Mrs Brimming?" he asked. Dimmy nodded, and Jack sped off, trying to remember the way to the back quarters.

He came back almost immediately with Miss Edie Lots who was looking rather scared. "I've found one of them," said Jack, pleased. "She says she didn't hear the bell, and doesn't believe anyone opened the door."

"Rubbish," said Dimmy. "Miss Lots, is everything ready for us to come in? You got Mrs Arnold's letter, I expect – and the one from the agent, telling of our change in plans."

"Oh yes. Yes," said Miss Edie, sounding rather breathless. "We heard that only the children were coming and a Miss Dimity. Yes. Everything is ready. You will choose what bedrooms you want yourself. And the packages have come – dozens of them! They are all in the kitchen. Yes."

"Thank you," said Dimmy. "We'll get straight in now, then – and I'll come and examine everything in the kitchen later on. Now, children – come upstairs and show me the bedrooms. What a truly magnificent place this is!"

Up the stairs they went in excitement, talking nineteen to the dozen. What fun they were going to have!

Settling Into The Castle

Ranni followed the children upstairs with the luggage. Dimmy thought she had better follow quickly too, before the children took unsuitable bedrooms for themselves! She marvelled as she went up the broad flight of stairs – what a wonderful place this was!

"What carpets! What hangings! What magnificent pictures!" she thought, leaning over the broad banister and looking down into the great hall. The front door was still open and sunlight flooded through it, gleaming on the suits of armour, standing on their pedestals.

"Not a speck of dust anywhere!" marvelled Dimmy. "Those caretakers may be strange but they do know how to take care of things!"

Ranni had put the luggage down on the great landing, and now passed Dimmy to fetch the rest of it. He stopped beside her.

"I would like a small room not far from my little master, the Prince," he said, politely. "Or one opening out of his, if that is possible."

"Very well, Ranni. I will see to that," said Dimmy, thinking for the hundredth time how devoted Ranni was to Paul. Servant – friend – guardian; Ranni was everything!

She hurried towards the sound of chattering and laughter. Where were those children?

They were in an enormous bedroom that looked out over the countryside for miles. Nora swung round to Dimmy, her eyes shining.

"Dimmy! Can Peggy and I have this room? It's wonderful! Look at the view!"

"I shouldn't think you can for one moment," said

Dimmy, amazed at the size of the room. "This must be one of the biggest rooms. Paul's mother should have it!"

"Oh no, Dimmy – there are much bigger rooms than this!" protested Nora. "Come and see!"

Feeling quite dazed, Dimmy followed Nora into room after room, all beautifully furnished, all beautifully kept. The views were marvellous.

Finally they came to a suite of smaller rooms, leading out of one another, but each with its own door to the landing. There were three of these, two of them double rooms and one single room.

"Now these would do beautifully for you five children," said Dimmy, at once. "No, don't argue, Nora – the room you wanted was far too big. Let me tell you this – you will probably have to keep it spotlessly clean and tidy yourself, if the caretakers are not going to take on the job – and you'd do much better to have these small rooms, which will be very easy to keep tidy."

"Oh," said Nora, disappointed. "Well – I suppose you're right, Dimmy. And it *would* be nice to have three rooms all together like this." She went to the door and shouted.

"Peggy! Mike! Come here – there are three rooms all together here!"

They all came running. Jack approved at once. "Yes – Mike and I could have this middle one – and you two girls the one to the left of us – and Paul the one to the right – the single room. Couldn't be better!"

He went to the window and looked out. "I never in my life saw such views!" he said. "Never! I say – is that a bit of the ruined village we can see? I'm sure I can see roof-tops and a chimney or two!"

They all crowded together at the window. "Yes!" said Mike. "It must be. Look – you can just make out a bit of the road there, too – the fork to the village comes about there. I say, we *must* go and explore it sometime."

Dimmy had wandered off. She wanted to find a room for

herself, and one for Ranni too. She found a small room for Ranni a little way down the corridor, but alas, it looked on to the hill at the back of the castle, and was rather dark, because the walls were so near the hillside itself. The hill rose up behind the castle like a cliff.

Only the tall tower rose high above the hilltop. Dimmy thought what a wonderful view there must be from that! She looked for a room for herself, hoping to find one with a view.

She found a tiny little room at the end of the corridor. It had no bed in it, but seemed more like a little sitting-room. She decided to move a bed into it from another room, and use the little room for herself – it had such a wonderful view that she felt she would rather have it than a bigger one without a view.

She went back to the children. They had called Ranni and he had brought their luggage in. Dimmy smiled at the big, bearded fellow. "I've found a room for you, Ranni," she said. "Quite nearby. But it hasn't a view."

However Ranni, brought up in a country of high mountains and sweeping valleys, had no wish for a view. He had had plenty of those in Baronia! He was very pleased with his little room, because it was so near Paul.

"There aren't any basins with running water," said Nora, looking at the great old-fashioned washstands. "Do we have to use these enormous jugs? I shall hardly be able to lift mine!"

"Use the bathrooms," said Mike. "I counted seven on this floor already! There's one just opposite our rooms. It's got a shower and everything."

"Dimmy, isn't this fun?" said Nora. "Have you got a room for yourself – a nice one? Oh Dimmy, won't it be lovely living in a castle like this? It will take me ages to find my way around properly."

Dimmy felt rather the same – but it was amazing how quickly they learnt where all the rooms were, and the quickest way here, there and everywhere! There were two main staircases, and two or three smaller ones.

"We can have a marvellous time chasing one another and playing hide-and-seek," said Mike. "All these staircases to get away on! You know, Paul, it's a very good idea to let us come here on our own, before your people come – we shan't have such fun when they're here, really, because all the rooms will be occupied, and people won't like us rushing everywhere."

"No, they won't," said Paul, thinking of the different way he would have to behave when his family came, with all their servants. "Let's make the most of it this week!"

Dimmy went down to see the three caretakers. She rang a bell from what she imagined to be the drawing-room, but nobody came. So she found her way to the enormous kitchens.

There were two fireplaces in the biggest kitchen, one with a fire, the other empty. Great cooking stoves lined the walls. Six or seven sinks showed up here and there. Dimmy paused at the door. Goodness – what a place!

Sitting at an open window at the far end were the three sisters. Dimmy had already seen the one called Edie Lots. She walked over to them.

They stood up as she came, looking nervous.

"Please sit down," said Dimmy, thinking what a queer trio they were. "I will sit with you too, and find out what is the best way to manage till Her Majesty, the Queen of Baronia, comes next week."

They all sat down. None of the three said a word. Dimmy talked pleasantly, and got Mrs Brimming to open her mouth at last.

She arranged that the three should look after the children, herself and Ranni, and should continue to clean the castle and keep it tidy until the Baronian servants came.

"Everything will go to rack and ruin then, I suppose!"

said Mrs Brimming, dolefully. "My son said it would. Those foreign servants!"

"That's not a fair thing to say," said Dimmy. "You will find that the Baronians will take a pride in the place and keep it beautifully. In any case, that is hardly your business. You may be sure that the Queen will see that nothing goes wrong. Now do please cheer up – after all, Lord Moon must try to make a little money out of a beautiful castle like this, empty for years!"

"My son says that Lord Moon wouldn't let it to foreigners if he knew about it," said Mrs Brimming. "He says it's only the agents that have let it, without consulting Lord Moon. He says—"

Dimmy began to feel as annoyed as Mrs Arnold had felt over this interfering son! "I'm afraid it is no business of your son's," she said. Then she remembered that one of the conditions Mrs Arnold had made was that the interfering fellow – what was his name – yes, Guy – should go away.

"I suppose your son is no longer here, now that the castle has been let?" she said.

"Of course he's not here," said Miss Edie Lots, in a loud voice. She glared at Dimmy, and seemed about to say a lot more – but Mrs Brimming nudged her sharply and she stopped.

Dimmy left them soon after that. "I suppose they all adore this Guy," she thought, as she went to find the children and help them to unpack. "Well, it's a good thing he's gone. He certainly wasn't in the kitchens. Now – which is the way to our rooms? Good gracious – it's a mile walk to find them, really it is!"

The children had begun their unpacking. They wouldn't let Dimmy help. "No, Dimmy – you've got your own unpacking to do," said Nora. "You always forget that we have to unpack our own things at school! We can do it all right now, honestly we can!"

"When do we have tea – and where?" called Mike. "I'm hungry already."

"I've arranged it for half-past four," said Dimmy. "And we're using the smallest room downstairs, off the right-hand side of the hall – the room where there are some queer old musical instruments on the walls."

"Oh yes – I know it," said Peggy. "It's a queer-shaped room – what do you call it – L-shaped."

"Yes – it's just like a letter L," said Jack. "With the bottom part of the L having windows all down the side. I vote we put a table there, and have our meals looking out of the window. We can see for miles then!"

They unpacked everything and arranged their things in the great drawers, leaving half of them empty, of course, because their clothes took up very little room!

"The drawers of these great chests are so enormous that I could almost get into one!" said Paul, coming into the boys' room, which was between his and the girls'. "Are you nearly ready? I had much more to unpack than you and I've finished first."

"Well, *we'd* have finished sooner if we'd just thrown everything higgledy-piggledy into drawers, like you have." said Mike. "Get off those jerseys, Paul. There's plenty of carpet to stand on without treading on my clothes!"

"Don't be so fussy," said Paul. "What time's tea? I could do with some."

But, like the others, he had to wait till half-past four. What should they do after that? Mike had an idea at once.

"The tower! We'll see if it's unlocked now. It jolly well ought to be!"

Queer Happenings

Mrs Brimming brought up a really delicious tea. The children approved of it so heartily, and said so in such loud voices, that Mrs Brimming actually smiled!

"Thank you, Brimmy," said Nora, unexpectedly. Dimmy looked at her sharply, and the others stared at Mrs Brimming, expecting her to object at once.

But to their surprise she didn't seem to mind at all. In fact, she actually smiled again. "Fancy your calling me that!" she said. "I haven't been called that since I was nurse to Lord Moon's youngest, years ago! They all called me Brimmy in those days!"

She then scurried out of the room like a frightened hen, evidently as surprised as the children that she had made such a long speech!

"What cheek to call her Brimmy when you've only seen her twice!" said Mike to Nora. "But you just hit her on a tender spot – didn't she, Dimmy?"

"Brimmy and Dimmy," said Nora, with a giggle. "I could make a nice rhyme up about Brimmy and Dimmy."

"Well, I'd rather you didn't," said Dimmy, pouring out tea. "I'm used to your silly ideas, but Mrs Brimming isn't. I'm quite sure she wouldn't like to hear you all singing a ridiculous song about her."

"All right," said Nora. "Anyway, there aren't any decent rhymes to Brimmy or Dimmy. I say – what a smashing chocolate cake. Nice and big too. Big enough for us all to have a second slice."

"You really mustn't finish that enormous cake today," said Dimmy. "I'm sure Mrs Brimming meant it to last us a whole week."

"Well, Brimy will have a whole lot of different ideas about us before the week is up," said Mike. "Where did these biscuits come from? They're not home-made."

"I looked at some of the piles of goods that have arrived," said Dimmy. "I told Mrs Brimming she could open what she thought would do for us – but she had already made this lovely chocolate cake."

"Well, I'm beginning to think she's not a bad sort, after all," said Jack. "What do you think, Paul?"

Paul thought that anyone who could make a chocolate cake as good as the one he was eating must be a good sort. Dimmy laughed. She listened to the friendly chatter of the five children, poured them out more cups of tea, cut slices of cake and sponge sandwich, and decided that they really were a nice set of children.

"What are you going to do after tea?" she asked.

"We're going to see the tower," said Mike promptly. "It ought to be unlocked now. Like to come, Dimmy?"

"I don't think so," said Dimmy. "I want to go and see that the beds are all made, and if they are aired properly. Mrs Brimming didn't know which rooms we were going to choose and I saw that she had piles of sheets airing by the fire – probably for us. I shall see to all that, and I'm sure she will help me. You go and explore the tower if you like."

"Right – we'll leave Brimmy and Dimmy to gossip together over sheets and pillow-cases," said Mike, getting up. "Everybody finished? Oh, sorry, Dimmy – I didn't see that your cup wasn't empty." He sat down again.

"Don't wait for me, please," said Dimmy. "I always enjoy a quiet cup after you've all gone! Go along now, and do whatever you want to do!"

"Dimmy's jolly glad to finish her tea in peace," said Nora, tickling the back of Dimmy's neck affectionately as she passed her chair. "She's been busy looking after us the whole of the meal. If you want any help with the beds, call us, Dimmy, and we'll come."

They trooped out of the room. Dimmy sat back peacefully, and poured out another cup of tea. They had had their meal in the curious L-shaped room as they had planned, and the table had been set in front of the windows, in the short bottom part of the L. Dimmy gazed out of the window at the view.

The room was silent. Dimmy couldn't even hear the voices of the children in the distance – she heard only the sound of her spoon stirring her tea slowly.

TWANG!

Dimmy jumped. The sound came so suddenly, and so very unexpectedly that for a minute she couldn't imagine what it was!

TWANG! There it was again. What could it be? Dimmy suddenly remembered the old musical instruments hung on the wall in the other part of the room – in the long part of the L. She smiled.

"Silly children!" she thought. "One of them has crept back to play a joke on me and make me jump. Mike, I expect! He's crept in and twanged one of the strings of some instrument. Silly boy."

She stirred her tea again, listening for a giggle.

TWANG! TWANG!

"I can hear you!" called out Dimmy, cheerily. "Twang all you like – I don't mind!"

DONG!

"Run away and play," called Dimmy. "Silly children!"

DONG!

Dimmy wondered what instrument made the "dong" noise. It was a queer sound – but then the musical instruments on the wall beyond were very queer-looking – old, foreign and most unusual. Perhaps the "dong" noise was made by that thing that looked like a drum but had stout strings stretched across it. Anyway, she wasn't going to bother to get up and see.

DONG!

"That's enough," said Dimmy. "You ought to know when a joke is played out."

She listened for a giggle, or the scuffle of feet creeping away, but she heard nothing. She began to drink her tea. No more of the twanging, donging noises came, and Dimmy was certain that whichever of the children had played the trick on her had crept away.

She went to see about the beds, and was soon in a deep discussion with Mrs Brimming about sheets and pillow-cases. She felt sure that the children were now busily exploring the tower.

But they weren't! They were all very angry indeed, because the tower door was still locked!

They had gone down the tapestry-covered corridor, and into the square-shaped room lined with great oak chests. Mike went straight to the tapestry that hung over the tower door to cover it.

He pulled it to one side, expecting to see the door.

He gaped in amazement, and turned startled eyes to the other four behind him. "It's gone!" he said. "There's no door here!"

The five looked hurriedly round the room. They could see no door at all – in fact, the whole wall was lined with chests. But about three feet from the tapestry hanging was a very tall chest, taller than the others.

"I bet it's behind that chest!" Jack said, and stepped over to it. "I *thought* that tapestry was hanging in a different place when I saw it just now. Give me a hand, Mike – we'll pull this chest away."

They tugged at it. It was astonishingly heavy, and needed all five of them to move it. Nobody thought of taking out the contents of the drawers to make the chest easier to handle!

Behind the chest, just as Jack had thought, was the tower door – tall, narrow – and locked!

"That's that awful man again!" said Jack, fiercely,

"It's gone! There's no door here!"

pulling at the ring handle. "What does he think he's doing? Fancy thinking he'd hide the door by putting a chest in front of it, and hanging the tapestry somewhere else. He must be mad. What's the point, anyhow?"

"The point is that he doesn't want anyone to go into the tower – because he's got some secret there," said Mike. The others nodded in agreement. Nora shook the handle, and then bent down and peered though the keyhole.

"I can see stone steps beyond the door," she said. "Oh how could that horrible man do such a thing! Whatever will your mother say, Paul, when she finds that this kind of thing is being done?"

"Perhaps by the time your mother's family comes, the door will be unlocked," said Jack slowly. "Maybe Mr Brimming hasn't had time to clear out of the tower – and thinks that he can stop us going in by tricks like this."

"Yes. I expect that's it," said Paul. "I bet he's made himself a kind of home in this tower – thinks of it as his own – and resents us coming. I bet he's got all his furniture in there still!"

"Well, if we suddenly find the key in the lock, and the tower is empty, we'll know we were right," said Jack. "He'll probably move out one dark night."

"It's *maddening*," said Peggy, shaking the handle in her turn, as if she thought that a little temper would make the door open. She put her mouth to the keyhole.

"Hey!" she shouted. "We know you're up there! Come down and unlock this door!"

Jack pulled her away. "Don't be so *silly*, Peggy," he said. "You wouldn't like it a bit if he came tearing down those stairs and flung the door open and glared at you out of his horrid eyes!"

Peggy looked at the door, rather alarmed. "No sound of footsteps!" she said, with a laugh. "He wouldn't hear my shouting, anyway. It wouldn't carry through that thick door and up those stone steps."

Mike was looking in the big chest they had hauled away from the door. "I'd like to know what makes it so jolly heavy," he said. "We *almost* couldn't drag it away. Look – rugs – cloth of some kind – and what's this in the bottom drawer of the chest, wrapped up in blue curtains?"

They all leaned over him as he knelt down, feeling in the big bottom drawer, He tugged at the cloth that wrapped up some great, heavy objects which could hardly be moved.

Nobody could move them an inch, and everyone grew very curious about what the heavy things could be. Jack took hold of a corner of one of the cloths and pulled hard until the heavy bundle unrolled.

"Rocks! Stones big enough to be called small rocks! My word, what a time he must have had, bringing them here to weight this chest down. I wonder the drawer didn't break – but these chests are very old and solid."

"No wonder we could hardly move the thing," said Paul. What are we going to do?"

"Leave the chest moved out of place so that Mr Guy Brimming can see we've discovered his little joke – a jolly silly one," said Jack. "He probably didn't reckon there'd be five of us to move it. Well! *Somehow* we've got to get into this tower – and it's certainly not going to be easy!"

Twang-Dong Again!

The five children left the chest where it was, pulled right away from the tower door. Guy Brimming would certainly know they had gone to explore the tower, found the door hidden, and discovered it behind the chest! Would he do anything further? They would wait and see.

They decided to go back to the L-shaped room and tell

Dimmy. She wasn't there, so they went to find her in the bedrooms upstairs, remembering that she was going to see to the beds. She was there, as they thought, just finishing Paul's room. She was alone.

"Oh Dimmy – have you done the beds all by yourself?" said Nora. "I'm sorry! I thought you'd be sure to call Peggy and me if you didn't have help."

"It's all right, dear – Mrs Brimming and one of the Lots came up to help me," said Dimmy. "I don't know which one – they're so alike, those two Lots. They've only just gone."

"We couldn't get into the tower, Dimmy," said Peggy, solemnly.

"The door was still locked," said Mike.

"And *some*body had tried to hide it by pulling a chest in front," said Paul. "What do you think of that?"

Dimmy laughed at their very solemn faces. "Well – I don't *really* think very much of it," she said. "I expect there are things in the tower that need to be cleaned, or perhaps cleared out. Maybe it's been used for storing all kinds of things in – and I've no doubt the tower will be unlocked and ready for anyone to use by the time Paul's family arrive next week."

"I think you're wrong, Dimmy," said Jack. "I think there's something *mysterious* about it. I'm sure it's something to do with that fellow Guy."

"You think a lot of foolish things," said Dimmy. "I'll mention it to Mrs Brimming – and you'll see, she'll have a quite ordinary explanation for it. Maybe the key is lost, as they said before."

"Well – but why was the door *hidden* this time?" persisted Jack. "And why was the chest that hid it weighted down with rocks so that it was almost impossible to move?"

"Rocks! Nonsense!" said Dimmy. "You're joking. And, by the way, talking of jokes – TWANG! DONG!"

She made a loud twanging sound with her mouth and

then a loud dong. The children stared at her in wonder. She laughed.

"Yes – you can look as inncent as you please!" she said. "But *I* know those innocent faces of yours! Aha! It was funny, wasn't it – TWANG! DONG!"

The children looked rather alarmed at this Twang-Dong speech. They stared at Dimmy, and then looked at one another.

"What exactly do you mean, Dimmy?" asked Nora at last. "Honestly, we can't imagine what you're getting at."

Dimmy looked rather annoyed. "Well, as you very well know, one of you – or maybe two or three of you, I don't know – crept back to the tea-room and twanged and donged one or two of the musical instruments on the wall," she said. "So don't deny it. It was a good joke, I agree, and the first time I jumped like anything. But don't pretend to be innocent now!"

"Not one of us went back to play a trick," said Jack, astonished. He looked round at the others. "We didn't, did we? We went straight to the tower door, and we've been there ever since. We don't know a thing about this twanging and donging."

Dimmy found it difficult to believe him. "Well, well – perhaps the instruments play a little tune by themselves," she said. "Anyway – I'd be glad to know which one of you it was, when you've made up your minds that the joke is now ended."

The five children left Dimmy and went down to the sitting-room, where they had had tea. They were very puzzled. "What on earth did Dimmy mean?" said Mike. "TWANG! DONG! I really thought she had gone suddenly dippy when she made those noises! We certainly don't know anything about them."

"Perhaps old musical instruments are like wicker chairs," said Peggy. "Perhaps their strings relax or something and make a noise."

"I never heard of such a thing before," said Mike. "Let's have a good look at them."

They stood beside the walls and looked at all the queer instruments – some were like big guitars, some like banjos, and there were tom-toms and tambourines – any amount of instruments were there, many of which the children had never seen before.

Jack touched a string, and it twanged softly. Soon they were all touching the various strings and knocking on the drums and tom-toms, so that a weird noise filled the room.

They got tired of it after a time. "I really think Dimmy must have fallen asleep or something, when we left her," said Jack. "Instruments just *don't* play themselves. Come on – let's have a game. Who says Racing Demon?"

Everyone did, and they took the cards from the cupboard where they had put their various games.

Dimmy came in, in the middle of the first game. "What a nice peaceful sight!" she said. "I'll get some mending to do, so don't ask me to play. I don't like those top-speed games!"

She got some sewing, and came to sit beside them at the window. The children were playing on the table where they had had tea. Dimmy glanced out of the window, marvelling at the wonderful view she could see for miles on miles. The sky was very blue, the distance was blue too. The sun was going down, and there was a golden light over everything.

Jack began to deal again. "Wait a moment before you begin another game," said Dimmy. "Look out there – did you ever see anything so lovely?"

They all gazed out of the window, and Nora began to make up a few lines of poetry in her mind. It was a very peaceful moment.

TWANG!

Everyone jumped violently and Dimmy dropped the pair of scissors she was holding.

"There!" said Dimmy. "That's the noise I heard before!"

"There!" said Dimmy, in a whisper. "That's the noise I heard before. Wasn't it one of you, then?"

"No – we told you it wasn't," said Nora. "And anyway, we're all here now. Not one of us has moved to the other part of the room, where the guitars and things are."

Nothing more happened. Jack got up and went round the bend of the L-shaped room into the long part where the walls held so many instruments. Nobody was there. The door was open and he shut it.

"Nobody there," he said, and sat down. "Maybe somebody crept in and twanged a guitar. I wonder who the joker is!"

He began to deal once more.

TWANG!

Everyone jumped again, it was so loud. Jack and Mike raced round the bend of the room. The door was still shut!

"But someone might have crept in, twanged, and gone out quickly," said Jack. "Look – there's a key in the door. We'll turn it and lock the door – then the joker will be completely done!"

He turned the key. Dimmy looked rather startled. She had quite thought that one of the children had played the joke on her after tea – but now she saw that they had told the truth. Somebody else was doing the twanging!

DONG!

Jack slapped his cards down. "This is silly!" he said. "I locked the door!"

Mike disappeared into the other part of the room. "It's still locked!" he called. "Well and truly locked. Can't be opened at all."

He took a look at the instruments on the wall, wondering which one had twanged. He looked for a quivering string, but could see none. He went back to the others, as puzzled as they were.

DONG!

"Blow it," said Jack. "*Who's* doing it?"

79

"I don't think anyone is," said Dimmy, picking up her scissors, which she had dropped again. "I think it's just one or two of the instruments doing it on their own – perhaps it's this hot weather – making them expand or something."

"Well, there doesn't seem anything else to think," said Peggy, "except—"

"Except what?" asked Jack, as Peggy stopped.

"Well – except that we heard that Queer Things Happen here," said Peggy. "Don't you remember what the waitress said at that hotel? 'Strange Noises – Queer Happenings.'"

"Don't!" said Nora. "I didn't believe it. And I don't want to believe it now."

"And do you remember she said that books jumped out of the bookshelves?" said Peggy. "Oh dear – I hope things don't begin to jump about."

"Now listen to me," said Dimmy, in a suddenly brisk voice, "this kind of talk is foolish and ridiculous. I don't want to hear any more of it. Fancy believing the silly tales of a waitress! Books jumping! Too silly for words!"

"Well – but we *did* hear a Queer Noise," said Peggy.

"I dare say we did – but we've decided that it's the hot weather making the strings of some instrument or other expand, and go twang and dong," said Dimmy.

DONG!

"Yes, just like that," said Dimmy firmly, as the curious dong noise came from round the bend of the room. "Nobody is there. The door is locked – and if the instruments like to sigh and make a noise because it's hot, what does it matter?"

TWANG!

"Well, I expect you're right, Dimmy," said Nora. "If it's only noises like that I don't mind a bit. Let's go on with the game!"

Jack began once more to deal, and they gathered up their cards, listening all the time for another twang or dong.

But none came! They began to forget about it and played with a lot of noise. Dimmy watched them, glad that they were no longer puzzled. But she was very puzzled indeed.

Was she right in thinking that the noises had been natural ones? Yes, of course she must be right. She looked out of the window at the view. The sun was sinking low.

Bang-bang!

Everyone jumped so much that half the cards slid off the table. Dimmy leapt to her feet. *Now* what was it?

A voice came from the other side of the door – a plaintive, puzzled voice.

"Please, Miss Dimity, we're bringing your supper, and the door's locked."

"Gosh – that was only Brimmy knocking at the door!" said Jack, in great relief. He ran to open it. Brimmy was there with a large tray, and behind her were the two solemn sisters, also with trays.

Nobody explained the locked door. It suddenly began to seem rather silly. At the sight of a very nice supper all six completely forgot both Twang and Dong, and willing hands took the trays and set the table!

"Aha!" said Jack. "A meal fit for a King – and certainly fit for a Prince! Dimmy – are we ready? One, two, three, begin!"

An Interesting Discovery

It was fun to go to bed that night in the little suite of three rooms. The doors between were left open so that shouting could go on between the three boys and the two girls.

Nobody felt sleepy at all. When they were all in pyjamas, the girls and Paul went to sit on the beds in the middle room to talk to Mike and Jack. It wasn't long before a pillow-fight began, of course. With shrieks and thuds the fight raged round the room, and a chair went over with a bang.

"We'll have Dimmy in if we make too much row," panted Mike. "Oh you beast, Paul – you've taken my pillow. Give it back!"

Thud! Biff! Giggles and shrieks, bare feet pattering all over the bedroom, and someone pinned in a corner! And then Nora gave an agonized yell.

"Paul! Ass! Your pillow's gone out of the window!"

There was a pause in the battle at once. Paul looked rather abashed as Mike rounded on him. "Idiot, Paul! What did you do that for?"

"It sort of flew out of my hand," explained Paul, and went to the window. He leaned out so far that Jack caught him by his pyjama trousers, afraid that he might pitch out and join the pillow. "I can see it," he said. "It's down on the grass below. I'll get it."

He ran to the door of his room and opened it. Dimmy was just coming up the corridor! She saw him and called out.

"Paul! You ought to be in bed long ago. What are you doing?"

"Just looking out," said Paul. "Are you coming to bed now, Dimmy?"

"Yes, I am – and I shall come along just before I get into bed and make sure you are all asleep," said Dimmy, firmly. "So if you have any ideas of playing catch or hide-and-seek round the castle corridors, just put them out of your head! I suppose you've been pillow-fighting or something – you look so hot and tousled."

"We've had a bit of a fight," said Paul, grinning. "Good night, Dimmy." He shut the door and went back to the others, who had leapt into their beds as soon as they had heard Dimmy's voice.

"It was Dimmy," said Paul, poking his head into the boys' room. "She's just going to bed – but she's coming

82

along last thing to see if we're alseep. Blow! What shall I do about the pillow? I don't like to go down and hunt for it now in case she comes along."

"Wait till she's been along and I'll go with you," said Mike. "It's getting dark now – we'll take our torches and slip out when it's safe. Get into bed now, for goodness' sake. Ranni will be along next!"

Mike was right. Ranni came along in about five minutes' time and quietly opened Paul's door to make sure he was in bed and asleep. There was no sound as Ranni switched on the light and saw a curled-up heap in Paul's bed. He went out quietly and shut the door. Paul heaved a sigh of relief.

When Dimmy came at last both the girls were fast asleep – and so was Paul! Dimmy had a word with Mike and Jack, said good night, and went out.

Mike sat up in bed. "Paul!" he called in a low voice. "Are you ready?"

No answer! Paul was far away, lost in delightful dreams of towers and castles and ruined villages. Mike scrambled out of bed and went to wake him – but Jack called him back.

"Let him be! He'll probably make some noise and wake up Ranni. We two will go. Got your torch?"

Without bothering to put on their dressing-gowns the two boys crept out of the room in slippers, each with his torch. The night was so warm that they felt hot even in pyjamas! It was dark now, too, and they crept along the dim corridors, flashing their torches when they came to the stretches of darkness between the lights which glowed dimly along the corridors at intervals.

"Better go out of the front door," whispered Mike. "We might bump into Brimmy or one of the Lots if we go towards the kitchen, and we're not sure yet where any other door is."

"Do you remember how the front door opened with-

83

They unbolted the great door.

out anyone there to open it, when we came today?" whispered Jack. "I'd forgotten it till now."

"Must have been one of the Lots, I expect," said Mike. "It would be just like them to scurry away as soon as they opened the door! Here we are – isn't it enormous?"

They unbolted the great door, hoping that no one would hear them. They turned the big key, and then twisted the handle. The door opened very quietly indeed, swinging back easily on its hinges.

The two boys went down the big flight of steps outside. "Round to the right," said Jack, in a low voice. "We'll keep close to the walls, and then we are bound to come to where the pillow fell."

The walls of the castle were not built in a straight line, but bulged out into odd shapes, sometimes rounded, sometimes square, as if the builder had planned queer-shaped rooms, or had planned towers that he had not completed.

"The pillow ought to be somewhere about here," whispered Jack, and shone his torch down on to the grass. Then he looked upwards to try to make out if they were under their bedroom windows.

He caught Mike's arm suddenly, and whispered in his ear. "Mike! The tower's over there, look – do you see what I see?"

Mike looked up – and saw the enormously high tower against the dark night sky, where stars shone, giving out a faint light. He gave a sudden exclamation.

"The windows! They're lighted! Somebody's in the tower!"

The two boys gazed up at the great tower. "Three of the narrow windows are lighted," whispered Jack. "Three! Somebody's very busy in there tonight!"

"Perhaps that man Guy is clearing out, as we thought," said Mike. "Clearing out his belongings, I mean."

"I wonder if it *is* that fellow," said Jack, gazing up, and wishing he could see into one of the windows just for a minute or two.

"Let's stay and watch for a bit – whoever is there might come to the window," said Mike. So they sat down on the thick grass and watched the lighted windows of the tower. Once they saw someone passing across a window, but couldn't make out if it was Guy or not.

They grew tired of watching, at last. "Let's get the pillow and go," said Jack, getting up. Then he had an idea and caught hold of Mike's arm. "Wait! What about sneaking along to that little square room where the tower door is, and seeing if the door's unlocked? We know someone is in the tower now."

"Yes! Smashing idea," said Mike, thrilled. "We might creep up the steps, even – and see what's going on. Come on – we'll go now."

They made their way back to the front door. It was still open, for which Jack was very thankful. He couldn't help thinking that a door which could apparently open by itself might also shut by itself! However, there it was, half-open just as they had left it.

They went in, shut, locked and bolted the door again, went past the silent suits of armour and then set off to the little square room. Down the tapestried passage they went, and into the square room.

It was in darkness, and neither boy could find a light switch. They turned on their torches, and at once weird shadows leapt round the walls. The boys flashed their torches to the place where the door should be. The chest was still out of its place, where they had left it. The tall, narrow door showed up plainly, set deeply in the wall.

Mike tiptoed to it and took hold of the handle. He turned it carefully. Then he groaned.

"No good!" he said. "It's still locked. Blow! No adventure tonight."

"We were silly to hope it would be open," said Jack. "That fellow wouldn't take any chances of being discovered in the tower, I'm sure. He'd be furious if he thought we had been out and had seen the lighted windows!"

"Well – it's no good waiting about here," said Mike. "Blow that fellow! I'd like to go and explore that tower more than anything else in the world! Why is he so secretive? Has he got something up there he doesn't want anyone to see? Why does he lock himself up?"

"I suppose because he knows he ought to have left the castle by now," said Jack. "I say – let's put something against the bottom of the door, so that when he opens it he pushes the obstacle away."

86

"What's the point of that?" asked Mike.

"Just to let him know we're about!" grinned Jack. "He'll know we're suspicious, he'll know we think there's someone up the tower, and that we'll be watching to see if the obstacle we put here is moved. He can certainly put it back again if he goes *out* of the door – but when he goes back he won't be able to – and we'll find it out of its place, and know that he's gone back up the tower again."

"All right – we'll get a rug out of one of the chests," said Mike. They got one, folded it lengthways, and shoved it firmly against the bottom of the door.

"Perhaps the door opens inwards *into* the tower," said Jack, "and not outwards, into this room. If it does, the rug won't prove anything. He could open the door, see the rug, and step over it without moving it."

"No. The door opens into this room," said Mike, and pointed to a curving line on the stone floor. "See where part of the bottom edge has scraped the stone each time it has been opened."

"Yes, you're right," said Jack, tucking the rug even more firmly against the door. He yawned widely. "Gosh, I'm sleepy now. Let's go to bed. Got the pillow?"

"Yes," said Mike, picking up the pillow from the floor. "Well, Paul's pillow certainly gave us the chance of making sure the tower is occupied!"

They went back to their rooms, keeping a sharp lookout for Ranni, who got up several times a night, as a rule, to see that his little master was safe! They didn't want to run into him.

The girls and Paul were still asleep. Mike put Paul's pillow at the end of his bed, and then he and Jack climbed thankfully between their sheets, and snuggled down.

"Good night," said Jack. "We'll ask Brimmy about the tower tomorrow, and see what she says!"

There was no answer. Mike was asleep already!

Jack Hears A Good Many Things

Next morning the two boys told the others about the lighted windows in the tower that they had seen the night before. The girls laughed when they heard about the rug that the boys had put in front of the door. "We'll go to the square room immediately after breakfast," they decided, "and see if it's still there."

But the rug had disappeared! The door was still shut and locked. Mike stared round the room. "Guy must have come out of the tower, seen the rug, and put it away somewhere. He just didn't bother to put it back. He doesn't care whether we suspect anything or not."

Jack was opening the many chests and peering inside. "Here it is!" he called at last. "Just chucked in here, still folded lengthways."

"Well – he knows we're on his track," said Nora, thrilled.

"I wish we were," said Jack. "As long as he slips in and out without anyone seeing him and challenging him, and as long as he keeps the tower locked up, we can't possibly do anything about it."

"We can ask Brimmy," said Nora. "She's doing some dusting and sweeping in the rooms downstairs. I saw her as we came here. Let's go and ask her."

They went to find Brimmy. She was on her knees, sweeping vigorously, her face very red.

"Excuse me, Brimmy," began Mike, "that tower door is still locked. Where's the key please?"

Brimmy looked up nervously, pushing some stray hairs away from her face. "The key?" she said. "Well now, perhaps it's still lost."

"It isn't," said Jack. "Somebody's been in and out of the tower door, so we know there must be a key."

"I daresay it's been found then," said Brimmy, beginning to sweep vigorously again. "There's – er – there's things in that tower that must be cleared out before the Queen comes."

"What things?" said Jack, determined to find out *some*thing. "Do they belong to Lord Moon? Are they very precious? Is that why they are locked up?"

"Maybe," said Brimmy, sounding annoyed as well as nervous. "There's things I don't want to talk about, so please don't ask so many questions. You're only renting the castle, not buying it! Everything will be unlocked, cleaned and ready for the Queen when she comes next week. You don't need the tower, and it's not safe for children."

"Why?" asked Nora.

"Oh, these questions!" said Brimmy, pushing more hair out of her eyes and looking really harassed. "Will you please leave me to my work, or I'll complain to Miss Dimity? I'm sure she wouldn't let you go up the tower, anyway, and risk falling out of those high windows. They're really dangerous."

At that moment Ranni appeared at the door. "Miss Dimity is going to take the car into Bolingblow for some things she needs," he said. "Would you like to come too?"

"Yes!" said everyone, and went out of the room, much to Mrs Brimming's relief.

"Listen – I'm not coming," said Jack, as soon as they were out of hearing. "You go, all of you – and I'll hide around somewhere. I've an idea that Brimmy will go and warn that Guy fellow, as soon as she thinks we're all safely out of the way. I might be able to find out something."

"Right," said Mike. "Well – we'll think of you snooping around while we're having big ice-creams!"

Jack hid in his room while the others went off. When they were safely gone he went cautiously into the long corridor outside his room. No one was about. He decided to go downstairs by one of the back staircases. He might hear Brimmy telling the two Miss Lots something.

The staircase led to what seemed to be staff bedrooms on the ground floor. Not a sound was to be heard. Jack passed the open doors of the bedrooms and went down an uncarpeted passage, glad that he had on rubber shoes.

He rounded a corner and came to an entrance to one of the kitchens. And then he heard voices! He stood at the half-open door, trying to make out if they were the women's voices.

Yes – they were certainly women's voices, worried and anxious. And then came a man's voice, raised as if in anger.

"Well, I can't! It won't be finished for some days. I can't help it. You'll have to make what excuses you can. It's your own fault for disobeying orders and letting people see over the place. But that tower will be locked, I tell you – so make what excuses you like about it. You don't know what you've done, letting these people into the castle just now!"

Then Jack heard angry footsteps on the stone kitchen floor, footsteps that sounded as bad-tempered and determined as the voice! The boy slid quietly behind a cupboard.

A man went by to the back stairs down which Jack had come. Jack peered out at him. Was it Guy? Yes, it was, he was sure of it. Jack debated with himself – should he follow him and see if he went back to the tower – he might even be able to see where the key was kept! No – it would be safely in his pocket, anyway. That was no good.

Jack decided that on the whole it might be foolish to follow the angry man. He stayed where he was for a

Was it Guy? Yes, it was, he was sure of it.

minute or two and then came out from his hiding-place. He went into the big kitchen. Brimmy was at the far end, weeping, and the two Miss Lots were standing by gloomily. Brimmy gave a little cry when she saw Jack.

"I thought you'd gone out! Surely you aren't all back yet!"

"I didn't go," said Jack. "What's the matter, Mrs Brimming? Why are you crying?"

"Oh – just one of my headaches, that's all," said Brimmy, dabbing her eyes. "Do you want something to do? Why don't you go and listen to the musical-box with a hundred tunes? Or go and look round the library?"

Jack saw that she wanted to get rid of him. Perhaps she was afraid he would ask her some awkward questions. He changed the subject.

"Do you know anything about that old ruined village?" he asked. "We thought we'd go and explore it one day. Why did everyone leave it?"

There was dead silence. Jack looked at the three women in surprise. They looked as if they didn't know what in the world to say!

"What's up?" said Jack. "Anything mysterious about the village?"

"No. No, of course not," said Miss Edie Lots in a suddenly loud voice. "There used to be mines there, you know – tin mines, I believe. And then something happened and they were given up, and the people drifted away to Bolingblow. That's why it's tumble-down, all in ruins. It's a horrid, lonely place – a place that no one in their senses would go near – especially at night!"

"I see," said Jack. "It sounds *most* interesting! We'll really have to go and explore it."

"Those old mines are dangerous," said Brimmy, joining in suddenly, her voice rather shaky. "If you fell down a shaft, that would be the end of you."

"We shouldn't be so silly," said Jack, wondering why

the three women seemed so worried. What was going on here? What was that man Guy doing? If only he could get into the tower!

"Well – I'll go and find the musical-box," said Jack, thinking that it would be fun to get it out and have it ready for the others when they came back. "Where is it?"

"I'll show you," said Miss Edie Lots, in her harsh, loud voice. She led the way, and soon Jack found himself in the hall, and then going down one of the corridors that led to the rooms near their own sitting-room.

"I say," he said, as he followed Miss Lots. "I say – a funny thing happened yesterday. You know those old musical instruments hanging on the wall in the room we've taken for our sitting-room, don't you? Well – they suddenly go TWANG! or DONG! – just like that! Queer, isn't it? Have you ever heard them?"

Miss Edie clutched at him, and Jack was surprised to see that she looked terrified. "You've heard them?" she said, in a loud whisper. "No! No! Oh, what dreadful thing is going to happen?"

"I've no idea," said Jack, politely. "What's up *now*? Why should anything dreadful happen because a bit of twanging and donging goes on?"

"It's the old legend," said Miss Edie, looking over her shoulder as if she expected a Twang or a Dong at any moment. "When those instruments make noises, something awful always happens!"

"What do you mean?" said Jack, with great interest. "Do you expect the castle to fall down or something – or the tower to blow up?"

"There's a legend – written in one of the old books in the library – that none but the Moon family may live here in peace," said Miss Edie. "They say that the spirit of the old castle gets angry and restless when others come, and queer things happen."

"I don't believe it," said Jack. "Beliefs like that belong to centuries ago, not to these days! You can't frighten *me* like that, Miss Lots!"

"I'm not trying to frighten you," said Miss Edie, forgetting to whisper in her annoyance with this unbelieving boy. "I've lived here all my life – I know that what I'm saying is true. I've seen dreadful things happen to those who have come here and defied the old legend. I could tell you many tales – people who have—"

"Save them up till the others come back, and then you can tell all of us," said Jack. "We'd absolutely love to hear those crazy old tales. They're such fun."

Miss Edie glared at him. She simply could not make out this smiling boy who disbelieved all she said. Most people were scared. She lowered her voice.

"The spirit of the old castle is restless again," she said, sounding really mysterious. "I can feel it! No wonder those noises came again. Now other things will happen. They always do"

"How smashing!" said Jack, sounding delighted. "What kind of things? My word, the others will be thrilled to hear all this!"

Miss Edie had now had enough of Jack. "I am not going to tell you things just for you to laugh at," she said, looking most unpleasant. "You can wait and see what happens – but be sure that my words will come true! Those noises always come first – a warning, no doubt."

"No doubt at all," agreed Jack, cheerfully. "Awfully kind of the old spirit of the castle to warn us in such an exciting way. Well – where's this musical-box? I'd like to set it going, if the spirit of the castle has no objection!"

All Very Peculiar

Miss Edie led him into a room that seemed very dark because it faced towards the hillside behind the castle, and not to the valley below.

"Do you want the light on?" she said, sounding cross. "The switch is over there."

"No thanks," said Jack. "Oh, is that the musical-box? My word, how enormous – and what a beauty!"

He went over to a long wooden box. It was about five feet long and a foot and half wide, and stood on a pedestal. Both box and pedestal were of walnut, and were beautifully carved. Little dancing figures ran all round the box and the pedestal too, carved by a clever and loving hand.

"How do you work it?" asked Jack, lifting up the lid, and peering inside at shining brass rollers set with myriads of tiny teeth.

There was no answer, and Jack looked round. Miss Edie had gone without a word! Jack grinned. Did she really think she could frighten him with those silly old tales? He wished the others could have been there to listen to everything.

"Now how does this box work?" he thought, bending over it. "Ah – here are the instructions on the lid. It has to be wound up. I wonder who made it. It must be very, very old!"

He wound it up carefully, and pushed back the lever that set it going. The roller went smoothly and slowly round, and the musical box began to play a merry old tune.

Its sweet, melodious music filled the room and Jack

listened, quite entranced. There was something unearthly and fairylike about the tinkling tunes that followed one after another, all different. The boy recognized some of them, but others he had never heard.

A sound disturbed him. He looked round the dim room into which no sunshine ever came. He saw that it was the same room that had the portrait of a long-ago Lord Moon over the mantlepiece. The face stared down at him, dark and forbidding, the black lock falling over the forehead. The eyes seemed to be looking straight at Jack, angrily and fiercely.

"Sorry if I'm disturbing you, Lord Moon," said Jack, politely to the portrait, as another tune began to play. "Please don't look so fierce!"

The same sound came again to Jack's ears through the tinkling of the music. It seemed as if it came from somewhere by the mantlepiece. Was it a hiss?

Jack walked over to the great fireplace. He listened. Then he looked up at the big portrait above his head. Lord Moon stared down as if he could say a great many things to this stupid boy who was disturbing his peace.

And then a curious thing happened. Lord Moon's eyes seemed to become alive! They glowed angrily, and seemed to flash with anger. Then came the hiss again!

Jack backed away. He was not a timid boy, and had plenty of courage – but this was very unexpected, and very eerie too, in that dim room, with the musical-box playing its tinkling music all the time.

He backed into a stool and fell over. When he got up and looked at the portrait again, the eyes no longer glowed, though Lord Moon still looked as unpleasant as ever.

Jack stared up, surprised to find his heart beating fast. Had he imagined those eyes? Was it some sudden trick of the light? The hissing noise had stopped now too. Jack frowned and walked back to the musical-box. He suddenly looked back over his shoulder at the portrait. Were those eyes looking at him, alive again and angry?

They were looking at him, certainly, but there was no glint in them now. "Imagination!" said Jack to himself. "Well, if that's the sort of effect this castle is going to have on me, I'd better be careful! I could have sworn those eyes came alive for a moment!"

The musical-box ran down with a slowing up of the music. Jack began to wind it up again. Then he heard a voice calling loudly.

"Jack! *Jack*! Where are you?"

He jumped violently – but then laughed at himself. It was only Mike's voice – they were back from Bolingblow already!

He ran out of the room and went to find the others. "Here he is!" cried Nora's voice, and she ran to meet him. "Jack, you ought to have come with us! We had meringues and ices both together. We brought you a meringue back. Here it is."

She gave it to him. He went into the L-shaped sitting-room where the others were. Dimmy was there too, and they were helping her to sort out the shopping she had bought.

"What have *you* been doing. Jack?" asked Dimmy. "You should have come with us!"

"I've been playing that musical-box with a hundred tunes," said Jack. "In the room where that portrait of a long-ago Lord Moon is – with the horrid eyes!"

Something in his voice made Mike look up. "Anything interesting?" said Mike. Jack nodded his head towards Dimmy, and Mike understood at once that Jack had something interesting to say, but not till they were alone. Fortunately Dimmy departed from the room with an armful of shopping in a short time, and left the children alone together.

"Jack! You've got something to tell us!" said Mike.

97

"What is it? Did you hear anything? Did something happen?"

"Yes – I heard plenty – and something *did* happen," said Jack. "Listen!"

He told the others what he had overheard Guy say to his mother and aunts. He told them what Miss Edie had said about the old legend of the spirit of the castle. Everyone laughed.

"Fancy trying to make us believe that the Twang and Dong came because the castle was angry we were here!" said Mike. "How idiotic!"

TWANG!

There was a startled silence. The sound echoed through the air and then was gone.

"H'm! That was timed very well," said Jack, noting that Nora and Paul looked scared. "Now then, spirit of the castle – what about a Dong?"

"Don't, Jack!" said Nora, anxiously.

No Dong came. "The spirit of the castle's gone a bit deaf," said Jack, cheerfully. "It didn't hear my request."

TWANG! Everyone jumped again. Jack ran round the bend of the room and examined every stringed instrument there. Not one had a vibrating string to show that someone had twanged it, or that it had somehow done it of its own accord.

Jack went back. He had suddenly remembered the gleaming eyes of the portrait. He glanced at Nora and Paul again. They both looked a bit scared, so Jack decided not to say anything in front of them about the portrait. He would tell Mike – and perhaps Peggy – when they were alone with him.

"Where's the musical-box?" said Nora. "Let's go and hear it."

But it was too late to do that because at that moment the two Miss Lots appeared with the midday meal. Dimmy appeared too.

"Oh thank you," she said. "Just put the trays down, and we'll set the table as usual. What a lovely meal!"

Meringues and ices did not seem to have spoilt anyone's appetite. The children looked joyfully at the trays left on the sideboard, lifting the lids that covered the various dishes.

"Cold ham. Tongue! Tomatoes – heaps of them, look. Hard-boiled eggs in salad. Potatoes in their jackets. And an enormous trifle with cherries on the top."

"Stop fiddling about with the lids," said Dimmy. "Come along, you two girls – set the table, please. Mike and Paul, you carry everything over carefully when the cloth is on."

They were soon sitting down and tucking in. It always amazed Dimmy to see how much the five could eat. It looked as if not a single crumb or fragment would be left.

"If anyone wants a biscuit or fruit, they are both on the sideboard," said Dimmy at the end of the meal.

Only Mike could manage any, and he went to take a plum. Just as he was taking it, one of the now familiar noises came from somewhere behind him.

DONG!

"There's the Dong you asked for," called Mike to Jack, glancing round quickly at each of the instruments on the wall. He took his plum back with him to the others. Nobody said anything about the noise, not even Dimmy, and a loud chatter arose as usual.

CRASH! That *did* make them all jump!

"Whatever was that?" said Dimmy. "It sounded round the bend of the room again, where the instruments are."

They all went to look. A big blue jar lay in fragments on the floor. "Look at that!" said Dimmy, vexed. "It's fallen from that shelf. But how could it have happened? What a pity!"

"It's a good thing you were here with us, Dimmy," said Mike. "You might have thought one of us had broken it! We'll have to tell Mrs Brimming. I wonder what made the jar jump off like that – it must have been too near the edge."

Jack remembered all that Miss Edie Lots had told him, and he couldn't help feeling a bit uncomfortable. They went back into the windowed corner, where they had meals. The girls began to clear the table, and stack the dirty plates and dishes on the trays for the caretakers to take down when they came.

Miss Edie Lots appeared in a short while, followed by Mrs Brimming. They stared in dismay at the broken jar; the fragments still lay on the carpet because there was no brush to sweep them up.

"I can't imagine how it happened," said Dimmy, "but we heard a crash, and when we came into this part of the room we saw this broken jar. It must have been too near the edge of the shelf it was on, and have fallen down."

"It was *well* back on its shelf," said Miss Edie. "I dusted this room myself this morning."

"Well, I'm sorry – but none of us had anything to do with it," said Dimmy. "I can't think how it could have happened."

"It's the beginning!" said Edie Lots, in a peculiar voice that made everyone look at her in surprise.

"The beginning of *what*?" asked Dimmy.

"All kinds of things," said Edie. "You'd best be gone before worse happens. The old legend is coming true again. You ask *him* what I said!" She nodded her head towards Jack. "I tell you, it's the beginning – you shouldn't have come to this castle. Bad things will happen!"

"Please don't be so silly," said Dimmy, coldly. "I cannot imagine what you are talking about. Take the trays and go!"

The Ruined Village

Mrs Brimming looked upset, and Edie Lots pursed up her lips and looked angry and most unpleasant. Dimmy turned to the children.

"I'm going upstairs for a rest. It really is so very hot this afternoon. What are you going to do ? Go for a walk?"

"Well – we might go and explore that old ruined village," said Mike. "We passed the fork to it again this morning and we felt we really must go and see it soon."

Edie Lots stared round at him and opened her mouth as if to say something. Dimmy saw her, and was determined that she shouldn't be allowed to talk again – such nonsense as she talked too! So she began to speak herself, and went on firmly until the trays had disappeared out of the room, carried by Brimmy and Edie!

Edie had no chance to say whatever it was she had meant to say – though Jack could have guessed! She would have tried to put them off going to the mines.

"I'm going upstairs now," said Dimmy. "Don't start off for your walk for half an hour or so – not *immediately* after your enormous lunch. Have a read."

"Let's go and play that musical-box, Jack," said Nora. "I do so love those tinkly musical-boxes. Does it really play a hundred tunes?"

"Well, I counted only thirty-three, and then you called me," said Jack. "All right – we'll go and count a few more. It's a lovely box – the finest I've ever heard."

They went along to the dim room with the portrait. Jack glanced up at it, half-afraid he might see those eyes gleaming again. But they were just as usual, staring down fiercely and broodingly. The children went over to the musical-box.

Jack started it. The silvery tune tinkled out, and all the children listened in delight. Just as it ended, Dimmy came quickly into the room.

"Have any of you been into my room? Surely you couldn't have played such a silly joke on me?"

All five stared at her in surprise. "What joke?" asked Jack, at last. "You *know* we haven't been upstairs since lunch-time, Dimmy."

"Well – it's very strange then," said Dimmy, frowning.

"What's happened?" asked Jack.

"The whole room is changed round," said Dimmy. "The bed is in a different place. My clothes are put into different drawers. The photos I brought with me are lying flat on their faces – and one of the vases on the chest has fallen down and smashed."

"Just like that other one did!" exclaimed Mike. "But Dimmy – who in the world could have done such a silly thing to your room? *Your* room, too! Honestly, not one of us would do such a thing."

"No, I don't think you would," said Dimmy. "Well, it must have been done in spite, perhaps – I really don't know! I can't think that one of the caretakers could have done it, grown women as they are – it's such a silly, spiteful thing. But I suppose one of them *might* have done it, just because we've arrived here and are making more work for them."

Dimmy went out of the room. The children looked at one another. "Poor old Dimmy," said Peggy. "I don't know how anyone could possibly feel spiteful towards *her* – she's so kind."

"I bet it's Guy," said Paul. "Or the spirit of the castle, whoever he may be! But he's a nasty fellow if he likes to smash Lord Moon's vases!"

The musical-box was still tinkling on. "Has anyone counted the tunes?" said Jack. "I forgot to."

"Yes, I have," said Peggy. "We've got to forty-one now. Oh listen – here's Cherry Ripe! We had it at school last term. It's a very old tune."

They were all listening to Cherry Ripe when Jack heard a noise by the mantlepiece. A distant hiss, just as he had heard before. He looked across uneasily.

Mike had heard it too, and Paul, but the girls were too engrossed in the musical-box. Paul suddenly gave a loud cry that made them all jump violently.

"Shut up, Paul," said Nora, crossly. "You nearly made me jump out of my skin!"

Paul was staring at the portrait. Mike and Jack were doing the same.

"Its eyes!" gulped Paul. "They came alive! They looked at me."

Nora and Peggy looked at the portrait too. "Don't be so silly," said Peggy. "You're imagining things! The eyes are horrid – but they're only *painted* ones that seem to look at you. Don't be such an ass, Paul."

CRASH!

A picture fell suddenly off the wall behind them, and made them all jump again. Jack stared at it. Then he went over and looked at the picture cord it had hung on. He at once saw that the broken ends were frayed.

"It's all right!" he said cheerfully to the others. "Nothing to do with the glowering Lord Moon – just frayed-out picture cord."

"Well, I don't like it," said Paul, who looked quite pale. "I *did* see those eyes gleaming just as if they were alive. Didn't *you*, Mike? You were looking too."

Jack frowned quickly at Mike. He didn't want him to say anything in front of the girls, who had neither of them seen the eyes glowing as if they were alive.

So Mike said nothing in answer to Paul, but suggested that it was time they went for their walk. "This room is getting on my nerves," he said. "I can't bear that fellow,

103

Lord Moon, glowering at us, and pictures falling down. Stop the musical-box, Jack, we'll go out."

"We got to forty-three tunes," said Peggy. "Listen – what's that hissing noise?"

Everyone had heard the hiss that time, for the musical-box was now silent. Jack gave the girls no chance of finding out what usually followed the hiss, and he hustled them out of the room. "It's nothing. Let's go, or we shan't have time to get to that old village."

The girls went out obediently. Jack glanced back into the room. Yes – those eyes were gleaming again, as if they were alive. Was it a trick? What a peculiar one, if so!

They made their way to the front door and went out into the sunshine, which seemed quite dazzling after the dim room where they had played the old musical-box. Ranni was outside, doing something to the car.

"Oh Ranni! What a bit of luck you're here with the car!" said Paul. He turned to Jack eagerly. "He could take us to the fork of the road in the car, Jack – it would save a lot of time. Then we need only walk up the fork to the old village. It's so frightfully hot this afternoon."

"Good idea," agreed Jack and they all got in. Ranni was quite willing to take them. He was bored with so little to do. The car swept off down the drive and out of the gates. It wasn't long before they were down the hill and at the fork of the road.

"I'll wait here," said Ranni. "I can do a little polishing till you come back."

The five of them set off up the rough road. It had never been much more than a village lane at any time, but now it was so overgrown that in places it was like a field. Only the hedges each side showed the children that they were in an old lane.

It took them a quarter of an hour to reach the village. What a desolate sight!

Every house was empty, the windows were broken, the

Every house was empty.

roofs had gaps in them where tiles had fallen off. A few houses had once been thatched, and there were great holes in the straw roofs.

"This must have been the main street," said Jack, stopping. "Is that a little church? What a shame to let it fall to bits like that."

"How silent and still it is!" said Nora. "Poor old village –no one to walk down the streets, or bang a door or call out cheerily."

"What's that over there?" said Mike, pointing. "A lot of tumble-down sheds and shacks – and that looks like some kind of old machinery."

"It's the mines, of course," said Jack. "Don't you remember – we heard there were mines here once, before the people all drifted away from the village. I suppose they were worked out. They were tin mines."

Nobody knew anything about tin mines. They walked over to the shacks, and looked at the old, rusted machinery. Jack came to a shaft driven deep into the earth. He looked down it.

"Come and see – here's where the miners went down," he said. "And there's another entrance over here – a bigger one."

"Let's go down!" said Mike.

This was just what Jack wanted to do, but Peggy and Nora looked doubtful. "Do *you* want to come, Paul – or would you like to stay and look after the girls?"

"They can look after themselves, can't they?" said Paul, indignantly. "Or go back to Ranni. But don't they *want* to come down?"

"Not particularly," said Nora. "It looks so dark and horrid down there. How do you get down?"

"There's an iron ladder," said Mike, peering down. "Gosh, it's pretty rusty, though. I wonder if it's safe?"

"This one's better!" called Jack, who was looking at the bigger shaft not far off. "This is much more recent, I should think. We'll try this one. I'll go down first."

He climbed down over the edge of the shaft. The others peered after him, excited. Tin mines! What did one find in tin mines? Nora had a vague picture of sheets of tin neatly stacked everywhere, which was very silly, of course. Mike thought of rocks with streaks of tin in them!

Jack called out to them when he was halfway down. "This ladder's fine. Come on, Mike and Paul!"

The other two boys followed him. The ladder seemed strong and in good order, surprisingly so, considering how long the village must have been deserted. Jack was now at the very bottom and was waiting for the other two.

They jumped down beside him, one by one. A hollow, most peculiar voice came down the shaft. "Are you all right, boys?"

"It's Peggy," said Jack. "How queer her voice sounds, echoing down that shaft!" He shouted up loudly. "Yes. We're at the bottom. There are tunnels everywhere. We'll have a quick look and come back again!"

"Don't get lost!" came Peggy's voice again, hollow and full of echoes.

The boys had their torches with them. Jack had switched his on as soon as he got to the bottom of the shaft. He flashed it round.

There were tunnels, as he had said, radiating out from the shaft. They seemed quite ordinary tunnels. Nothing glinted in the walls, no metal shone anywhere. Jack shone his torch into each one.

"Which shall we take?" he said. "This is going to be quite an adventure!"

Down In The Mines

The three boys decided to take a fairly wide tunnel, and they went down it. The roof was low, and Jack, the tallest, had to walk with his head bent. They came to a cave-like room after a time, out of which two tunnels led.

"Look," said Jack, picking up a bent knife. "This must have belonged to one of the old workers – and that broken mug too."

They shone their torches round. The roof of the cave was shored up by big timbers, but one had given way and that side of the cave had collapsed.

"I hope these timbers will hold up the roof till we get back!" said Mike, shining his torch on them. "They must be very old now. Look – there's some funny old machine they must have used – all rusty and falling to bits."

They took the right-hand tunnel and went on. "We could spend a long time exploring these old mines," said Jack. "There seem to be heaps of tunnels. Hallo, what's this?"

They had come up to what looked like a rough wall, blocking the tunnel. They shone their torches on it. "It's not a wall," said Mike. "It's a fall from the roof. Blow! We can't go any farther this way."

Jack kicked at the heap of rubble, and it fell all round him. Another lot then fell from the roof, and rubble and stones rolled round the boys' feet.

"There's a hole in the middle of all this stuff," said Jack. "I'll shine my torch through and see if there's anything to be seen."

He was just about to do so when Mike gave an exclamation. "Jack! Don't shine your torch through. There's a light the other side of this rubble wall! Look – you can see it shining through the hole. What can it be?"

Jack stared in surprise. Yes – through the hole that had appeared in the fallen rubble came a dim light. He set his eye to the hole in excitement.

He saw a strange sight. Beyond the fall of rubble was a spacious cave, and from it led another tunnel. Jack could see the opening to it, dark and shadowy.

On the floor of the cave burned a fire. It burned slowly and clearly, sending up vivid green flames from its deep-red heart. What it was burning Jack could not see – nothing so far as he could make out!

The fire made a noise, almost as if squibs or small fireworks were going off in it all the time. After every little explosion a purple tinge came into the green flames, and they sent off circles of greenish-purple that floated away like smoke-rings.

Jack gazed and gazed, filled with amazement. What was all this? What was this strange fire, and why was it burning here, in the old mines? Did anyone know of it?

"Let *me* see," said Mike, impatiently, and pushed Jack aside. He put his eye to the hole in his turn, and gave a loud cry of wonder.

"Gosh! Whatever is it? A fire – a green fire, burning all by itself!"

Paul elbowed him away in excitement. "My turn to see!" he said, and then fell silent in amazement as he gazed through the hole at the leaping flames, and heard the crick-crick-crack of the constant explosions.

Jack pulled him away after a minute or two. "My turn again," he said, and gazed earnestly through the hole. The others, leaning close against him, felt him suddenly stiffen and catch his breath.

"What is it? What is it?" whispered Mike and Paul, and tried to pull Jack away so that they too might see – but Jack resisted them, and went on looking.

109

Then he started back suddenly, just as the others heard a deep roaring noise from behind the rubble. A curious tingling came into their arms and legs, and they began to rub them quickly.

"What did you see? Tell us!" said Mike, rubbing his legs which felt as if they had pins and needles from the top to the bottom.

"I saw a figure," said Jack, rubbing his legs too. "Gosh, why have I suddenly got pins and needles? I saw a very strange figure, with a hood right over his face so that I couldn't see it. He wore very loose things, and very big gloves, so I couldn't see his skin at all. He poured something on the fire, and it made that sudden roaring noise, and its flames changed to brilliant purple. I simply couldn't look at them!"

Mike went to peep again. But, how bitterly disappointing – the fire had disappeared! Not a flame was to be seen, although the curious roaring noise still went on. Then in the tunnel beyond, lighted by a strange glow, he saw two figures – not one, as Jack had seen, but two.

They came forward slowly with what looked like a small broom. One of them swept gently over the place where the fire had been, and a little heap of stuff appeared, gleaming and glowing in its own light. What colour was it?

Mike didn't know! He wasn't sure that he had ever seen a colour quite like that before. Was it green – purple – blue? No, none of these.

The men swept the little heap into a curious narrow shovel made of some glittering metal that seemed to make the heap of glowing dust disappear as soon as it touched it. Then one of them put a bag or sack over the shovel, and the two of them disappeared down the tunnel.

Mike told the others all this. They sat back in their own tunnel, amazed and rather alarmed. What had they seen? What was happening in these old ruined mines?

"I wish I could get rid of these pins and needles in my

He poured something on the fire!

111

arms and legs," said Jack, rubbing vigorously again. "As soon as I stop rubbing, the feeling gets worse."

"Same here," said Mike. "Jack – what do you make of all this?"

"Nothing," said Jack. "I'm absolutely stumped. These are only old tin mines – *tin*, mark you – quite ordinary stuff. And yet we find this queer affair going on – a strange and most peculiar fire of green flames, that cricks and crack – and roars – and sends off rings of curious colour. Then for no reason at all that we can see, it dies down – and what's left is collected by a couple of men in the strangest clothes I ever saw!"

"Do you suppose that fellow Guy has anything to do with this?" asked Paul, after a pause.

"He might have," said Jack. "But how do the men get into that cave? Not through the way *we* came, or they would have removed this wall of rubble. I wish we could find the right way in. Then we could perhaps hide and watch everything properly. Yes, and see who the men are, and where they take the shovelful of stuff to."

"Well – I don't feel inclined to wander through all these mazy tunnels and get lost for ever," said Mike. "Couldn't we get a map of the old mines? If so, we might trace out a way to the cave we've just been looking at."

"Yes. That's a good idea," said Jack. "We'll do that – and I bet I know where we could get a map from, too! In that old library! This land probably belongs to Lord Moon, and we're sure to be able to find a book – or books – about the castle and all this property, in the castle library. I've no doubt that he made a lot of money out of the tin dug from here – or some of the Lord Moons did. I expect the mines had fallen into ruin long before the present one inherited the castle."

Mike glanced at his watch to see what the time was. "Surely it's more than half-past three?" he said, astonished. "Oh – it's stopped."

To their surprise the watches of the others had stopped too. "Better get back," said Jack. "The girls will be worried. I suppose that queer fire stopped our watches – and gave us these pins and needles too!"

They each took one more look through the hole, and then, as they could see absolutely nothing at all now, except for a faint glow from the floor of the next cave, they made their way back to the foot of the shaft they had entered by.

Nora and Peggy were leaning over the top, feeling anxious. They heard Nora shouting as they came to the bottom of the shaft.

"Mike! *Jack*!"

"Coming!" yelled the three boys, and then they heard Ranni's deep voice booming down.

"It gets late. Hurry, please."

They climbed up, and were very glad indeed to find themselves in the sunshine once more. But how their pins and needles tickled and pricked when the sun fell on their arms and legs! The three boys rubbed and scratched at top speed, much to the amazement of the girls.

"You have been too long, and such a pit is dangerous," said Ranni, severely, to Paul. "I was just coming to fetch you, little Prince. I have left the car waiting at the fork."

"Our watches stopped," said Paul. He turned to the girls. "Have your watches stopped too, by any chance?" he asked.

"No," said Nora, glancing at hers and then at Peggy's. "What did you see down there? Anything thrilling?"

"Gosh, yes," said Jack. "We'll tell you when we get back to the car."

The girls listened in the greatest astonishment when the boys related their adventure. Ranni, at the wheel, heard every word, and he was horrified.

He stopped the car and turned himself round to face the children at the back. "You will not come here again," he said, sternly. "If this tale is true, this place is not for you. I will not have my little master mixed up in such dangers."

"They're not dangers," said Jack. "We weren't in any danger, Ranni, really we weren't!"

Ranni thought differently. "Something goes on here," he said. "Something secret. It is not for children to meddle with it. Jack – you must promise me never to go down those shafts again, nor to take Paul with you."

"Oh Ranni!" said Jack, protestingly. "I can't promise that, Ranni. I mean – we really must discover what all this means."

"You will promise me," said Ranni, unmoved. "If you do not, I will tell Miss Dimity, and she shall take you back home."

"You're jolly mean, Ranni," said Jack. But he knew Ranni of old. There was nothing for it but to promise!

"All right – we won't go down the beastly shafts again," he said, sulkily.

"Nor will you come to the village," persisted Ranni who was taking no chances.

"All right," said Jack again. "Anyone would think we were six years old and wanted looking after. Go on – let's get back."

Ranni drove off, satisfied. Jack made a few plans, which he outlined to the others. "Even though we've had to promise Ranni we won't go to the village, there's no reason why we shouldn't find out a bit more about the mines from old maps. We'll go to the castle library after tea!"

"And have books jumping on us from the shelves!" said Nora, with a giggle. "Like that waitress said!"

"Well, it will all add to the fun," said Jack. "I say – don't let's say anything about what we saw in that mine, when we get back to Dimmy. She *might* whisk us back home – there's no knowing what she'll do if she thinks there's something we can't cope with."

"Oh, my pins and needles!" groaned Mike. "How long will they last? Honestly, mine are worse than ever!"

"Here we are!" said Nora, as the car swept in at the gates. "You're lucky, you boys, even though you've got pins and needles – you've had a fine adventure, and we haven't!"

114

Pins And Needles – And Jumping Books!

Dimmy was wondering what had happened to them all, because they were so late back to tea. She sat at the tea-table, occasionally looking out of the window to see if the children were coming.

She was most relieved when she saw them walking into the room. "Ah – here you are," she said. "Have you had a good afternoon?"

"Yes. We went to the old village – where the tin mines are," said Mike. "Ranni took us in the car. Sorry we're late. We did quite a bit of exploring. It's a queer old place, that village."

"Yes," said Nora, who really *had* explored it with Peggy, while the boys had been down the mine. "The tumble-down houses are all covered with ramblers and blackberry sprays, and tall-growing weeds, Dimmy. It's a sad sort of place, really – not a soul there. Only birds, and one or two rabbits we saw scampering around."

"Go and wash," said Dimmy, "and then come back quickly. Mrs Brimming has managed to provide another good meal for you!"

They were soon sitting down at the table, washed and brushed. The boys had bathed their arms and legs in cold water to try to get rid of the pins and needles that still attacked them. The water helped them at first, but as soon as they sat at the table, the pins and needles came back again so fiercely that the three boys wriggled and rubbed themselves in pain.

"What *is* the matter?" said Dimmy. "Have you been stung by something?"

"No," said Mike.

"It's just pins and needles," said Jack. "It came on us suddenly in the village. But it won't stop!"

When Brimmy came to take the tea-tray, Dimmy spoke to her about the boys' pins and needles.

"Do you think they've been stung by something?" she said, anxiously. "I can't make it out. Look at them – they can't keep still for a minute. They're wriggling and squirming all the time."

"They've been near the mines!" said Brimmy, at once. "Been down into them too, I wouldn't be surprised! You can do only one thing, Miss Dimity. Put them to bed, and I'll give you some lotion I have so that you can soak bandages for their arms and legs. That will soon put them right."

"But what *is* this pins and needles?" said Dimmy. "Why should it come on them like this?"

"It's the illness that drove the people away from that old village," said Brimmy. "It came all of a sudden, they say. The men were working the mines as usual – and for some reason a great fire came. When it died down, the men went to work down in the mines again – but when they came up they all had this pins and needles."

"Good gracious!" said Dimmy. "Is it dangerous?"

"Oh no, Miss," said Brimmy. "These boys will soon get rid of it if they lie quiet with this lotion on their limbs. But when it first came to the village it soon attacked every man, woman and child in the place, and only when they got away from the place did the attacks stop."

"What caused these attacks then?" said Dimmy, most interested.

"I don't rightly know," said Brimmy. "They do say that the great fire had something to do with it – it set loose radiations or something down in the mine, and these seeped up into the air above, and gave the village people this pins and needles in their limbs – a kind of tickling and prickling that drove them nearly crazy!"

116

"And so they left the village, did they?" asked Jack.

"Yes. The place got a bad name," said Brimmy. "No one would work the mines, and so there was no money to be earned. In three years' time there wasn't a soul there – and it's been going to rack and ruin ever since. My, that's over a hundred years ago now! I remember my grandmother telling me how it all happened in her grandad's time. I did warn these children not to go there, Miss Dimity – but they're headstrong, aren't they?"

Dimmy wasn't going to say anything against the five children! "Perhaps you'll get that lotion you kindly said you'd let us have," she suggested. "Nora, go with Mrs Brimming and bring it back."

Dimmy thought that the three boys would be sure to make a fuss at having to go to bed at once, but they did not. "Pins and needles can be most terribly tiring when it doesn't stop at all!" complained Mike, rubbing his arms hard. "It's quite funny when you have it for a little while – but not when you've got to put up with it for hours!"

"You're right," said Jack, feelingly. "It's like hiccups – quite comical for a few minutes, but alarming after half an hour!"

They went to their rooms to undress. Dimmy said she would bring the lotion as soon as she had it. The boys opened their doors – and then stared.

Their rooms were completely changed round, just as Dimmy's had been! The beds were by the window, the clothes had been taken out of drawers and arranged on the tops of the chests, the vase of flowers was on the floor, and their shoes were on the window-sill.

"This is crazy!" said Jack, staring round. A shout from Paul told him that his room was the same. They went into the girls' room – and that was changed round too.

"Mad!" said Mike. "Who's doing it? And why?"

"If it's the spirit of the castle, he's been pretty busy!" said Paul.

117

"Stuff!" said Jack. "This is no spirit – this is someone spiteful. But what's the point?"

"All part of the Queer Happenings that the waitress foretold, I suppose," said Mike, taking his shoes from the window-sill. "Look here – let's change the rooms round quickly and put everything tidy. Don't let Dimmy see what's happened. If she gets the wind up we'll all be taken back home – and I'm *jolly well going* to find out a bit more myself."

"Hear, hear!" said the other two.

"Mike, go and put the girls' room right, I'll do ours, and Paul can do his," said Jack. "Buck up! Dimmy will be here in a trice."

They hurried as much as their pins and needles would let them! They had got their rooms right, and were just beginning to undress when Dimmy came in with a big bottle of green lotion and some strips of old sheet for bandages. She looked reproachfully at them.

"Oh! I did think you'd all be in bed! I suppose you've been monkeying about, as usual. I don't think you're as bad as you make out."

"We *are*," said Mike. "Look at my leg – I've scratched it almost raw already! Come on, do me first, Dimmy. I'm in bed now."

Dimmy put the bandages soaked with the green lotion on his legs and arms, wrapping them round loosely. Mike lay back in great relief. "That's super! Oh, how heavenly! That lotion feels as cold as ice. I can hardly feel the pins and needles now."

"Mrs Brimming says you'll be as right as rain in the morning," said Dimmy. "I must say it's very extraordinary – the whole tale of the village is queer. In fact, I think quite a lot of things are extraordinary here. I've half a mind to take you all back home."

Mike sat up, shocked. "Oh *no*, Dimmy! Don't be such a spoil-sport! It's grand here. There – you've made my pins

118

and needles come back again by saying such a worrying thing."

"Rubbish!" said Dimmy, and began to bandage Jack. "Lie down, Mike, I'll leave the lotion near you, so that when the bandages dry off, you can soak them again. Do you want any books?"

"The girls will get us some from the library," said Mike, making up his mind to get Nora and Peggy to bring up some books about the castle and the mines too, if they could find them. "Ask Nora and Peggy to come up, will you, Dimmy?"

The girls came up and said yes, of course they would go down to the great library and try to find some books for the boys. So down they went. They bumped into Edie Lots as they came to the library door. She had a duster in her hand, and they imagined she must have been dusting the books.

She stood with her back against the library door as they came up, her face unsmiling.

"Oh – er – do you mind moving, we want to go into the library," said Peggy, seeing that Edie was standing there for them to pass her.

Edie stood aside and even opened the door for them. "What kind of books do you want?" she said. "There are no books for children here."

"Well – we thought we'd like to read up about the old castle – and the old village," said Nora. "Goodness – what thousands of books there are! We'll never be able to find what we want here. It would be like looking for a needle in a haystack!"

"I'll help you," said Edie obligingly. "I've dusted these books so often I almost know their titles by heart. You sit down there now, for a minute. I'll get the little ladder from the cupboard outside, so that I can climb up to the shelf where the books are that you want."

She disappeared. The girls did not sit down, they began to wander round, reading out the titles of the books at

119

High up on a shelf a book was tilting itself over.

random. Nora suddenly gave a cry, and Peggy turned round quickly. Nora had her hand to her head.

"Peggy! You threw a book at me!" said Nora crossly. "It hit me on the head."

"I didn't throw one," said Peggy in astonishment. They bent down to pick up the book – and immediately another crashed down beside them, hitting Peggy's foot. She swung round, alarmed. Where were the books coming from? Then she clutched Nora's arm, and pointed. High on a shelf a book was tilting itself over – then it seemed to spring from its place, and landed about two feet away from the children.

"This is just what the waitress said happened to the man who came here to see some of the old books," said Peggy in a whisper. "Look out – here's another!"

Sure enough, yet another book tilted itself backwards, and then with a spring was off the shelf and on the floor in a heap, lying wide open. It was near Nora and she glanced down fearfully at it.

On the open pages she saw a map. She picked up the book at once. A map! Would it show the mines?

She looked at the title. It was difficult to read because the lettering was old and dim. *"A History of Moon Castle and its Lands,"* she read. "Gosh, this is just the book we want, Peggy!"

Miss Edie came in, carrying a small library ladder. She stopped when she saw the books on the floor. "Now don't you treat the books like that!" she said angrily. "I won't have it!"

"They jumped off the shelves themselves," said Nora, not expecting to be believed. But Edie did believe her! She threw the ladder down and ran off at top speed, looking scared out of her life! Was she pretending, or was she really scared? She certainly looked terrified!

"Let's take this book to the boys and go and tell them about the jumping ones!" said Nora. "Whatever will they say!"

Some Exciting Map-Reading

The boys were feeling very much more comfortable. As long as they kept their bandages soaked with the green lotion they had no more pins and needles – but if they got out of bed and walked about, then back came the prickling at once!

They were very pleased to see the girls. Ranni had been in, and had put Paul's bed into the middle room with Mike and Jack, so all three were now together.

"Ha! You've brought a book!" said Mike, and reached out to get it. "A history of the castle – and its lands! Good work! This is just what we wanted. How clever of you to find it so quickly."

"We didn't find it," said Nora. "We didn't even look for it. It leapt straight off a shelf and fell at our feet!"

"Don't be an ass," said Mike, opening the book. "That's only the waitress's tale!"

"It's her tale, certainly – but it's ours too," said Peggy. "Do listen, Mike. It *really* happened!"

Now the girls had the whole attention of all three boys, of course! They listened as the two girls told their strange little story. Then, in their turn, they told Peggy and Nora how they had found all three rooms changed round, with everything in a different place.

"I can't make out what's happening," said Mike. "It looks as if we're being driven away from here – but I'm not going! I'm sticking it out till Paul's family comes. If things are still odd then, well, your father can go into the matter, Paul. But I feel somehow, from what Jack overheard this morning, that it's the next few days that are important to somebody – Guy, perhaps – or the two men we saw down in the mines. We just don't know."

They began to discuss everything again – the Twang-Dong noises – the way the rooms had been upset – the books flying off the shelves – the hissing noise in the room where the musical-box was, and then Mike mentioned the gleaming eyes of the portrait, forgetting that the girls hadn't seen them. They listened, finding this difficult to believe.

"It must have been some effect of light," said Peggy.

"It wasn't," said Paul. "That room's so dark."

"Well, I give it up," said Peggy. "In fact, I give everything up. I just don't understand a thing. If the castle really had a spirit of its own I'd understand what's happened, because it might not like us, and might want us to go – but I can't believe in spirits of that kind!"

"Nor can I," said Jack, and the others said the same, except Paul. Paul had been brought up in far-off Baronia, a wild land of mountains and forests, where legends were believed in, and strange things actually happened. But here – well, here it was just impossible. And yet – what *was* happening then?

Mike was looking through the book. The pages, solid with small print, were not easy to read, so Mike was looking for maps.

He found a section of them, unexpectedly clearly drawn. Some of them opened out into big sheets, like motoring maps. Mike opened one and spread it out over his bed. Paul left his bed and clambered on to Mike's to see. Soon all the children were poring over bits of the big map.

"It's the castle," said Mike. "Here's a plan of the downstairs floor. Let's find our L-shaped sitting-room."

They found it at last – then they found the library – the room with the musical-box – the one with the clock like a church. They found the different staircases. What a maze of rooms this castle possessed!

They examined the next plan, which showed the first floor, where their own rooms were. "Here's our suite of

123

rooms," said Mike, pointing. "One – two – three – all connected. And there's Ranni's room – and this must be Dimmy's. Look – what's this extra door shown here – opening into Paul's room? *Is* there a door there – look, it would be in the wall on the right-hand side of your bed, Paul. Did you notice a door there? I didn't."

"I'll go and see," said Paul, and leapt off the bed. He took a few steps and then hobbled back again. "Oooh, my pins and needles!" he said. "As soon as I take a step or two they come back worse than ever. Peggy, you go and look. I'm sure there isn't a door. I'd have noticed it, I know."

Peggy and Nora went off to Paul's room at once and looked at the right-hand wall. No – there was no door there. The room was panelled all round, but, except for the door that led out to the corridor and the one that led into the middle room of the suite, there was no other door to be seen.

"No door," they reported when they came back. "Either it's a mistake on the map, or else there was once a door and it's been removed and the wall panelled over."

"Where did the extra door once lead to?" asked Jack with interest. "Let me see now – if it had been in the right-hand wall of Paul's room, it would have led into that blue bathroom next to it, wouldn't it? Well, I suppose there wouldn't have been a bathroom there in the old days – so I daresay when the bathroom was built, the old door was done away with."

"You mean, the door just led into the room that was there *before* the bathroom?" said Peggy. "Let's have another look. It's marked with a T. I wonder why."

"Let me fold this map up," said Mike impatiently. "Take your hand off, Peggy. I'll shake out the next map."

He shook it out, and there was an excited exclamation at once. "It's the tower! A map of the old tower!"

So it was. The children pored over it with great interest. The tower was shown in a diagram, as if it were cut in half from top to bottom, and the children could quite clearly see how it was built, and could imagine what it was like inside.

"There's the door at the bottom – the one that's locked," said Mike, pointing. "Then the stone stairway is shown – quite big, really – then the room on the first floor, look – how strange, it's quite round. I wonder how big it looks in reality? It looks fairly small here. Then up goes the staircase again, from just outside the room – it gets wider above and then narrows again to the second-storey room."

"I rather imagined the tower was like that inside," said Paul. "It's a bit like one we have in a castle in Baronia. Look – up go the stairs to the third–floor room, and up again to the roof. What a view there would be from there!"

"These square marks in each room must be the fireplaces," said Mike, pointing. "And this line must be the chimney, connecting all the fireplaces, and leading the smoke somewhere out at the top."

Nora put her finger on a small door-shaped drawing shown in the fireplace on the second floor.

"What's that?" she said. "It can't be the door that shuts off the staircase outside the room, because that's shown here, look. And yet it *looks* like a door. What's that mark on it?"

"It looks like a letter T," said Jack.

That rang a bell in Peggy's mind at once. "T! Well, that secret door in Paul's room – the one we couldn't find – was marked with T too, when it was shown on the other map," she said. "T – T for Tower perhaps."

"Why should a door leading off Paul's room be marked with T for Tower?" said Mike scornfully.

"Well – it might have been a door that at one time *led* to the tower," said Peggy, sticking up for herself. "I mean – there might have been a passage from this suite to the tower at some time – the tower isn't so very far from this suite of rooms!"

Mike looked at her, thinking hard. "You know – she

might be right," he said to the others. "Wait now – let's see the other maps."

There were no other big maps, except one for the attics, which was not very interesting. But there was a curious little map, marked ALL COMMUNICATIONS, which puzzled the children for some time.

"'All communications' – that *might* mean such things as stairways, passages, corridors and so on, connecting one part of the castle to the other," said Mike. "This is rather a muddled map if it means those though. I can't make out any of the staircases, for instance."

"Communications might mean *secret* ways," said Paul suddenly. "All old castles have secret ways and secret doors. Ours has in Baronia. They were once used for all kinds of things – hiding-places – escape routes – ways to get in by when the castle was surrounded by enemies. I expect Moon Castle has got its own secret communications too!"

"You're probably right," said Mike, looking suddenly excited. He pored over the map again, and then traced a curving line with his finger. "This line is marked with T at this end – and T at the other," he said. "It might be showing the two doors and the connecting passage between Paul's room and the tower. I *say*! Wouldn't it be super if we could find a secret way into the tower?"

There was a hush of excitement, and then Paul pounded on the bed. "We must find it! We must! We could creep in on Guy then, and see what he is doing. We *must* find it!"

"Well – look at this," said Jack, pointing to the map again. "It looks as if the passage from that secret door in Paul's room leads inside the walls somewhere, and then comes out to another door – or perhaps an opening of some kind – *inside the chimney* of one of the tower rooms. What does everybody think?"

Everybody was only too anxious to think that Jack was right!

"I know how we can tell if we're right," said Mike. "We

could measure the width inside of Paul's room, and the width of the bathroom, and see what they come to, together – and then we could measure the walls of both, *outside*, in the corridor – and if that measurement is bigger than our first one, we'll know it includes a secret passage in between the two rooms!"

"Gosh – what a super idea!" said Peggy. "I'll get a tape-measure out of my work-basket this very minute!"

She soon found one, and she and Nora measured Paul's room from wall to wall – exactly fourteen feet. Nora popped her head into Mike's room. "Fourteen feet exactly," she said. "Now we're going to measure the bathroom."

They measured it carefully, and came back to report. "Eight feet," said Nora. "Eight and fourteen make twenty-two. Now we'll measure the walls *outside* the rooms, in the corridor, and see what we make the length there."

Carefully they measured the walls that stretched along the corridor, outside Paul's room and then the bathroom. They counted in excitement – and then raced back into Mike's room.

"The measurements are different! The inner walls measure twenty-two feet – but the outer ones measure twenty-four! What do you think of *that*?"

Mike looked excited. "Two feet missing! Just the width for a secret passage. Good work, girls. There *is* a passage that starts somewhere in Paul's room, goes between his room and the bathroom – and then curves away behind walls to the tower!"

"Shall we go and find the secret door now?" said Paul excitedly, and leapt out of bed again. But he was soon back groaning. The boys had forgotten to soak their bandages when they had got dry, and now their pins and needles were coming back badly. Poor Paul had started his up again at once by jumping out of bed.

"We'll have to leave the secret door for tonight," said Mike dolefully. "No, Peggy – you're not going to look for secret doors without us, so don't think it. It'll be something to do tomorrow. My word – we'll have some fun!"

In The Middle Of The Night

All the five children felt really excited that night when bedtime came. Nobody could sleep. As for Paul, he tossed and turned, wondering where in the world the secret door could be in his room – if there still was one!

"But there must be!" he thought. "Because we know there is a space in the walls between this room and the bathroom next door."

He had, of course, not been able to stop himself from tapping his wall, and banging it here and there to see if there *was* a door in the panelling! It certainly sounded hollow – there was no doubt about that!

He had to get into bed before he had really examined the right-hand wall properly, because his pins and needles came back again with a rush. Mike heard the tapping and called from the next room.

"Paul! No probing about for that secret door now! You just wait till everybody can hunt for it!"

"Right!" said Paul, safely in bed, stretching his tingling legs out straight and rubbing his arms. Ranni had moved his bed back into his room again, though Paul had wanted to stay in Mike and Jack's room for the night.

"I shall come in two or three times, little master, to see that you are all right," said big Ranni, who had been most concerned about Paul's legs. "Do not be frightened if you see me standing by you."

"I wish you wouldn't fuss so, Ranni," said Paul. But it was of no use to say that. Paul had been put into Ranni's care, and the big Baronian was by his side as much as possible.

Everyone went to sleep at last, the girls first, because they had no pins and needles to bother them. Paul tossed and turned for some time and then he too went to sleep.

He woke very suddenly, some hours later, and sat up wondering what had awakened him. In his dreams he thought he had heard a loud click.

He saw a figure over by the window, and lay down again. "Bother you, Ranni," he murmured. "You woke me up!" He lay watching Ranni, and then his eyes began to close. He wondered if Ranni would come and fuss him about his bandages, and decided to pretend to be asleep.

He heard no further sound for a minute or two and then opened his eyes again. He could not see anyone now – perhaps Ranni had gone. Good!

Another loud click made him open sleepy eyes again – that must be Ranni going out of the room. He thought he saw a shadow moving high up on the wall, and tried to wake himself up enough to see more clearly. No – he couldn't – he was too sleepy. Clicks and shadows and Ranni all merged into a muddled dream.

He didn't hear low voices in the next room. It was Mike and Jack talking. They too had awakened suddenly, though they didn't know why. Mike thought he heard a sound in the room, and strained his eyes to see where it came from. The room appeared to be very dark indeed – not the slightest light came from the window, and Mike couldn't see even one star in the sky.

Jack spoke in a low voice. "You awake, Mike? How are your pins and needles?"

"Not too good," said Mike. "I'm awfully sleepy and I don't want to get out of bed – but I simply *must* get that lotion and soak my bandages again."

He saw a dark figure over by the window.

"Yes, I must too," said Jack. "Blow these pins and needles. It's most peculiar to get them like this, just because we went down those mines."

There was a creaking of the two beds as the boys sat up. Mike felt for the torch he always had by his bedside. He couldn't find it.

"Put *your* torch on," he said to Jack. "I can't find mine."

"Right," said Jack, and fumbled about for it. But he couldn't find his either! "Where on earth did I put it?" he grumbled. "Oh for a bedside lamp to put on! Living in a castle is great, but I do miss some things we have at home. *Where's* my torch?"

"It's most awfully dark tonight!" said Mike. "Surprising, really, because when we went to sleep it was such a starry night – no moon, but millions of stars. It must have clouded up."

Jack got out of bed, determined to find his torch. "I may have left it on the window-sill," he said. "Ooooh – my pins and needles!"

He went towards the window and fumbled for the window-sill. He couldn't find it! Something thick and soft and heavy hung over it.

"I say!" said Jack suddenly, "who's pulled the curtains over our windows? No wonder we couldn't see a thing! These great heavy curtains are pulled across, making the room as black as pitch and frightfully stuffy. No wonder I was so hot in bed!"

"Well, *I* didn't pull them!" said Mike. "You know I hate sleeping with a shut window or pulled curtains. I suppose Dimmy came in and did that."

"But whatever for?" said Jack. "She's just the one that's all against it! Well, I'm going to pull them back again and get a bit of air. I bet it's a beautiful starry night."

There was a soft rattle of curtain rings as the heavy curtains were pulled across the window. Jack leaned out, taking deep breaths of the warm night-air. The sky was full of stars.

131

"That's better," said Mike, getting out of bed. "I can breathe now. Why, the room's quite light, there are so many stars!"

He leaned out of the window with Jack. It was really a beautiful night. The boys soon felt, however, that they must get some more lotion on their bandages – the pins and needles were beginning to prickle unbearably! They turned to find the bottle.

"We can see by the starlight, really," said Jack. "But I do wish I could find my torch. I *know* I put it by my bed!"

They got the sponge, soaked it with the lotion, and dabbed the sponge over their bandages. "That's better already," said Jack.

They went to the window for one last look out at the lovely night. Both boys at once saw something that made them stare and draw in their breath quickly.

"Look! What is it!" said Jack, startled.

"A light – a sort of glow – shimmering over the ruined village!" said Mike, amazed. "What colour is it? It's the same colour as that little heap of stuff we saw that the men swept up after the roaring fire!"

"Yes," said Jack, his eyes on the soft, shimmering haze that hung over the rooftops of the village far below. "My word – this is really very peculiar, Mike. What *is* going on here – and down in those mines? I'm sure it's something that man Guy is mixed up in."

"Some experiment, perhaps," said Mike. "If so, that's the reason why he doesn't like people renting the castle or even coming to look over it. And now that he knows the Baronians are coming here in a few days, he's got to finish up whatever this experiment is, and clear out. No wonder he's angry!"

The strangely coloured haze began to fade, though it still shimmered beautifully. The boys watched till it completely disappeared. "What a sight!" said Mike, going back to bed. "I bet he would be annoyed if he thought we'd seen that!

It's a thing he can't hide – something that would make people enquire into it if they saw it – and then his little experiments, or whatever they are, would be found out!"

"Gosh – of course – he *didn't* want us to see it!" said Jack. "That's why the curtains were drawn across the window, so that if we woke we shouldn't see a thing! That's why our torches are gone, so that if we woke we couldn't put them on and discover the curtains blocking out the light!"

"Well, of all the cheek!" said Mike, sitting up indignantly in bed. "Coming in here – drawing our curtains – hiding our torches! I say – do you suppose he did the same in the girls' room – and Paul's?"

"I bet he did," said Jack. "I'm going to look." He soon reported that Mike was right. The curtains had been carefully pulled across in each room! "I've dragged them back again," said Jack. "I expect you heard me. What's he done with our precious torches? If he's taken them away with him I *shall* be wild!"

"Well – we've seen what he didn't mean us to see," said Mike, pleased. "We're one up on him! I say – he must be quite scared of us, mustn't he – trying to stop us discovering what he's up to!"

"He knows we're snooping round," said Jack, getting into bed and lying down. "He must have found that rug we put against the tower door to see if he came in and out – he saw we'd moved the chest there, when he put it to hide the tower door."

"Fancy him daring to come along here in the middle of the night, and take our torches and draw our curtains." said Mike. "He would have to pass Ranni's door – and Ranni sleeps like a dog, with one ear always open."

"He may have come through that secret door – the one we haven't found yet," said Jack, sitting up straight again. "Down the secret passage, straight from the tower! He wouldn't need to pass anyone's door then – or bump into anybody. I bet that's what he did!"

"Gosh! I shall never get to sleep tonight now," said Mike. "What a place this is! Twang-dongs, breaking vases, jumping books, gleaming eyes, secret doors, peculiar mines – well, we've had a good many adventures, Jack – but this beats the lot!"

"And we're only just in the middle of it so far," said Jack. "Come on – we really must go to sleep, Mike. We *must* find that secret door in Paul's room tomorrow. It will be very, very well-hidden, I'm sure – but we'll find it!"

They settled themselves down to sleep. Their pins and needles had subsided again. They lay and looked through the uncurtained window into the starry sky, puzzling out this and that, feeling little surges of excitement now and again.

They went to sleep at last, and woke late in the morning. The girls were already up and about. Peggy heard Jack speaking to Mike and went in. "Hallo, sleepy-heads!" she said. "We're just going down to breakfast. How are your legs?"

"Well – they feel absolutely all right," said Jack, getting out of bed and trying them. "Not a twinge! Not a pin, not a needle! Good!"

"Then you don't want to stay in bed for the day or anything?" said Nora, pleased.

"Good gracious, no!" said Mike, leaping out too. "We're quite all right. I say – anyone lost their torches?"

"Yes," said Peggy and Nora together. "Ours have both gone. We thought you'd borrowed them."

Paul poked his head in at the door. "Are your legs all right?" he asked. "Mine are. Did I hear someone ask about torches? Mine's gone too!"

"Blow!" said Mike. "Not one of us has got a torch then. All right, girls, don't look so puzzled. Jack and I have got a bit of news for you – something that happened in the night, while you were snoring your heads off!

134

We're in the very middle of an adventure – the strangest one we've ever had. Just wait till Jack and I are dressed, and we'll tell you all about it – and we'll have to Make Plans. Aha, Plans! We're going to be very, very busy today!"

Where Is The Secret Door?

Dimmy was pleased to find that the boys' legs and arms were better. She told Brimmy so when she and Edie Lots came to collect the breakfast trays.

"That lotion is very good," she said. "I've never heard of anyone keeping a lotion for pins and needles before! How did you hear of it? Do you suffer from pins and needles yourself?"

"No. But my son does," said Brimmy, and Mike nudged Jack at once. "I bet he does," he said, in a low voice, and Jack grinned. "I bet he gets it every time he goes down those mines!"

"It's a pity it's raining," went on Brimmy. "It'll keep the children in."

"We've got plenty to do," said Jack at once, and winked at the others. They laughed. They knew what Jack's wink meant – they were going to hunt for that secret door in Paul's room. The girls and Paul had now heard of all the happenings of the night before, and were feeling very thrilled.

"Where are you going to play?" Dimmy asked the children after breakfast. "You can be in here, if you like, now the breakfast is cleared."

"Well – we rather thought we'd just go up to our suite of rooms and look for something we've lost," said Jack. "So

135

you can sew here in peace, Dimmy. Anyway, we've got a game or two up there, so there's no need to disturb you with our shouts and yells!"

"You don't disturb me," said Dimmy. "But if you want to go up to your rooms, you can. But wait till they are dusted and cleaned. And by the way, you must put that book back into the library that you borrowed last night."

"Oh yes – I'll fetch it now," said Jack. "You four go and wait for me in the library." He sped off, and the others went to the library.

"I hope some books do a bit of jumping," said Nora. She looked up at the shelves. "Books – we're here!"

But, most disappointingly, nothing happened. The books that had fallen out the day before had been picked up and put away in their places. Only one gap showed in the shelves, and that was where the *History of Moon Castle* had leapt from!

Jack came in with the big book. He shut the door and looked round the room. "Any circus performances yet?" he said. The girls shook their heads.

"No. Most boring," said Nora. "The books are behaving just like books!"

There came a knock at the door. "Come in!" said Jack. The door opened and Edie Lots looked in. "I thought I heard you," she said. "Will you please not throw the books about as you did yesterday. Some are very valuable."

"We didn't throw them, you know we didn't," said Nora. "We told you what happened and you rushed off looking scared!"

Edie said nothing to that. She noticed the big book in Jack's hand. "Oh, you've come to put that back," she said. "I'll fetch the ladder for you – it belongs to that high shelf there."

She went off and in a minute or two came back with the ladder. She set it up against the shelves, and then went out again.

"She's a misery," said Mike. "I don't like her. I don't like any of them much. Well – does anyone want to have a squint at this book again before I put it back?"

"Let's not talk too loud," said Peggy, suddenly. "I have a feeling that Edie may be listening at the door. I'd like to have one more look at the book – where that secret passage to the tower is." She dropped her voice at the last words, so that no eavesdropper could hear her.

They all pored over the maps once again. "It's a pity it doesn't show the mines too," said Jack. "I'd like a book about those mines."

CRASH! They all jumped. A book lay near them, half-open, on its face. "Welcome, dear book!" said Jack. "Are you by any chance a book about the mines?"

He picked it up – but it wasn't. It was called *Rolland, the Duke of Barlingford. A History of his Horses.*

"Sorry, Duke Rolland," said Jack, "but your horses don't really interest me. Nice of you to throw yourself at my head, though!"

"Jack – look," whispered Mike, and Jack turned quickly. He saw that Mike and the others were staring at a picture over the mantelpiece. It was swinging slowly to and fro! It was a dark picture, of mountains and hills, of no interest at all – except that it was swinging to and fro like a pendulum!

Jack walked up to it and took hold of it. It stopped swinging immediately.

"I don't like it," said Nora. "It's worse than jumping books!"

THUD! CRASH!

The children swung round. Two more books lay on the ground – and then Jack caught sight of another one tilting up on the shelf. Over it went and down it came!

He took the ladder, put it below the shelf where the book had fallen from, and climbed up. He could see nothing that could cause the books to jump out.

"All the books have come from the same side of the

room, and from the same shelf-level," said Paul. "That's queer, isn't it?" Oh my goodness, there goes the picture again!"

Sure enough it had begun to swing, though more slowly than before. Jack stood on the ladder and watched it. What was the point of all these silly happenings? "Pass the books back to me," he said to Mike. "I'll put them in their places."

He put the last one in its place, and climbed down again, expecting more to fall out immediately.

"Let's get out of here," said Nora. "I really don't like all these happenings."

"Come on then – we'll go upstairs. Our rooms will be done by now, I expect," said Mike. So they left the library and went up to their suite of rooms. Mrs Brimming was just coming out of them with a duster and a brush and pan.

"I've finished them," she said. "Now I'm going to do Miss Dimity's."

The five children went into the rooms. Jack locked the outer doors of all three rooms. "If we're going to hunt for a secret door, we don't want anyone bursting in just as we've found it!" he said.

They all felt excited. They went into Paul's room and looked at the right-hand wall. It was panelled from floor to ceiling. At first sight it seemed impossible that there should be a door at all.

"I wonder you didn't hear the fellow coming through the secret door into your room last night," said Jack to Paul.

"Well – I did hear a click once or twice," said Paul. "But I thought it was Ranni coming into my room and going out again. He stood over there by the window – I saw his outline."

Jack thought for a moment. "Well, perhaps that *was* Ranni, Paul. The man who came in by the secret door drew all our curtains across the window, as you know – so you wouldn't have been able to see his outline there, if the curtains were drawn. The man must have come after Ranni had been."

"Or else Paul saw him by the window just *before* he drew the curtains," said Nora. Jack nodded.

"Yes – that might be," he said. "Now come on – let's find this door. And mind – we don't give up till we've got it."

They each went to a portion of the right-hand wall, and began to search the panelling carefully. They pushed this panel and that. They pressed, they tapped. They leaned against the panels, they tried to shove them sideways.

"Well – we're not very successful," said Jack, at last. "I've examined my portion of the wall as high as six feet – but as far as I can see it's all ordinary panelling – no secrets anywhere. Let's change over places and try our hands at each other's bits of wall."

So they changed places, and began all over again. What a probing and tapping and pressing there was! The smallest knot of wood was examined, the tiniest crack!

In the middle of it all somebody tried the handle of the boys' door, and then tapped sharply on it. The five children, intent on their search, jumped in fright.

But it was only Dimmy, bringing up biscuits and plums for their elevenses. She was cross because the door was locked. Peggy flew to open it.

"What do you want to lock this door for?" demanded Dimmy.

"To keep out Brimmy and the Lots," said Jack, truthfully. "They're always snooping about. Oh thanks, Dimmy. You're a brick – chocolate biscuits and plums – I could do with those."

Dimmy went, and the children took a rest from their labours and ate all the biscuits and the plums, sitting on Mike's bed. They were very disappointed.

"We've been over an hour looking for that wretched

door," said Jack. "We *know* it must be there! It's pretty certain our night-visitor came through it from the tower passage. Why can't we find it then?"

"We'll try again," said Mike. He hated giving up anything. "Come on. I bet we'll find it this time."

But they did not. They had to give it up at last. "There's not a single inch we haven't examined," said Jack, with a groan. "It's beaten us. I really don't feel that I can possibly look panelling in the face again – I'm fed up with it!"

Everyone was. "Let's go out," said Nora. "It's stopped raining, and the sun's out. I hope to goodness nobody comes along while we're out and changes our rooms round again. That's such a silly trick."

"We'll lock the doors," said Jack, "and take the keys with us."

So when they left their rooms they locked each of the three corridor doors, though they left the ones connecting them wide open. Off they went into the sunshine, and wandered all round the enormous castle, exploring it thoroughly from the outside.

"It's almost lunch-time," said Nora, at last. "We must go in. Gosh, I'm filthy! Let's go straight up and wash, as soon as we get in. Dimmy will have a fit if she sees us like this."

They went up the stairs and came to their rooms. Jack took the keys out of his pocket. He unlocked the girls' room door and they all went in.

"Everything's all right," said Jack, pleased. "No change-round this time. Whoever the joker is, he or she couldn't get in today, because the doors were all locked. Good!"

"Look – my torch is back!" said Nora suddenly, pointing to the table beside her bed. "So is Peggy's."

"So's mine!" said Mike, running into the middle room, "and Jack's. But – the doors were all locked, weren't they?"

"They were," said Jack. "So – whoever brought back the torches came through the secret door – the one we couldn't

140

find. There's no other way in. It *is* there! It *is*! And he came through it. Oh, why can't we find it? Paul – can't you think of *anything* that might help? You're the one that heard the clicks, and saw a man. Think hard – tell us everything you heard or saw."

"I have," said Paul, frowning hard, trying to remember the least detail. "I just remember a last click, that I thought was Ranni going out of the room – and a sort of shadow high up on the wall – and—"

"A shadow! High up on the wall! That's it, that's it!" cried Jack, his eyes shining. "This entrance must be high up, of course – higher than we looked – that shadow must have been the secret visitor going back through the door – but a door that is set high up in the wall! We'll find it now – we will!"

A Strange Night Journey

The children could not stop then and there to look for the door, because it was past their lunch-time already. Dimmy would be coming to look for them, not at all pleased. In excitement they flew to the bathroom, washed their hands, and then rushed back to brush their hair.

Downstairs they went, to find Dimmy just about to set out to fetch them, looking most annoyed. Peggy caught her round the waist and gave her a sudden hug, which stopped Dimmy's scolding at once. She couldn't help laughing, as Peggy nearly swung her over.

"Don't be so violent," she said. "And please set the table quickly. The meal has been here for ten minutes."

All the children longed to discuss the secret door, and longed even more to set to work and find it, but, of course.

141

they did not want to discuss it in front of Dimmy. They would have to answer so many, many questions if they did. It was their secret, and they hugged it to themselves all lunch-time.

"I've told Ranni to be here with the car at two o'clock," said Dimmy, dropping a sudden bombshell. "Mrs Brimming has told me of a glorious bathing-pool about six miles from here, and, as it's so very hot today, I thought you would all enjoy a really good bathe. We're taking our tea with us, and our supper too!"

To her great surprise nobody seemed at all pleased. She did not know their tremendous impatience to get back to hunting for the secret door, now that they thought they knew where it was! She looked round, surprised at the lack of excitment.

"Don't you *want* to go?" she said. "What funny children you are! I thought you'd love it. I suppose you had made other plans. Well, never mind, your plans can wait till tomorrow. I've ordered the picnic tea and supper now. Fetch your bathing-things quickly after lunch, because I don't want to keep Ranni waiting."

Jack saw that Dimmy was disappointed because they didn't seem pleased. He was kind-hearted enough to pretend that he was thrilled, and he kicked the others under the table to make them follow his lead.

They played up valiantly, and soon Dimmy was thinking that she had been mistaken – the children really did want to go! Actually, when they went to fetch their bathing-things, they began to feel excited about the unexpected treat. A bathe would be heavenly this hot weather – and a picnic tea *and* supper would be heavenly too!

"The secret door won't run away," Jack said. "It will still be there, waiting for us this evening. We'll find it all right, now we are sure it's higher up in the panelling than we searched. I never thought of that. Let's enjoy ourselves, and look forward to a good hunt this evening!"

So they went off happily, and had a really wonderful time, bathing in a pool as blue as forget-me-nots, lying to dry themselves in the hot sun, and then bathing again and again. The picnic was better than they had hoped – and as for the supper, even Dimmy was amazed to see what Mrs Brimming had provided. They all enjoyed themselves thoroughly.

They were very tired when they got back. They had done so much swimming that their arms and legs ached all over! "You must go straight to bed," said Dimmy, seeing them yawn one after another. "You've had a lovely day – so have I – and we're all burnt a deeper brown than ever!"

They said good night to Dimmy and went upstairs. Their enthusiasm for the secret door was not quite so high as it had been. In fact, only Jack and Mike seemed able to hunt for it!

"We'll get into bed," said Peggy. "Nora and I can hardly stand. Do you mind looking for the door by yourselves, you and Mike, Jack? I'm sure Paul won't want to stand on chairs with you and tap the walls above his head! He can hardly keep awake."

"You get into bed, and Paul too – and Mike and I will tell you as soon as we've spotted the door," said Jack. "Good thing we've got our torches back. We can see what we're doing now."

The girls got into bed – and so did Paul, although he felt he really ought to go and help the two boys. He lay and watched them put chairs against the wall, and then, quite suddenly, fell fast asleep.

"Blow," said Jack, looking at him. "I meant to have asked him if there was a chair standing close to the wall when he woke up this morning; because it seems to me that whoever climbed back through the high-up door would certainly have to have a chair to stand on!"

"Yes, you're right," said Mike. "I remember seeing one, Jack – just about here, it was! Let's stand on one here and see if there's anything queer high up on the panelling above."

They put one of Paul's chairs in the place Mike pointed out, and Jack stood on it. He felt round the panelling there, and was lucky, almost at once!

"I've got something!" he said, in a low, excited voice. "A knob! I'm pressing it – gosh, this whole big panel is moving!"

Mike shone his torch up from below, his heart beating in excitement. Yes – a big panel had moved with a loud click to one side, and a dark gap showed in the wall. They had found the secret door! What a well-hidden one! Who would think of looking high up in the panelling for an entrance?

"Mike! See if the girls are awake," said Jack. "We'll tell them. Don't wake Paul. He's absolutely sound asleep. We'd have to yell the place down to wake him."

Mike went into the girls' room with his torch and came back immediately. "Sound asleep too," he reported. "I shook Nora, but she didn't even stir! We'd better go exploring alone, Jack. Anyway, it's probably better there should be only two of us!"

"Right," said Jack. "I think we'd better get a couple of our suitcases to put on this chair, to stand on. I don't see how we can climb into this hole unless we get a bit nearer to it!"

Mike fetched two suitcases and put them on the chair. It was easy to clamber into the hole then! Jack went first, making quite a noise, but Paul didn't even move!

"There are steps this other side," said Jack, feeling with his foot. "That's good! Pass me my torch, Mike. I've left it down there."

Mike passed it to him and Jack shone it into the passage. "Yes – it's a proper passage," he said. "About eighteen inches wide. I'll go down the steps. You get through and follow."

Mike clambered through the queer high-up door, and

Jack went first.

followed Jack down the steps into the passage. The steps were more like a ladder clamped to the wall, but were quite easy to get down.

Now the two boys stood one behind the other in the passage. They both felt exultant. They had found the way! Now where would this lead to? To a chimney of the tower? And if so, what would they find there? A way out into a room? And who would be in the room?

They began to make their way along the passage. It was

145

hot and stuffy. It ran straight for a little way and then bent sharply to the right. "I think we're walking behind the walls of some of the rooms on this floor," said Jack. "Hallo, we go downwards here – there's a slope."

They went downwards, and then very sharply upwards. The passage wound in and out, just as had been shown on the plan. And then, quite abruptly it stopped!

It came to an end against a stone wall. Up the wall some iron staples were set, evidently meant for climbing. "We go up here," said Jack, in a low voice, flashing his torch upwards.

They went up a little distance and then Jack stopped. "Can't go any farther up," he said. "There's a stone roof. But there's a grille or something here, just at the side of the iron staples. It's got a kind of handle. I'll pull it back. I hope it doesn't make a noise!"

He pulled it slowly back. It made not the slightest sound, and Jack guessed that it was well oiled. No doubt this was the way that the night-visitor used whenever he wanted to visit the three-room suite, or any other of the rooms on that floor, for any purpose!

Jack looked through the opening left by the sliding grille. He could see nothing but utter blackness. Was he looking into the chimney-piece of the room in the tower, which had been marked with a T door on the map? He must be! He listened. He could not hear a sound nor see a light.

"I'm climbing through the opening," he whispered to Mike, below him. "I think it's safe. Stay there till you hear a low whistle, then come up."

Jack climbed through the opening and felt about for some way to get down. His feet found some stone ledges, and he stepped down cautiously, not daring to put his torch on yet. He put out his hands and touched cold stone in front of him, at the back of him and at the sides! He decided to flick his torch on and off quickly.

When he did so he saw at once that he was standing

upright in a big chimney, his feet in the empty stone fireplace. He had only to bend down, walk forward, and he would be out in one of the tower rooms!

He bent down. There was pitch darkness in the room, but in a short time Jack made out a small strip of starry sky! He knew he was looking at one of the narrow tower windows, with the stars shining through it.

He gave a low whistle, and heard the sounds of Mike climbing up, then scrambling through the grille and down the stone ledges. Soon the two boys stood together in the dark room. Jack switched on his torch. The room was a sitting room – very comfortably furnished indeed. Nobody was there.

"What a lot of armchairs!" whispered Jack. "Guy believes in making himself comfortable. What do we do now?"

"Find the stone tower-stairway and go up it," whispered back Mike. "There are more rooms above. We know that from the map. Come on. The stairway will be outside that door over there."

They went carefully to the door and opened it. Outside was a dim light, evidently for lighting up the stairway. Jack fumbled round the curved stone wall until he found a switch, and turned off the light. "We shan't run so much risk of being spotted if we go up in the dark," he whispered. "Be careful, now. We don't know what we might come up against!"

They went silently up the stone steps in their rubber shoes. The stairway appeared to wind round and round the inside of the tower walls. They came to a door, which was a little ajar. The room beyond was in darkness.

Jack listened but could hear nothing. He pushed the door open, and looked in. He was sure nobody was there. He flashed on his torch quickly, and stared in astonishment.

"A bedroom!" he whispered to Mike. "But look at the beds – heaps of them! Whoever lives up here? Goodness, it

147

He flashed on his torch.

isn't only that Guy fellow – it's a whole lot of people. What *can* they be doing in this tower?"

"There's another room above this," whispered Mike, whose heart was thumping like a piston. "Perhaps something will be going on there."

They left the bedroom and went up the stone stairs again. Before they came to the next door, they heard loud voices!

They stopped at once, and pressed close together, hardly breathing. Some kind of quarrel was going on in that top room of the tower.

There were angry shouts in a foreign language. Then came the sound of something being flung over – a table perhaps?

"Who are they?" whispered Jack. "There sounds to be quite a lot. I vote we creep up and listen! Come on!"

A Truly Adventurous Time

The two boys crept up the few remaining stone steps and came to another door which, like the rest, was a little ajar. There was a small platform outside this door, and from it a narrower stairway led upwards.

Jack put his mouth to Mike's ear. "We'll scoot up these steps if anyone comes rushing out. They're not likely to think there's anyone up there at this time of night. I expect it only leads to the roof of the tower."

Mike nodded. He set his eye to the crack of the door, and so did Jack. The crack was wide and gave the boys a very good view of the whole room. They were astonished to see so many men.

Half of them were in the curious garb that the boys had seen being worn by the figures in the mine. Their heads

149

were hidden in a hood which had eye-holes covered by some stiff, transparent material. Jack thought it was probably to protect their eyes from the heat.

The other half were in ordinary clothes, but wore overalls over them. Jack gave Mike a nudge as he recognized Guy in overalls. There was no mistaking that ugly face with its fierce eyes!

It was plain that everyone was angry with Guy. They shouted at him in strange tongues. They shook their fists and threatened him. He stood there, glowering.

"You told us we were safe here, and could do our work in secret. You told us no one ever came to this castle, or to the mines. And now, before our work is finished, you say we have to clear out of this tower!"

Someone yelled something in a foreign language and Guy scowled.

"I've told you it's no fault of mine," he said. "We've been here, unseen, for nearly two years now – thanks to the help my mother and aunts have given me – ever since I first discovered the priceless metal in that old mine. I put you on to it, didn't I? I've helped you with my knowledge. But I tell you, if we stay here in this tower now, everything will be discovered. The place has been let – and the tower has got to be opened."

More yells. Then a quiet-looking man spoke up. "What you suggest, then, is that you take the stuff that is ready, and hide it away. And we leave this tower and go to live down in the mines, working there till the castle is empty of its tenants, and we can come back again and live in the tower while we finish our work?"

"Yes. And that's the only sensible thing to do," said Guy. "You know that. Lord Moon owns the castle – and the mines and everything in them, valuable or not. He thinks they are only tin mines – we know better. Because of that strange fire years ago, which drove the miners away and gave them that curious tingling disease, a new metal was formed. We've called it 'Stellastepheny', and it's going to be one of the most powerful and valuable in the world . . ."

More shouts, and someone pounded on a table.

"And you want us to let you go off and sell it, while we go down and live in the mines!" shouted one of the men in the hoods. "We don't trust you, Guy Brimming. We never did. You're not straight."

Guy looked round at them bitterly. "Not straight? And which of *you* is straight? Not one! Well, either you trust me, and we save something out of this – or you don't trust me, and all our work will be lost forever."

There was a heated discussion in all kinds of languages. Then the quiet-spoken man gave the verdict.

"All right. We *have* to trust you. Let's finish the last lot of stuff, and you can take it with the other. Then we'll take the secret way to the mines and stay there, at work, till we hear from you that things are safe. We've plenty of food down there."

"You're wise," said Guy, his face surly and unpleasant. "Get cracking, then. I want to go tonight. I'd hoped to scare the fools who want the castle – but they won't be scared. I daren't stay any longer."

"Right," said the quiet man. "We'll finish off this last lot of stuff, and you can take it and go. Then tomorrow we'll heave all the beds down into the cellars underneath the tower, so that no one suspects anything when they see the room. The other furniture won't matter. Then we'll clear up here. But tonight we must go to the mines. We all saw that light over the ruined village after we'd left last night. There will be many things to do there at once."

There was a good deal of muttering, but it was plain that everyone was now agreed. Jack and Mike watched the next proceedings in the greatest wonder.

One of the men put what looked like a glass cylinder in the middle of the floor. He clamped it down, and attached some glass tubes to it. Then the men in the loose robes and hoods brought up two or three narrow shovels covered in bags of some kind.

"Stand back," they said to the men in overalls. "Cover your faces."

Everyone stood back. Some of the men turned round to face the wall, and crouched down. Jack and Mike felt rather frightened, but they could not stop watching.

The hooded men uncovered their narrow shovels quickly and emptied the curious, shining, misty stuff on them into the wide opening at the top of the glass cylinder. Another man poured some colourless liquid into the tubes as the shimmering material slid into the cylinder.

And then the whole room seemed to disappear! A shimmering radiance came instead, that blotted out every single thing – a radiance that was of the same strange, unknown colour that the boys had seen hanging over the ruined village the night before.

Mike and Jack gazed through the crack, fascinated and entranced. What was this? They could see nothing at all in the room but this unearthly light. Men, chairs, floor, walls – everything was gone.

Jack's eyes began to hurt him. So did Mike's. They put their hands over them and stumbled away from the door and a little way up the stone steps. They sat down, unable to see for some time. No wonder the men had been told to cover their eyes!

"If that radiant stuff makes 'Stellastepheny' or whatever they called it, it's really wonderful," whispered Jack, at last. "I've never in my life seen anything like it."

"Listen – somebody's coming to the door," said Mike, clutching Jack's arm. "It must be Guy, with the stuff he wants to get away with tonight."

Somebody stumbled out of the open door and down the stone steps. The boys saw vaguely that he carried a metal box under his arm. Was the precious "Stellastepheny" in that? It must be.

"Let's follow and see if he goes out of the tower door at the bottom," whispered Jack. So they followed, and when they came to the bedroom, they saw that a light was there. Guy must have gone into that room. Perhaps he was getting a few of his clothes?

And then Jack did something so quickly that Mike could not at first make out what he was doing. He ran down the two steps to the door, shut it firmly, and turned a key that stuck out from the lock! There was a startled cry from inside, and an angry voice shouted:

"Who's that? What are you doing?" Then footsteps could be heard running over to the door. The man inside pulled at it violently, shouting again when he found it locked.

"Oh Jack! You've caught him! You've got him prisoner!" said Mike, in amazed delight. "He can't get out of that room. He can't even be heard in the room above."

"It won't matter if he is," said Jack. "I'm taking the key!" He took the key and put it into his pocket!

"What do we do now?" whispered Mike, his voice shaking with excitement.

"Shall we follow the men to the mine?" said Jack.

"No. Let's lock them into the top room, like you've locked Guy into this one," said Mike, almost choking over his brilliant idea.

"Come on, then!" said Jack, quite beside himself with all these sudden thrills. They raced up the stairs and came to the top room again. They peered cautiously through the crack.

The men were there, evidently getting ready to go, for all of them now had on the loose, hooded clothes. Jack saw that he must lock them in at once or they would be coming out. He banged the door, and felt for the key.

There wasn't one! Angry shouts came from inside, and Jack caught Mike's arm. "We must hide! There's no key!"

He pulled Mike up the steps that ascended to the roof, just as the door was wrenched open, and a man came out, looking very weird in his hooded garb.

153

"Who's that?" shouted the man. "Who's monkeying about with the door? Is it you, Guy?"

A murmur came from behind him, and he was pushed forward. "Of course it's Guy. Who else could it be? What's he doing, staying on here still? Come on, let's go down after him and see what he's up to."

Then the whole crowd of men poured down the stairs, never dreaming that two scared boys were on the stone steps just a little way above them!

They made a great noise, clattering down the stairs — such a noise that when Guy shouted to them as they passed the locked bedroom door, not one of them heard him. The boys, following down cautiously afterwards, heard him clearly, and grinned.

The men clattered right down to the foot of the tower, and then stopped. "He's not here. He's gone through the tower, after all," said one of them. "It must have been the wind that banged that top door shut! My, we must be scary to act like this!"

Another man produced a big key and fitted it into the tower door. He unlocked it and went out into the little square room beyond. The others followed.

One man gave a sudden exclamation. "I've forgotten to get my notes out of the sitting-room. I'll go and get them and catch you up. Give me the key and I'll lock the tower door behind me when I've got my notes."

He was given the key. Jack and Mike fled back up the steps, as silently as they could. If that man was coming to get something from the room above they would be caught if they did not get out of the way!

The man came up the stairs, slowly and heavily. He had not heard the boys. They shot past the door of the sitting-room and stood on the steps above, shaking with excitement. The man went into the room and switched on a torch. They heard him opening a drawer.

"Come on — we'll go down," said Jack, in a sudden

whisper. "It's our chance to get out of the tower before he locks it – and watch where he goes. There must be a secret way to the mines, as we thought!"

They ran silently down the steps to the very bottom, went out of the tall, narrow tower door, and crouched at the side of a chest, waiting.

Soon they heard footsteps and the man came down again. He pushed through the doorway, lighting his way with a torch, shut the door and locked it carefully. The boys watched breathlessly. What was he going to do?

He went to the side of the little square room, fumbled behind a chest and pulled at something there. In the very middle of the floor a big stone slid quietly downwards, as silently as if it had been oiled. The boys stared at the gap in the floor lit by the light of the man's torch. They were really amazed. Why, they had trodden over that stone a dozen times!

The man went over to the hole, sat down on the edge of it and let himself down carefully into the gap. He disappeared. After a few seconds the boys came out from their hiding-place and switched on a torch. Just as they flashed it they saw the stone rising slowly and silently back into place!

"Look at that!" said Jack. "I'm not sure we aren't in some peculiar kind of dream, Mike! What are we going to do now?"

"Follow that man!" said Mike promptly. Jack shook his head. "Too dangerous," he said. "I'd like to – but we might get lost underground trying to find where the man has gone. He's got too good a start. I know what we'll do!"

"What?" said Mike.

"Help me pull a heavy chest right over the stone that goes up and down!" said Jack. "Then none of the men will be able to get out. They'll be caught! If they lower the stone it won't provide a way out – because the chest will be on top! We'll have got them properly!"

So the two boys hauled one of the biggest chests right

over the stone trap door, and then stared at one another in delight.

"We've got Guy locked up in the bedroom of the tower —and we've blocked the way out for the others – unless they like to find their way through that wall of rubble we found in the mines, and come up the shaft. But I bet they won't do that!" Mike rubbed his hands in glee.

"*Now* what do we do?" said Jack. "Go to bed? Everyone is a prisoner, so we might as well! We'll tell Dimmy and Ranni in the morning – what a surprise for them, and the others, too! Come on."

"I hope we shan't wake up and find it's all a dream," said Mike. "Honestly, it's been one of the most adventurous nights we've ever had!"

An Exciting Finish

Next morning Mike and Jack were still sound asleep when the others were fully awake. It was Paul who woke them.

He came running into the boys' room. "I say, what happened last night? You found the secret entrance and never woke me! It's still open in my room. *I say*!"

The girls joined him, thrilled to hear his news. Mike and Jack woke up with a jump. Jack immediately remembered the happenings of the night before, and gave Mike an excited punch.

"I say, Mike, I wonder how all our prisoners are!"

Mike grinned, remembering everything in a rush. Goodness! What a night! Then Paul and the girls began to clamour to know all about the secret door, and if the boys had gone into the passage, and *what had happened*?

They could hardly believe their ears when the boys told

them. They listened, their eyes nearly falling out of their heads. All those men! Living in the tower too! and Guy finding out about that precious stuff, whatever it was – and getting men to work the mines for it, keeping it a dead secret.

"And he's locked up in the tower bedroom, you say!" cried Nora, with a squeal. "How *did* you think of such a thing! And all those men imprisoned underground! Quick – let's find Dimmy and Ranni!"

Dimmy was surprised to find five such excited children descending on her, as she sat waiting for them to come to breakfast. "Dimmy, Dimmy! Listen to what Jack and Mike have found out!" shouted Nora.

"I'm fetching Ranni," said Paul. "He ought to hear all this too," and he sped off, coming back with the big Baronian, who looked very puzzled at this sudden call.

Breakfast was forgotten as the children poured out their tale. Dimmy listened, almost speechless with astonishment. Ranni listened too, nodding his great head from time to time, and finally bursting into a great guffaw of laughter as he heard how Guy had been locked up in the tower bedroom.

He laughed still more when he heard how the two boys had put a heavy chest over the entrance to the underground passage to the mines. Then he looked grave.

"I should not laugh," he said apologetically to Dimmy, who looked very serious, and felt it. "There has been danger here for us – great danger. I can see that. Many things are clear to me now which puzzled me before."

"And to me too," said Dimmy soberly. "Well – the children seem to have managed everything very well without our help – but I think we should get the police in now, Ranni."

"Yes," said Ranni. "This is a serious busniess. Lord Moon must be told. He must fly back from America, or wherever he is."

"I had better ring for Mrs Brimming and the Lots," said Dimmy. "I am sure they knew all about this."

They did, of course. They were three frightened women as they stood before Dimmy and Ranni, and answered their stern questions.

Mrs Brimming wept bitterly and would not stop. Her two tall sisters were frightened, but Edie Lots was defiant as well.

"Don't blame my sister, Mrs Brimming," she said. "She never wanted her son to do this. But I urged him on. He's clever! He should be one of the greatest scientists in the world. He should—"

"He won't be," said Dimmy. "He has done wrong. The mines are not his, and he had no right to bring all those men here and put them into the tower like that. What will Lord Moon say when he knows all this?"

Mrs Brimming sobbed more loudly. The children felt sorry for her. Edie Lots spoke loudly.

"Lord Moon never comes here. He has no use for his castle or for the mines. Why shouldn't my nephew use them?"

"It is foolish to talk like that," said Dimmy. "Don't you realize that all of you will get into serious trouble over this?"

"I suppose all those queer happenings were caused by you three?" said Jack. "The jumping books – and Twang-Dong noises and so on. You wanted to scare us away, didn't you?"

"Yes," said Edie Lots, still defiant. "But I was the only one who worked them. My sisters wouldn't. My nephew Guy invented them – I tell you, he's a genius – and he showed me how to work them. The front door opening by itself – that's done by a wire. And the jumping books – there's a little passage behind the library bookcases, and Guy made some small holes in the back of one of the shelves; so that when I went into the passage behind I could poke my finger into a book, and send it leaping off the shelf."

"Very simple!" said Jack. "We didn't look for small holes at the back of the shelf! What about the Twang-Dong noises? How did the instruments on the wall make *them*?"

"They didn't," said Edie Lots, sounding quite proud. "There's a mechanical device up the chimney. When it goes off, it makes those two noises at intervals."

"Gosh! So that's why we could never spot who did it – even when the door was locked!" said Mike. "Oh – and what about those gleaming eyes in Lord Moon's portrait?"

"The canvas eyes have been scraped very thin, and then painted again, and a hole made in each," said Edie Lots. "And there is a light behind each eye that can be turned on from outside the room. I waited ouside when you were inside, and kept turning the light on and off. And the hissing noise was made by a bellows worked at the same time. My nephew thought of all those things."

"And did you change the rooms round – and break the vases?" asked Dimmy, entering suddenly into this extraordinary conversation.

"I did everything," said Edie, proudly. "I made the picture swing too. Guy arranged that." Her tall sister hung her head, and Mrs Brimming still sobbed, heart-broken. But Edie was proud and glad. She had helped her beloved nephew, and that was all she cared about!

"Oh well – it's rather disappointing – everything has got quite a reasonable explanation!" said Peggy. "But goodness me, some people would have been very scared!"

"Some people were," said Edie, and the children thought of the man who had gone to the library to look at the old books. How pleased the sisters must have been when he spread the tale of Queer Happenings about!

Nobody seemed to want any breakfast at all! Dimmy dismissed the three caretakers, and began to pour out the tea. Ranni sat down to join them, his arm round Paul. He seemed to think that Paul had escaped great dangers and must now be guarded every minute!

They talked soberly for some time. "I think you should take the car and go and inform the police, Ranni," said Dimmy. "I don't see that this will make any difference to Her Majesty the Queen of Baronia coming here, as arranged – but we must get this business settled up before she comes."

"Yes. Guy will have to come out of the tower bedroom, for instance!" said Nora.

Ranni got up to go. The children made a very poor breakfast, they were so excited and so eager to talk. They watched for Ranni to come with the police, and were thrilled when they heard the car hooting below to tell them he was back.

Things happened very quickly after that. Ranni had told the police most of the strange story. Two men were dispatched to get the angry Guy from the tower bedroom. They forced the tower door easily enough, and went up the stone stairs, having been presented with the bedroom key by Jack. Soon a very dishevelled Guy was being hustled into a police car, angry, astonished and bewildered.

His weeping mother and two aunts were not allowed to speak to him. Nothing was being done about them for the time being. Lord Moon would decide everything when he returned the next day, called back from America. He was flying over, most astonished at what the police had told him on the telephone.

As for the underground miners, they were soon rounded up by a most formidable posse of police. Jack and Mike got permission to go down the secret passage to the mines, behind the police, provided they stayed close to Ranni. Much to Paul's anger Ranni would not allow him to come.

The heavy chest was moved away from the stone trap door. Mike went to the side of the room and fumbled behind the same chest he had seen the man go to. He found an iron lever sticking a little way out of the wall. He pulled it – and lo and behold, the stone in the middle of the floor slid downwards, and exposed the opening to the secret passage!

Down they all went. The underground passage was not a pleasant one, for most of the way it was narrow, low-roofed and dripping wet. It led down the hill, meandering about. Ranni thought it must have been the bed of an underground stream, which had more or less dried up and left its bed as a tunnel.

They came into the mines at last, and at once the passage became dry and the roof rose high. The boys soon found themselves in a little tunnel near the place where they had seen the wonderful, roaring fire. It was just opposite the wall of rubble from behind which they had watched such a strange sight.

The men were all gathered together in the main cave, puzzled and anxious. They had been back to the trap door entrance, and had moved the stone trap door, to get out and back into the tower. But, of course, they had found the way blocked by the heavy chest, and had not dared to try to move it. In fact, they had no idea what it was! They had closed the stone trap door again and retreated into the mines.

When they saw the uniforms of the police, a murmur went up from the miners, who looked very strange in their queer hooded garments. Ranni was quite startled to see them!

The men had been expecting something like this ever since they had found the trap door blocked. They felt sure that Guy was at the bottom of it, and were ready to give away everything, to get even with him! It was not until they had told the police every single bit of information they knew that they were told that Guy was a prisoner too – and had been locked up all night in the tower bedroom!

"If only the men had known, they could have escaped

that way," said Jack, pointing to the wall of rubble on the opposite side of the cave. "They could have knocked down the rubble and escaped up a shaft. We knew that – but they didn't!"

"The things you kids know just don't bear thinking about," said a tall policeman, with a grin. "Keep behind your red-bearded friend, now – we don't need your help in front."

The prisoners were all taken away in police cars. Ranni and Dimmy sighed with relief. Goodness gracious – to think of all the secrets that had been going on in Moon Castle!

"I think we'll take the car and go into Bolingblow for lunch," said Dimmy, heaving an enormous sigh. "I'm sure Mrs Brimming and her sisters won't be able to provide anything like a lunch today!"

"Yes, let's go," said Nora, at once. "We can tell that waitress she was quite right. There *were* Queer Happenings and Noises in Moon Castle. Do let's."

"You're not to say a single word to her," said Dimmy. "It's nothing to do with her. We don't want the news all over the town, exaggerated and garbled – we'd never hear the last of it!"

"Dimmy – come and see the tower," begged Jack.

"No, thank you," said Dimmy, firmly. "I don't feel strong enough today to tackle that awful tower – though I *would* like to see the view from the top."

"My mother is still coming, isn't she?" said Paul anxiously. "You haven't put her off, have you, Dimmy?"

"On the contrary," said Dimmy. "I had a letter from her this morning – which, in all the excitement, I forgot to mention – and as your brothers are quite well again, they're all coming tomorrow! What do you think of that?"

"Smashing!" said Mike, at once. "It was going to be dull, now this adventure is over, waiting and waiting for them to come. Now we'll have hardly any waiting at all. Couldn't be better!"

"In fact, we've cleared up all the mysteries at exactly the right moment," said Jack. "Aren't we clever, Dimmy?"

Dimmy wouldn't say they were. She laughed and ruffled Jack's hair

TWANG!

"Oh, my goodness – don't say that awful Twang-Dong is still going!" cried Dimmy. "I can't bear it!"

DONG!

The children roared with laughter. Jack went round the bend of the L-shaped room and looked up the chimney, shining his torch there.

He put up his hand and pulled down a curious little contrivance of metal, springs and tiny hammers.

"There you are," he said, putting it on the table. "The Twang-Dong itself. One of the mysterious secrets of Moon Castle!"

"Hurrah for Moon Castle!" said Nora. "And hurrah for all its secrets, Twang-Dongs and everything!"

The Twang-Dong made a curious noise. Its mechanism seemed to be running down. It slowly raised one of its little hammers and struck the metal beneath.

DONG!

"It's finished," said Jack. "Finished – like this adventure. Well, it was GRAND FUN while it lasted!"

The Treasure Hunters

The Treasure Hunters was first published in this edition
in the U.K. in hardback in 1976 by William Collins
Sons & Co. Ltd, and in paperback in 1983 in Armada.

Copyright © Enid Blyton 1976

CHAPTER 1

Granny's Old House

Jeffery was sticking some stamps into his album when Susan and John came tearing into the playroom.

"Jeffery! What do you think! We're going to stay with Granny and Granpa in their old, old house!" cried Susan.

"Really?" said Jeffery, surprised and pleased. "How do you know?"

"Because Daddy said so," said Susan, dancing round the room. "Isn't it lovely! John has never been to Granny's, and I hardly remember the house – but you've told us so much about it, Jeffery, that I feel as if I know it inside and out!"

Mother came into the room, and smiled at the three excited faces.

"Yes," she said, "it *is* fun for you, isn't it? Daddy's father and mother are such dear old people, and you will be very happy with them for a few weeks. Daddy is taking me away for a while, because the doctor says I need strong sea air – and Granny and Granpa have offered to have you till we come back."

"Let me see their letter, Mother!" begged Jeffery. He took it and read it.

"We shall so love to have our grandchildren," he read. "Especially as this may be the last year we shall be able to live here. It will almost break our hearts to leave this old house, which has been in our family for three hundred years."

"Oh, Mother!" said Jeffery, looking up in dismay. "Are they really leaving their old home? I thought Daddy said it would be his and ours some day."

"Yes, we thought so too," said Mother. "But you see, since the War, things have been very difficult, and Granny and Granpa have very little money. They will have to sell the old place, and live in a smaller house."

"Well, it's a good thing we're going to stay with them whilst they've still got the old house," said Jeffery. "I remember it quite well, Mother – it's simply lovely!"

"I've never been there," said John, who was the youngest. "Last time you and Susan went I had chicken pox."

"I don't remember it *very* well," said Susan, "but

Jeffery has told us all about it heaps of times. I'm longing to go!"

"Well, you haven't long to wait!" said Mother. "You are going tomorrow! So I am going to be very, very busy today, packing for you all!"

"Tomorrow!" cried Susan, jumping for joy. "Oh, how lovely! I must go and pack for my dolls."

Tomorrow came very quickly indeed. In no time at all the three children were packed into Daddy's car, with the luggage behind, and off they went! Mother sat in front with Daddy, and the three children were behind.

"You'll love Granny's old house," said Jeffery, as they sped along. "It's the sort of place where all kinds of things have happened, you know – and where you feel anything might still happen."

"Oh, I *do* love places like that," said Susan, happily. "Are there good walks round, Jeffery?"

"Most exciting ones," said Jeffery. "There is a deep, dark wood nearby, where we can go exploring. And there is a river that flows through the wood and makes part of it very marshy. And there is a lovely farm, where Farmer Timbles lives, and his wife – she's fat and kind, and she makes the most lovely cakes."

"We'll go there to tea then!" said Susan, jumping up and down on the seat. "This will be a lovely holiday."

"I hope you will remember to be quiet in the house, and to be kind and obedient to your grandparents," said Daddy. "They have had a lot of trouble lately, and it is kind of them to have you."

"We really will do our best," promised John. "Jeffery, was there a dog at Granny's? Or a cat?"

"There was a dog called Rags," said Jeffery, who never forgot anything. "He was a darling, but he may not be there now."

"You'll soon see!" said Mother. "We are nearly there!"

"Look! That's the wood I was telling you about," said Jeffery. The children pressed their noses against the car window and peered out. They saw a thick, dark wood with one or two narrow paths running into it. It looked very exciting.

The car turned into a drive between two big gate-posts. On the top of each sat a stone eagle.

"We're here, we're here!" shouted Jeffery, remembering the eagles from his last visit.

The car ran up a winding drive and stopped before a lovely old house. It was long and rather low, with very tall chimneys. The windows shone with leaded panes, and the sides of the house came out to form a sunny courtyard, in which walked some white fantail pigeons.

With a flutter of snowy wings the pigeons flew to the roof, and sat there cooing. "Rookity-coo," they said, peering down at the visitors in surprise. "Rookity-coo!"

"Isn't it lovely!" said Susan, jumping out of the car. The old house glowed red in the sunshine and seemed to welcome the children. It had known many children's feet in the years it had stood, and had heard many children's voices. Now here were more children of the same family, and the house was glad to welcome their pattering feet and to hear their happy calls.

"Granny! There's Granny!" cried Jeffery, and he ran to meet the pretty old lady who stood on the steps to greet them. She was small and round and smiling, and she wore a funny little cap on her white hair.

Granpa came up behind her. He wore a pointed white beard, and had a thick mop of silvery hair. He ran down the steps to kiss Mother.

"Welcome to Greylings Manor!" he said to them all. "It may be the last time we shall welcome you here – but we hope it will be the happiest!"

The children hugged their grandmother and kissed their grandfather. They knew them very well, for the two old people had often been to stay at the children's home. They were fond of them, and were very glad to see them again.

"Isn't it a lovely place, John?" said Jeffery, as he took his brother and sister up to their rooms. "We have been given the two little rooms up in the roof – good! I had one before, and it's so exciting there."

He opened a door. The others went in. They found themselves in a low-roofed room, with latticed windows that looked out on to the sunny garden at the back of the house. The walls of the room were crooked, the ceiling was crooked, and the big beams that ran here and there were crooked too! "It's like a room in a fairy-tale!" said Susan, delighted. "I love the whitewashed walls and the uneven floor. Is this my room or yours?"

"It's our room," said Jeffery. "John and I sleep here, and you have the little room that leads off it.

Open that low door there in the corner and you'll see your room, Susan."

Susan opened a low door that came no higher than her shoulder. She stooped and went through it. She came into a small room that seemed like a doll's room! It was almost round, had a ceiling that sloped right down to the floor at one side, and two tiny windows that let in the sun. A white pigeon sat on a small slanting roof outside one window, and cooed softly.

"It's simply lovely!" said Susan. "Oh, I know what you mean when you say this is a house where things might happen, Jeffery! It's like the beginning of a story!"

Susan spoke more truly than she knew. It *was* the beginning of a story – but the children didn't know it yet!

They washed, and then went downstairs. Mother and Daddy were talking out in the garden with Granny and Granpa.

"They don't want to be disturbed," said Jeffery. "I'll show you the rest of the house!"

The other two followed him. It was the most exciting house in the world. For one thing there were three separate staircases! One was the main one, a wide, winding stair that went from the big landing to the hall. Another led from the kitchens to the servants' rooms, and a third, most mysterious, led from a door in the dining-room, behind the wall, and up to the children's room, entering Susan's room unexpectedly from a cupboard!

"How simply thrilling!" said Susan, as she went up the tiny stairway, so narrow and dark, and came out of the little cupboard in her room!

172

There were old family pictures to see – there was great-grandfather, looking rather stern. Great-great-grandmother, looking very pretty indeed in a blue bonnet, stared at them from her frame.

"She's like *you*, Susan," said Jeffery. So she was. She had just the same deep-blue eyes and golden hair.

They were still looking at the pictures when Granny called them.

"Mother and Daddy are leaving now!" she called. "Come and say goodbye."

The children ran downstairs. They hugged their parents, wished them a lovely holiday, and then watched them get back into the car. Daddy started the engine and called to them.

"Be good now! We'll write to you!"

"Goodbye, dears!" cried Mother, and she waved her hand. The car swept down the drive and disappeared out of the eagle-gates. They were gone!

"Our holiday has begun!" cried Susan, and she jumped up and down the steps. The boys turned to Granny.

"Where is Rags? Is he still here with you?" they asked.

"He's out with one of the maids," said Granny. "Look – here he comes! My goodness, he'll be delighted to see so many children to play with!"

He was! He was a rough-haired fox terrier, with bright eyes, a wagging tail, and a black spot on his white back. He tore up to the children, barked loudly, flung himself on each of them in turn, and licked whatever leg or hand he could find.

"You're just the same darling old dog!" said Jeffery, pleased. He patted him hard. "We'll go for some good walks together, Rags, old boy!"

"Woof!" said Rags, in delight, and rolled over on his back with all four paws in the air.

"Ridiculous dog!" said Granpa, tickling him with his foot. "I suppose you'll forget all about the old people, now you've got three youngsters to tear about with! Ah – there's the dinner-bell! I'm sure we could all do with something to eat!"

Indoors they all went, and took their places in the long, low dining room. Rags lay down on Jeffery's foot. He was just as happy as the children!

CHAPTER 2

The Greylings Treasure

For the next few days the children and Rags had a fine
time, tearing round the garden, going into all the sheds
and outbuildings, eating peas in the kitchen garden,
and hunting for ripening strawberries.

When Rags was not with them, Whiskers, the big
black cat, sauntered along beside them. The fantail
pigeons disappeared like a cloud of snowflakes when
they saw Whiskers – but at other times they were tame
and would come flying down on the children's shoulders and hands.

"This is such a lovely place," said Susan, looking back at the old house, as she went out of the little white gate that led to the kitchen garden. "How I wish that Granny and Granpa could go on living here, and that it would be Daddy's later on – and ours too, when we are grown up."

"Look – there is a car coming up the drive!" said Jeffery. The three children watched to see who would get out of the car. It might be someone they knew. But it wasn't.

The chauffeur got out and opened the door of the car. A very grandly-dressed lady appeared, followed by a tall man. They went up the steps to the front door.

The children went into the kitchen garden as soon as the visitors disappeared into the house. They thought no more about them at all – until later on in the morning.

Jeffery was playing hide-and-seek with the others. He had gone into a little hedged garden that Granny called her own. In it she had planted all her very favourite flowers, and here her pigeons came to be fed each day from her hands.

Jeffery pushed his way into the middle of the thick yew hedge. He was sure that the others would never find him there! He stayed there, quite still, and waited for the other two to hunt for him.

Whilst he was there Granny came into her garden. She sat down on her white seat, and looked into her little pond, where white water-lilies were showing.

Jeffery thought at first that Granny's footsteps were those of Susan or John, and he kept as still as could be. But when the footsteps stopped, and nobody spoke or called, he carefully parted the green boughs and peeped to see who was there.

"Oh! It's only Granny!" he thought. And then he got a shock!

Granny was crying! Tears ran down her apple-cheeks, and she mopped them up with a tiny lace handkerchief. Jeffery stared in horror. He had never seen a grown-up cry before, and it was dreadful to see tears rolling down Granny's cheeks. Whatever could be making her so unhappy?

He struggled out of the hedge at once. Granny heard him, wiped her eyes quickly, and then looked round in surprise. She tried to smile when she saw the hot, dirty face peeping out of the hedge.

"Oh, Jeffery dear!" she said. "You did make me jump! Are you playing hide-and-seek?"

"Yes," said Jeffery. He ran up to his grandmother. "What's the matter?" he asked. "Why are you crying? Has somebody been unkind to you? Just wait till I see them, that's all!"

He looked so fierce that Granny couldn't help laughing, though she still had tears in her eyes.

"No," she said. "Nobody's been unkind. But – did you see those visitors this morning, Jeffery?"

"Yes," said Jeffery. "Did *they* make you cry?"

"In a way they did," said Granny. "You see – they came to look over Greylings Manor – to buy it – and it made me feel sad to think that Granpa and I will have to go. It has always belonged to the Greyling family – and now it must go to strangers. Poor old house – it will not like that!"

"But Granny, have you lost all your money, or

something?" asked Jeffery. "Why must you suddenly go?"

"We haven't *suddenly* lost our money," said Granny. "The family has been unlucky, as the years went by. First, the Greylings Treasure was lost."

"The Greylings Treasure!" cried Jeffery, excited. "What's that? I haven't heard of that!"

"Here he is!" suddenly cried Susan's voice and she came running into Granny's hedged garden. "He isn't even hiding. Catch him!"

"No, Susan, don't," said Jeffery. "I'm not playing now. Granny is telling me something marvellous – about the Greylings Treasure!"

"Whatever's that?" said Susan and John in surprise. They came to sit beside Granny on the white seat. The old lady went on with her story.

"Well," she said, "the Greylings Treasure was brought back from India two hundred and fifty years ago by an adventurous Greyling – Hugh Greyling. He had done a good turn to an Indian Prince, and the Prince gave him some wonderful presents."

"What were they?" asked Susan.

"There were strings of pearls, diamonds set in marvellous metals, a golden cup studded with rubies and sapphires, and other smaller things," said Granny. "There is a book all about this Treasure in the library."

"I shall read it!" said Jeffery, thrilled.

"Well," said Granny, "this treasure was in the Greyling family for some years, and then civil war broke out. You know what civil war is, don't you?"

"It's a war when a country fights against itself,"

said Jeffery. "Families against families. Daddy says it's the worst of all wars."

"It is," said Granny. "Well, in this civil war the Greyling family was afraid that their enemies would steal the Treasure. So Jeffery Greyling – yes, he had your name Jeffery, and he was very like you to look at – well, this old Jeffery of long ago took the Treasure to hide it away safely. He left the house with it – and never came back!"

"What happened to him?" asked John, in surprise.

"Nobody knows," said Granny. "We think he was killed by his enemies. But anyway, the Treasure was never found or heard of again."

"What do you think happened to it?" asked Jeffery.

"Either Jeffery Greyling hid it somewhere in safety, where it was never found again – and then died before he could tell anyone about it, or else his enemies took it and kept it for themselves," said Granny. "But I don't think that is so because somebody would have been sure to have seen the Treasure, and sooner or later it would have been talked about."

"Oh, Granny! Do you mean to say that you think it's still hidden somewhere?" asked Jeffery, in astonishment.

"I sometimes think so," said Granny. "When the Indian Prince gave your great-great-great-great-great-grandfather the Treasure he told him that as long as the golden cup was drunk out of by the Greyling family once a year, good fortune, health, and happiness would remain with the family. But if the cup passed out of the family, and was not used by them, these gifts would pass away too."

"It sounds like a fairy-tale," said Susan, who loved magic and mystery. "Granny, did the tale come true?"

"Well, in a way it did," said Granny. "I don't believe in these old sayings of good and bad luck, you know – but ever since the Treasure went, the Greylings have been unlucky. They have lost their money through the years, they have had illness and sorrow – and now, alas, Granpa and I have so little money left that we must give up the old Manor House, and go to live somewhere else."

"Wait a little longer till I'm grown-up, and I'll earn heaps of money and give it to you!" cried John.

"I'm afraid we can't wait as long as that, John!" said Granny, putting her arm round him. "We shall have to go before Christmas. Those people who came today have offered to buy the house at a good price, and to take the two farms, as well, that go with it."

"Dear old Greylings," said Jeffery, looking at the old house, with its tall chimneys. "I'd hate to think it wouldn't be Greylings any more. If only we had that Treasure now, Granny! You could stay here then, and needn't worry."

"I'd like to see that book that tells us about the Treasure," said Susan.

"I'll show it to you when you go indoors," said Granny. So, that evening, the three children pored over an old book, in which were rough pictures of the Indian Treasure. The golden lucky-cup was clearly drawn and the children looked at it in wonder. It had precious stones set around the middle, and all down the handle. Someone had coloured the picture, and the cup shone as if the stones were real!

The children could not understand the reading in the book, for the lettering was very old, and had faded with the years. They looked at the pictures of great brooches and necklaces and pins, and how they wished they all belonged to the family now!

"It's the most exciting tale I've heard," said Susan. "Granny, I feel as if I must go hunting for the lost Treasure straight away!"

"Many people have hunted," said Granny, with a smile. "But nobody has found it. No – I'm afraid it was captured by enemies all those years ago, smuggled away, and then sold. It's gone for ever now."

But Susan wouldn't let herself think that. She loved to imagine all kinds of things. "I shall pretend it can be found!" she said. "I shall pretend to go hunting for it every day! I shall be a Treasure Hunter!"

"We will, too," said the boys, who liked Susan's pretends.

"My three Treasure Hunters!" said Granny, with a laugh. "Well, hunt all you like – but don't get into *too* much mischief!"

CHAPTER 3

Adventure in the Woods

The boys did not really take the treasure hunt seriously, but Susan did. You should have seen her hunting the next day! She tapped the walls of the old house to see if she could find hollow places, behind which treasure might be hidden. She went into the attics and got herself covered with dust and cobwebs, hunting everywhere in the corners.

"You're silly," said John at last. "All these places have been hunted in for years and years. Granny says there only was one secret passage, and that was the staircase to your room, which was found and opened long ago, and isn't secret any more."

"Children, you really *must* go out of doors," called Granny. "It is far too lovely a day for you to spend in the house."

"But, Granny, we're Treasure-Hunting!" cried Susan.

"Well, you must hunt outside," said Granny. "Go along – out of the house you go, all of you!"

So the three hunters had to go out of the house, and they wandered over to the gate of the kitchen garden. Tipps, the gardener, was there and he waved them away.

"Don't you come in here this morning!" he shouted. "You ate half a row of my best peas yesterday and you'll just keep out today!"

"Bother!" said John. "I felt just like a few peas. What shall we do?"

"Let's go treasure-hunting in the wood!" said Susan eagerly. "We haven't been there yet. We could follow one of those little paths, couldn't we, and see where it leads to."

"We shall get lost," said Jeffery.

"Well, we can take Rags with us," said Susan. "Rags always knows the way home. Come on, Rags. We're going hunting! Hunting! Treasure-hunting, Rags!"

"Woof, woof!" said Rags, thinking that Susan meant rabbit-hunting. So all four of them set off for the woods. They went down the drive and out of the eagle-gates. They turned to the left and soon came to the wood.

They went in under the trees. There was a green light in the wood, very cool and lovely. The trees were so thick overhead that only tiny specks of sunlight got through and these lay like specks of gold on the ground below.

Rabbit-paths ran everywhere. Rags rushed excitedly about, following first one and then another. The children followed quite a wide rabbit-path, thinking it was a real path.

But it wasn't. It stopped at a big rabbit-hole and Rags almost disappeared down it, barking in excitement. The children had to pull him out.

"Well, we can't go down the hole," said John, laughing. "That's where the path leads to. Where shall we go now?"

"Let's go deeper into the wood," said Susan. "It feels mysterious and exciting. You don't know what we might find!"

"Well, you won't find fairies or witches, if that is what you're thinking of," said Jeffery, laughing.

"Listen – what's that noise?" said Susan, stopping suddenly. They all stopped. There was a rushing noise that was not the sound of the wind in the trees.

"It sounds like water," said Jeffery, puzzled. "Oh – of course! I told you there was a river that ran through the wood, didn't I? It wanders in and out and we must be quite near it."

He led the way between the tall trees. The ground became rather wet and marshy, and the children had to tread carefully.

"There it is!" said Jeffery at last. He pointed to where a dark green stream flowed swiftly along between tree-grown banks. The children went to it.

It was deep, and flowed quickly. Susan thought it looked queer.

"Let's follow the banks," she said. "I'd like to see where it goes."

So they followed the stream. It was difficult, because bushes grew so thickly on the bank in some places that they had to leave the stream, go a good way round the bushes and then come back to the water.

It grew wider and shallower as they followed its banks deeper into the wood. It lost its deep green colour and became brown. It bubbled and gurgled, and in its depths quick fishes darted about.

Then suddenly the stream widened out into a large pool, like a small lake. At one end of the pool the stream flowed in, at the other it flowed out.

"Isn't it lovely!" said Susan, in surprise. "I wonder how it made itself into a pond. It looks so round that it seems as if someone made it."

"Whoever would make a lake in the middle of a wood?" said John scornfully. "Ooh look – what a marvellous water-lily that is!"

Water-lilies covered the pond. They were of many colours. The wild yellow one grew there, but deep red and paler pink ones lay on the water also.

"I wish I could pick that deep red lily and take it back for Granny," said Jeffery, looking at the one that John had pointed to.

"It's deep," said Susan, looking into the water. "You couldn't paddle out to it."

Jeffery made his way round the pond, looking to see if there was any shallower place. "There's a big flat

rock here," he said. "And another under the water. I might be able to stand on that, and reach it."

The flat rock was green with slime. Jeffery stood carefully on it, barefooted, and then stepped to the flat stone below – and then he felt about with his foot and said, "I do believe there's another flat stone below this one as well. It's just like steps!"

"They *are* steps!" said Susan, in surprise. She had scraped the green slime off with a stone, and below the slime was white marble! "Look, Jeffery – they are real steps. Steps that somebody put here for the pond."

Jeffery stared down in surprise. Susan was right. Jeffery forgot all about the red water-lily and began to scrape the steps.

"Well, why should anyone build steps here?" he said. "You only put marble steps by a pond if you want to feed swans – or go boating – or if you have a house nearby that you sit in to look over the water."

"Swans wouldn't come here," said Susan. "They like more open water. And there aren't any boats."

"No – but there might have been once," said Jeffery. "I say – I wonder if there ever was a summer-house – or boating-house, or something, near here. After all, if somebody took the trouble to build marble steps here, they might have built a little summerhouse for themselves as well!"

"Let's look!" said Susan. So the three children began to hunt around the pond. The trees and bushes were so thick that it was difficult to make their way here and there.

Suddenly Susan gave a shout. "I say! Look here! What do you think this is?"

The boys scrambled over to where Susan was standing. She was pulling at some thick ivy.

"Look," she said. "There's brick under this ivy. I believe the ivy, the brambles, and the honeysuckle have grown all together here, and hidden a building of some sort!"

The boys excitedly looked about. It certainly seemed as if the great bramble and ivy cluster might be growing over something. They peeped here and there, but they could find no proper building.

"It's like the Castle of the Sleeping Beauty," said Susan, "all overgrown with thorns. Oh, Jeffery, look, look!"

Jeffery and John looked. Rags had gone after a rabbit, and had scraped hard at the bottom of the great ivy tangle. Where he had scraped, stone steps showed – steps that must lead down to the pond!

"So there *must* be some sort of a building beneath this tangle of bushes!" cried Jeffery. "There must! Steps wouldn't lead down from nothing. There must have been a tiny house of some sort here, with steps leading down to the pool. However can we find out?"

"We'll have to borrow an axe from Tipps," said Susan, thrilled. "Then we can chop away the ivy and the other creepers, and see if there's a house underneath."

"Well, there won't be a Sleeping Beauty inside, so don't hope for that, Susan!" said Jeffery, grinning. "I expect it's just a tumbledown hut built by somebody long ago who loved to come and dream in the wood."

"Jeffery, let's go back and get an axe now, this very minute," begged Susan. "Look – when I pull away the ivy here, there is more stone or brick underneath. I *know* there's a secret house here.''

''All right,'' said Jeffery, who was longing to find out more himself. ''We'll go back now, this very minute.''

So back they went, making their way over the marshy ground. They would never have taken the right path if Rags had not shown them the way! But he trotted ahead, sniffing, and soon led them to the rabbit-path they had first followed.

When they were at last out of the dark, green wood, they scampered along at top speed, up the drive and into Tipp's garden shed. He was there, potting plants.

''Tipps! Would you please lend us your axe?'' asked Jeffery. ''The one you chop wood with.''

''Indeed no,'' said Tipps. ''I'll not lend you something to chop off your fingers!''

''Oh, Tipps! We aren't as silly as that!'' said Susan. ''Please do lend us the axe. It's for something secret and important – something we found in the wood.''

''Oh, well – I suppose you want to chop up a dead tree,'' said Tipps. ''Listen now – I'll lend the axe to Jeffery because he's the oldest and biggest – but none of you are to use it except him. See?''

''All right, Tipps,'' said Susan and John. Jeffery took the axe, and they made their way out of the shed. But just as they turned their steps towards the front gate, a bell rang.

''Bother!'' said John. ''That's for dinner.''

''Let's miss dinner and go and chop,'' said Susan, who was always ready to do mad things.

''Don't be silly,'' said Jeffery, putting the axe

carefully into the middle of the yew hedge to hide it. "We don't want to have Granny and Granpa hunting all over the place for us, and Tipps telling them he's lent us the chopper. No – we'll go in and have our dinner – and then we'll spend the afternoon in the wood, chopping!"

So they went in to their dinner. It was stew, and treacle tart, and the three children ate hungrily. It was exciting to think of the axe hidden in the hedge, waiting to chop away creepers that had grown around a secret house.

"How you do gobble today!" said Granpa, in astonishment. "Now, now, eat properly, or you'll be ill!"

"Granny, we found a pond in the middle of the wood this morning," said Susan, who could never keep quiet about anything.

"Did you?" said Granny. "Well, there did use to be one, I believe. There was supposed to be a summerhouse there too long years ago, but that seems to have disappeared now. The river has made the wood so marshy that it is no longer a pleasure to walk there, as it used to be years and years ago. Be careful if you go into the wood very far – it is very boggy."

"We'll put wellingtons on" said Jeffery. He frowned at Susan to stop her saying any more. So often she said too much, and then their adventures were stopped by the growns-ups before they had even begun!

They slipped away from the dining room as soon as they could. "I'm going to have a quiet nap," said Granny. "So keep away from the house, won't you?"

"Oh, yes, we'll be far away from Greylings this afternoon!" said Susan. She ran to join the boys. Jeffery was taking the axe from the hedge. It shone bright and sharp.

"Come on," he said. "We've got plenty of time this afternoon. We'll see what we can find!"

So off they went again with Rags, who was delighted to go hunting rabbits once more. The children did not find it very easy to make their way to the river, but once they found it, it was easy to follow.

"Look! There's the pool again!" said Susan, jumping for joy, and landing in such a boggy patch that the boys had to pull her out. "Come on! Do some chopping, Jeffery!"

CHAPTER 4

The Little Secret House

Jeffery went to the overgrown clump and began to chop away at the ivy stems. Some of them were very thick. He chopped hard above the steps where Rags had found a rabbit-hole.

He hadn't chopped for long before he gave a shout. "Yes! Look – there is a house of some sort under all this ivy. I'm chopping by the door. Come and pull away the stems for me."

Susan and John went to help Jeffery. He had chopped so hard that he was very hot, and his face was wet.

He took out his handkerchief and mopped his forehead.

Susan and John began to tear away the broken stems of ivy. They were more careful with the blackberry sprays, because they were prickly. The honeysuckle came away more easily, for its stems were thin and brittle.

"Yes!" said Susan, excited. "There *is* a door behind here. Oh, Jeffery! Fancy there being a little secret house hidden under all this ivy and creeper – a house forgotten long ago and never used except by the rabbits."

Jeffery laughed. He took up his axe again. "Well, the rabbits must be getting a shock now," he said. "Stand away, you two. I don't want to chop your heads off!"

"Let *me* have a turn!" begged Susan, who was simply longing to chop too. But Jeffery shook his head firmly.

"Certainly not, Susan," he said. "You know quite well that we promised I would be the only one to chop. I'm the oldest and the biggest, and I know how to use the axe. Goodness knows what *you* might do, Susan, if you began chopping!"

Jeffery chopped hard. Some of the ivy stems were as thick as the trunks of small trees. The roots that these stems had put out held firmly to the door underneath – but once Jeffery had chopped the stems in half, it was easy to pull away the brown roots that clung everywhere.

"Jeffery, we've made quite a hole already!" said Susan, dancing about in excitement. "Oh, Jeffery, hurry! Soon there will be enough room for us to creep through."

"Well, I'm hurrying as much as I can," said Jeffery. "But it's jolly hard work."

Crash! Crash! The axe cut through one stem after another, and at last there was a hole big enough for anyone to crawl through, about the middle of the doorway. Jeffery twisted a handkerchief round his hand and bent back some of the more prickly sprays that the others couldn't manage.

He poked the axe in through the hole. There was a wooden door behind. "I can see the handle!" said Jeffery, in excitement.

He slipped his hand along the door and tried the handle. It would not even turn!

"It won't move," said Jeffery.

"Let *me* try," said John. "My wrist is very strong – perhaps *I* can turn the handle."

But none of them could. It was stiff with the rust of many many years, and would not move. The three children were terribly disappointed.

"Let's see if we can find a window and chop the ivy away from that," said John. "We can get in through a window."

So they tried to find a window – but the creeping ivy and brambles were so thick that it was quite impossible to guess where a window might be.

Scratched and pricked all over their arms and legs, the children looked at one another and wondered what to do.

"There *must* be some way we can get in!" said John.

"Yes – there *is*!" cried Susan. "I know what to do!"

"What?" asked the boys.

"Chop down the door, of course!" shouted Susan, in excitement. "Can't you chop a big enough hole in the door for us to squeeze through, Jeffery?"

"But do you think we *ought* to do that?" said Jeffery. "I mean – after all, it's a door, and it isn't right to chop holes in doors."

"It can't matter with *this* door." said John, eager to try Susan's idea. "It must be nearly falling to pieces as it is! Go on, Jeffery – chop a hole in it! We'll never get in if you don't. I simply can't wait any longer!"

Jeffery didn't want to wait either. He lifted the axe and chopped at the door with it. The wood was quite rotten and gave way easily. The axe went through it at once. A few strokes, and there was a large hole in the door, through which the children could easily squeeze!

"Good!" said Jeffery, panting. "I say – doesn't it look dark inside there?"

"I guess it's full of spiders and earwigs!" said Susan, staring at the dark hole in the door. "It's a good thing we none of us mind them. Who's going in first?"

Nobody seemed quite so keen on going in after all! It really did look dark and mysterious through the hole in the door. It smelt a bit funny too.

"I believe I've got a candle-end somewhere in my pocket!" said Jeffery suddenly. He always carried a strange collection of things about with him. "You never know when any of them may come in useful," he would say, when the others teased him about them. He felt in first one pocket and then another – and then brought out a candle-end – about two inches of red candle.

"I've got some matches somewhere too," he said.

"Oh, do hurry, Jeffery!" said Susan, always the impatient one. "I want to see inside this strange, secret little house. Fancy finding a house all hidden and covered with creeper, that nobody has been inside for years and years and years!"

Jeffery found his matches, and lighted the candle-end. He held the candle inside the hole in the door. The three children pressed round it to see inside the queer woodland house.

It did indeed look very mysterious. It was full of dark shadows. It looked small, high and round. A bench ran round it, and there was a small fireplace or hearth at the back. A table was against the wall at one side, with something on it. The children could not see what it was.

"Let's go in!" whispered Susan.

"What are you whispering for?" whispered back John.

"I don't know – but it seems funny to talk out loud now!" said Susan, still in a whisper.

Jeffery squeezed in through the hole first. He said "Oh! what's that!" and quickly climbed out again.

"What do you mean? What's the matter?" asked John, half-frightened.

"Something touched my face," said Jeffery. "I didn't like it!"

"It was a spider's web, you silly!" said Susan. She laughed, and the sound seemed to make things bright and ordinary again. "You baby, Jeffery! Fancy being frightened of a spider's web!"

"Well, it didn't feel nice touching my cheek like that," said Jeffery. "You go in first, Susan, if you think a spider's web is so funny! Take the candle!"

So Susan climbed in through the hole in the door, brushing aside the hanging spiders' webs with her hand. She held the candle up and looked round the queer little house.

It had had two windows, but both these were blocked up with ivy and other creepers. The bench round the wall was thick with the dust of many, many years. So was the table. Susan held the candle up and looked to see what was on the table.

"Jeffery, the people who were here last drank out of these glasses!" she said. "There are two here – all dirty and dusty. Oh, isn't it strange to come here and find glasses still on the table!"

By this time the two boys had crept into the little house too, and were staring round in excitement.

"Those glasses are like the very old ones that Granny keeps in the cupboard in the drawing room!" said Jeffery, picking one up. "She won't use them because she says they are old and rare – how pleased she will be to have two more!"

"Look at the fireplace," said Susan, holding the candle to it. "There are the remains of a fire there. What fun it must have been to come to this house on a cold day, light a fire, and sit here in the middle of the wood, with the lovely pool gleaming below!"

"Yes, mustn't it," said Jeffery. "I'd like it myself! I'd love a little secret house like this. The squirrels would come to it – and the robins. The rabbits would peep inside, and perhaps a hedgehog would walk in, and sniff around.''

"That does sound lovely," said Susan, delighted. "Poor little house – hidden away and forgotten all these years. Let's make it ours!"

"Oh, yes!" cried the boys, thrilled with the idea.

"We'll clear away the ivy from the windows, and let the light through," said Susan, busy planning as she loved to do. "We'll bring a brush and sweep the dust away. We'll clean up the whole house – and we'll make a fire here one day, and boil a kettle for tea!"

"What fun!" shouted Jeffery, and he jumped for joy. A long spider's thread caught his ear, and he rubbed it away. "I'd like to clear away these clinging cobwebs," he said. "I really don't like them!"

"Let's go home again now," said Susan. "The candle won't last any more. It's running down on my fingers now and the wax is very hot. We'll bring candles here when we come, and keep them on the mantelpiece. Let's take the two old glasses with us."

Off they went back home, carrying the two glasses carefully. They whistled to Rags, who had been chasing rabbits the whole of the time, and then made their way through the dim wood. What an exciting day they had had!

CHAPTER 5

The House Gets a Spring-clean

Granny and Granpa were thrilled to hear about the secret house in the woods, but Granny was not at all pleased to hear of the axe.

"You are not allowed to use such dangerous things," she said to Jeffery. "Tipps is foolish to let you have an axe. You must not use that again, Jeffery."

"All right, Granny," said Jeffery. "But I am really very careful, you know, and after all, I shall soon be twelve!"

"Look, Granny, here are the glasses," said Susan – and she put them on the table. She had carefully washed them, and polished them with a clean cloth. They shone beautifully. Granny gave a cry of delight and picked them up.

"Look, Thomas!" she said to Granpa. "Two of those beautiful, heavy old glasses that we have in my cupboard over there. How lovely! These are rare, now, children, and I am delighted to have them. They are over a hundred years old!"

She put them proudly in her glass-fronted cupboard in the corner of the drawing room. They were fat glasses, short and very heavy – the children wished they could use them each day for their lemonade but Granny wouldn't hear of it!

"Granny, we are going to make that little secret house our very own," said Jeffrey. "We are going to clean it up, and keep a few books and things there. We shall clean up the steps that lead down to the pond – and then, when it is all ready, you must come and have tea with us there!"

"We can boil a kettle on the little hearth," said Susan, jumping round like a grasshopper. "We can make a fire! There's a table there too, and a bench round the wall. Oh, it really is a most exciting little house!"

"Well, I can't see why you shouldn't make it your own house if you want to," said Granny. "Greylings Wood is ours, and the house was ours too – so you can have it for a playhouse, if you like."

For the next few days the children spent all their time in the wood, going to and from their new house, carrying brooms and pans and cloths! Jane the house-maid was quite cross at the disappearance of so many of her cleaning things, and the children had to promise to bring them all back safely when they had finished with them.

Susan took charge of the cleaning, as she was the girl. They all went to the house the next day, and climbed in through the door again. This time they had plenty of candles and two candlesticks. They put two candles into the stands and stood them on the little mantelpiece. They lighted the house up well.

"You two boys had better see what you can do about the windows," said Susan. "It would be a good thing to let some light and air into the house. It still smells old and musty."

"We mustn't have the axe this time," said Jeffery, staring at the windows. "But I could borrow Tipps' little saw, and saw through the ivy stems. It wouldn't take long."

So Jeffery ran back to Greylings and borrowed the saw. He and John took it in turns to saw the thick stems, and soon they were able to pull the ivy and brambles away from the window, and to let in air and light.

There was no glass in the windows – they were simply round holes in the rather thick wall. Whilst the boys were clearing the two windows Susan got busy with the cleaning. The house was dustier than any-where she had ever seen!

Rags was thrilled with the house. He jumped in and out of the hole in the door a dozen times in an hour, and trotted all round the house, sniffing everywhere.

He would have liked to live there always, surrounded by rabbits!

Susan removed all the cobwebs first. They hung down from the roof, they stretched here and there, and were grey with dust. They were soon down! Big spiders scuttled away. A robin hopped in at the hole in the door, and flew to the mantelpiece. He carolled a tiny song as if to say, "I'll help with the spiders!"

But he didn't. He flew out again, and sat on a branch outside, watching the children with his bright black eyes.

Susan swept down the walls with her broom. She swept the mantelpiece, the bench, and table. When she had got all the dust on to the floor, she began to sweep that into her pan.

The dust made the children sneeze. They blew their noses, and then settled down to their work again. It was fun.

"Get some water from the pool, John, will you?" asked Susan, when she had swept up all the dust she could find. "I want to do a little scrubbing now!"

"I'll help you," said John, who liked to scrub.

"Well, I've got two scrubbing brushes here, so you can have one," said Susan happily. It was lovely having a secret house like this, making it their very own.

John fetched a pail of water from the pond. The children had found that there was a complete flight of overgrown steps leading down from the little house to the pool. Jeffery was determined to clean them and uncover them all as soon as he had finished the windows.

There was a lot to do, but the children enjoyed every minute. The sun was very hot in the garden of Greylings, but here in the wood, it was cool and green. The children had brought lemonade with them, and they drank it when they felt too hot.

Susan scrubbed the floor, the bench, and the table. The floor was of brightly-coloured tiles, set in a pattern, and at some time had had a rug over it, for Susan found threads of it still left.

"I say! What a lovely floor!" said Jeffery, looking in from one of the window-holes. "It looks beautiful now! Who would have thought there was a floor like that!"

It took the children three days to get the little house really nice. At the end of that time it was lovely!

Jeffery had managed to get the door to open now, and had cleared away all the creepers over the doorway, so that light came in there as well as in at the windows. Tipp's saw was not so quick at clearing ivy as the axe, but that couldn't be helped.

John had cleared the steps that led down to the pool. He had torn away the creeping roots that hid them, and had cleared them of earth and moss. They were of white marble and shone beautifully. John was proud of them.

Susan had made the house look really lovely. Everything was clean there now. The brightly-coloured tiles shone on the floor. The table and bench were quite clean, and the fireplace was cleared too, and was neatly laid ready for a fire, with paper, twigs, and old wood that the boys had found outside.

They begged an old rug from Granny for the floor.

They brought along a little vase which they filled with flowers for the middle of the table. Susan even brought an old clock that she had found in a cupboard. It had belonged to Granpa, and one of its legs was broken. It had not been worth mending and had been put away in a cupboard.

John mended its leg. Susan wound it up and it went. So to the secret house it was carried, and there it stood on the mantelpiece, ticking away cheerfully!

"I always think a clock makes a house feel cosy and lived-in," said Susan happily. "Doesn't it all look nice? Let's have tea here tomorrow! We won't ask Granny and Granpa yet. We'll wait till we're sure the fire goes all right, and the chimney doesn't smoke. We'll try tomorrow!"

Rags was most interested in the house. He ran in and out, and Susan did wish he could be taught to wipe his feet. He seemed to take a delight in running in the muddiest places he could find, and then walking over the clean floor of the little house!

The next day the children brought along the things for tea at the house. Susan carried a kettle of water to boil for tea. The boys brought a picnic basket full of food. Inside there were unbreakable cups and plates which Granny had given them to keep in their house.

"Isn't this fun!" said Susan, as she put a gay little cloth on the table. "Jeffery, do let *me* light the fire, please, to boil the kettle! After all, I did lay it ready."

Everybody wanted to light the fire, but Susan was allowed to do it. She knelt down and put a lighted match to the paper. It flared up at once. The twigs began to crackle. The wood soon caught fire, and a lovely glow filled the hearth.

But it wasn't so lovely after a little while. Smoke began to pour out from the fireplace, and filled the little house. The children coughed.

"Oh dear! It's smoking!" said Susan. "What a nuisance! Do you suppose we ought to have swept the chimney?"

"Well, I shouldn't have thought the fire was used often enough to make the chimney really sooty," said Jeffery.

Susan poked the lighted wood to the back of the fireplace, hoping that the smoke would soon go up the chimney. But it didn't. It went pouring out into the room. Soon the children's eyes began to smart, and they choked with the stinging smoke.

"Wood smoke is always horrid," said Jeffery, going outside to wipe his streaming eyes. "This won't do, Susan. We'll have to put out the fire. We can't boil water for tea today. We'll have to do that when we've put the chimney right."

"I expect it's stuffed up with ivy stems and leaves," said John. He kicked the fire out, and soon only a few wisps of smoke rose from the hearth.

But it was impossible to have tea in the smoky house. Susan was very disappointed about it. She took the tea outside, and they sat on the steps, looking down to the little pond, and ate their egg sandwiches, ginger cake, and chocolate biscuits there. They drank the water out of the kettle, pouring it into their cups.

"This is really a lovely place!" said Susan. "Look how the sun comes slanting through the trees just there, and lights up the pond. What a lot of water-lilies there are today!"

"There's a red squirrel watching us," said John in a low voice. "Don't move. He's in that hazel tree over there."

The children watched the big-eyed creature. He sat on the branch, his bushy tail curled up behind him. Then with a light bound he leapt to the ground and scampered up the steps to them. Rags saw him and would have pounced on him, but Jeffery had him by the collar.

Susan held out a bit of chocolate biscuit. The squirrel took it in a tiny paw and then bounded into the trees, carrying it in his mouth.

"He likes chocolate!" said Susan. "Oh, isn't he sweet! I'd like to tell him to live in our little house when we are not there. He can be our caretaker!"

As the shadows began to grow longer, one or two rabbits came slipping out of their holes. They sat not far off, washing their ears, bending them down as they cleaned them. The children watched, keeping quite still. Rags whined, and longed to chase them, but they would not let him.

"We *are* lucky to have a little house all to ourselves in the wood," said John. "All the animals and birds will soon be tame for us and we can feed them and make friends with them!"

The robin was already very tame. It took crumbs from Susan's hand, and did not seem at all afraid. A big freckled thrush sat nearby and eyed the children warily, turning its head first to one side and then another.

"It looks at us first out of one eye and then out of the other!" said Jeffery, with a laugh. He threw the thrush a bit of bread – but the robin flew down and got it before the thrush stirred from the branch.

"I could stay here all evening," said Susan. "But I'd really like to see what's the matter with that chimney, Jeffery. I'd like to put it right before Granny and Granpa come to tea!"

"Well, we'll have a look at it now," said Jeffery, getting up. The squirrel bounded up a tree as he moved, and the rabbits shot into their holes, showing white bobtails. Rags raced after them at once, and began to scrape earth into the air in a great shower!

"Have you got the brush here that you had yesterday, Susan?" said Jeffery. "The one with a long handle, I mean. I could put that up the chimney to see if there is anything stopping it up."

"Yes, there it is," said Susan. "In the corner."

Jeffery took it. He went to the fireplace and knelt down beside it. "I expect there is a bird's nest or something stopping it up," he said. "It is a very short chimney, and it should be quite easy to clear."

He put the broom up – and at once a shower of twigs and moss and leaves came down. It all fell into the fireplace. "A bird's nest," said Jeffery. He pushed the brush up as high as he could. Another shower of twigs and moss came down.

"Go outside and see if the brush is sticking out of the chimney," said Jeffery to John. John went out and looked. He came back.

"Yes," he said. "I can just see it. The chimney should be clear now."

207

"Right," said Jeffery. He pulled the brush down – but the end of it stuck against something in the chimney. Jeffery tugged hard, but the brush-end would not come.

"Blow!" he said. "What's the matter with it?" He put his head up the chimney and felt about with his hand. To his surprise he found something sticking out halfway across the chimney. This was what the brush had caught on.

Jeffery felt round it. It felt like a box or something. He grew excited.

"I say!" he called. "There's a sort of opening in the side of this chimney – a kind of hidey-hole, I should think! And there's something been stuffed into it – something too big for the hole – so that it sticks out half across the chimney!"

"Oh, Jeffery! Get it down, quick, get it down!" shouted John and Susan.

"I'll try," said Jeffery. "It seems to have stuck. No – here it comes!"

CHAPTER 6

A Most Exciting Discovery

He had tugged so hard at the box that it had moved from its place. He slid it out from the hole. It was heavy and Jeffery could not hold it in one hand. The box slid down the chimney and landed in the back of the fireplace with a crash.

"Gracious!" said Susan. "What a funny old box!"

"Isn't it exciting!" said John, almost beside himself with joy. "Is it the Treasure?"

"Of course not!" said Jeffery. "The box is too small to hold the Treasure! But it may hold something exciting, all the same."

It was an iron box, with a stiff clasp in front. On the top of the box was a raised letter – G.

"G for Greylings," said Susan, tracing the letter with her finger. "This is an old Greylings box. Open it Jeffery, quickly! Whatever can be inside it?"

It was not easy to open. The years had made the clasp very stiff, and Jeffery had to get a knife from the picnic basket to force it open.

"Shake it, John, and see if it rattles," said Susan eagerly. "Perhaps it might have a few old brooches inside."

John shook it – but it did not rattle.

"It sounds empty!" he said. "Oh dear – I do hope it isn't!"

Jeffery took the box from John, and began to work at the stiff fastening. It suddenly gave way, and Jeffery opened the lid. The three children peered inside in excitement.

"There's nothing inside it at all!" said Jeffery in the greatest disappointment. "Look – it is empty!"

So it was. Nothing was to be seen except the sides and bottom of the box itself.

John was puzzled. "But Jeffery," he said, "why should anyone want to hide a box in a secret chimney-hole, if there was nothing in it?"

"How should *I* know?" said Jeffery gloomily. "It must have been hidden there over a hundred years ago. Perhaps more. A silly joke, perhaps."

"It couldn't have been a joke," said Susan, taking the box from Jeffery. "Nobody sticks things up chimneys for a joke! Do you suppose there *was* something

210

in the box – and somebody found it – and put the box back again after taking out the things inside?"

"Well, that's an idea," said Jeffery. "But how disappointing for us!"

Then Susan made a discovery. "Look, Jeffery," she said, holding up the box. "Doesn't it seem to you as if the box ought to be bigger inside than it is?"

"Whatever do you mean?" asked the boys.

"Well," said Susan, "if you look at the outside of the box it seems quite big – but if you look, *inside*, it doesn't look *big enough*!"

"You mean – there might be a secret bottom to it!" cried Jeffery, and he snatched the box from Susan. He examined it very carefully – and then he nodded. "Yes – there *is* a false bottom to it. You're right, Susan. How clever of you!"

"How can we open the secret part?" cried John, going red with excitement.

"I don't know," said Jeffery, busy pressing and tapping to see if he could open it. "My goodness! Suppose there is something really thrilling here after all!"

Susan and John could hardly keep their hands off the box as Jeffery tried to open the bottom part. It was no good – he coudn't do it.

He gave it to John, and John tried. Then Susan had a try. But no matter what they did they couldn't open the bottom of the box.

"It's some clever little trick, I'm sure," said Jeffery, in despair. "Oh, I *do* wish we could find it."

Susan grew impatient. She turned the box upside down and banged it with her fist. It slipped from her knee and fell on to the floor.

"Susan, be careful!" cried Jeffery – and then he stopped, and stared at the box. It had fallen upside down, and as Jeffery stared, he saw that the bottom of the box had slid crooked! Somehow or other in its fall, the secret spring had been touched, and the bottom was now loose!

Jeffery grabbed the box. He pressed on the bottom of it, as he held it upside down. The bottom slid away neatly, and the three children saw a small narrow space inside, hidden between the false bottom and the real one.

And this time there was something inside! Yes, there really was!

It wasn't brooches or anything like that – it was a sheet of thick parchment-like paper, doubled over. Just that and nothing more.

"A bit of paper," said Jeffery, taking it out very carefully. It fell in two as he touched it, breaking at the fold. It was very, very old.

"What does it say?" asked Susan, bending over to see it.

"It's a map," said John. "What a funny old map!"

"So it is," said Jeffery. "But what's it a map *of*?"

"Goodness knows!" said Susan. "And what's this one word on the map – just here? It's such old, old printing that I can't even read it!"

"What's that first letter?" said Jeffery, trying to make it out. "It's a J, I think. J – and that's an R, I believe. J – R – there's no word beginning with Jr."

"J – R – is that an E?" wondered Susan. "It's a funny one! And the next letter is certainly an A. Jrea – worse than ever!"

"And then comes an F," said Jeffery. "Jr – eaf – it must be some foreign language!"

"There are some more letters after that," said John. "I give it up! But I know what we'll do – we'll ask someone who can read old writing, and see if they can tell us what the word is. Perhaps if we know what the word is, we should know what the map means."

"Gracious! Look at the time!" said Susan. "Granny will be wondering whatever has happened to us! We'd better pack up and go home."

So they packed up their things, and, leaving the kettle behind for another day, they went to Greylings, carrying the old box with them. What a find they had had!

When they got to Greylings, they found a car in the drive. "It's the same one that came the other day," said Jeffery, looking at it. "It belongs to those people who want to buy the house."

"Well, Granny and Granpa will be busy with them, then," said Susan. "We'd better go into the study and wait till the visitors have gone."

So into the study they went – and, of course, they got out the strange map, pieced it together once more – and tried to find out what the word said.

"If only we could find out!" sighed Susan. And then a voice behind her said, "And what do you want to find out, little girl?"

The children looked round. They saw that Granny had brought a gentleman into the room – the man who wanted to buy the house. She was showing him the study once more, and the children had not heard the door open.

Jeffery did not want to say anything about the map. He tried to take it off the table – but as it was in half, he only managed to get one piece before the man leaned over the table to look.

"I want to know what that word says," said Susan, in her clear voice. "We've been puzzling and puzzling over it. It's an old map we found today, hidden in this old iron box, up the chimney of our secret house in the woods."

Granny looked surprised. So did the man. He bent over the piece of parchment at once. "Where's the word?" he said. "Ah – well, let me see. That first letter is a T."

"T! We thought it was a J," said Susan.

"T – R – E – A – S——" read the man.

"S!" said Susan scornfully. "That's not S, it's F."

"In the old days the letter S was written like an F," said the man. Then he jumped, because Jeffery gave a shout. He didn't mean to shout, but he couldn't help it. If the first letter was a T – and the fifth was an S – then he knew what the word was!

But he didn't say it. He tried to take the paper out of man's hand – but the man held on to it. "Wait, wait," he said "I haven't finished. T – R – E – A – S – U – R – E. The word is Treasure! How very interesting!"

The three children's faces went red with excitement and joy. "So it's a map showing where the Treasure was hidden!" thought Jeffery to himself. "We can puzzle it out – and perhaps find the Treasure for Granny!"

"May I take this old piece of paper to a friend of mine who is extremely clever at puzzling out old papers?'' said the gentleman, suddenly, turning politely to Granny. ''I could perhaps find out a good deal more for you, Mrs Greyling, and it might be most interesting.''

''Well – its kind of you,'' said Granny, not knowing quite what to do. ''But I'd rather like to keep the paper and show it to my husband.''

''Very well,'' said the man, ''I'll take it with me now, show it to my friend at once, and send it back to you tonight, with a note telling you what he says about it.''

But Jeffery did not want the precious paper to go out of his sight. ''Please, it's mine,'' he said. ''I want it. We found it ourselves.''

''Of course, of course, my dear boy,'' said the man, smiling at Jeffery. ''I quite understand your feelings. I will only keep the paper an hour – my friend is staying at a hotel nearby, and will tell me at once his opinion of it – whether it is genuinely old or not – and if it contains anything of importance to you. Your grandmother has been so kind to me that I would like to do her this little service, if I may.''

Poor Granny could do nothing but smile and thank him. She did indeed think it was kind of him, but she was sorry because she guessed that the children wanted to show her their find and talk about it as soon as the man had gone. But as she hoped he would buy Greylings, she did not like to offend him.

''Take it, by all means,'' said Granny politely. ''It would be kind of you to find out exactly what the paper means – if it *does* mean anything!''

The man patted Jeffery on the shoulder. The boy

was angry, and looked it. What right had this man to go off with their precious paper?

He went almost at once, carrying the parchment carefully in his hand.

The children clustered together as soon as Granny took the man out of the room to his car.

"What did you want to go and tell our secret to a stranger for, you stupid, silly girl?" said Jeffery to Susan. "Now see what you've done! He's guessed it's something to do with the long-lost Greylings Treasure – and he's got the map. At least – he's only got half of it, thank goodness! I was quick enough to get the other half, and hide it behind my back before he saw it. So he won't be able to tell much from *his* half!"

"That was quick of you, Jeffery," said John. "But really, Susan *is* an idiot to go and blurt out our secret like that."

"I'm sorry," said Susan, looking ready to cry. "I didn't think. I really felt so excited."

"Well, Susan, if that's a map showing where the Treasure was hidden, we don't want strangers going after it and finding it," said Jeffery. "I should have thought you would have been sharp enough to keep your tongue quiet."

"Don't grumble at me so, Jeffery," said Susan, who hated her big brother to think she was silly. "I'm very, very sorry, really I am."

"Well, don't say a word another time," said Jeffery. "We must just wait and see what happens now – I hope the man brings back our paper all right."

CHAPTER 7

Mr Pots of Money

Granny was told all about the finding of the box, and she called Granpa to hear about it when he came in. They looked at the old iron box with the big letter G on it. They exclaimed over the secret bottom, where the paper had been hidden. And Granpa longed for the man to bring back the parchment so that he might see the map himself.

"I shan't tell *any*one that we've got the other half of the map," said Jeffery to the others, when they were alone once more. "Not *any*one. This is *our* secret – and if there's going to be any finding of the Treasure, *we're* going to do it. See?''

The other saw quite well and they agreed heartily with Jeffery. They waited impatiently for the man to come back.

"Supposing he doesn't?" said Susan. "Supposing he keeps the paper for himself, and tries to get the Treasure?"

"Oh, don't be so silly, Susan," said Jeffery, who still felt cross with her. "How can he find anything if *we've* got one half of the map? Do use your brains."

"I *am* using them," said Susan indignantly. "He might be able to make out enough, just by using his half. It looked to me to be the most important half."

"Here he is again!" cried John, from the window. "And he's got the map. Good!"

The man was shown into the study again, and Granny and Granpa came too, eager to hear what was said.

"I've taken the paper to my friend to puzzle out," said the man, whose name was Mr Potts. "He says there is no doubt at all that it is an old map, which shows the whereabouts of some Treasure."

"Really!" said Granny, thrilled.

"Yes," said Mr Potts, his big moustaches seeming to bristle with excitement too. "But my friend, who is used to dealing with old documents like this, says that there is only half of the real map here. He says there should be another half."

"Dear dear," said Granny, looking round the room as if she expected the other half to come floating down to her. "Now where can that be? In the box, do you think?"

"Quite likely," said the man eagerly. "May I look and see?"

Jeffery gave a secret wink at the others. He handed Mr Potts the box. He felt quite safe in doing that because he knew quite well that there was nothing in the box at all! The other half of the old map was at that moment in the top drawer of the desk in the corner! Jeffery had slipped it there as soon as he had seen Mr Potts coming up the steps again.

Mr Potts shook the box. He opened and shut the false bottom. He peered into the secret hiding-place and scraped round it with a pencil. There was nothing there at all.

"No," he said. "It's quite empty. But I am perfectly certain there must be another half to this old map. Until it is found, no one will be able to hunt for the Treasure. Do *you* know where it is?" he said very suddenly, wheeling round on Susan.

Susan had no idea where Jeffery had put the map. She shook her head. "No," she said, "I don't know where it is at all."

"Do *you*?" asked the man, staring at John. John went very red. Like Susan, he had no idea where the half was but he couldn't help blushing.

"I don't know at all where it is," he said.

Mr Potts turned to ask Jeffery – but that sharp boy had guessed he would be asked, and he had slipped out of the room. He wasn't going to tell an untruth – but he was jolly sure he wasn't going to tell the truth to Mr Potts either!

"I wonder if you children are telling the truth," said Mr Potts, looking at the blushing John.

That made Granny angry. "Mr Potts," she said, "I think you forget that they are my grandchildren. They are all truthful children, I can assure you."

"Sorry, Mrs Greyling," said the man, with a laugh. "This boy went so red I thought he wasn't telling the truth."

"May we have our map back, please," asked Susan, trying to make Mr Potts stop staring at John, who was looking more and more uncomfortable.

"Certainly," said Mr Potts. "Here it is. But it isn't much use to you or to anybody unless the other half can be found."

He gave the map to Susan. "That word is certainly 'Treasure'," he said. "And I should think that if we could find the other half of the map, and piece it together, there's a good chance of coming across the Greylings Treasure. You were good enough to tell me the old story the other day, Mrs Greyling, and I was *most* interested in it!"

"Well, thank you for your help," said Granpa.

"May I ask a favour?" said Mr Potts, smiling very charmingly at Granpa. "If you *should* come across the other half of the map, let me show it to my friend, and he will work it out for you, and help you to find the Treasure. It needs someone very learned in old documents to trace out the meaning of them – and I should be delighted to help you if I could, by getting my friend to do his best for you."

"Thank you," said Granpa again. "We will certainly promise to let you see the other half, if we find it."

"Where did you say you found the box?" asked Mr Potts, turning to Susan.

220

Susan told him, rather sulkily. She didn't want to tell him any more than she could help, after Jeffery's scolding – but if she didn't tell him, Granny would – so she didn't see that it mattered.

"Very interesting, very, very interesting," said Mr Potts, when he heard about the secret house, and the hole in the chimney. "You are very lucky children! Well – don't forget to let me know if you find the other half of the map, will you?"

He patted Susan on the shoulder, smiled at her most beautifully, and then said goodbye. As soon as he was gone Susan stamped her foot.

"Horrid man! Patting me and smiling at me with a nasty treacly smile! He'd like to get the treasure himself, I know he would!"

Jeffery slipped into the room, grinning.

"Hallo!" he said. "He's just gone! Isn't he dreadful? Fancy Greylings Manor being *his!* I just simply couldn't bear it!"

"He's frightfully rich, Granny says," said John.

"Well, Potts is a good name for him then," said Jeffery, grinning again. "Mr Pots of Money!"

The others laughed. "You were clever to slip out of the room before you could be asked if you knew where the other half was," said Susan. "John went awfully red. I really thought Mr Pots of Money would guess that he knew about the other bit of map."

"Where's the half he brought?" asked Jeffery. John gave it to him "Oh, good – well now we'll be able to fit the pieces together and see what *we* can puzzle out. We may not be clever and learned, like Mr

Potts' friend is – but I hope we're smart enough to see what this map means!"

"Let's go up to our roon to look at it," said John. "If dear Mr Potts comes back suddenly, he might see we have two bits. And I say – suppose Granpa sees them! He has promised to let Mr Potts see the other half."

"Well, we musn't let him or Granny see the half then," said Jeffery. "Now remember, Susan – don't you go and give the game away!"

"Of course I shan't!" said Susan crossly. "Don't keep saying things like that, Jeffery."

"Come on. Let's go up to our room and have a good look at the map again," said John. So they set out to go upstairs – but Granny and Granpa were in the hall, near the stairs. Suppose they stopped the children and asked them about the other half of the map, whilst they still thought of it?

"Susan! We'll go up to our rooms by that secret staircase that leads into your room," said Jeffery. "Quick! Come into the dining room before we're seen."

They slipped unseen into the dining room and went up the funny, narrow stairs that wound up to Susan's room. All three children stepped out of Susan's cupboard, laughing.

"It's fun to come up those old stairs!" said Susan. "There's a table in your room, Jeffery. Let's go and put the map there and really study it hard. Now that we know it may be a map of where the Treasure was hidden, it is much, much more exciting!"

Soon the three children were bending over the funny

old document. Jeffery hurriedly stuck the back of the halves together with gummed paper, so that they could see everything better.

"Look!" he said suddenly. "Do you see this half that Mr Potts took away? Compare it with the other half – and you'll see that every line on Mr Potts's piece looks dented – as if someone had run a pencil over every bit of the map! Do you know what has been done?"

"No, what?" asked Susan, puzzled.

"Somebody has traced the map," said Jeffery. "They wanted a copy of it – so they laid tracing paper over it, and pencilled a copy! The lines would show through the tracing paper quite clearly. It's like when we trace maps at school. Mr Potts has got a copy of this! No wonder he was willing to bring it back so quickly!"

"That means he thinks it's a proper map, showing where the Treasure *is*," said John slowly.

"It shows something else too," said Jeffery. "It shows that he means to try and find it! Why would he take a copy of it if he didn't want to find it! No – he believes in Greylings Treasure – and he believes in our map. Thank *goodness* he only saw half!"

"Do you think he may try to get the other half?" asked John solemnly.

"I hope not!" said Jeffery. "But you never know. Do you know what I'm going to do? I'm going to take a tracing of the map myself – and then put the real map into some good safe place so that we don't need to use it. We'll hide the tracing too, except when we use it."

"Do the copy now," said John. "I can see Granny and Granpa in the garden, and Mr Potts has gone. Then we can hide the real map away."

Jeffery got some tracing paper and sharpened a pencil.

In ten minutes he had carefully traced the map on the paper, which he folded and put into his pocket.

"Now we'll hide the *real* map!" he said.

"Where?" asked Susan.

"It had better be somewhere quite simple," said Jeffery. "Difficult places are always searched. *I* know! We'll put the map in your dolls' house, Susan! I'm sure no one would think of looking there!"

Jeffery got some drawing pins, and knelt down on the floor. He carefully pinned the two halves of the map on to two ceilings in Susan's dolls' house – on the bedroom ceiling, and on the kitchen ceiling!

"Nobody, nobody would *ever* think of looking there!" said Susan, in delight. And, indeed, it was a clever place.

The bell rang for supper.

"Now we shan't have any time to work out the map!" said Jeffery. "Bother! We'll do it afterwards, when we're in bed! You can come into our room, Susan, and we'll see if we can work out the map. We'd better wash now, and change into something clean. Hurry!"

CHAPTER 8

Where is the Winding Road?

At supper that night Granny and Granpa asked the
children all kinds of questions about the secret house
and the iron box. They were really just as excited as the
three children.

Jeffery said nothing at all about the other half of the
map. Granpa wanted to see the piece that Mr Potts
had had, and Jeffery took out his copy of it.

"I've put the map in a safe place," said the boy.
"You see, Granpa, if people keep handling it, it will
fall to pieces, it's so old!"

"Quite right, my boy," said Granpa, taking the tracing. "Very sensible of you."

The children went early up to bed that evening, for they all so badly wanted to study the complete map and see if they could puzzle it out. As soon as Susan was undressed and had her dressing-gown on, she slipped into the boys' room.

They were already in bed. They had lighted their bedside lamp, and their two heads were close together, looking hard at the map.

Susan climbed into bed beside them and looked too.

"It's an odd sort of map," said Jeffery. "Look at this curving snake thing – it must be a road! And then there are three big trees. Well, those trees are probably dead by now and fallen down. But it's possible they may still be standing in a row somewhere."

"And look at this funny hump-shaped thing," said John, pointing with his finger. "Is it a hill? There aren't any hills like that round here, are there?"

"There might be," said Jeffery. "We haven't explored everywhere yet, you know. And goodness knows what might be in that deep wood of ours! It's almost a forest, it's so thick and so big."

"Then what's this funny little drawing down here?" said Susan, pointing to what looked like a roughly drawn church. "It's got a row of queer little lines beneath it – steps up to it, I suppose."

"It's very odd," said Jeffery, his face red with trying to make out the map. "I read it like this – first we have to go down a winding road or lane. Then we come somewhere where there are three big trees in a line. Then we come to a hump-backed hill. Near there

226

we shall find a little church or building of some sort – and perhaps the Treasure is hidden somewhere about there."

"That sounds splendid, Jeffery!" said Susan, her eyes shining with excitement. "I wonder where the winding road is?"

"We'll get a map of the district," said Jeffery. "It will show us all the winding roads there are. We should come to the three big trees at the fourth bend in the road. If you count, you'll see there are four bends in the drawing."

"Yes. So there are," said Susan. "You are clever, Jeffery! Oh, I'm longing to go exploring now. Where can we get a map to see if there are any winding roads round here?"

"I believe there's one in Granpa's study," said John. "I saw Granpa looking at it the other day. Shall I slip down and fetch it?"

"Yes," said Jeffery. "Go down Susan's little staircase, John. You won't be seen then, perhaps."

John slipped out of bed. He ran into Susan's room, opened her cupboard door, and went down the curious little stair. He stopped at the bottom to listen if there was anyone in the dining room. He could hear nothing. He stepped into the dining room, ran to the door and then crept into the study, which was nearby. He could hear the radio murmuring in the drawing room.

"Good!" thought John. "If I do make a bit of a noise, no one will hear me if the radio is on!"

He opened the glass front of the bookcase. It made a click as it ran back. But nobody heard. John hurriedly looked down the row of books. He was sure the map had been put back there.

It had. There it was. "Map of the Greylings Lands."

He took it out of the bookcase, shut the glass front, which made a most alarming click again, and then ran back to the staircase. He was up it and into Susan's bedroom in a trice.

"Good boy!" said Jeffery, pleased, when John danced in, holding up the map. "You've been jolly quick. But what a row you made! We heard the click of the bookcase up here!"

"Yes, I know – I couldn't help it," said John. "But the radio is on, so Granny won't hear anything. Come on, let's see if we can find this winding road."

They opened the big folding-map. It showed the whole of the land held by the Greyling family. There were the two farms, the Manor House and its grounds, the Greylings Wood, and the roads around and through the property.

"It's jolly big," said Jeffery. "I hate to think of it all going to Mr Pots of Money. He's not the right person to have it. I bet he'd turn the people out of the farms, and cut down all that lovely wood to sell for timber!"

"Look – would you call *that* a winding road?" asked Susan, pointing to a place called Cuckoo Lane.

"It's not *very* winding," said Jeffery. "And it only seems to have three bends, not four. Let's see if there's a road that winds more than that."

They studied the Greylings map from end to end. They looked at every road, every lane. They even

228

studied the field paths that were shown running here and there.

"Well, it's funny, but Cuckoo Lane seems to be absolutely the only road or lane that winds at all," said Jeffery at last. "Maybe we shall find that it has more bends than the map shows. The other roads are either straight, or just sort of wavy – no proper bends."

"Well, you see, it's very flat ground around here," said John. "People can walk straight from place to place. When there are hills, the roads wind a bit."

"What shall we do tomorrow?" said Susan. "Shall we go to Cuckoo Lane, and see if we can find four bends in it – and maybe three enormous trees, and a hill somewhere?"

"Yes – that's what we'll do," said Jeffery. "We'll go tomorrow morning – and in the afternoon we'll ask Granny and Granpa to have tea at the secret house with us. It will be fun!"

There was the sound of someone coming up the stairs to the landing outside. "Quick, Susan – it's Granny!" whispered John. "Get back to bed!"

Susan almost fell out of bed, in her hurry. She shot across the room, slipped into her bedroom and jumped into bed as Granny opened the boys' door.

"I heard you talking, my dears," said Granny. "It's quite time you put out your light and went to sleep. You will wake Susan if you talk like this."

Jeffery giggled. He knew quite well that he wouldn't wake Susan – she was wide enough awake already! He snuggled down under the clothes with John. Granny bent over them and kissed them goodnight.

Then she tiptoed into Susan's room, and softly

kissed her too. Susan didn't make a sound. But you should have heard those three children giggling as soon as Granny went downstairs!

"Susan, I hope we don't keep you awake with our talking!" called John.

"Be quiet, John," said Jeffery. "You'll have Granny back again, if you shout like that. We'd better go to sleep. Well, goodnight, Susan. I expect we'll all dream of the winding lane and the Treasure!"

CHAPTER 9

A Visit to Timbles' Farm

The next day the children asked their Granny and Granpa if they would go to tea at the little house.

"Yes, we'd love to," said Granny. "We're longing to see it! We'll all have tea there at four. What are you going to do this morning?"

"We're going for a walk, Granny," said Jeffery. "Unless you want us to do anything for you?"

"No," said Granny. "It would be nice for you to go for a walk. Where are you going?"

"Along Cuckoo Lane, I think," said Jeffery.

231

"We'll take old Rags – that is, if he can walk after such a huge breakfast!"

"You shouldn't feed him at meal times," said Granny. "He gets so many scraps now that he's getting quite fat. Aren't you, Rags?"

"Woof!" said Rags, leaping about the room like a kangaroo, excited because he had heard the wonderful word "walk"!

"You will pass near Farmer Timbles' house," said Granpa, looking up from his paper. "Go in and see Mrs Timbles. She will be delighted to welcome you."

The children set off as soon after breakfast as they could. Rags pranced ahead of them, barking at the sparrows in the roadway. Jeffery had with him the copy of the map.

They went down the drive, out through the gates. The stone eagles sat on the gateposts, looking over the road as they had done for three or four hundred years. They were so old that they had begun to crumble away here and there.

Down the road went the children, followed by Rags, till they came to a stile. They climbed over it and went across a large field. There was a stile at the other end, and then a narrow path that ran between two tall hedges.

"We come into Cuckoo Lane at the end of this path," said Jeffery, looking at the big map.

They were soon in Cuckoo Lane. It began at two cottages nearby and then wandered away across a common to Farmer Timbles' house.

"Now, it begins *here*," said Jeffery, standing at the cottage gates. "We'll follow it carefully and count the bends."

They set off down the lane. On one side was a low hedge of hawthorn. On the other there was nothing – the common stretched away, soft and heathery.

"Here's *one* bend," said Susan, as they rounded a corner. "Good! But oh dear – the lane looks awfully straight now, doesn't it, Jeffery? It looks straight almost as far as Farmer Timbles' house."

"Well, maybe it goes past his house, after all," said Jeffery. "There may be a few bends we can't see."

Down the lane they went again, passing a duck-pond and Jeffery thought they might call that another bend. Then, just as it came to Farmer Timbles' house, it wound round to his front gate.

"That's three bends, anyway," said Susan, pleased. "Jeffery, let's just see if the path goes on, before we go and call on Mrs Timbles."

So they went to see if the lane went on anywhere, or whether it stopped at the farm.

To their great disappointment it seemed to stop at the farm gate! Only field paths were to be seen after that.

"Isn't it tiresome?" said Susan. "But perhaps, Jeffery, the old map is wrong – maybe there should have been only *three* bends shown?"

"Perhaps so," said Jeffery. "But what I'd like to see is some big trees! It's rather wild land here – too much common – and I can't see any big tree except that one over there by the farmhouse – and that's not really very big."

"And where's the hill?" asked John, looking all round. "The land is so flat here. I can't see a hill anywhere!"

233

"It's very disappointing," said Jeffery. "But let's go in and see if Mrs Timbles is anywhere about. She may be able to tell us if the lane ever went any farther than this. After all, this map is very, very old, you know, and lanes can disappear easily enough, if they are not used."

They went into the farmyard. It was a lovely place. Cows lowed in a shed nearby. Pigs grunted in a big sty. Hens clucked all over the place, and from somewhere not far off came the curious sounds of turkeys gobbling.

"There's Mrs Timbles, with the turkeys!" said Jeffery. "Hallo, Mrs Timbles! We've all come to see you!"

Mrs Timbles shut the door of the turkey-house. She beamed at the three children, who liked her at once. She was fat and round, and her face shone like a large, red, polished apple.

"Well, I never!" she said. "The three little Greylings! Welcome, my dears – I'm right glad to see you all! I was wondering when I'd get a sight of your merry faces. How like your father you all are! Ah, I remember him here as a boy – and a monkey he was too! Let all my turkeys out one day, he did, and such a time we had getting them back."

"Did Daddy really do that?" said Jeffery, in the greatest surprise. He couldn't imagine his father doing anything so naughty. "Oh, I must ask him about it!"

"Yes, you ask him if he remembers Mrs Timbles' turkeys!" said the farmer's wife, with a laugh. "It was this very house he let them out of! The rascal!"

"Why don't you let them loose like the hens and the

ducks?" asked Susan, who felt sorry for the big birds shut up in the house. There was wire-netting round two sides, but they did look very crowded together inside, she thought.

"You mustn't let turkeys touch the ground," said Mrs Timbles. "If they get wet feet, they're done for! But come along, we don't want to stand here talking about my greedy turkeys! You come along in and I'll see if I can find a few cakes for you, and something to drink!"

They followed her into the sunny farmhouse. They sat down in a great kitchen, whose floor was tiled with old red bricks, so clean that it seemed a shame to tread on them. At one end burned a cheerful wood fire. Bright red geraniums flowered on the windowsill, and cups and saucers with a bright red pattern seemed to flower on the dresser!

"It's a lovely kitchen," said Susan, looking round it. "When I'm grown up I shall have a kitchen like this, and I shall live in it like you do. It's nicer than drawing rooms and dining rooms."

Mrs Timbles disappeared into a larder as big as Granny's study. She brought out some ginger buns, some tarts that were so full of home-made jam that they ran over, and a great jug of something that looked a little like lemonade, but wasn't.

"It's nettle beer, my dears," said Mrs Timbles. "Nettle lemonade! Made of the youngest leaves of the hedgerow nettles, according to an old, old recipe that my great-grandmother had from Greylings Manor when she was cook there a hundred years ago!"

The children tasted the nettle drink and thought it

was simply lovely. They ate all the buns and the tarts and were very sorry when they were finished. They were too polite to ask for any more. Rags sat beside them, licking up any crumbs that were dropped!

"I'll not give you more to eat," said Mrs Timbles, who knew quite well what the children were thinking. "I've plenty to offer you – but I know you'll not be eating any dinner if you have too much now! And what will your Granny say to me then?"

The children laughed. They loved being in the old kitchen and having such a feast. The farmhouse felt as old as the Manor House.

"*Is* it very old?" asked Susan, looking up at the enormous black beams that ran across the ceiling and in the walls of the kitchen.

"Very, very old," said Mrs Timbles. "As old as Greylings Manor. Ah, children, I'm grieved to hear that the old mistress is going, and the old master. We've belonged to Greylings, we Timbles, as long as anyone knows. We don't want to belong to strangers!"

"Isn't it a pity that the Greylings Treasure can't be found?" said Jeffery. "Then Granpa would be rich."

"The Greylings Treasure has been lost this many years," said Mrs Timbles, gathering up the dirty plates. "Many a man has hunted for that, my dears. But it's my belief it went years and years ago. It will never be found now."

"Is the lane old that goes to your house, Mrs Timbles?" asked Jeffery.

"As old as the house, I guess," said the farmer's wife.

"Did it ever go farther than the house?" asked Jeffery.

"No, never," said Mrs Timbles. "It had no need to. There's no house beyond this one. It only runs between the two cottages down the way, and our farm."

The children were disappointed to hear that. But they did not tell Mrs Timbles why they wanted to know. They got up to see the young chicks and ducklings at the back of the farm, and to look at the lambs frisking in the fields beyond.

"What's that old place just there?" asked Susan, pointing to a tumbledown stone hut, with no roof, not far off. Lambs were playing in and out of it.

"No one knows," said Mrs Timbles. "It's been like that for years. I did hear say that there was something funny about it, but I never found out what. There's not much left of it now."

"Let's go and look at it," said Susan. But there was no time.

"We must hurry back," said Jeffery. "We've been all the morning! Rags, Rags! Stop sniffing about, and come along home!"

They said goodbye to Mrs Timbles, who begged them to come again soon. They hurried down the lane, counting the bends again.

"It's no good, there are only three," said Jeffery. "And one of those isn't much of a bend really. And there aren't any big trees about and I didn't see any hill at all, did you? I looked and looked everywhere, when we went round the farm."

"So did I," said John, looking gloomy. "I'm afraid this lane isn't the right one. Well, we'll have to think again, that's all!"

237

CHAPTER 10

Somebody Else is Treasure-hunting!

That afternoon the three children and their grand-parents went to picnic in the little house.

Granny didn't at all like the marshy ground she had to cross, and John had to keep putting down handfuls of twigs on the muddiest bits for Granny to walk on.

Rags came with them, of course, quite beside him-self with joy at chasing rabbits again. His tail wagged the whole time, and his tongue hung out of his mouth.

"We'll make a fire again this afternoon," said

Susan happily. She loved making fires. "I hope the chimney won't smoke this time."

"It shouldn't smoke now," said Jeffery. "It was the birds' nests and the iron box that made it smoke, because they stopped up the chimney."

Granny and Granpa were amazed when they saw the secret house, and looked at the doorway and windows which the children had cleared by chopping and sawing away the ivy and brambles.

"I *had* heard of this place," said Granpa. "But even when *I* was a boy it had disappeared. I remember looking for it, and thinking it must have fallen to pieces. But it must have been overgrown like this, even then, and I didn't see it."

Susan went to lay the fire – and then she stopped and stared. The fireplace was not as she had left it! It had been full of birds'-nest twigs and leaves and moss. But now it wasn't! The mess had been cleared out of the fireplace, and was all over the floor.

"Look," said Susan to the boys. "Somebody has been here!"

The boys stared at the fireplace. They, too, remembered that it had not been cleared when they had left the day before. How strange!

"Why should all that mess have been moved away from the hearth!" wondered Jeffery. "Well – for one reason only!"

"What?" asked John.

"Because *some*body was hunting all around for something!" said Jeffery. "Somebody has been looking for the other half of the map! Yes – that's what happened. They've looked up the chinmey – and

239

cleared the hearth to hunt for it, too. And look – they've caught their sleeve on this old nail!''

The nail stuck out from the mantelpiece and on this hung a small piece of blue cloth.

''Mr Potts wore a blue suit yesterday,'' said Jeffery. ''And I guess he's been here hunting – and tore his suit! Serve him right!''

''Well, he didn't find much!'' said John. ''I wish I'd caught him.''

''I don't,'' said Jeffery. ''He might be rather unpleasant! I don't like him!''

The children didn't tell their grandparents what they had discovered. They quickly cleared away the mess, and Susan laid and lighted a fire in the hearth. This time it burnt beautifully and didn't smoke at all. The children were very pleased. Susan put the kettle on the fire to boil.

They had a lovely picnic, except that Rags discovered the chocolate buns, which John had stupidly put on the floor for a moment. Rags quite thought the plate was meant for him, and he ate six of the buns before he was noticed! Then he was driven out of the house in disgrace, and spent his time pawing in the pool at a big fish he could see below the water.

''I know he'll fall in,'' said Susan. But he didn't. He wasn't fond enough of water for that!

''Well,'' said Granny, when the picnic was over, ''that was a real treat. I think you've cleaned the house beautifully, Susan darling. You will be able to have it as your own hidey-hole whilst you are at Greylings!''

''The pool is very pretty from here,'' said Granpa, sitting on a step and looking down at the lilies. ''I like

240

the bit of the stream you can see too. It winds in and out beautifully between the trees."

"Yes, doesn't it," said Susan – and then a thought struck her.

It was such a wonderful thought that she went red at once. She beckoned to Jeffery and took him behind the little house. He was puzzled at her excited face.

"Jeffery! Did you hear what Granpa said?" whispered Susan.

"Of course," said Jeffery. "But I didn't see anything in it!"

"But, Jeffery! When he said the stream *winds in and out beautifully*, didn't you think of anything!" cried Susan, forgetting to whisper. "Don't you see? We've been looking for a winding lane – but it's a river in the map, not a lane!"

"Gracious! I believe you're right!" said Jeffery, thrilled. "Yes – why didn't we think of that before? The river, of course. At its fourth bend – goodness, we'll have some more exploring to do tomorrow!"

They told John, who came up to see what the excitement was. He glowed with delight. "Of course, of course!" he said. "We *are* idiots not to have thought of that. Good old Granpa! He gave us the right idea and didn't know it!"

Granny was puzzled to know why the children seemed so excited when they went home that evening. But they didn't say a word! No – this was their own secret, and they meant to do their exploring without anyone knowing.

"And now that we know somebody else is doing a bit of exploring too, we'll keep our secret all the tighter!'' said Jeffery, remembering the fireplace in the little house. "Mr Potts has been to our little house – but he doesn't know any more than he did before!''

"Well,'' said Granny, when they reached home, "that was a very pleasant outing. You were clever to discover that hidden house, children – it is really most exciting. I can imagine how thrilled you were to find the iron box in the chimney too – and the old map. It is a great pity that there is only half of it.''

"Well, the other half may turn up,'' said Granpa. "If so, we'll let that fellow Potts have it and see if his learned friend can make out what it all means. *I'm* afraid it doesn't mean anything.''

The children looked at one another, but they said nothing. Susan longed to tell everything, but she knew she mustn't.

They went up to their rooms – and Susan made a queer discovery! She opened one of her drawers to get a clean handkerchief – and to her great surprise she found that the drawer was most untidy!

"Which of you boys has been untidying my drawers?'' she shouted to the two in the next room.

Neither of the boys had even been in the room. Susan opened the other drawers – they were none of them as neat as she had left them. She was puzzled.

"I only tidied them this morning,'' she said. "Granny scolded me yesterday because they were untidy, and I spent ages putting them nice – now they're all higgledy-piggledy again.''

Jeffery came to see. Then he went to the big chest of drawers that the boys shared in their room, and opened the top drawer, and the next one.

"Look here!" he said. "Someone has been through my drawers too. This is pretty queer."

Susan went into the boys' room and they looked at one another. They each thought the same thing.

"It's Mr Potts, or somebody belonging to him," said John slowly. "They've been looking for the other half of the map. They guessed we've got it, because I went so red yesterday when they questioned me about it."

"So they came and hunted through our things whilst we were out," said Jeffery. "The burglars!"

"Jeffery! You don't think they've found the halves of the map, do you?" said Susan suddenly.

"Good gracious! I hope not!" said Jeffery. He rushed to the dolls' house and knelt down. He switched on the little electric lamps that lighted the house and looked inside. He gave a sigh of relief.

"No, it's all right," he said. "They're here, safe on the ceilings. It's a good thing we thought of such a good place!"

"Let's go downstairs and find out if Mr Potts called," said John. So they went down. In the hall they found Jane, the housemaid, arranging some flowers.

"Hallo, Jane," said Jeffery. "Did anyone call whilst we were out this afternoon?"

"Yes, Master Jeffery. Mr Potts came, and another gentleman," said Jane. "They said they would like to see you children. They were sorry you were out."

"Did they come into the house?" asked Jeffery. "Or did they go off straightaway in their car?"

"Mr Potts asked if his friend might use the

telephone," said Jane. "So I showed Mr Potts into the dining room and took his friend to the hall telephone. He was there such a time!"

"Was Mr Potts waiting in the dining room all that time?" asked John.

"I expect so," said Jane.

The children ran off. "I bet he *didn't* wait in the dining room all that time!" said Jeffery. "He slipped up the little staircase to Susan's room and had a good hunt round while his friend was pretending to telephone. He's a clever one, is Mr Potts!"

"Jeffery, I don't think you ought to carry the map-tracing about with you," said Susan seriously. "Suppose he caught you and searched you. He'd find it!"

"You're right, Susan," said Jeffery. "Well, I know something to trick dear Mr Potts! I shall make up a false map, and keep it in my pocket! Then, if he does catch me and search me for the map, he'll get on the wrong track – because he'll have a false map to follow!"

"That's clever, Jeffery," said Susan. "You had better do it tonight – and we'll burn the tracing you made, after looking at it very carefully and learning it by heart! We can always turn the dolls' house upside down and study the map on the ceilings, if we forget anything!'

So that night Jeffery made a false map. At least, half of it was quite correct, because Mr Potts had seen the half with the words "Treasure" on it – but the other half was a real muddle!

Jeffery drew four more bends in the river instead of two, on the first half. He drew six more trees, a few small bushes, and then something that looked like a piece of bread-and-butter with a bite out of it!

"Whatever's that?" asked Susan in surprise.

"I don't know!" said Jeffery with a laugh. "Just something to puzzle Mr Potts, that's all!"

He burnt the other tracing, after the three of them had studied it very carefully indeed, and had learnt it so well that any one of them could have drawn it correctly from memory. Then Jeffery slipped the false map into his pocket.

"Now, Mr Potts can find it if he likes!' he said.

"Jeffery, can we go and find the four bends of the river tomorrow?' asked Susan. "I'm longing to do some more exploring."

"Yes, rather!' said Jeffery. "We'll go treasure-hunting again for all we're worth!"

CHAPTER 11

The Children Follow the Map

The next day the three children set off once more with Rags. They had wanted to stay out to a picnic lunch but Granny had said no.

"Mr and Mrs Potts have kindly asked you all to tea this afternoon," said Granny. "So I will take you in the car. I want you home for lunch, so that you can tidy yourselves and change into something nice afterwards."

"Oh, what a nuisance!" said Susan. "I don't like Mr Potts."

"Well, you may like his house and grounds!" said Granny. "He has a wonderful lake, so he tells me, and four boats. He says you can go out in one."

"Oh, good," said John, who loved boating. "That won't be so bad."

"All the same, it's a waste of time when we have so much exploring to do," said Jeffery, as they got ready to go to Greylings Wood.

Rags knew the way very well to the secret house now, and set off on the usual path at once. But Jeffery called him back. "Hie, Rags, old boy! We're not going that way today!"

"Which way are we going then?" asked Susan, surprised.

"We want to find out where the river enters the wood," said Jeffery. "I think we must count the bends from when it enters the trees. I asked Tipps this morning where it went into the wood, and he said we had to go down the road for about a mile – then we'd see it under a bridge."

So Rags and the children went down the road in the sunshine. After about twenty minutes' walk they came to a small stone bridge that spanned the little river.

"Here it is," said Jeffery. "Come on – we'll leave the road here and go into the wood."

There was no hedge, and no railing. The children simply walked among the trees and followed the stream. It ran quite straight for a little way and then curved slightly.

"Is this one of the bends, do you think?" asked Susan excitedly.

Jeffery shook his head.

"No," he said. "We must look for fairly big bends, I think. They were very curved ones in the map."

A pleasant path ran by the bank of the stream for some way. Then the path stopped at an old wooden seat, and the children had to scramble along through an overgrown part of the wood for some time.

Just after the wooden seat the stream took a great turn to the left, almost doubling over on itself.

"The first bend!" said Jeffery, pleased. They followed the curve as best they could, and almost at once the river curved again, this time to the right.

"The second bend!" said Susan. "We're getting on, boys!"

They were in a part of the wood that they did not know – but after they had followed the stream for a little while longer they suddenly came to the piece they knew, that led to the pond by their secret house!

Susan was very surprised. The boys laughed at her. "But, Susan, you must have known that we would come to it some time," said Jeffery. "After all, it's the same river!"

"Yes, I know," said Susan. "But I just didn't think we'd arrive here somehow. Well, there's a fine bend just beyond the pond, Jeffery – that's the third one!"

They scrambled round the pond, and tried to follow the third bend. But it was quite impossible because the ground was so marshy just there that they sank almost up to their knees. Rags hated it. He stood and barked loudly at the children.

"He thinks we're quite mad!" said John. "Come on, Rags, old fellow. Don't get left behind."

Rags ran off round the trees. "We'd better follow

him," said Jeffery, pulling his foot out of a muddy hole. "We can't possibly go this way. We shall come to the river another way, and perhaps miss this marshy bit."

So they followed Rags between the trees on drier ground. The dog seemed to know that they did not want to go very far from the water, for, as soon as possible, he led them back to it.

Jeffery stood on the bank and looked up the river, the way they had come. It was almost straight after the third big curve.

"Only one more bend, and then we should come to the three big trees or the humpy hill," said Jeffery. "Come on. It's drier here."

They were now able to follow the stream better. Great beeches grew all around, and the undergrowth was scarce. Some of the beech trees were so old and knotted that they seemed to have queer faces in their wrinkles.

At last the children came to the fourth bend. This was a good one. The river swung round to the right and then the children saw before them a marvellous avenue of trees, planted in two straight rows, with what must once have been a grassy lane between them.

Now the space between them was no longer a lane but was completely overgrown with bushes and undergrowths of all kinds. But it was easy to see what a fine avenue it must have been, for the trees still stood there in their places, swaying in their two long rows.

"Somebody planted this avenue a long time ago," said Jeffery. "Perhaps they liked to ride here – or maybe it was a proper roadway at one time, leading to somewhere."

"The only difficulty is – where are our three big trees?" said John. "With so many trees it's difficult to know which are the right three!"

Jeffery stared at the trees. He noticed that they were not so big as some of the others they had passed on their way through the wood.

"I don't think these trees are more than a hundred years old," he said at last. "So they couldn't have been planted at the time that map was drawn. It's three much bigger, much older trees we must look for – more like those enormous old beeches we passed a little time back."

"Do you think it might be three of those that we want?" said Susan.

"Of course not," said Jeffery. "We want three trees *after* the fourth bend in the stream, not before. We must hunt about the place for three enormous old trees. I only hope they haven't died or been cut down."

They made their way through the trees, looking for three together. Susan came across a great old tree, with such a thick trunk that she felt sure the tree must be about three hundred years old! It had a knotty, wrinkled trunk.

"Here's a very, very old tree," called Susan. "Oh, and look – here's another not far off. They are two of the oldest trees we've seen."

"Where's the third?" said Jeffery, looking around. "These two are certainly enormous – and look, Susan, look, John, there's the stump of a third old tree! In between these two we've found – see? There were *three* trees here once – but one must have died

250

and been cut down. Thank goodness its stump was left to show us where it grew!"

The children stared at the two gnarled old giants and the stump of the third. They were in a slanting line, just as the map had shown.

"There are no other trees in a slanting line as far as I can see," said Jeffery, hunting around. "They are either in straight lines, like those in the avenue, or they are just growing anywhere. These must be the three!"

"Well, now we must look for the humpy hill," said John. "How will these trees help us? Do we have to follow the direction in which they are pointing?"

"Either that – or we climb one of the trees and see what we can find!" said Jeffery.

"Climb up the biggest one!" said Susan.

"I'll climb this one and you climb that one," said John to Jeffery. So each boy climbed up one of the old, old trees. They had to be careful because the twigs were brittle, and some of the boughs were quite dead.

But at last they got to the top. And then Jeffery gave a shout.

"I can see something!"

"What?" shouted Susan, at the bottom.

"A humpy hill!" cried Jeffery.

"Oooh!" said Susan, almost beside herself with excitement. "Where is it?"

"It's in the very thickest part of the wood, I should think!" said Jeffery. "Wait a minute – I've got my compass. I'll set it so that I know exactly in which direction the hill is."

John could see nothing from his tree. His view towards the hill was hidden by Jeffery's enormous

tree. He climbed down quickly. Jeffery climbed down too, slipping on one bough, and grazing his knee rather badly.

But he was too excited to do any more than mop his knee with his handkerchief. "It's funny," he said. "The hill sticks up just above the top of the trees – and it's not got any trees on it at all, as far as I could see. It's just a grassy hill. It's buried so deep in the wood that no one would ever find it unless they knew it was there. Oh I say, aren't we getting on!"

"Have we got time to go and find the hill?" asked Susan, leaping round in joy. She could never keep still when she was excited.

"Stop, Susan," said Jeffery. "You make me feel giddy. Well, I don't think we really *have* got time! But all the same, we'll *make* time! We'll have a *look* at the humpy hill, even if we can do no more than that today!"

He showed the others his compass. "I've got to keep the needle pointing exactly *there*," he said, showing them the little swinging needle in its round glass case. "If I do, and we follow the direction, we are bound to come to the humpy hill. I say – isn't this thrilling!"

They set off in the direction to which the needle pointed – due north. It was difficult going, for the wood grew very thick indeed, and the children had to force their way through. The beech trees had given way to oak, hazel, and birch, and the undergrowth, untrimmed for years, had grown thick and matted.

Soon their legs were scratched, and their clothes were torn. But they would not stop. It was far too exciting!

After forcing their way though the wood for about twenty minutes they came suddenly to the hill. It was very queer, for it had no trees on it at all, and yet there seemed no reason why trees should not grow there. It rose very steeply from the ground of the wood, covered with grass and bracken.

"Well – there's the hill!" said Jeffery in delight. "We *are* reading the map well!"

CHAPTER 12

Rags is a Great Help!

The three children looked at the queer, humpy hill. A rabbit peeped out of a burrow and popped back. Rags was up the hill like a flash of lightning and put his head down the hole.

"Shall we climb the hill?" asked Susan.

"Well, we shall be awfully late for lunch," said Jeffery, looking at his wristwatch. "But we simply must go on a bit farther and see if we can find that church-like place!"

So they climbed up the hill, seeing little rabbit-paths

255

here and there. When they got to the top they exclaimed in surprise. They were level with the tops of the trees, and they looked over the top of the wood, seeing the swaying branches for miles! It was a lovely sight.

They could see no sign of any little church anywhere. They looked on all sides of the hill, but there was no building of any sort or kind. It was really disappointing.

"I say, I hope we're not going to lose the trail just as we've followed the map so well," said Jeffery. "But I can't see any building, can you, John?"

"No, I can't," said John gloomily. "Let's go down the other side of the hill and hunt around a bit, Jeffery. Perhaps the church was built among the trees, and is hidden from us."

So down the other side of the steep, humpy hill they went, and spied around to see what they could find. They found nothing at all.

It was Rags who found something! He shot after a rabbit that had ventured too near him, and when it rushed under a bush, he rushed after it and began to scrape there for it, thinking it had gone into the ground! Jeffery pulled him out – and then called to the others.

"Come and look here – Rags has scraped out a big old stone, as grey as our gateposts!"

They crowded round to look. They scraped away more of the moss and creeper, and sure enough, it was an old stone.

"I guess that was once part of a wall," said Jeffery. "What *sillies* we are! That old building shown in the map must have fallen down long, long ago! All we shall find will be the great squares of stone, like this one, that it was built of. Let's look.''

They began to hunt, scraping away moss here and there, and pulling away brambles – and at last they found enough stones to show where some building had been. It could not have been a very large building, for the children found a rough outline of the shape, guided by the great stones they had unearthed round about.

''Well, this was the building all right,'' said Jeffery. ''The thing is now – *where* is the flight of steps that led up to it? You remember the lines that looked like steps in the picture, don't you, you two?''

They remembered quite well. ''I don't see how there could possibly have been any steps to this building,'' said Susan, puzzled. ''It's built flat on the ground. If it had been built on the hill, there might have been steps leading up to it, as there are to our secret house, from the pond – but you can't have a flight of steps if you build on the ground itself!''

Jeffery was puzzled and disappointed. It was too bad that they had found everything except the steps! He looked at his watch and gave a shout. ''Goodness! It's one o'clock already – and lunch is at one. We *shall* get into a row! Come on – we must go at once. We'll come back tomorrow.''

''Isn't there a shorter way home?'' asked John, thinking with dismay of the very thick wood they would once more have to force their way through.

''Well, if there is, we don't know it!'' said Jeffery. ''Hie, Rags! Where are you going? Come back!''

Rags was trotting off in another direction. He took no notice of Jeffery at all.

"RAGS!" yelled Jeffery angrily. "Don't pretend to be deaf. Come here! You'll be lost if you go wandering off by yourself when we're so far from home!"

Rags stopped and looked back at the other. He cocked his ears up, and put on a most cheeky expression. But he didn't come back.

"I'll go after him and get him," said Jeffery, angry. "He'll make us later than ever."

So he ran after Rags – who at once began trotting off again in the opposite direction. It was most annoying. Jeffery called and shouted, and ran after the little dog, but he still would not come.

Then Jeffery noticed that Rags really did seem to know the way he was going, and he stopped and thought. "I say!" he called. "I think old Rags knows another way home! After all, he's lived here all his life and gone rabbiting in the woods hundreds of times. I expect he knows all the shortest ways home. Shall we follow him?"

"Yes," said Susan. So all three children followed Rags, who wagged his tail, very pleased. He led them through the wood, leaving behind the very thick part, and then, most unexpectedly, came out at the field behind Farmer Timbles' house! It was most astonishing.

"Good gracious!" said Jeffery, amazed. "Who would have thought we were so near the farm? Well, that's jolly good, I must say – we can run home all the way from here, instead of scrambling through the wood. It will be a shorter way to come tomorrow too."

They set off home at a trot, and arrived at a quarter to two, dirty, tired, hungry and with their clothes torn and scratched. Granny was very cross indeed.

"You naughty children!" she said, coming out of the dining room and catching them just as they were creeping upstairs to wash and change. "Three-quarters of an hour late! You don't deserve any dinner at all! And just look at your clothes – and what *have* you done to your knee, Jeffery?"

"Oh, nothing much, Granny," said Jeffery, looking down at his badly-grazed knee, which he had forgotten all about. "I climbed a tree and slipped as I was climbing down again. Really it's nothing."

"I give you five minutes to wash and put on something clean," said Granny. "If you are not down by then I shall send out the dinner and you can have bread and butter instead."

They all shot upstairs, and soon taps were running and clothes were being hurriedly changed. They rushed into the dining room just in time!

"Now I don't want you to speak a word," said Granny, still very cross with them. "Eat your dinners, and try to make up for your bad behaviour."

So they ate hungrily, and didn't say a word. Granpa had had his dinner and was in the garden, smoking.

"You will be ready at three o'clock to go with me in the car to Mr Potts' house," said Granny, when they had finished. "It is nearly half-past two now. Wash again, a little more carefully, bind up that awful knee, Jeffery, do your hairs properly, put on your best things, and be down in time. You had better begin to get ready now – it is nearly half-past two."

"Bother Mr Potts," grumbled Susan, as they went upstairs. She was very tired with her exciting morning, and would have liked to take a book and go and read in the hammock.

At three o'clock they were all ready, looking very clean, neat and well-dressed. Jeffery had bandaged his knee with a clean handkerchief.

"Now, are we all ready?" said Granny, appearing down the stairs. "Yes – you look nice, all of you. Now please behave yourselves, and don't climb trees or anything this afternoon!"

The children were glad to see that Granny was smiling again. She was never cross for very long for she was very sweet-tempered. They all got into the car and set off.

Mr Potts' house was more like a mansion. It was simply enormous, and the grounds were marvellously laid out. There was the lake that Granny had told them about, and a few small boats moored at the bank.

Mr and Mrs Potts greeted them all very heartily. Mrs Potts was rather fat, and had more rings on her fingers than Susan had ever seen anyone wear before. She had six ropes of pearls round her neck, and bright earrings dangled in her ears.

"They must be very rich people," said John to Susan, in a low voice. "I wonder what they want to buy Greylings for, when they've got an enormous place like this?"

The children were told that they might go out in the boat, with Mr Potts to help them to row. They would much rather have gone by themselves, but it would not have been polite to say so.

They all got into the little boat. It was painted red, and was very pretty. There were two pairs of oars. Jeffery took one pair and Mr Potts took the other.

"It's quite a way, to row round the lake," said Mr Potts. "I'll show you some ducks' nests, and a little waterfall we've made."

It certainly was quite a long way round the lake! John took the oars after a bit, and then Susan had a turn. They saw three ducks' nests, all with eggs in, and came to the little waterfall, which was very pretty.

Mr Potts talked a lot. He tried to be very nice to them indeed. He noticed Jeffery's bandage, and spoke to him about it.

"Hurt yourself, Jeffery?" he asked.

"Nothing much," said Jeffery.

"He did it this morning," said Susan, who always liked to talk when she could. "He was climbing a most enormous tree – right to the very top he went – and when he came down, he slipped and grazed his knee badly."

"A most enormous tree?" said Mr Potts. "And where was that? In the wood?"

"Yes," said Susan. "Ever so far in the wood. We followed . . ."

She stopped and gave a cry of pain. John had punched her in the back to stop her saying any more. He knew what Susan was like once she begun talking. She never knew when to stop!

"Dear me, why did you stop your sister telling me about your adventures this morning?" asked Mr Potts "I am most interested. Do go on, my dear."

But Susan would say no more. She bit her lip and

hoped that Jeffery wouldn't scold her afterwards. Why was she so silly as to tell things she had much better say nothing about?

"Well, we'd better be getting back," said Mr Potts, seeing that none of the children was going to say any more about their morning adventures. "I'm afraid this is rather a dull afternoon for you, after all your tree-climbing this morning!"

But it wasn't so dull after all – because something most unexpected suddenly happened!

CHAPTER 13

Mr Potts is Clever

Mr Potts and Jeffery rowed back to the bank. Susan got out first, and then John. Then Jeffery stood up – but suddenly the boat wobbled violently – and Jeffery fell straight over the side into the water!

It wasn't at all deep – Jeffery could stand quite easily. But he got a shock and came up gasping and spluttering. Mr Potts looked *most* alarmed and grabbed him at once. He pulled him into the boat and then helped him to the bank.

"Oh, Jeffery, are you all right?" cried Susan,

who had been really frightened.

"Of *course* I'm all right!" said Jeffery, half cross at the fuss. "I can't imagine how I fell in. The boat rocked like anything and I lost my balance, that's all."

Granny and Mrs Potts came hurrying up when they saw what had happened. Mrs Potts was dreadfully upset.

"Oh, my dear boy, you are so wet!" she cried. "Come along in at once and take your wet things off. Mr Potts has some shorts you can have, and a vest and pullover. Dear, dear, I *am* sorry this has happened."

"Now don't get upset, my dear," said Mr Potts to his wife. "*I'll* see to the boy. He won't be any the worse for his wetting, and I can easily get him dry clothing. Come along, Jeffery – we'll see what we can do for you."

Susan and John went with Jeffery. Mrs Potts sank down on a garden seat, looking quite pale. Granny found that she had to comfort her, because she really looked as if she would burst into tears!

"Such a thing to happen!" she kept saying. "Such a thing to happen!"

Mr Potts took the children into an enormous kitchen, where three maids were at work. They were astonished to see the children with Mr Potts, but at once saw what had happened.

"I'll take his wet clothes off, sir," said a kindly-faced cook, bustling forward.

"No thank you," said Jeffery firmly. "I can take them off myself. I hope I shan't make your kitchen floor too wet, though."

He stripped off his wet clothes, and took the big warm towel that Mr Potts offered him. It wasn't long before he was quite dry. Mr Potts picked up the wet clothes and went through the door with them. "I'll get you some dry ones," he said.

"Oh, sir! Let *me* take the clothes!" cried the house-parlourmaid, running after him. "I'll dry them and press them."

But Mr Potts took no notice of her and disappeared quickly. The cook went to the scullery, and the third maid went into the garden. The house-parlourmaid followed Mr Potts after a minute, and the children found themselves alone.

"Jeffery! You *were* a silly!" whispered Susan. "It's the first time you've ever fallen out of a boat!"

"And so would *you* fall out if the boat was rocked violently just as you were standing on one foot, ready to step out," answered Jeffery crossly. "That boat was rocked on purpose – by Mr Potts. He *wanted* me to fall in the water!"

"Oh, Jeffery! But why?" asked Susan, horrified.

"So that I would have to change my wet clothes under his eyes – and he could take them away – and run through my pockets to see if he could find any signs of the *map*!" said Jeffery.

The other two stared at him in silence. They hadn't for one moment thought of such a thing – but now they saw that it was very likely to be true. After all, the clothes had been whisked off by Mr Potts, although it was the maid's job to take them and dry them.

"But, Jeffery ——" said John, beginning to

giggle, "you had the false map in your pocket – the one we made up!"

"I know that," said Jeffery with a laugh. He pulled the big towel round him more closely. "Old Pots of Money will have to use his brains to work out *that* map, won't he!"

"What a good thing you didn't have the proper tracing in your pocket," began Susan. But Jeffery nudged her, for he had heard footsteps. The house-parlourmaid came back with some dry clothes – some rather big shorts belonging to Mr Potts, a vest, and a yellow pullover.

"Has Mr Potts got my wet clothes?" asked Jeffery.

"Yes, he has," said the maid rather indignantly. "He won't let me hang them out, he's doing them himself!"

Jeffery winked at the others. "Well, I've no doubt he has some good reason for seeing to them himself," he said. The others giggled. They knew what Jeffery meant. But the maid didn't, and she looked annoyed. She tossed her head, sniffed, and went to join the cook in the scullery.

Jeffery felt rather odd in his big clothes. Granny laughed when she saw him. Mrs Potts patted him kindly and said, "Well, I expect you'd all like some tea now. I can see Edith bringing it out on the terrace. Come along."

They went to the magnificent terrace that overlooked the lake – and there, set out on low tables, was the most scrumptious tea that the children had ever seen.

There were great ripe strawberries, and rich cream.

There were the most exciting sandwiches imaginable, honey in the comb, looking like golden syrup, a chocolate cake as big as a Christmas cake, little iced cakes of all kinds, a jam sandwich stuffed with cream as well, and a dish of the most exciting biscuits. And, to end up with, the maid brought out a tray full of strawberry and vanilla ice creams.

"Well, this was worth falling into the pond for," said Jeffery, as he ate his second ice cream, and wished that he could manage a third.

"I'm so glad you enjoyed your tea," said Mrs Potts, who had eaten just as much as the children. Susan thought it wasn't surprising that she was so fat, if she ate gorgeous teas like this every day. She wished she could have tea like that every day herself – but Granny would say it wasn't good for her, she knew!

The car came round for them after tea and they said goodbye and thank you, and got into it. Mr Potts promised to send Jeffery's clothes back the next day.

"That will just give him nice time to dry our false map and copy it out!" said Jeffery, with a grin, as they sat in the car waiting for Granny to finish saying goodbye.

They drove home, feeling rather full up. Granny gave a sigh as they turned in at their stone gateposts. "Dear old Greylings Manor!" she said, as the beautiful old house came into sight. "I am sorry to think you will soon no longer be ours. Mr Potts will be your master instead!"

"What does old Pots of Money want to buy your house for, Granny?" asked Jeffery. "His own is far bigger and grander."

"Jeffery! Don't call him that!" said Granny,

looking half-shocked and half-amused. "You must call people by their right names."

"Well, it *is* his right name," said Jeffery. "He *has* got pots of money, hasn't he?"

"Yes – I suppose he has," said Granny. "He doesn't want Greylings Manor for himself though – he wants it for his daughter, who is soon getting married."

They swept up to the steps and jumped out. "Now you'd better go and do something quiet," said Granny. "After that enormous tea you won't want to climb trees or run races, I hope. And if you don't come to supper, I shall quite understand. I am sure you can't possibly manage any more to eat today!"

But, dear me, by the time that supper was on the table, the children were quite ready for it! Granny seemed very surprised indeed, but she gave them just as big helpings as usual.

The next day a parcel arrived for Jeffery from Mr Potts. It was his clothes, all dry now, and neatly pressed. He ran his hands through his pockets. Everything was there – string, handkerchief, two bits of toffee, an unusual stone he had picked up, a pencil stump, a broken rubber, a notebook – and the map! Yes, that was there as well.

"Carefully copied, I'm quite sure!" said Jeffery, putting it back again with a grin. "Well, Mr Potts may be smart – but we're smarter! I didn't guess he'd get me into the lake – but we were ready for him, anyway. We did that map just in time for him!"

"I wish tomorrow would come quickly," said Susan. "I do want to hunt round that ruined building again – what's left of it! I simply can't *think* why there are those steps shown on the map, if there are none to be seen by the building."

"Perhaps they are not steps," said Jeffery.

"Well, what else can they be?" asked John.

"I can't think!" said Jeffery, frowning. "No – they *must* be steps. But yet there never, never could have been steps there, if the building was set on the level ground, as it seems to have been."

John was thinking hard. He looked up. "I suppose, Jeffery, there couldn't have been steps leading underground from the building, could there?" he asked. "You know – steps going down to a cellar, or something, from *inside* the building?"

Susan and Jeffery stared at John in surprise. Then Jeffery smacked his hand down on a nearby table. "Of course!" he said. "Of course! *That's* what we've got to look for! Steps going *down* from the building – not steps going *up* to it! Good for you, John!"

"Tomorrow we'll take forks and spades," said John excitedly. "We'll probe all over the ground and see if we can uncover a floor of some sort. And then we'll see if there are any signs of steps going underground!"

"Now I shan't be able to go to sleep tonight!" said Susan, her eyes shining. "I shall keep on and on thinking of tomorrow!"

But she did go to sleep, and she dreamt of finding a wonderful place where beautiful treasures were stored – but just as she was going to take what she wanted, Mr Potts popped up and drove her away! Susan woke up with a jump, feeling very angry with Mr Potts.

CHAPTER 14

A Thrilling Morning

The next morning Jeffery went to ask Tipps to lend him a garden fork and two spades.

"I got into trouble over lending you the axe," said Tipps. "I don't think I'd better lend you anything else."

"Oh, go on, Tipps, please do," begged John. He saw Granny in the distance and called to her. "Granny! May we borrow some gardening tools, please? Tipps says he had better not lend them to us."

"Well, so long as it's not an axe or a scythe," said

Granny. "I'm glad to hear you want to do some gardening!"

"Dear old Granny's got remarkable hearing," said Jeffery. "Nobody said a word about doing any gardening! Anyway, Tipps, let us have the things we want, now that Granny says we can."

They marched off with the tools, hoping that Granny wouldn't call them and ask where they were going to garden. Jeffery slipped indoors for his torch. He thought that if they *did* find steps going underground, they would want a little light to see them!

"We'll go the short way," said Jeffery. "We won't scramble all through the wood again. Where's Rags? Hie, Rags, come on – you can take us the way you took us yesterday!"

As they marched down the drive to the gates, Mr Potts' car came in. Mr Potts saw the children and stopped the car.

"I just came to ask if Jeffery was all right after his wetting yesterday," he called, showing all his white teeth in a wide smile. "But I see you are, Jeffery. Dear me, wherever are you going with those spades and forks?"

The children couldn't think what to say. Then Jeffery spoke up.

"We're going to the farm," he said. This was quite true. They had to pass the farm – and they meant to call in for a moment to see Mrs Timbles.

"Oh! You're going to help the farmer, are you?" said Mr Potts. This wasn't exactly a question, so nobody answered it. But John, of course, went as red as a tomato. He always did if he felt awkward or guilty about anything. Mr Potts noticed his red face at once.

"Have you found the other piece of that map?" he said suddenly.

Now this was a very difficult question to answer. If Jeffery said yes, Mr Potts would ask him for it and would see that it was different from the copy he had found in Jeffery's pocket. If he said no, it was an untruth, and Jeffery, like the others, hated untruths.

The three stared at Mr Potts, quite tongue-tied – and then Rags saved them! He suddenly saw a stray hen and barked loudly at it. He rushed at it, and the frightened creature fluttered into the hedge.

"Excuse us, sir – we must rescue the hen!" cried Jeffery gladly, and he darted off. The others went too and left Mr Potts in his car, looking annoyed.

"Quick, Rags, scare the old hen through the hedge," whispered John, "then we can squeeze through after it and disappear!"

Rags was delighted to find that for a change the children were encouraging him to bark at a hen, instead of scolding him for it. He went completely mad, barked his head almost off, leapt round like a kangaroo, and made the hen almost faint with fear. The children made as much noise as they could, too, shouting to the hen and to one another, as they pretended to shoo away Rags and catch the poor hen.

They squeezed through the hedge, and although they could hear Mr Potts calling to them, they took no notice and shouted all the more loudly. At last they began to giggle. Jeffery hurriedly picked up the hen, and tore off with it, afraid that Mr Potts would leave the car and come after them.

But he didn't. They heard the car going up the drive. Jeffery set the hen down when he came to the hen-run, and it ran to join the others, squawking out its adventures at the top of its voice. Rags barked joyfully. He had had a wonderful time.

"Poor old hen!" said Susan, sorry for the clucking bird. "But it did save us from a very awkward moment, Jeffery."

"It did," said Jeffery. "Come on. We'd better slip off quickly before old Pots of Money catches us again."

So once more they set off, this time without anyone stopping them. They came to Farmer Timbles' house, and stopped for a few minutes to talk to Mrs Timbles. She was most astonished to see their spades and forks.

"What in the world are you going to do?" she asked.

"It's a secret, Mrs Timbles!" said John. "We'll tell you all about it one day."

"All right, I'll wait till then!" said the farmer's wife. "Would you like some of my new cakes?"

"Well, if you'd let us take a few with us, we'd be *very* pleased," said Jeffery. "But we can't stop long today, because we have a busy morning in front of us!"

"I'll pop some into a bag for you," said Mrs Timbles kindly, and she did. The children were thrilled when they saw her put at least twelve cakes into the bag for them.

They set off again with Rags, who was very much interested in the bag of cakes. Jeffery sent him on in front, hoping that he would be sensible enough to take them the way they had come yesterday.

He did take them the right way. He was a very clever dog, and loved trying to read the children's thoughts. He trotted ahead, and it was not long before the children came to the humpy hill, and found the place where they had uncovered so many old grey stones the day before.

"Now the thing to do is to jab about with the fork and see what we can feel underneath all this moss and stuff growing on what must have been the floor of the building," said Jeffery. So, taking the long-pronged fork, he began to jab strongly here and there.

Each time he jabbed, the fork struck something hard. He stopped, and looked at the others. "There must be a proper floor all underneath here," he said. "A tiled floor perhaps, like our secret house has. We'll clear it if we can."

Jeffery was right. Under the moss, the grass and the bracken was a tiled floor. The tiles were small, and even after so many years were still bright in colour. Rags helped as much as he could, scraping away with his feet in excitement.

After a great deal of hard work the children had most of the floor uncovered. Many of the tiles were broken. Some were missing altogether.

Then John uncovered a flat slab of stone, quite different from the coloured tiles.

"Look!" he said. "Here's something different. A big slab of stone – and it's got some old pattern on it."

Susan and Jeffery came beside John to see what the pattern was. Jeffery gave a shout.

"Don't you know what the pattern is, sillies? It's the

Greylings eagle – just like the ones on the gateposts, only flat instead of rounded. That shows this was a Greylings building."

"Why do you suppose they laid a flat stone here suddenly, in the middle of the coloured tiles?" asked John. "It seems odd to me."

"It *is* odd," said Jeffery, "But I bet I can explain the oddness! I guess there's the flight of steps underneath that slab!"

"Oooh, really?" said Susan and John in delight. "Goody!"

"The thing is – how are we going to get it up to see?" wondered Jeffery. "It looks jolly heavy. I wonder if there's an iron ring or anything that we can pull it up by? Let's clear the whole slab properly and see."

They cleared it from end to end – but not a sign of any iron ring was to be seen. Jeffery stood on the slab and jumped on it to see if he could make it move.

The slab moved at once. There was a creaking, cracking noise as if something underneath was breaking, and Jeffery leapt off the slab in alarm. The children stared at it. Something below the slab of stone had given way, and it was lying all crooked, a little below the surface of the ground.

"Now what did it do that for?" said Jeffery. "It did give me a shock when it moved like that – and did you hear that funny breaking noise?"

"Perhaps, Jeffery, the stone is placed on wooden supports or something," said John. "And maybe they have rotted with the years, and when you jumped on the stone, the wood cracked and gave way."

"I think you're right," said Jeffery, kicking at the

275

stone with his foot. "I don't like to tread on it again. I wonder how we could move it?"

"There's a big stone over there, that was once part of the wall," said John. "I think we could all three carry it between us – then we could drop it down on the slab and see if that would move it!"

"Good idea," said Jeffery. They went to the big square stone and with great difficulty lifted it up. They staggered with it to the slab, and then, at a word from Jeffery, dropped it right on to the flat stone.

The result was most startling. The heavy stone struck the slab, which at once gave way, and, with a crash, it disappeared entirely, taking the heavy stone with it! The children found themselves staring into a big black hole!

"Golly!" said Jeffery, in the greatest astonishment. "Look at that!"

"The flight of steps must be down there," said John excitedly. He bent over to see. Jeffery took out his little torch and flashed it downwards into the hole.

It was a deep hole, with an old stairway leading downwards. "So we were right!" said Jeffery, in delight. "John! Susan! Down there is where the Greylings Treasure is hidden! I'm sure of it!"

Susan was so excited that she almost fell down the hole. Jeffery pulled her back. "Don't be silly," he said. "The whole place is rotten with age – if you miss your step you'll crash down there and hurt yourself. Look – can you see the slab of stone right down there, on the floor and the other stone beside it?"

Yes, they could see them both. They examined the entrance too, where the slab had been, and saw that the flat stone had rested on wood, which, as John had said, had become rotten, and had given way when Jeffery jumped on the stone.

"I want to go down the steps," said Susan. "Jeffery, do let me be the first one."

"Certainly not," said Jeffery. "Those steps may look all right, but they may be quite rotten too. *I* shall try them first."

"Well, be carefull, then, Jeff," said John anxiously. Jeffery stuck his torch in his pocket and sat down at the entrance to the hole. He tried the top step with his foot. With a crack it broke away at once, and the splinters went down below. Jeffery tried the next step. That broke too. The steps were as rotten as deadwood in a tree struck by lightning.

"Blow! The steps are no use at all," said Jeffery. "They wouldn't bear the weight of a mouse!"

"Well, how shall we get down then?" asked Susan, so anxious to explore underground that she simply could not keep still.

"We'll have to get a rope," said Jeffery. Both the others looked most disappointed at once. They couldn't bear the thought of going home and leaving the exciting hole even for an hour!

"Couldn't we jump down and chance it?" said John.

"Don't be so stupid," said Jeffery. "You'd break your leg to start with, and you'd never climb out again! Rags, go away. You'll fall in."

"Well, let's go home quickly and get the rope," said

277

John impatiently. "Anyway, it's almost dinner time. We'd better not be late again – though I'm sure we shall. We can come back after dinner."

"Come on, then," said Jeffery, and he turned to go. "Gracious! We *are* late again! Run!"

CHAPTER 15

An Unexpected Punishment

They hadn't gone very far before a thought came into John's head. "I say," he said, stopping, "do you think we ought to leave that hole open like that? Suppose anyone came along and saw it – and got down before we did?"

"Yes – you're right, John," said Jeffery. "We ought to have thrown bracken and branches over it to hide it. Let's go back and do it quickly – it won't take a minute!"

But a great surprise awaited them as they made their

way back through the trees. The sound of voices came to them!

Jeffery put his hand on Rags' collar at once, in case he should bark.

"Sh!" he said to the others. "Don't make a sound. Take Rags, John, and I'll creep up and see who it is."

Jeffery crept silently from bush to bush, keeping himself completely hidden – and at last he came in sight of the ruined building. He had a dreadful shock! Mr Potts was there, with another man! They were looking in the hole and talking in excitement.

"Those children are smart!" said Mr Potts. "They've found the very place. That map in the boy's pocket was wrong. We've been on a regular wild goose chase this morning, following goodness knows how many bends in the river! It's a good thing we heard their voices, and came to see what they were doing!"

"We'd never have found this by ourselves," said the second man. "This little hill is well-hidden, and the old building is fallen to pieces. Those are the steps shown in the map, Potts – no doubt of it. But they're quite rotten. We'd better come back again with a rope."

"Well, those kids will be back after lunch," said Mr Potts, rubbing his chin and thinking. "Let me see – how can we stop them? I know! I'll get my wife to phone up the old lady and invite the children to go for a picnic somewhere! Then they will be out of the way. I can't come back here after lunch, as I've business to see to – but we'll be here early in the morning before those kids are about."

"Well, come on then," said the other man. "I wish

we knew a short way back – I hate wading in that marshy bit! I'm soaked to the knees!"

Jeffery couldn't help grinning. He wasn't going to show them the other way back! He waited until the men had disappeared round the humpy hill and then he shot back to the others. He told them all he had heard. They listened in rage.

"*Well!*" said Susan. "So he thinks he'll get the Treasure before we do, does he? He thinks he'll get us nicely out of the way for the rest of the day! Well, he won't. We'll refuse to go to the picnic!"

"Quite right," said John. "We've simply *got* to get here this afternoon. Then, when he arrives early to-morrow morning, he'll find nothing at all!"

"I say, we *must* go!" said Jeffery. "It's five to one! You know what a row we got into yesterday!"

They simply raced home, carrying the spades and fork, hoping Granny wouldn't be too cross.

But she was. She was very angry indeed, and worse, still, Granpa was in a rage too.

"Half-past one!" said Granpa, as they trooped into the hall. "Is that what you call being punctual? Two days running! Disgraceful! Really disgraceful!"

"We're awfully sorry, Granpa," said Jeffery.

"Being sorry isn't enough," said Granpa, looking really fierce. "Your Granny orders nice meals for you and then you keep the whole household waiting like this."

"It is really very naughty of you all," said Granny. "I've a good mind to send the dinner out and make you have bread and butter – but I'm sure you are all very hungry, and I don't like to do that."

"But you'll be punished all the same!" said Granpa, looking very fierce still. "Oh yes! You'll go up to your rooms after lunch and there you'll stay for the rest of the day. You'll have your tea up there and no supper! Bad children! I'm angry with you!"

Granpa stalked out of the hall and the children stared after him in dismay. What! Spend the rest of the day in their bedrooms, when they had such important work to do after lunch? They couldn't!

"Granpa!" called Jeffery. "Please forgive us. Just this once. You see. . ."

"I never listen to excuses," said Granpa. "You'll just do as you are told and say no more."

Susan began to cry with tiredness and disappointment. She stamped her foot. "It's too bad, it's too bad!" she shouted. "Granpa, you're unkind! You ought to listen to Jeffery."

"*Susan*!" said Granpa, in a shocked voice. "Don't be rude. I shall send you all up to your rooms immediately if I have any more nonsense."

Susan didn't want to make the boys lose their lunch, so she wiped her eyes and said no more. They went meekly into the dining room and sat down.

"You musn't make Granpa angry by arguing with him, Susan," said Granny, serving out big helpings of cold meat, potatoes, and salad. "You have really been very thoughtless, coming in late again like this, and you deserve to be punished. Now I don't want to hear a word from any of you. Eat up your dinner quietly."

Granny took up the paper and sat down. The children were very hungry indeed, and they ate quickly. Just as Granny had finished ladling out the raspberries and cream for pudding, the telephone bell rang.

The maid came into the room after a minute. "Mr Potts on the telephone, Madam," she said. Granny got up and went into the hall. The telephone was in the hall cloakroom. Granny left the door open, and the children could hear every word she said.

"Good afternoon, Mr Potts," she said. Then she listened. "Oh, it's very kind of Mrs Potts to offer to take the children for such a lovely picnic, but I'm sorry to say they can't come. No, they really can't, Mr Potts. . . . No, they are not ill . . . as a matter of fact, they have been rather naughty, and they have been told to keep to their rooms for the rest of the day. What? Yes – I'm afraid they will be indoors – they will not be allowed out at all . . . so you see they can't possibly go to the picnic – but please thank Mrs Potts for me. Another day perhaps."

Then Granny listened again as Mr Potts spoke for some time.

"Well, I'm glad you have really decided to buy Greylings," said Granny. "Yes – the papers will be ready for us to sign tomorrow. Our lawyer will be here, and if you like to come tomorrow morning at ten o'clock, the whole matter can be finally settled. Yes . . . yes . . . goodbye."

Granny put back the receiver. The children longed to speak to one another and say what they thought, but they had been told not to talk. Oh dear! So everything was to be settled at ten o'clock tomorrow morning. It was dreadful. Tears trickled down poor Susan's face and fell into her raspberry juice.

Granny came back. "Mrs Potts wanted to know if

you could go for a picnic with her this afternoon," she said. "Now you see what you have missed by being so silly!"

"I don't want to go picnicking with Mrs Potts," said Susan. "I'm glad we're not going! I don't like Mr and Mrs Pots of Money!"

"Susan! Don't talk like that!" said Granny sharply. "Mr Potts is buying Greylings Manor, and you will have to be polite to him if you ever want to come and see the old place again."

"Granny! Please don't let him buy it!" said Jeffery. "Granny, we're going to find the Treasure for you, really we are!"

"Don't talk nonsense, dear," said Granny. "I suppose you are thinking of that old map? Well, I'm sure it doesn't mean anything at all."

"Oh, but, Granny, really we . . ." began Jeffery, but Granny wouldn't let him say any more.

"That's quite enough, Jeffery," she said. "Have you all finished? Well, go up to your rooms then. And remember that you are to stay there for the rest of the day. Tea will be sent up to you, but you'll have to go without supper – and I do hope you will remember that when you are guests in somebody's house the least you can do is to be punctual for meals!"

"We're very sorry, Granny," said John humbly, hoping that Granny would change her mind. "Couldn't we just stay in our rooms till tea time and then take Rags for a walk?"

"Certainly not," said Granpa, who had come in at that moment. "I never heard of such a thing! Go along now – and can I trust you not to leave your rooms – or must you be locked in?"

"You can trust us," said Jeffery, his cheeks going red. "We promise to stay in our rooms for the rest of the day."

"Very well," said Granpa. "I trust you. The Greylings never break their word."

The children went upstairs slowly and sadly. They sat in the boys' room and looked at one another dolefully.

"This is the worst bit of luck that could happen!" said Jeffery. "Who would have thought that Granpa would be so fierce?"

"Well, what about Granny?" said John. "She was fierce too. And all the time we're trying so hard to find the Treasure for them."

"Yes, but grown-ups don't think of things like that," said Jeffery. "Oh, do stop crying, Susan. I can't think where you get all your tears from. I really can't!"

There was a scraping at the door, and Rags whined outside.

"The dear old dog!" said John, jumping up. "He wants to share our punishment too! Good old Rags."

Rags came in and jumped up on to Jeffery's knee. He licked the boy's chin.

"Jeffery, I suppose we can't possibly go to the woods?" said John, in a timid voice. "I feel as if we *must* – don't you think Granpa would understand, once we had got the Treasure?"

"I know enough of Granpa to know that he would rather lose the Treasure than have any of us breaking

285

our word," said Jeffery. "We've given our word of honour, John, and we can't possibly break it. Don't even think of it! It would be an awful thing to do, and I'd hate myself for it."

"Yes – you're right," said John, in a miserable voice. "Oh, how I wish Mr Potts was at the bottom of his own silly lake!"

That made Jeffery laugh. "That's where he tried to put *me* yesterday!" he said. "Well, old Pots of Money knows we are safely out of the way now, picnic or no picnic – so he's safe to attend to his business this afternoon. If only we could have borrowed a rope and gone down that hole – we'd have been down it by now if it hadn't been for this silly punishment!"

"I'm tired," said Susan. "I'm going to lie on my bed and have a nap."

But no sooner had she laid herself down than an idea came to her. She jumped off her bed and ran to the boys.

"I've got an idea!" she said.

CHAPTER 16

An Underground Adventure

The boys looked at Susan. "What is it?" asked Jeffery doubtfully. He didn't think there *could* be any good ideas just at the moment.

"Well, listen, Jeff," said Susan. "We've promised to stay in our rooms for the rest of the day, haven't we?"

"Yes," said the boys.

"But we haven't promised to stay in them all night long!" cried Susan. "Mr Potts is going to explore that underground place early in the morning – well, why can't we go *tonight*? We can take torches. We shall be quite all right. It would be just as dark down in that hole in the daytime as in the night, so it won't make a bit of difference, really.''

"Well! That *is* an idea!'' said Jeffery, really thrilled. "Why didn't we think of it before? Of course – we shan't be breaking any promise if we go there tonight. We'll go!''

"We'll go!'' shouted John, and he banged his eiderdown so hard that the feathers flew out of it.

"We'll creep down Susan's secret stairs so that no one will hear us!'' said Jeffery.

"We'll take our touches! We'll find a strong rope! We'll get the Treasure before old Pots of Money!'' shouted John.

"Sh!'' said Susan, delighted that her idea was thought so much of. "You'll tell everyone in the house what we're going to do if you shout like that!''

"I feel much happier, now,'' said John. "What shall we do till tea time, Jeffery?''

"I think we'd better try and have a nap,'' said Jeffery. "It looks as if we shall be up half the night!''

So they all three lay on their beds and shut their eyes. The smell of the early roses outside the window came in. Bees hummed loudly. Everything was peaceful, and soon the children, happy again now, were fast asleep. They had worked so hard that morning, digging and scraping, that they were really tired out.

They did not awake until Jane, the housemaid, came knocking at the boys' door with their tea. She came in and set the tray down on the table.

"And what have *you* been doing to get sent to your

288

rooms like this?'' she said. "Late for lunch, I suppose. There's nothing that makes your granpa crosser than that!''

"Oooh, what a nice tea you have brought us, Jane!'' said Susan, looking at the tray of things. "Egg sandwiches – my very favourite ones! And what are these – potted meat. Thank you, Jane!''

"And ginger biscuits and seed cake!'' said John. "Well, I shan't mind going without my supper now.''

"You'll never be able to eat all this,'' said Jane. "Ring when you've finished and I'll fetch your tray.''

"Thanks, Jane,'' said Jeffery. Jane left the room, and the three children drew up their chairs and began their tea.

They enjoyed it. They talked about what they were going to do that night. It was very exciting.

"I think we'd better keep slices of that seed cake for tonight,'' said John. "We shall be awfully hungry if we go exploring at midnight!''

So they cut three enormous slices and put them in the top drawer of the chest. Then they rang for Jane.

"Good gracious!'' she said, when she came in and saw what a lot they had eaten. "Nearly everything gone! *You* won't miss your suppers!''

She went, carrying the tray. The children found some cards and played Happy Families until seven o'clock. Then Granny came in.

"Well,'' she said, "I'm sorry to have had to punish you like this – but you will please remember in future not to be late for meals, won't you?''

"Yes, Granny,'' they all said.

"You had better go to bed now,'' said Granny.

"You are not coming down to supper. I will say goodnight – and I hope tomorrow you will turn over a new leaf, and we shall all be happy together again. It upsets me to have to treat you like this – but I promised your mother I wouldn't spoil you. You are usually such *very* good children!"

They kissed their Granny goodnight and listened to her going down the stairs to the hall.

"It's not worth while getting undressed," said Susan.

"Yes, we'd better," said Jeffery. "Granny may come up again for something – or even Granpa – and we don't want to get into any more trouble. We can easily dress again about midnight."

So they undressed and got into bed. But none of them could go to sleep! They talked to one another and listened to the hall clock chiming the hours and the half-hours.

"Granny's gone to bed now," said Susan. "I heard her door click. It must be eleven o'clock."

It was. The clock struck eleven almost at once. The children talked again until midnight – and then, when the hall clock chimed, they slipped out of bed.

"Don't make a sound," said Jeffery. "If we drop anything on the floor it may waken Granny or Granpa."

So they were very quiet indeed. They were soon dressed. Jeffery took the slices of cake out of the drawer and they all ate them. The cake tasted delicious at that time of night!

"We had some supper after all," said John, with a grin.

They took their torches, and opened Susan's cupboard. The top of her secret stair was there, and one by one they crept down the tiny winding stairway to the dining room. They crept out of the dining room and went to the garden door at the side of the house. It was locked. They unlocked it and stepped outside.

"Good! There's a bright moon," said Jeffery. That was lucky. The moonlight lay on the ground like pools of silvery water, and everywhere was bright.

"Where is Rags?" asked Jeffery. Jane had taken him down with her at tea time, and he had not come back.

"In his kennel, I expect," said John. So they went to the kennel and there was Rags, staring at them in delighted astonishment. What! A walk at this time of night! Well, he was quite ready for it! He slipped out and joined the children.

"Now for a rope," said Jeffery. They went to Tipps' shed and shone their torches round. They soon found that there was quite a big coil in one corner. It was thick and strong, just what they wanted.

Jeffery picked it up. It was heavy. He flung it over his shoulder, and thought he could carry it quite easily like that. Then, with Rags at their heels, they set off for Timbles' Farm, for that was the shortest way to the ruined building.

They had to use their torches in the wood for it was dark there. They arrived at the hole, and pulled away the branches and bracken that covered it. Mr Potts had put them back, for he did not want anyone else to find the hole.

"I'll go down first," said Jeffery. He tied the rope

to a tree-trunk nearby, and then let the other end fall down the hole. Then he let himself carefully down the rope, swung on it, and slid down slowly to the ground below.

"Come on!" he shouted to the others, flashing his torch around. "There's a passage here. It smells a bit musty, but it's all right – not blocked up, or anything."

The other slid down the rope. Jeffery helped Susan, who was so excited that she might have fallen. They all three switched on their torches and looked around.

In front of them was a narrow passage, with the roof just above their heads.

"I believe it leads into that hill!' said Jeffery. "You know – the little humpy hill."

He was right – it did! The children followed the passage, which was very narrow in parts, and at last came out into a curious oblong room, hewn out of the very heart of the hill!

It was strange to stand there in the light of their torches, and look round at a room where no one had been for many, many years.

"This must have been a hiding-place for the Greylings at some time or other," said Jeffery. "In the old days people were often ill-treated because of their religion, and maybe this room was a hidey-hole for long-ago Greylings. It's a marvellous place – right in the heart of a wood – and in the heart of a hill!"

"Where is the Treasure, do you suppose?" asked John, looking round. They flashed their torches everywhere. The room was furnished very plainly with strong wooden benches and an old narrow table. On a shelf old plates and mugs still stood, dusty and cobwebby. The floor was tiled like the floor above. There was no fireplace at all.

"I can't see anywhere for Treasure to be hidden," said Jeffery. "I say! Wouldn't it be too disappointing to have come all this way, to the very end of the map, and find that the Treasure wasn't here after all!"

"Jeff, look – there's an old wooden door in that corner," said Susan suddenly. She shone her torch there and the boys saw what she meant. They had not noticed the door before, because the walls were of earth and the door was as brown as the earth.

"I say! I wonder if that's a cupboard or anything!" said Jeffery, in excitement. He went over to the door. It was fast shut, and seemed to be bolted on the other side.

"Funny!" said Jeffery. "How could it be bolted the *other* side. People wouldn't bolt themselves in a cupboard surely!"

"The door is as rotten as those steps were," said John. He aimed a kick at the lower part of the old door. It gave way and the wood broke at once. John kicked again, and soon there was an enormous hole in the door!

Jeffery put his hand in at the hole and felt about for bolts. He found them but they were too stiff to undo. So he and John kicked at the door until it had almost been kicked away, and the three children could easily squeeze through the hole.

It wasn't a cupboard. It was the entrance to another passage, a little wider than the first one, and leading in the opposite direction.

"Come in – let's see if we can find anything here," said Jeffery. He walked a few steps and then came to a stop. In his way, stopping up the passage, lay a great wooden box, with bands of iron round it. The lock had rusted, and the lid was loose.

The children shone their torches on it and looked at one another, very thrilled. Was it – could it be – the Treasure, at last?

CHAPTER 17

The Treasure at Last!

"I hardly dare to lift up the lid in case the box is empty!" said Jeffery, in a whisper. Nobody knew why he whispered, but it seemed the right thing to do. He lifted up the lid – and then, oh what a marvellous sight!

The Greylings Treasure lay in an old box! Somehow or other the dust and the damp had kept away from the box, and the Treasure shone undimmed. Great brooches, wonderful necklaces, jewelled pins – and loveliest of all, the wonderful Greylings cup made of pure gold, with its handle and the middle studded with precious stones! Jeffery lifted it out.

"Look!" he said. "Oh, look! The very cup that we saw pictured in that old book. The lucky-cup! It's been here for years and years. Oh, what will Granny say? She'll be rich! She won't need to sell Greylings after all!"

Susan began to jump up and down in excitement. She forgot that the roof was so near her head and she jumped right into it. But she was so happy that she didn't even feel the bump. She knelt down by the box and put her fingers among the jewels.

"Pearls for Granny! Brooches for Mummy! Lots of lovely things for everyone," she said. "Oooh! This is wonderful! How clever we are, aren't we, Jeffery?"

"I think we are rather," said Jeffery. "After all, people have been hunting for this lost Treasure for years and years – and now three children have found it!"

"Won't Mr Potts be angry when he hears that we got here first and found everything!" said John. "And he'll be angrier still when he finds that Granny won't need to sell her dear old house to him after all! Oh! I'm longing to get home and wake up Granny and Granpa and tell them everything!"

"Listen," said Jeffery suddenly. "What's that noise?"

They all listened. "It's Rags barking," said John, in surprise. "What's he barking at?"

"Suppose somebody is coming through the woods," said Susan, clutching Jeffery. "Suppose it's Mr Potts and the other man, coming at night? What will he say when he finds us here?"

Jeffery ran back into the oblong room, and then made his way down the first passage. He shone his torch up to the top of the entrance hole. Rags looked down, wagging his tail. He gave a short yelp.

"Is there somebody coming, Rags, old boy?" said Jeffery. "Come on down with me. Jump!"

Rags jumped into Jeffery's arms. He was very glad to be with his little master. Jeffery listened and at last heard something. It was the sound of people scrambling through the wood! In the silent night the sound could be heard very clearly.

Jeffery thought quickly. There was no time to get out. Was there any good hiding-place up the second passage for them? Could they take the Treasure with them and hide it? But how could they carry that heavy box?

He took out his pocket-knife and cut a good piece of loose rope from the rope that hung through the hole. It might be useful. Then, hearing voices coming nearer, he shot back to the others.

"Sounds like Potts and one or two more," he said. "Come on. Let's see if this passage has got any sort of hiding-place for us."

"How are we going to take the Treasure with us?" asked John.

Jeffery quickly tied the rope round the big box. He knotted it at the top, leaving two long ends, which he looped firmly. He gave one loop to John and took the other himself.

"We can carry the box between us," he said. "It's too heavy for one person – but we can easily carry it like this, swung on the rope."

"Good idea," said John. "Get out of the way, Rags, old boy. You don't want this box on your head!"

Susan had crept to the old room and had listened to see what was happening. She heard somebody at the entrance to the hole.

"Hallo! Look here!" came Mr Potts' voice. "Somebody's dropped a rope down. I didn't see it this morning, did you?"

"No," said another voice. "I suppose those kids aren't down there now, are they?"

"They'll be sorry for themselves if they are!" said Mr Potts, in an angry voice. "Making false maps and trying to throw us off the trail – stupid little idiots!"

Susan waited to hear no more. She fled up the second passage to tell the boys.

"Oh, here you are," said Jeffery impatiently. "We wondered where you were. Don't go disappearing like that just when we've got to escape."

Susan told the boys what she had heard. The three of them set off up the second passage, the boys carrying the box between them.

"I only hope this passage *leads* somewhere!" said Jeffery. The underground way ran straight for some time then turned to the left. It was dark, musty, and low. The three torches threw a bright light in the dark tunnel.

The passage suddenly split into two ways – one to the right and one going straight on.

"Blow!" said Jeffery. "Which way ought we to go, I wonder?"

John anxiously shone his torch up first one way and

then the other. "The right-hand way seems a bit wider," he said. "Let's go that way."

"Right," said Jeffery. "Susan, have you a handkerchief? Well, throw it down on the ground just a little way up the *other* passage, will you?"

"Whatever for?" asked Susan, in surprise.

"So that old Pots of Money will think we've gone up that way, and follow the wrong path," said Jeffery.

Susan laughed. "You *are* clever, Jeffery!" she said. She threw her little white handkerchief down on the ground a little way up the passage. Then the three of them, with Rags nuzzling against their legs, took the right-hand tunnel.

It went on for ages. Once they came to where part of the roof had fallen in, and had to climb over a heap of stones and earth.

"I feel like a rabbit running through a burrow," said Susan.

"With foxes behind us," said John.

"Oh, don't!" said Susan. "I hope Mr Potts has gone up the wrong passage."

Mr Potts had! He and his friends – there were two of them this time – had jumped down the hole, found the strange underground room, and squeezed through the broken door that led up the second passage. But when they came to the splitting of the ways, they caught sight of Susan's handkerchief, just as Jeffery had hoped they would.

"They've gone up there," said Mr Potts. And up the wrong passage they had gone! But before they had gone very far the passage came to an end in a small cupboard-like room, whose walls were of stone. It was quite empty, though, hundreds of years before, it had been used for storing and hiding many things.

By the time that Mr Potts and his friends had turned back and gone to follow the children's passage, the three treasure-finders had got a long way ahead.

"I simply can't *imagine* where this is leading us to," said Jeffery, putting down the box for a moment. It was really very heavy, and though the two boys were strong their arms were aching badly.

They went on again after a bit. Rags ran ahead, thinking that all this was a fine adventure! Every time he turned round his eyes gleamed like the head-lamps of a small car in the light of their torches.

Suddenly the passage came to an end – and facing the children were a few rough steps of stone.

"Hallo – look at this!" said Jeffery. "We've come somewhere at last."

John shone his torch overhead. The stone steps led to a square stone slab that lay flat in the earthy roof above their heads.

"Why, it looks as if there's a slab of stone at the entrance here, just like the one we moved," said Jeffery.

"But not nearly so big," said John. "Get up the steps, Jeff, and try to heave up the stone with me."

Both boys went up the steps. They bent double and heaved with their backs against the slab. It seemed to move a little.

"Jeffery! John! They're coming! I can hear them!" suddenly cried Susan. "We shall be caught. Oh, do hurry!"

There was the sound of voices and footsteps to be

heard a good way along the passage. Jeffery and John pushed at the stone slab with all their strength. Rags ran back along the passage, barking loudly and fiercely.

"That's right, Rags! Keep them there! Don't let them pass!" shouted Susan. Rags felt grand. He tore down the passage till he saw Mr Potts and his friend and then the plucky little dog stood in front of them, barking, growling, and showing his teeth. He would *not* let them pass!

The children heard Mr Potts' voice shouting to them.

"You naughty children! What are you doing here at this time of night? Call your dog off. He's making himself a nuisance!"

The children didn't say a word. Jeffery heaved up with all his might – and the roots of the grasses that had been clinging to the stone slab and keeping it tightly in place, all gave way. The stone lifted up – and Jeffery put his head out into the cool night air!

"Golly! It's open!" said John, thrilled. "Just in time too! Come on, Jeff – hand out the box. Susan, come along. Leave Rags there to bark and give us a start!"

The children all climbed out of the hole. They stood there in the bright moonlight for a moment, wondering where they were. And then Jeffery suddenly knew!

"We're near Timbles' Farm!" he cried. "Look – there it is, down there, beyond the field gate. Do you know where we are – we've come up inside that funny little ruined stone hut we saw the other day in the field. We wondered what it was! Fancy! There's an underground way between the old building in the wood and this one – and we've found it!''

"Oh, do come on," said John, who was very much afraid of being caught. "Let's go down to the farm and wake Mrs Timbles up. She'll look after us!''

"Come on then," said Jeffery, thinking it would be very nice to see plump Mrs Timbles. They half-stumbled, half-ran down the slope of the field, the boys still carrying the box between them.

When they came to the pig-sty, Jeffery put the box down. "Let's hide the Treasure here," he said. "Nobody would guess it was in a pig-sty!''

The others giggled. It seemed funny to hide treasure with the pigs – but as Jeffery said, no one would ever think of looking there!

So under the straw of the pig-sty went the old box. The pigs grunted sleepily in surprise. Jeffery stood up and stretched his tired back.

"Look! There are Mr Potts and friends," he said. "Let's go and wake the farmer! I feel as if I'd like a grown-up on our side now!''

CHAPTER 18

Safe at Timbles' Farm

In the bright moonlight the children could see the three men running over the sloping field. What the men were going to do the children couldn't imagine – perhaps they would take away the Treasure – perhaps they would be very angry indeed – they might march them all the way home, and tell some dreadful story to Granny and Granpa.

"Come on, let's bang on the farm door," said Jeffery. "No one will find the Treasure in the pig-sty."

They ran round the farmhouse, and Jeffery banged on the big knocker there. The sound thundered through the night. Crash! Crash! Crash!

A window was flung up and the farmer looked out in astonishment.

"Who's there?" he shouted.

"It's us!" shouted back Jeffery. "We're in trouble – somebody is chasing us. Let us in!"

"Good gracious – it's the Greylings children!" said Mrs Timbles' voice, and her head appeared by the side of the farmer's. "I'll go down and let them in, Fred."

In half a minute the big bolts were being drawn back, and the great wooden door was opened. The children pressed inside and Jeffery banged the door. He could see the three men coming up the path.

"Now, my dears, what is all this?" said Mrs Timbles, in the greatest astonishment. She looked very queer because she had on an enormous white night-gown, with a pink shawl thrown over it, and her hair was hanging loose round her plump red face.

Before the children could answer there came another knocking at the door. Mrs Timbles jumped.

"Bless us all!" she said. "Who's that now?"

The farmer came into the hall; he had pulled on his breeches, and put on some bedroom slippers. He looked just as amazed as his wife.

"Fred! There's someone at the door again!" said Mrs Timbles.

"Ay! I can hear them," said the farmer. "I'll open before they knock my door down."

The children went into the big kitchen with Mrs Timbles. She lighted the oil lamp, and poked the fire which still showed red.

"Why, you're shivering!" she said, looking at them. "You can't be cold this warm night."

"We're shivering with excitement," said Jeffery. "Oh, Mrs Timbles, take care of us, won't you?"

"Of course, of course," said Mrs Timbles, in still greater surprise. "You're safe here."

The farmer brought Mr Potts and his two friends into the kitchen. Mr Potts looked very angry. He glared at the three children, who stood close to fat Mrs Timbles.

"Now what's all this about?" asked Farmer Timbles, looking sternly at the three men. "Have you been frightening these children?"

"Let me explain," said Mr Potts. "I have bought Greylings Manor, and . . ."

"You haven't bought it yet!" said Jeffery.

"Don't interrupt, my boy!" said Mr Potts. "The final papers are being signed tomorrow – but I regard myself as the owner of Greylings lands now. Everything is settled."

"Well, what's all that got to do with you being out at this time of night?" asked Farmer Timbles.

"My friends and I are interested in the old ruins belonging to Greylings," said Mr Potts. "Naturally those belong to us, as well as the house and grounds. Well, we have been doing a little exploring, and these children have very strangely and rudely been trying to interfere with our affairs. My friend here is an authority on old books, china, jewellery, and so on, and I

305

have promised to let him have any old Greylings property to examine."

"You're not telling the story truthfully," said Jeffery, boiling with rage.

"My dear boy, don't be rude," said Mr Potts. "As you can see, Farmer, these children are quite out of hand. Well, we have been looking for some old things that belong to the property – and we have reason to believe that these children have stolen them tonight. This is a very serious matter, Farmer, as you will see – but if the children are willing to hand us back our property now, we will not make any more trouble about it."

"They didn't bring anything in here with them at all," said Mrs Timbles. "And let me tell you, sir, that these children are not the sort to steal! I never heard of such a thing!"

"Mrs Timbles! It was the Greylings Treasure we found!" said Jeffery. "It's Granny's and Granpa's! It doesn't belong to Mr Potts. We found it tonight! They were after it too – these three men!"

"The Greylings Treasure!" said Mrs Timbles, in the greatest surprise. "Well, I never did! The Greylings Treasure! Are you sure, Master Jeffery?"

"*Quite* sure," said Jeffery. "We looked it up in an old book, and saw the pictures of some of the things – and they were there, in the old box!"

"Well, my boy, you must let us have the box," said Mr Potts. "I tell you, I have bought Greylings, and anything found on the property is mine. You will get into serious trouble over this, if you don't give me what belongs to me."

"That's so," said one of the men.

"I don't care!" Jeffery almost shouted. "You shan't have it!"

"Well, Jeffery, give us the box to put somewhere safe just for tonight," said Mr Potts. "Then tomorrow we will all go into the matter with your Granny and Grandfather. You will see that I am right. Now, be a sensible boy and tell us where you put the Treasure."

"Well, lad, I think maybe you'd better do that," said Farmer Timbles. "If this gentleman *has* bought the property, you'd better be careful."

"I will *not* give up the Treasure!" said Jeffery.

"No, we won't!" cried Susan and John. They were all quite certain about that.

"Then we shall find it ourselves," said Mr Potts, looking furious. "And you will get into trouble, all three of you. I'll see that you do – you interfering little wretches!"

The men went into the hall and out of the front door. They began to hunt about in the moonlight for the box of Treasure. The children flew to the window of the front room and watched them. Would they look in the pig-sty?

They did go to it – but the sty smelt and the men didn't even open the gate. They did not think for one moment that the children would have chosen such a peculiar place!

Mr Potts suddenly grew tired of the search. "Come on," he said to the others. "We'll have something to say about this tomorrow!"

To the children's great delight they saw the three

men going away. Then, and not till then, did they pour out their extraordinary story to Mrs Timbles and the astonished farmer.

Jeffery and John went out to the pig-sty to get the box. It was covered with straw, and did not smell very nice – but who cared for that! How the children enjoyed Farmer Timbles' surprise when they opened the box and displayed the marvellous things inside! Mrs Timbles too, could not believe her eyes. She would not even touch the things – she just stared and stared at them, saying, "I never saw such a thing! Never in my life!" over and over again.

"So, you see, we've got the lost Treasure at last!" said Susan, jumping round the kitchen like a frog. "Isn't it awfully exciting, Mrs Timbles?"

"I never heard of such a thing!" said Mrs Timbles, and her plump face looked even redder than usual with the surprise and excitement.

"Well, I'm going to take you children back home," said Farmer Timbles, getting up.

"Oh, couldn't the little things stay here for the night?" said Mrs Timbles. "They'll be tired out."

Jeffery did not at all like being called a little thing, but he was so delighted at the thought of staying the night at the farm, that he felt he didn't mind anything. The children looked at the farmer anxiously.

"Well, let them stay if you want to," said Farmer Timbles. "I'm not wanting to dress and go out at this time of night! We will telephone to the Manor early tomorrow morning, before the children are missed."

So that night the children cuddled down in soft

goose-feather beds at Timbles' Farm. They were terribly excited and terribly tired – but very, very happy. They didn't care what Mr Potts said – the Treasure was theirs!

CHAPTER 19

Good Luck to the Greylings!

The children's grandparents were immensely astonished when the telephone rang early the next morning,
and the news was told to them. At first they simply
couldn't understand it – but when they heard Jeffery's
voice on the phone, telling them that he had found the
Treasure, the two old people sat down and stared at
one another in astonishment.

Farmer Timbles told his wife to give the children
some breakfast, but for once the three were really too
excited to eat anything. They swallowed down the

creamy coffee that kind Mrs Timbles made, and then begged the farmer to take them home in his pony-cart.

They were afraid of meeting Mr Potts on the way home! They wanted to get the Treasure safely to Greylings Manor. So Farmer Timbles put the fat brown pony in the little cart, and brought it round to the front door.

He and Jeffery put the box in the cart. Then they said goodbye to Mrs Timbles and climbed into the little cart themselves. It was a bit of a squash but nobody minded.

"Gee up there!" said Farmer Timbles, and the pony trotted down the farm lane. "Clickitty-clack, clickitty-clack," went her hooves.

Granny and Granpa were waiting excitedly for the children. They really couldn't believe it was true! They had telephoned to a friend of Granpa's, an old man who was very wise about long-ago things, and knew whether they were real or not.

He had arrived just before the children came. His name was Mr Frost, and his hair was as white as his name. He, too, was very excited, for if the children really had the old Greylings Treasure, it was very wonderful.

The pony-cart clattered up the drive. The children sprang out, and the farmer lifted the old box on to his shoulder. Granny opened the front door and the children rushed to meet her.

"Granny! We've got the Treasure!"

"Granny! We've had such an adventure!"

"We've found the Treasure, Granny!"

"What a noise!" said Granny, and she led the way

to the study, where Mr Frost sat talking to Granpa. Granpa had got out the old book that showed the Treasure, and he and Mr Frost were examining the pictures carefully.

Farmer Timbles put the old wooden box gently down on the table. "It's been in the pig-sty," he said, with his large smile. "I'm afraid it doesn't smell very good."

Nobody minded that! Granpa flung back the lid and everyone looked inside. For a moment there wasn't a sound to be heard. Then, to everyone's surprise, Granny began to cry! She cried quite quietly, and the tears rolled down her soft pink cheeks one after another.

"What's the matter, Granny?" asked Susan, in alarm, putting her arms round the old lady.

"Nothing, dear – just tears of happiness," said Granny. "It's so wonderful – just as we were thinking of selling Greylings, you find the Treasure!"

Mr Frost looked quite amazed. With his long thin fingers he took first one thing and then another out of the box. Soon the table was covered with precious jewels, and the wonderful golden cup shone in the midst of them.

"Yes," said Mr Frost, in a low voice, "yes! This is all old – very old. Wonderful stuff. Marvellous! And to think it has remained unspoilt and undiscovered all these years!"

"It is worth a lot of money?" asked Susan.

"It is worth a fortune!" said Mr Frost. "It is almost priceless! This cup alone is worth thousands of pounds."

"Ooooh!" said the children, and looked with wide eyes at the dull gold of the carved cup, with its precious rubies and sapphires shining and glowing around it.

"But I shan't sell this cup," said Granpa. "The famous Greylings cup, found after so many years! It is unbelievable! The lucky-cup is back where it belongs!"

"Granny, you won't have to sell Greylings now, will you?" asked John.

"No, we shan't," said Granny. "We shan't have to leave our dear old home – it will be your father's – and yours – and your children's!"

"Mr Potts said that it was his, last night," said Jeffery. "I knew he wasn't telling the truth."

"Well, he almost was," said Granpa. "Except for my signing one document, and Mr Potts signing another, the sale was completed. I'm not sure even now that we shall not have some difficulty in drawing back from the sale. We shall see what our lawyers say. I have no doubt that we shall find a way out all right."

"It seems to me that this man's strange behaviour will not sound too good when it is told to your lawyers," said Mr Frost suddenly. He had listened very carefully to all that the children had said. "I think, my dear sir, that you will find Mr Potts will not want anything said about his behaviour, and will not make any more trouble."

"He did make Jeffery fall into the lake," said Susan. "We are sure of that."

"Yes. He is not a charming friend to have at all!" said Mr Frost. "I shall be interested to hear what he has to say about all this."

313

Susan, who had been listening impatiently to all the talk, suddenly went quite mad! "But we've got the Treasure, the Treasure, the Treasure!" she yelled, dancing round like a top. "Nobody can take that away from us! It's ours, it belongs to the Greylings! Hurrah! Hurrah!"

She took up two pearl necklaces and hung them round her neck. She pinned two enormous brooches to the front of her frock. She put an enormous bracelet round her wrist, and took the golden cup into her hand.

Everyone watched her and laughed.

"*I've* got the Treasure! *I've* got the Treasure!" she sang, and danced round the room again. Just at that moment the door opened, and Jane showed in Mr Potts and his lawyer! Susan almost bumped into them.

Mr Potts stared at Susan in amazement when he saw all the jewellery she wore. "The Greylings Treasure!" he said. "So you *did* find it after all! I began to think last night, when we hunted round the farm for it, that you had made up the tale of finding it, just to annoy us!"

"It was in the pig-sty, the pig-sty, the pig-sty!" chanted Susan.

Mr Potts suddenly remembered Granny and Granpa and bowed stiffly to them.

"I have brought my lawyer to hand you my cheque for Greylings," he said. "And, Mr Greyling, as your property is now mine, I also claim the Greylings Treasure."

The children held their breath. What would Granpa say to that?

Granpa offered the box of cigarettes most politely to

Mr Potts. "I'm afraid," he said, "that there will be no sale. I can't accept your cheque, as now that the Treasure has been found, there is no need for me to part with Greylings Manor. I very much regret that you have been put to so much unnecessary trouble. I shall be pleased to pay you whatever sum our lawyers agree upon to make up for the trouble you have been put to."

"But this won't do, this won't do!" said Mr Potts, in a rage. "You can't get away with things like that! I'll soon show you that you can't behave like this to me."

"Mr Potts," said Granpa, in a voice like icy cold water, "if I have any nonsense from you, my lawyers will hear my grandchildren's tale of your very peculiar behaviour this last week – and I do not think you would want that made public. I quite understand your disappointment over the sale – and over the Treasure – but I do feel very glad that Greylings Manor is not going to belong to your family! I think, if I may say so, that it deserves a better fate!"

Mr Potts listened to all this with a furious face. He went red – and then white – and then red again. He tried to speak. He swallowed hard. He looked as if he were going to burst – and then, with a noise that sounded like the squawk of an angry hen, he stamped from the room. His lawyer followed him, looking worried.

The front door banged. There was the noise of a car being started up. It sounded as angry as Mr Potts had looked.

Then the car drove off down the drive. Everyone heaved a sigh of relief.

"Horrid man!" said John.

"I feel rather guilty about him," said Granpa. "The sale *was* almost completed – and I would have considered myself bound to go on with it, if it had been any other man. But I have heard such strange tales about Mr Potts lately that I feel he is not the right owner for Greylings – and now that I have heard how he has scared you children, and tried to get the Treasure for himself, before the sale was really completed, I am glad we have defeated him!"

"Oh, Granny! Oh, Granpa! Isn't everything lovely!" cried Susan, who was still wearing a great deal of jewellery. "Oh, I'm so happy! Greylings belongs to Greylings – and we can go on coming here as often as we like!"

"You certainly can!" said Granny, hugging the excited little girl. "You all deserve a reward for being so clever!"

"We've got our reward," said Jeffery. "We've got the Treasure. Oh, Granny, it *was* such fun hunting for it! You nearly stopped us finding it yesterday, though, when you sent us to our rooms!"

"Poor children!" said Granny. "No wonder you were late for lunch! You should have told us all that you were doing, and then we would have understood!"

"Well – it was rather fun having a secret," said John.

"Woof!" said Rags, who had been quite bewildered by all the excitement. He had hidden under the table, and now he came out and licked Jeffery's legs.

"Rags was a *great* help, Granny!" said John, patting the little dog. "We simply couldn't have done without him."

"I think," said Granpa, beaming round at everyone, "I think that such an exciting day needs a celebration – what about going out to the ice cream shop and ordering the largest and most delicious ices they have?"

"Oooh, good!" shouted the children – and off they all went in the car to eat chocolate, strawberry, and vanilla ices – and what do you think Granpa did? He had taken with him the golden Greylings cup – and he had it filled with iced ginger-beer at the shop!

"Now we must all drink from the lucky-cup!" he said. "Just as the Greylings did long years ago. And each year we must all meet and drink from it again, and we'll hope that good fortune and happiness will come to everyone of the Greylings family!"

Then all of them drank from it and said the same words – "Good luck to Greylings – and may it always belong to – a Greyling!"

Smuggler Ben

Smuggler Ben was first published in a single volume in
the U.K. in hardback in 1943 by T. Werner Laurie Ltd.
First published as part of *Mystery Stories* in hardback in
1976 by William Collins Sons & Co. Ltd, and in
paperback in 1982 in Armada.

Copyright © Enid Blyton 1943

CHAPTER ONE

THE COTTAGE BY THE SEA

Three children got out of a bus and looked around them in excitement. Their mother smiled to see their glowing faces.

"Well, here we are!" she said. "How do you like it?"

"Is this the cottage we're going to live in for four weeks?" said Alec, going up to the little white gate. "Mother! It's perfect!"

The two girls, Hilary and Frances, looked at the small square cottage, and agreed with their brother. Red roses climbed all over the cottage even to the chimneys. The thatched roof came down low over the ground floor windows, and in the thatch itself other little windows jutted out.

"I wonder which is our bedroom," said Hilary, looking up at the roof. "I hope that one is – because it will look out over the sea."

"Well, let's go in and see," said Mother. "Help with the suitcases, Alec. I hope the heavy luggage has already arrived."

They opened the white gate of Sea Cottage and went up the little stone path. It was set with orange marigolds at each side, and hundreds of the bright red-gold flowers looked up at the children as they passed.

The cottage was very small inside. The front door opened straight on to the little sitting room. Beyond was a tiny dark kitchen. To the left was another room, whose walls were covered with bookshelves lined with books. The children stared at them in surprise.

"The man who owns this house is someone who is interested in olden times," said Mother, "so most of these books are about long-ago days, I expect. They belong to Professor Rondel. He said that you might dip into any of the books if you liked, on condition that you put them back very carefully in the right place."

"Well, I don't think *I* shall want to do any dipping into these books!" said Hilary.

"No – dipping in the sea will suit *you* better!" laughed Frances. "Mother, let's see our bedrooms now."

They went upstairs. There were three bedrooms, one very tiny indeed. Two were at the front and one was at the back. A small one and a large one were at the front, and a much bigger one behind.

"I shall have this big one," said Mother. "Then if Daddy comes down there will be plenty of room for him, too. Alec, you can have the tiny room overlooking the sea. And you two girls can have the one next to it."

"That overlooks the sea, too!" said Hilary joyfully. "But, Mother – wouldn't *you* like a room that looks out over the sea? Yours won't."

"I shall see the sea out of this little side window," said Mother, going to it. "And anyway, I shall get a wonderful view of the moors at the back. You know how I love them, especially now when the heather is out."

The children gazed out at the moors ablaze with purple heather. It was really a lovely spot.

"Blue sea in front and purple heather behind," said Alec. "What can anyone want better than that?"

"Well – tea for one thing," said Frances. "I'm most terribly hungry. Mother, could we have something to eat before we do anything?"

"If you like," said Mother. "We can do the unpacking afterwards. Alec, there is a tiny village down the road there, with about two shops and a few fishermen's cottages. Go with the girls and see if you can buy something for tea."

They chattered down the narrow wooden stairway and ran out of the front door and down the path between the marigolds. They went down the sandy road, where blue chicory blossomed by the wayside and red poppies danced.

"Isn't it heavenly!" cried Hilary. "We're at the seaside – and the holidays are just beginning. We've never been to such a lovely little place before. It's much, much nicer than the big places we've been to. I don't want bands and piers and steamers and things. I only want the yellow sands, and big rocky cliffs, and water as blue as this."

"I vote we go down to the beach after tea, when we've helped Mother to unpack," said Alec. "The tide will be going out then. It comes right up to the cliffs now. Look at it splashing high up the rocks!"

The children peered over the edge of the cliff and saw the white spray flying high. It was lovely to watch. The gulls soared above their heads, making laughing cries as they went.

"I would love to be a gull for a little while," said Frances longingly. "Just think how glorious it would be to glide along on the wind like that for ages and ages. Sometimes I dream I'm doing that."

"So do I," said Hilary. "It's a lovely feeling. Well, come on. It's no good standing here when we're getting things for tea. I'm awfully hungry."

"You always are," said Alec. "I never knew such a girl. All right – come on, Frances. We can do all the exploring we want to after tea."

They ran off. Sand got into their shoes, but they liked it. It was all part of the seashore, and there wasn't anything at the sea that they didn't like. They felt very happy.

They came to the village – though really it could hardly be called a village. There were two shops. One was a tiny baker's, which was also the little post office. The other was a general store that sold everything from pokers to strings of sausages. It was a most fascinating shop

"It even sells foreign stamps," said Alec, looking at some packets in the window. "And look – that's a fine boat. I might buy that if I've got enough money."

Hilary went to the baker's. She bought a large crusty loaf, a big cake and some currant buns. She asked for their butter and jam at the other store. The little old lady who served her smiled at the children.

"So you've come to Sea Cottage, have you?" she said. "Well, I hope you have a good holiday. And mind you come along to see me every day, for I sell sweets, chocolates and ice creams, as well as all the other things you see."

"Oooh!" said Hilary. "Well, we'll certainly come and see you then!"

They had a look at the other little cottages in the village. Fishing nets were drying outside most of them. And one or two of them were being mended. A boy of about Alec's age was mending one. He stared at the children as they passed. They didn't know whether to smile or not.

"He looks a bit fierce, doesn't he?" said Hilary. They looked back at the boy. He did look rather fierce. He was very, very dark, and his face and hands were burnt almost black. He wore an old blue jersey and long trousers, rather ragged, which he had tied up at the ankles. He was barefooted, but beside him were big sea boots.

"I don't think I like him much," said Frances. "He looks rather rough."

"Well, he won't bother *us* much," said Alec. "He's only a fisherboy. Anyway, if he starts to be rough, *I* shall be rough, too — and he won't like that!"

"You wouldn't be nearly as strong as that fisherboy," said Hilary.

"Yes, I would!" said Alec at once.

"No, you wouldn't," said Hilary. "I bet he's got muscles like iron!"

"Shut up, you two," said Alec. "It's too lovely a day

325

to quarrel. Come on – let's get back home. I want my tea."

They sat in the garden to have their tea. Mother had brought out a table and stools, and the four of them sat there happily, eating big crusty slices of bread and butter and jam, watching the white tops of the blue waves as they swept up the shore.

"The beach looks a bit dangerous for bathing," said Mother. "I'm glad you are all good swimmers. Alec, you must see that you find out what times are best for bathing. Don't let the girls go in if it's dangerous."

"We can just wear swimming costumes, Mother, can't we?" said Alec. "And go barefoot?"

"Well, you won't want to go barefoot on those rocky cliffs, surely!" said Mother. "You can do as you like. But just be sensible, that's all."

"We'll help you to unpack now," said Hilary, getting up.

"Gracious, Hilary – you don't mean to say you've had enough tea yet?" said Alec, pretending to be surprised. "You've only had seven pieces of bread and jam, three pieces of cake and two currant buns!"

Hilary pulled Alec's hair hard and he yelled. Then they all went indoors. Mother said she would clear away the tea when they had gone down to the beach.

In half an hour all the unpacking was done and the children were free to go down to the beach. The tide was now out quite a long way and there was plenty of golden sand to run on.

"Come on!" said Alec impatiently. "Let's go. We won't change into swimming things now, it will waste time. We'll go as we are!"

So off they sped, down the marigold path, through the

white gate, and into the sandy lane. A small path led across the grassy cliff top to where steep steps had been cut in the cliff itself in order that people might get up and down.

"Down we go!" said Alec. "My word – doesn't the sea look grand. I've never seen it so blue in my life!"

CHAPTER TWO

A HORRID BOY — AND A DISAPPOINTMENT

They reached the beach. It was wet from the tide and gleamed brightly as they walked on it. Their feet made little prints on it that faded almost as soon as they were made. Gleaming shells lay here and there, as pink as sunset.

There were big rocks sticking up everywhere, and around them were deep and shallow pools. The children loved paddling in them because they were so warm. They ran down to the edge of the sea and let the white edges of the waves curl over their toes. It was all lovely.

"The fishing boats are out," said Alec, shading his

eyes as he saw the boats setting out on the tide, their white sails gleaming in the sun. "And listen — is that a motorboat?"

It was. One came shooting by at a great pace, and then another. They came from the big seaside town not far off where many trippers went. The children watched them fly past, the white spray flying into the air.

They wandered along by the sea, exploring all the rock pools, picking up shells and splashing in the edge of the water. They saw nobody at all until they rounded a rocky corner of the beach and came to a small cove, well hidden between two jutting-out arms of the cliff.

They heard the sound of whistling, and stopped. Sitting beside a small boat, doing something to it, was the fisherboy they had seen before tea.

He now had on his sea boots, a red fisherman's cap with a tassel hanging down, and a bright red scarf tied round his trousers.

"That's the same boy we saw before," said Alec.

The boy heard the sound of voices on the breeze and looked up. He scowled, and his dark face looked savage. He stood up and looked threateningly towards the three children.

"Well, he looks fiercer than ever," said Hilary, at last. "What's the matter with him, I wonder? He doesn't look at all pleased to see us."

"Let's go on and take no notice of him," said Alec. "He's no right to glare at us like that. We're doing no harm!"

So the three children walked into the hidden cove, not looking at the fisherboy at all. But as soon as they had taken three or four steps, the boy shouted at them loudly.

"Hey, you there! Keep out of this cove!"

The children stopped. "Why should we?" said Alec.

"Because it belongs to me," said the boy. "You keep out of this. It's been my cove for years, and no one's come here. I won't have you trippers coming into it and spoiling it."

"We're *not* trippers!" cried Hilary indignantly. "We're staying at Sea Cottage for a whole month."

"Well, you're trippers for a month then instead of for a day!" said the boy sulkily. "Clear off! I tell you. This is my own place here. I don't want anyone else in it. If you come here I'll set on you and beat you off."

The boy really looked so fierce that the children felt quite frightened. Then out of his belt he took a gleaming knife. That settled things for the two girls. They weren't going to have any quarrel with a savage boy who held such a sharp knife.

But Alec was furious. "How dare you threaten us with a knife!" he shouted. "You're a coward. I haven't a knife or I'd fight you."

"Alec! Come away!" begged Frances, clutching hold of her brother. "Do come away. I think that boy's mad. He looks it anyway."

The boy stood watching them, feeling the sharp edge of his knife with his thumb. His sullen face looked as black as thunder.

Frances and Hilary dragged Alec off round the rocky corner. He struggled with them to get free, and they tore his flannel shirt.

"Now look what you've done!" he cried angrily. "Let me go!"

"Alec, it's seven o'clock already and Mother said we were to be back by then," said Hilary, looking at her watch. "Let's go back. We can settle with that horrid boy another day."

Alec shook himself free and set off home with the girls rather sulkily. He felt that the evening had been spoilt. It had all been so lovely — and now that nasty boy had spoilt everything.

The girls told their mother about the boy, and she was astonished. "Well, he certainly does sound rather mad," she said. "For goodness' sake don't start quarrelling with him. Leave him alone."

"But, Mother, if he won't let us go into the little coves, it's not fair," said Hilary.

Mother laughed. "Don't worry about that!" she said. "There will be plenty of times when he's busy elsewhere, and the places you want to go to will be empty. Sometimes the people who live in a place do resent others coming to stay in it for a while."

"Mother, could we have a boat, do you think?" asked Alec. "It would be such fun."

"I'll go and see about one for you tomorrow," said Mother. "Now it's time you all went to bed. Hilary is yawning so widely that I can almost count her teeth!"

They were all tired. They fell into bed and went to sleep at once, although Hilary badly wanted to lie awake for a time and listen to the lovely noise the sea made outside her window. But she simply couldn't keep her eyes open, and in about half a minute she was as sound asleep as the other two.

It was lovely to wake up in the morning and remember everything. Frances woke first and sat up. She saw the blue sea shining in the distance and she gave Hilary a sharp dig.

"Hilary! Wake up! We're at the seaside!"

Hilary woke with a jump. She sat up, too, and gazed out to the sea, over which white gulls were soaring. She felt so happy that she could hardly speak. Then Alec appeared at the door in his swimming trunks. He had nothing else on at all, and his face was excited.

"I'm going for a dip," he said in a low voice. "Are you coming? Don't wake Mother. It's early."

The girls almost fell out of bed in their excitement. They pulled on swimming costumes, and then crept out of the cottage with Alec.

It was about half-past six. The world looked clean and new. "Just as if it has been freshly washed," said Hilary, sniffing the sharp, salt breeze. "Look at those pink clouds over there! And did you ever see such a clear blue as the sea is this morning. Ooooh – it's cold!"

It *was* cold. The children ran into the water a little way and then stopped and shivered. Alec plunged right under and came up, shaking the drops from his hair. "Come on!" he yelled. "It's gorgeous once you're in!"

The girls were soon right under, and the three of them spent twenty minutes swimming out and back, diving under the water and catching each other's legs, then floating happily on their backs, looking up into the clear morning sky.

"Time to come out," said Alec, at last. "Come on. Race you up the cliff!"

But they had to go slowly up the cliff, for the steps really were very steep. They burst into the cottage to find Mother up and bustling round to get breakfast ready.

At half-past seven they were all having breakfast. Afterwards Mother said she would tidy round the house

and then do the shopping. The girls and Alec must make their own beds, just as they did at home.

"When we are down in the village I'll make inquiries about a boat for you," promised Mother, when at last the beds were made, the kitchen and sitting room tidied and set in order. "Now, are we ready? Bring that big basket, Alec. I shall want that."

"Mother, we must buy spades," said Alec. "That sand would be gorgeous to dig in."

"Gracious! Aren't you too big to dig?" said Mother. The children laughed.

"Mother, you're not too big either! Don't you remember how you helped us to dig that simply enormous castle last year, with the big moat round it? It had steps all the way up it and was simply lovely."

They set off joyously, Alec swinging the basket. They did a lot of shopping at the little general store, and the little old lady beamed at them.

"Do you know where I can arrange about hiring a boat for my children?" Mother asked her.

"Well," said the old lady, whose name was Mrs Polsett, "I really don't know. We use all our boats hereabouts, you know. You could ask Samuel. He lives in the cottage over yonder. He's got a small boat as well as a fishing boat. Maybe he'd let the children have it."

So Mother went across to where Samuel was sitting mending a great fishing net. He was an old man with bright blue eyes and a wrinkled face like a shrivelled brown apple. He touched his forehead when Mother spoke to him.

"Have you a boat I could hire for my children?" Mother asked.

Samuel shook his head. "No, Mum," he said. "I have

got one, it's true – but I'm not hiring it out any more. Some boys had it last year, and they lost the oars and made a great hole in the bottom. I lost more money on that there boat than I made."

"Well, I'm sure my three children would be very careful indeed," said Mother, seeing the disappointed faces around her. "Won't you lend it to them for a week and see how they get on? I will pay you well."

"No, thank you kindly, Mum," said Samuel firmly.

"Is there anyone else who has a boat to spare?" said Alec, feeling rather desperate, for he had really set his heart on a boat.

"No one that I know of," said Samuel. "Some of us lost our small boats in a big storm this year, when the sea came right over the cliffs, the waves were so big. Maybe I'll take the children out in my fishing boat if they're well behaved."

"Thank you," said Hilary. But they all looked very disappointed, because going out in somebody else's boat wasn't a bit the same as having their own.

"We'll just go back to old Mrs Polsett's shop and see if she knows of anyone else with a boat," said Mother. So back they went.

But the old lady shook her head.

"The only other person who has a boat – and it's not much of a boat, all patched and mended," she said, "is Smuggler Ben."

"Smuggler Ben!" said Alec. "Is there a smuggler here? Where does he live?"

"Oh, he's not a real smuggler!" said Mrs Polsett, with a laugh. "He's my grandson. But he's just mad on tales of the old-time smugglers, and he likes to pretend he's one. There were smugglers' caves here, you know, somewhere about the beach. I dare say Ben knows them. Nobody else does now."

The children felt terribly excited. Smugglers — and caves! And who was Smuggler Ben? They felt that they would very much like to know him. And he had a boat, too. He would be a fine person to know!

"Is Smuggler Ben grown-up?" asked Alec.

"Bless you, no!" said Mrs Polsett. "He's much the same age as you. Look — there he goes — down the street there!"

The children turned to look. And as soon as they saw the boy, their hearts sank.

"It's the nasty boy with the knife!" said Hilary sadly. "*He* won't lend us his boat."

"Don't you worry about his knife," said old Mrs Polsett. "It's all pretence with him. He's just play-acting most of the time. He always wishes he could have been a smuggler, and he's for ever pretending he is one. There's no harm in him. He's a good boy for work — and when he wants to play, well, let him play as he likes, I say! He doesn't get into mischief like most boys do. He goes off exploring the cliffs, and rows in his boat half the time. But he does keep himself to himself. Shall I ask him if he'll lend you his boat sometimes?"

"No, thank you," said Alec politely. He was sure the boy would refuse rudely, and Alec wasn't going to give him the chance to do that.

They walked back to Sea Cottage. They felt sad about the boat — but their spirits rose as they saw their swimming costumes lying on the grass, bone-dry.

"What about another swim before lunch?" cried Alec. "Come on, Mother. You must come, too!"

So down to the sea they all went again, and by the squeals, shrieks and shouts, four people had a really wonderful time!

CHAPTER THREE

HILARY HAS AN ADVENTURE

One evening, after tea, Frances and Alec wanted to go
for a long walk. "Coming, Hilary?" they said. Hilary
shook her head.

"No," she said. "I'm a bit tired with all my swimming
today. I'll take a book and go and sit on the cliff top till
you come back."

So Alec went off with Frances, and Hilary took her
book and went to find a nice place to sit. She could see
miles and miles of restless blue sea from the cliff. It was
really marvellous. She walked on the cliff edge towards
the east, found a big gorse bush and sat down beside it
for shelter. She opened her book.

When she looked up, something nearby caught her eye. It looked like a little-worn path going straight to the cliff edge. "A rabbit path, I suppose," said Hilary to herself. "But fancy the rabbits going right over the steep cliff edge like that! I suppose there must be a hole there that they pop into."

She got up to look – and to her great surprise saw what looked like a narrow, rocky path going down the cliff side, very steep indeed! In a sandy ledge a little way down was the print of a bare foot.

"Well, *someone* has plainly gone down this steep path!" thought Hilary. "I wonder who it was. I wonder where it leads to. I've a good mind to find out!"

She began to go down the path. It really was very steep and rather dangerous. At one extremely dangerous part someone had driven in iron bars and stretched a piece of strong rope from bar to bar. Hilary was glad to get hold of it, for her feet were sliding down by themselves and she was afraid she was going to fall.

When she was about three-quarters of the way down she heard the sound of someone whistling very quietly. She stopped and tried to peer down to see who was on the beach.

"Why, this path leads down to that little cove we saw the other day!" she thought excitedly. "The one where the rude boy was. Oh, I hope he isn't there now!"

He was! He was sitting on his upturned boat, whittling at something with his sharp knife. Hilary turned rather pale when she saw the knife. It was all very well for old Mrs Polsett to say that her grandson was only play-acting – but Hilary was sure that Ben really felt himself to be somebody fierce – and he might act like that, too.

As she stood and watched him, unseen, she saw the

sharp knife slip. The boy gave a cry of pain and clutched his left hand. He had cut it very badly indeed. Blood began to drip on to the sand.

The boy felt in his pocket for something to bind up his hand. But he could find nothing. He pressed the cut together, but it went on bleeding. Hilary was tender-hearted and she couldn't bear to see the boy's face all screwed up in pain, and do nothing about it.

She forgot to be afraid of him. She went down the last piece of cliff and jumped down on the sand. The boy heard her and turned, his face one big scowl. Hilary ran up to him.

She had a big clean handkerchief in her pocket, and she took this out. "I'll tie up your hand for you," she said. "I say – what an *awful* cut! I should howl like anything if I did that to myself."

The boy scowled at her again. "What are you doing here?" he said. "Where are the others?"

"I'm alone," said Hilary. "I found that funny steep path and came down it to see where it led to. And I saw you cut your hand. Give it to me. Come on, Ben – hold it out and let me tie it up. You might bleed to death if you go on like this."

The boy held out his cut hand. "How do you know my name is Ben?" he said in a surly voice.

"Never mind how I know!" said Hilary. "You're Smuggler Ben! What a marvellous name! Don't you wish you really *were* a smuggler? I do! I'm just reading a book about smuggling and it's terribly exciting."

"What book?" asked the boy.

Hilary bound up his hand well, and then showed him the book. "It's all about hidden caves and smugglers coming in at night and things like that," she said. "I'll lend it to you if you like."

The boy stared at her. He couldn't help liking this little girl with her straight eyes and clear, kind little voice. His hand felt much more comfortable now, too. He was grateful to her. He took the book and looked through the pages.

"I'd like to read it after you," he said more graciously. "I can't get enough books. Do you really like smuggling and that kind of thing?"

"Of course," said Hilary. "I like anything adventurous like that. Is it true that there are smugglers' caves along this coast somewhere?"

The boy stopped before he answered. "If I tell you, will you keep it a secret?" he said, at last.

"Well – I could tell the others, couldn't I?" said Hilary. "We all share everything, you know, Alec and Frances and I."

"No, I don't want you to tell anyone," said the boy. "It's my own secret. I wouldn't mind sharing it with you, because you've helped me, and you like smuggling, too. But I don't want the others to know.

"Then don't tell me," said Hilary, disappointed. "You see, it would be mean of me to keep an exciting thing like that from the others. I just couldn't do it. You'd know how I feel if you had brothers and sisters. You just have to share exciting things."

"I haven't got any brothers or sisters," said the boy. "I wish I had. I always play alone. There aren't any boys of my age in our village – only girls, and I don't like girls. They're silly."

"Oh well, if you think that, I'll go," said Hilary, offended. She turned to go, but the boy caught her arm.

"No, don't go. I didn't mean that *you* were silly. I don't think you are. I think you're sensible. Let me tell you one of my secrets."

"Not unless I can share it with the others," said Hilary. "I'm simply longing to know – but I don't want to leave the others out of it."

"Are they as sensible as you are?" asked Ben.

"Of course," said Hilary. "As a matter of fact, Frances, my sister, is nicer than I am. I'm always losing my temper and she doesn't. You can trust us, Ben, really you can."

"Well," said Ben slowly, "I'll let you all into my secret then. I'll show you something that will make your stare! Come here tomorrow, down that little path. I'll be here, and just see if I don't astonish you."

Hilary's eyes shone. She felt excited. She caught hold of Ben's arm and looked at him eagerly.

"You're a sport!" she said. "I like you, Smuggler Ben. Let's all be smugglers, shall we?"

Ben smiled for the first time. His brown face changed completely, and his dark eyes twinkled. "All right," he said. "We'll all be. That would be more fun than playing alone, if I can trust you all not to say a word to any grown-up. They might interfere. And now I'll tell you one little secret – and you can tell the others if you like. I know where the old smugglers' caves are!"

"Ben!" cried Hilary, her eyes shining with excitement. "Do you really? I wondered if you did. Oh, I say, isn't that simply marvellous! Will you show us them tomorrow? Oh, do say you will."

"You wait and see," said Ben. He turned his boat the right way up and dragged it down the beach.

"Where are you going?" called Hilary.

"Back home in my boat," said Ben. "I've got to go out fishing with my uncle tonight. Would you like to come back in my boat with me? It'll save you climbing up that steep path."

"Oh, I'd love to!" said Hilary joyfully. "You know, Ben, we tried and tried to hire a boat of our own, but we couldn't. We were so terribly disappointed. Can I get in? You push her out."

Ben pushed the boat out on to the waves and then got in himself. But when he took the oars he found that his cut hand was far too painful to handle the left oar. He bit his lip and went a little pale under his tan.

"What's the matter?" said Hilary. "Oh, it's your hand. Well, let me take the oars. I can row. Yes, I can, Ben! You'll only make your cut bleed again."

Ben gave up his seat and the girl took the oars. She rowed very well indeed, and the oars cut cleanly into the water. The boat flew along over the waves.

"You don't row badly for a girl," said Ben.

"Well, we live near a river at home," said Hilary, "and we are often out in our uncle's boat. We can all row. So you can guess how disappointed we were when we found that we couldn't get a boat here for ourselves."

Ben was silent for a little while. Then he spoke again. "Well – I don't mind lending you my boat sometimes, if you like. When I'm out fishing, you can have it – but don't you dare to spoil it in any way. I know it's only an old boat, but I love it."

Hilary stopped rowing and looked at Ben in delight. "I say, you really are a brick!" she said. "Do you mean it?"

"I always mean what I say." said Ben gruffly. "You lend me your books – and I'll lend you my boat."

Hilary rowed all round the cliffs until she came to the beach she knew. She rowed inshore and the two got out. She and Ben pulled the boat right up the beach and turned it upside down.

"I must go now," said Ben. "My uncle's waiting for me. See you tomorrow."

He went off, and Hilary turned to go home. At the top of the beach she saw Frances and Alec staring at her in amazement.

"Hilary! Were you with that awful boy in his boat?" cried Frances. "However did you dare?"

"He isn't awful after all," said Hilary. "He's quite nice. He's got wonderful secrets – simply wonderful. And he says we can use his boat when he doesn't want it!"

The other two stared open-mouthed. They simply couldn't believe all this. Why, that boy had threatened them with a knife – he couldn't possibly be nice enough to lend them his boat.

"I'll tell you all about it," said Hilary, as they set off up the cliff path. "You see, I found a little secret way down to that cove we saw – and Ben was there."

She told them the whole story and they listened in silence.

"Things always happen to you, Hilary," said Frances rather enviously. "Well, I must say this is all very exciting. I can hardly wait till tomorrow. Do you really think Smuggler Ben will show us those caves? I wonder where they are? I hope they aren't miles away!"

"Well, we'll see," said Hilary happily. They went home hungry to their supper – and in bed that night each of them dreamt of caves and smugglers and all kinds of exciting things. This holiday promised to be more thrilling than they had imagined.

CHAPTER FOUR

AN EXCITING EVENING

The children told their mother about Ben. She was amused.

"So the fierce little boy has turned out to be quite ordinary after all!" she said. "Well, I must say I'm glad. I didn't very much like to think of a little savage rushing about the shore armed with a sharp knife. I think it's very nice of him to lend you his boat. You had better bring him in to a meal, and then I can see him for myself."

"Oh, thanks, Mother," said Hilary. "I say – do you think we could get ourselves some fishermen's hats, like

343

Ben wears – and have you got a bright-coloured scarf or sash that you could lend us, Mother? Or three, if you've got them. We're going to play smugglers, and it would be fun to dress up a bit. Ben does. He looks awfully grand in his tasselled hat and sash and big boots."

"Hilary, you don't seriously think I am going to hand you out all my precious scarves, do you?" said Mother. "I'll give you some money to go and buy three cheap hats and scarves with, if you like – and you can all wear your wellingtons if you want big boots. But I draw the line at getting you sharp knives like Ben. Look how even he cut himself today!"

The children were delighted to think they could buy something they could dress up in. The next morning they set off to Mrs Polsett's and asked to see fishermen's hats. She had a few and brought them out. "I knitted them myself," she said. "Here's a red one with a yellow tassel. That would suit you fine, Miss Hilary."

So it did. Hilary pulled it on and swung the tasselled end over her left ear just as she had seen Ben do.

Frances chose a blue one with a red tassel and Alec chose a green one with a brown tassel. Then they bought some very cheap scarves to tie round their waists.

They went back home, pulled on their wellingtons, and put on their hats and sashes.

They looked grand.

Hilary showed them where the little narrow path ran down the steep cliff.

"Goodness," said Alec, peering over the edge. "What a terrifying way down! I feel half-afraid of falling. I'm sure I can never get down those steep bits."

"There's a rope tied there," said Hilary, going down

first. "Come on. Ben will be waiting. I saw his boat out on the water as we came along the cliff."

They all went down the path slowly for fear of falling. When they jumped down the last rocky step into the little cove, they saw Ben there waiting for them, sitting on his little boat. He was dressed just as they were, except that his boots were real sea boots, and he wore trousers tucked well down into them. He didn't move as they came up, nor did he smile.

"Hello, Ben!" said Hilary. "I've brought my brother and sister as you said I could. This is Alec, and this is Frances. I've told them what you said. We're all terribly excited."

"Did you tell them it's all a deep secret?" said Ben, looking at Hilary. "They won't give it away?"

"Of course we won't," said Alec indignantly. "That would spoil all the fun. I say – can we call you Smuggler Ben? It sounds fine."

Ben looked pleased. "Yes, you can," he said. "And remember, I'm the captain. You've got to obey my orders."

"Oh," said Alec, not liking this idea quite so much. "Well – all right. Lead on. Show us your secret."

"You know, don't you, that there really were smugglers here in the old days?" said Ben. "They came up the coast quietly on dark nights, bringing in all kinds of goods. Folk here knew they came, but they were afraid of them. They used to take the goods to the old caves here, and hide them there till they could get rid of them overland."

"And do you really know where the caves are?" said Alec eagerly. "My word, Smuggler Ben – you're a wonder!"

Smuggler Ben smiled and his brown face changed at once. "Come on," he said. "I'll show you something that will surprise you!"

He led the way up the beach to the cliffs at the back. "Now," he said, "the entrance to the old caves is somewhere in this little cove. Before I show you, see if you can find it!"

"In the cove!" cried Hilary. "Oh, I guess we shall soon find it then!"

The three children began to hunt carefully along the rocky cliff. They ran into narrow caves and out again. They came to a big cave, went into that and came out again. It seemed nothing but a large cave, narrowing at the back. There were no more caves after that one, and the children turned in disappointment to Ben.

"You don't mean that these little caves and that one big one are the old smuggling caves do you?" said Hilary. "Because they are just like heaps of other caves we have seen at the seaside."

"No, I don't mean that," said Ben. "Now, you come with me and I'll show you something exciting."

He led them into the big cave. He took them to the right of it and then jumped up to a rocky ledge which was just about shoulder high. In half a moment he had completely disappeared! Hilary felt about up the ledge and called to him in bewilderment.

"Ben! Smuggler Ben! Where have you gone?"

There was no answer. The three children stared up at the ledge. Alec jumped up to it. He felt all along it, up and down and sideways. He simply couldn't imagine where Ben had gone to!

There was a low laugh behind them. The children turned in surprise – and there was Ben, standing at the entrance to the big cave, laughing all over his brown face at their surprise.

"Ben! What happened? Where did you disappear to? And how did you get back to the entrance without us seeing you?" cried Hilary. "It's like magic. Do tell us. Quick!"

"Well, I'll show you," said Ben. "I found it out quite by accident. One day I came into this cave and fell asleep. When I woke up, the tide was high and was already coming into the cave. I was trapped. I couldn't possibly get out, because I knew I'd be dashed against the rocks outside, the sea was so stormy."

"So you climbed up on to this ledge!" cried Hilary.

"Yes, I did," said Ben. "It was the only thing to do. I just hoped and hoped the sea wouldn't fill the cave up completely, or I knew I'd be drowned. Well, I crouched there for ages, the sea getting higher and higher up till it reached the ledge."

"Gracious!" said Frances, shivering. "You must have been afraid."

"I was, rather," said Ben. "Well, I rolled right to the back of the ledge, and put up my hand to catch hold of any bit of jutting-out rock that I could – and instead of knocking against rock, my hand went into space!"

"What do you mean?" said Alec in astonishment.

"Come and see," said Ben, and he took a torch out of his pocket. All the children climbed on to the ledge, and squeezed together there, watching the beam of Ben's torch. He directed it upwards – and then, to their amazement, they saw a perfectly round hole going upwards right at the far corner of the rocky ledge. It didn't look very big.

"See that?" said Ben. "Well, when I felt my hand

going up that hole I slid over to this corner and put my arm right up the hole. And this is what I found."

He shone his torch up the rounded hole in the rock. The three children peered up, one after another.

Driven into the rock were great thick nails, one above the other. "See those?" said Ben. "Well, I reckon they were put there by some old-time smuggler."

"Did you get up the hole?" asked Alec.

"You bet I did!" said Ben. "And pretty quick, too, for the sea was washing inches above the ledge by that time and I was soaked through. I squeezed myself up, got my feet on those nails – they're sort of steps up, you see – and climbed up the hole by feeling for the nails with my feet."

"Where does the hole lead to?" asked Frances in excitement.

"You'd better come and see," said Ben, with a sudden grin. The children asked nothing better than that, and at once Alec put his head up the hole. It was not such a tight fit as he expected. He was easily able to climb up. There were about twenty nails for footholds and then they stopped. There was another ledge to climb out on. The boy dragged himself there, and looked down.

"Can't see a thing!" he called. "Come on up, Smuggler Ben, and bring your torch."

"I'll give Hilary my torch," said Ben. "She can shine it for you up there when she's up, and shine it down for us to climb up by, too. Go on, Hilary."

So Hilary went up next with the torch – and when she shone it around her at the top, she and Alec gave a shout of astonishment.

They were on a ledge near the ceiling of a most enormous cave. It looked almost as big as a church to

"*Real* smugglers have been here!" said Hilary, in a whisper

the children. The floor was of rock, not of sand. Queer lights shone in the walls. They came from the twinkling bits of metal in the rocks.

"Frances! Hurry," cried Hilary. "It's marvellous here."

Soon all four children were standing on the ledge, looking down into the great cave. In it, on the floor, were many boxes of all kinds – small, big, square, oblong. Bits of rope were scattered about, too, and an old broken lantern lay in a corner.

"*Real* smugglers have been here!" said Hilary in a whisper.

"What are you whispering for?" said Alec with a laugh. "Afraid they will hear you?"

"No – but it all seems so mysterious," said Hilary. "Let's get down to the floor of the cave. How do we get there?"

"Jump," said Ben.

So they jumped. They ran to the boxes and opened the lids.

"No good," said Ben. "I've done that long ago. They're quite empty. I often come to play smugglers here when I'm by myself. Isn't it a fine place?"

"Simply marvellous!" said Alec. "Let's all come here and play tomorrow. We can bring candles and something to eat and drink. It would be gorgeous."

"Oooh, yes," said Hilary. So they planned everything in excitement, and then climbed back to the ledge, and down through the hole into the first cave. Out they went into the sunshine. Ben smiled as much as the rest.

"It's fun to share my secret with you," he told the others half-shyly. "It will be grand to play smugglers all together, instead of just by myself. I'll bring some sandwiches tomorrow, and some plums. You bring anything you can, too. It shall be our own secret smugglers' cave – and we're the smugglers!"

CHAPTER FIVE

YET ANOTHER SECRET

The next day the four children met together in the big
cave. They felt very thrilled as they climbed up the hole
and then jumped down into the smuggler's cave. They
had brought candles and food with them, and Alec had
bottles of home-made lemonade on his back in a leather
bag.

They played smugglers to their hearts' content. Ben
ordered them about, and called them "My men", and
everyone enjoyed the game thoroughly. At last, Alec sat
down on a big box and said he was tired of playing.

"I'd like something to eat," he said. "Let's use this big
box for a table."

They set the things out on the table. And then Hilary looked in a puzzled way at the box.

"What's up?" asked Alec, seeing her look.

"Well, I'm just wondering something," said Hilary. "How in the world did the smugglers get this big box up the small round hole to this cave? After all, that hole only just takes us comfortably – surely this box would never have got through it."

Frances and Alec stared at the box. They felt puzzled, too. It was quite certain that no one could have carried such a big box through the hole. They looked at Ben.

"Have you ever thought of that!" Alec asked him.

"Plenty of times," said Ben. "And, what's more, I know the answer!"

"Tell us!" begged Hilary. "Is there another way into this cave?"

Smuggler Ben nodded. "Yes," he said. "I'll show it to you if you like. I just wanted to see if any of my three men were clever enough to think of such a thing. Come on – I'll show you the other way in. Didn't you wonder yesterday how it was that I came back into the other cave after I'd disappeared up the hole?"

He stood up and the others rose, too, all excited. Ben went to the back of the cave. It seemed to the children as if the wall there was quite continuous – but it wasn't. There was a fold in it – and in the fold was a passage! It was wide, but low, and the children had to crouch down almost double to get into it. But almost immediately it rose high and they could stand. Smuggler Ben switched on his torch, and the children saw that the passage was quite short and led into yet another cave. This was small and ran right down to the rocky side of the cliff very steeply, more like a wide passage than a cave.

The children went down the long cave and came to a rocky inlet of water. "When the tide comes in, it sweeps right through this cave," said Ben, "and I reckon that this is where the smugglers brought in their goods – by boat. The boat would be guided into this watery passage at high tide, and beached at the far end, where the tide didn't reach. Then the things could easily be taken into the big cave. The smugglers left a way of escape for themselves down the hole we climbed through from the first cave – you know, where the nails are driven into the rock."

"This gets more and more exciting!" said Alec. "Anything more, Ben? Don't keep it from us. Tell us everything!"

"Well, there is one thing more," said Ben, "but it just beats me. Maybe the four of us together could do something about it though. Come along and I'll show you."

He led them back to the little passage between the big cave and the one they were in. He climbed up the wall a little way and then disappeared. The others followed him.

There was another passage leading off into the darkness there, back into the cliff. Ben shone his torch down it as the others crowded on his heels.

"Let's go up it!" cried Alec excitedly.

"We can't," said Ben, and he shone his torch before him. "The passage walls have fallen in just along there – look!"

So they had. The passage ended in a heap of stones, soil and sand. It was completely blocked up.

"Can't we clear it?" cried Alec.

"Well, we might, as there are so many of us," said

Ben. "I didn't feel like tackling it all by myself, I must say. For one thing I didn't know how far back the passage was blocked. It might have fallen in for a long way."

"I wonder where it leads to," said Alec. "It seems to go straight back. I say – isn't this thrilling!"

"We'll come and dig it out tomorrow," said Hilary, her eyes dancing. "We'll bring our spades – and a sack or something to put the stones and soil in. Then we can drag it away and empty it."

"Be here tomorrow after tea," said Smuggler Ben, laughing. "I'll bring my uncle's big spade. That's a powerful one – it will soon dig away the soil."

So the next day the children crowded into the cave with spades and sacks. They used the ordinary way in, climbing up the hole by the nails and jumping into the cave from the high ledge. Then they made their way into the low passage, and climbed up where the roof rose high, till they came to the blocked-up passage. They went on by the light of their torches and came to the big fall of stones and soil.

"Now, men, to work!" said Smuggler Ben, and the gang set to work with a will. The boys shovelled away the soil and stones, and the girls filled the sacks. Then the boys dragged them down the passage, let them fall into the opening between the two caves, climbed down, dragged the sacks into the large cave and emptied them into a corner. Then back they went again to do some more digging.

"What's the time?" said Alec, at last. "I feel as if we've been working for hours. We mustn't forget that high tide is at half-past seven. We've got to get out before then."

Hilary looked at her watch. "It's all right," she said. "It's only half-past six. We've plenty of time."

"Gracious! Hasn't the time gone slowly!" said Frances in surprise. "Come on – we can do a lot more!"

They went on working, and after a time Ben began to feel rather uncomfortable. "Hilary, what's the time now?" he said. "I'm sure it must be getting near high tide."

Hilary glanced at her watch again. "It's half-past six," she said in surprise.

"But you said that before!" cried Ben. "Has your watch stopped?"

It had! Hilary held it to her ear and cried out in dismay. "Yes! It's stopped. Oh blow! I wonder what the right time is."

"Quick! We'd better go and see how the tide is," said Ben, and he dropped his spade and rushed to the entrance of the blocked-up passage. He dropped down and went into the big cave, and then climbed up to the ledge, and then down by the nail studded hole on to the ledge in the first cave.

But even as he climbed down to the ledge, he felt the wash of water over his foot. "Golly! The tide's almost in!" he yelled. "We're caught! We can't get out!"

He climbed back and stood in the big cave with the others. They looked at him, half-frightened.

"Don't be scared," said Smuggler Ben. "It only means we'll have to wait a few hours till the tide goes down. I hope your mother won't worry."

"She's out tonight," said Alec. "She won't know. Does the water come in here, Ben?"

"Of course not," said Ben. "This cave is too high up.

Well – let's sit down, have some chocolate and a rest, and then, we might as well get on with our job."

Time went on. The boys went to see if the tide was falling, but it was still very high. It was getting dark outside. The boys stood at the end of the long, narrow cave, up which the sea now rushed deeply. And as they stood there, they heard a strange noise coming nearer and nearer.

"Whatever's that?" said Alec in astonishment.

"It sounds like a motorboat," said Ben.

"It can't be," said Alec.

But it was. A small motorboat suddenly loomed out of the darkness and worked itself very carefully up the narrow passage and into the long cave, which was now full of deep water! The boys were at first too startled to move. They heard men and women talking in low voices.

"Is this the place?"

"Yes – step out just there. Wait till the wave goes back. That's it – now step out."

Ben clutched hold of Alec's arm and pulled him silently away, back into the entrance between the caves. Up they went in the blocked passage. The girls called out to them: "What's the tide like?"

"Sh!" said Smuggler Ben, so fiercely that the girls were quite frightened. They stared at Ben with big eyes. The boy told them in a whisper what he and Alec had seen.

"Something's going on," he said mysteriously. "I don't know what. But it makes me suspicious when strange motorboats come to our coasts late at night like this and run into a little-known cave. After all, our country is at war – they may be up to no good, these people. They may be enemies!"

All the children felt a shivery feeling down their backs when Ben said this. Hilary felt that it was just a bit *too* exciting. "What do you mean?" she whispered.

"I don't exactly know," said Ben. "All I know for certain is that it's plain somebody else knows of these caves and plans to use them for something. I don't know what. And it's up to us to find out!"

"Oooh! I wish we could!" said Hilary, at once. "What are we going to do now? Wait here?"

"Alec and I will go down to the beginning of this passage," said Ben. "Maybe the people don't know about it. We'll see if we can hear what they say."

So they crept down to the beginning of the passage and leaned over to listen. Three or four people had now gone into the big cave, but to Ben's great disappointment they were talking in a strange language, and he could not understand a word.

Then came something he *did* understand! One of the women spoke in English. "We will bring them on Thursday night," she said. "When the tide is full."

Another man answered. Then the people went back to their motorboat, and the boys soon heard the whirring of the engine as it made its way carefully out of the long, narrow cave.

"They're using that cave rather like a boathouse," said Ben. "Golly, I wonder how they knew about it. And what are they bringing in on Thursday night?"

"Smuggled goods, do you think?" said Alec, hot with excitement. "People always smuggle things in wartime. Mother said so. They're smugglers, Ben – smugglers of nowadays! And they're using the old smugglers' caves again. I say – isn't this awfully exciting?"

"Yes, it is," said Smuggler Ben. "We'd better come

here on Thursday night, Alec. We'll have to see what happens. We simply must. Can you slip away about midnight, do you think?"

"Of course!" said Alec. "You bet! And the girls, too! We'll all be here! And we'll watch to see exactly what happens. Fancy spying on real smugglers, Ben. What a thrill!"

CHAPTER SIX

A QUEER DISCOVERY

Mother was in by the time the children got back home, and she was very worried indeed about them.

"Mother, it's all right," said Alec, going over to her. "We just got caught by the tide, that's all, playing in caves. But we were quite safe. We just waited till the tide went down."

"Now listen, Alec," said Mother, "this just won't do. I shall forbid you to play in those caves if you get caught another time and worry me like this. I imagined you all drowning or something."

"We're awfully sorry, Mother," said Hilary, putting

her arms round her. "Really, we wouldn't have worried you for anything. Look – my watch stopped at half-past six, and that put us all wrong about the tide."

"Very well," said Mother. "I'll forgive you this time – but I warn you, if you worry me again like this you won't be allowed to set foot in a single cave!"

The next day it poured with rain, which was very disappointing. Alec ran down to the village to see what Ben was doing. The two girls talked excitedly about what had happened the night before.

"Mother says will you come and spend the day with us?" said Alec. "Do come. You'll like Mother, she's a dear."

The two boys went back to Sea Cottage. The girls welcomed them, and Mother shook hands with Ben very politely.

"I'm glad you can come for the day," she said. "You'd better go up to the girls' bedroom and play there. I want the sitting room to do some writing in this morning."

So they all went up to the bedroom above, and sat down to talk. "It's nice of Mother to send us up here," said Hilary. "We can talk in peace. What are our plans for Thursday, Captain?"

"Well, I don't quite know," said Ben slowly. "You see, we've got to be there at midnight, haven't we? – but we simply must be there a good time before that, because of the tide. You see, we can't get into either cave if the tide is up. We'd be dashed to pieces."

The children stared at Smuggler Ben in dismay. None of them had thought of that.

"What time would we have to be there?" asked Alec.

"We'd have to be there about half-past nine, as far as

I can reckon," said Ben. "Can you leave by that time? What would your mother say?"

"Mother wouldn't let us, I'm sure of that," said Hilary in disappointment. "She was so dreadfully worried about us last night. I'm quite sure if we told her what we wanted to do, she would say 'no' at once."

"She isn't in bed by that time, then?" said Ben.

The children shook their heads. All four were puzzled and disappointed. They couldn't think how to get over the difficulty. There was no way out of the cottage except through the sitting room door – and Mother would be in the room, writing or reading, at the time they wanted to go out. "What about getting out of the window?" said Alec, going over to look. But that was quite impossible, too. It was too far to jump, and, anyway, Mother would be sure to hear any noise they made.

"It looks as if I'll have to go alone," said Ben gloomily, "It's funny – I used to like doing everything all by myself, you know – but I don't like it now at all. I want to be with my three men!"

"Oh, Ben – it would be awful thinking of you down in those caves finding out what was happening – and us in our bed, wanting and longing to be with you!" cried Hilary.

"Well, I simply don't know what else to do," said Ben. "If you can't come, you can't. And certainly I wouldn't let you come after your mother had gone to bed, because by that time the tide would be up, and you'd simply be washed away as soon as you set foot on the beach. No – I'll go alone – and I'll come and tell you what's happened the next morning."

The children felt terribly disappointed and gloomy. "Let's go downstairs into the little study place that's lined with books," said Hilary, at last. "I looked into one of the books the other day, and it seemed to be all about this district in the old days. Maybe we might find some bits about smugglers."

Ben brightened up at once. "That would be fine," he said. "I know Professor Rondel was supposed to have a heap of books about this district. He was a funny man – never talked to anyone. I didn't like him."

The children went downstairs. Mother called out to them: "Where are you going?"

"Into the book room," said Hilary, opening the sitting room door. "We may, mayn't we?"

"Yes, but be sure to take care of any book you use, and put it back into its right place," said Mother. They promised this and then went into the little study.

"My word! What hundreds of books!" said Ben in amazement. The walls were lined with them, almost from floor to ceiling. The boy ran his eyes along the shelves. He picked out a book and looked at it.

"Here's a book about the moors behind here," he said. "And maps, too. Look – I've been along here – and crossed that stream just there."

The children looked. "We ought to go for some walks with you over those lovely moors, Ben," said Alec. "I'd like that."

Hilary took down one or two books and looked through them, too, trying to find something exciting to read. She found nothing and put them back. Frances showed her a book on the top shelf.

"Look," she said, "do you think that would be any good? It's called *Old-Time Smugglers' Haunts*."

"It might be interesting," said Hilary, and stood on a chair to get the book. It was big and old and smelt musty. The girl jumped down with it and opened it on the table. The first picture she saw made her cry out.

"Oh, look – here's an old picture of this village! Here are the cliffs – and there are the old, old houses that the fishermen still live in!"

She was quite right. Underneath the picture was written: "A little-known smugglers' haunt. See page 66."

They turned to page sixty-six, and found printed there an account of the caves in the little cove on the beach. "The best-known smuggler of those days was a dark, fiery man named Smuggler Ben," said the book. The children exclaimed in surprise and looked at Ben.

"How funny!" they cried. "Did you know that, Ben?"

"No," said Ben. "My name is really Benjamin, of course, but everyone calls me Ben. I'm dark, too. I wonder if Smuggler Ben was an ancestor of mine – you know, some sort of relation a hundred or more years ago?"

"Quite likely," said Alec. "I wish we could find a picture of him to see if he's like you."

But they couldn't. They turned over the pages of the book and gave it up. But before they shut it Ben took hold of it. He had an idea.

"I wonder if by chance there's a mention of that blocked-up passage," he said. "It would be fun to know where it comes out, wouldn't it?"

He looked carefully through the book. He came again to page sixty-six, and looked at it closely. "Someone has written a note in the margin of this page," he said, holding it up to the light. "It's written in pencil, very faintly. I can hardly make it out."

The children did make it out at last. "For more information, see page 87 of *Days of Smugglers*," the note said. The children looked at one another.

"That would be a book," said Alec, moving to the shelves. "Let's see who can find it first."

Hilary found it. She was always the sharpest of the three. It was a small book, bound in black, and the print was rather faded. She turned to page eighty-seven. The book was all about the district they were staying in, and on page eighty-seven was a description of the old caves. And then came something that excited the children very much. "Read it out, Ben, read it out!" cried Alec. "It's important."

So Ben read it out. "'From a well-hidden opening between two old smugglers' caves is a curious passage, partly natural, partly man-made, probably by the smugglers themselves. This runs steadily upwards through the cliffs, and eventually stops not far from a little stream. A well-hidden hole leads upwards on to the moor. This was probably the way the smugglers used when they took their goods from the caves, over the country.'"

The children stared at one another, trembling with excitement. "So that's where the passage goes to!" said Alec. "My word – if only we could find the other end! Ben, have you any idea at all where it ends?"

"None at all," said Ben. "But it wouldn't be very difficult to find out! We know whereabouts the beginnings of the passage are – and if we follow a more or less straight line inland till we come to a stream on the moors, we might be able to spot the hole!"

"I say! Let's go now, at once, this very minute!" cried Hilary, shouting in her excitement.

"Shut up, silly," said Alec. "Do you want to tell everyone our secrets? It's almost dinnertime. We can't go now. But I vote we go immediately afterwards!"

"Professor Rondel must have known all about those

caves," said Ben thoughtfully. "I suppose he couldn't have anything to do with the strange people we overheard last night? No – that's too far-fetched. But the whole thing is very strange. I do hope we shall be able to find the entrance to the other end of that secret passage."

Mother called the children at that moment. "Dinner!" she cried. "Come along, bookworms, and have a little something to eat."

They were all hungry. They went to wash and make themselves tidy, and then sat down and ate a most enormous meal. Ben liked the children's mother very much. She talked and laughed, and he didn't feel a bit shy of her.

"You know, Alec and the girls really thought you were going after them with that knife of yours," she said.

Ben went red. "I did feel rather fierce that day," he said. "But it's awful when people come and spoil your secret places, isn't it? Now I'm glad they came, because they're the first friends I've ever had. We're having a fine time."

Mother looked out of the window as the children finished up the last of the jam tarts.

"It's clearing up," she said. "I think you all ought to go out. It will be very wet underfoot but you can put on your wellingtons. Why don't you go out on the moors for a change?"

"Oh *yes*, we will!" cried all four children at once. Mother was rather astonished.

"Well, you don't usually welcome any suggestion of walking in the wet," she said. "I believe you've got some sort of secret plan!"

But nobody told her what it was!

CHAPTER SEVEN

GOOD HUNTING

After dinner the children put on their boots and macs. They pulled on their sou'westers, and said goodbye to their mother, and set off.

"Now for a good old hunt," said Ben. "First let's go to the cliff that juts over my little cove. Then we'll try to make out where the passage begins underground and set off from that spot."

It wasn't long before they were over the cove. The wind whipped their faces, and overhead the clouds scudded by. Ben went to about the middle of the cliff over the cove and stood there.

"I should say that the blocked-up passage runs roughly under here," he said. "Now let's think. Does it run quite straight from where it begins? It curves a bit, doesn't it?"

"Yes, but it soon curved back again to the blocked-up part," said Alec eagerly. "So you can count it about straight to there. Let's walk in a straight line from here till we think we've come over the blocked-up bit."

They walked over the cliff inland, foot-deep in purple-heather. Then Ben stopped. "I reckon we must just about be over the blocked-up bit," he said. "Now listen – we've got to look for a stream. There are four of us. We'll all part company and go off in different directions to look for the stream. Give a yell if you find one."

Soon Alec gave a yell. "There's a kind of stream here! It runs along for a little way and then disappears into a sort of little gully. I expect it makes its way down through the cliff somewhere and springs out into the sea. Would this be the stream, do you think?"

Everyone ran to where Alec stood. Ben looked down at the little brown rivulet. It was certainly very small.

"It's been bigger once upon a time," he said, pointing to where the bed was dry and wide. "Maybe this is the one. There doesn't seem to be another, anyway."

"We'll hunt about around here for an opening of some sort," said Alec, his face red with excitement.

They all hunted about, and it was Hilary who found it – quite by accident!

She was walking over the heather, her eyes glancing round for any hole, when her foot went right through into space! She had trodden on what she thought was good solid ground, over which heather grew – but almost at once she sank on one knee as her foot went through some sort of hole!

"I say! My foot's gone through a hole here," she yelled. "Is it the one! It went right through it. I nearly sprained my ankle."

The others came up. Ben pulled Hilary up and then parted the heather to see. Certainly a big hole was there – and certainly it seemed to go down a good way.

The children tugged away at armfuls of heather and soon got the tough roots out. The sides of the hole fell away as they took out the heather. Ben switched his torch on when it was fairly large. There seemed to be quite a big drop down.

"We'd better slide down a rope," he said.

"We haven't got one," said Alec.

"I've got one round my waist," said Ben, and undid a piece of strong rope from under his red belt. A stout gorse bush stood not far off, and Ben wound it round the strong stem at the bottom, pricking himself badly but not seeming to feel it at all.

"I'll go down," he said. He took hold of the rope and lay down on the heather. Then he put his legs into the hole and let himself go, holding tightly to the rope. He slid into the hole, and went a good way down.

"See anything?" yelled Alec.

"Yes. There *is* an underground channel here of some sort!" came Ben's voice, rather muffled. "I believe we're onto the right one. Wait a minute. I'm going to kick away a bit with my feet, and get some of the loose soil away."

After a bit Ben's voice came again, full of excitement.

"Come on down! There's a kind of underground

channel, worn away by water. I reckon a stream must have run here at some time."

One by one the excited children slipped down the rope. They found what Ben had said – a kind of underground channel or tunnel plainly made by water of some kind in far-off days. Ben had his torch and the others had theirs. They switched them on.

Ben led the way. It was a curious path to take. Sometimes the roof was so low that the children had to crouch down, and once they had to go on hands and knees. Ben showed them the marks of tools in places where rocks jutted into the channel.

"Those marks were made by the smugglers, I reckon," he said. "They found this way and made it into a usable passage. They must have found it difficult getting some of their goods along here."

"I expect they unpacked those boxes we saw and carried the goods on their backs in bags or sacks," said Frances, seeing the picture clearly in her mind. "Ooooh – isn't it strange to think that heaps of smugglers have gone up this dark passage carrying smuggled goods years and years ago!"

They went on for a good way and then suddenly came to an impassable bit where the roof had fallen in. They stopped.

"Well, here we are," said Ben, "we've come to the blocked-up part once more. Now the thing is – how far along is it blocked-up – just a few yards, easy to clear – or a quarter of a mile?"

"I don't see how we can tell," said Alec. The four children stood and looked at the fallen stones and soil. It was most annoying to think they could get no farther.

"I know!" said Hilary suddenly. "I know! One of us

"Yes, there *is* an underground channel here of some sort!"

could go in at the other end of the passage and yell. Then, if we can hear anything, we shall know the blockage isn't stretching very far!"

"Good idea, Hilary," said Ben, pleased. "Yes, that really *is* a good idea. I'd better be the one to go because I can go quickly. It'll take me a little time, so you must be patient. I shall yell loudly when I get up to the blocked bit, and then I shall knock on some stones with my spade. We did leave the spades there, didn't we?"

"We did," said Alec. "I say – this is getting awfully exciting, isn't it?"

Ben squeezed past the others and made his way up the channel. He climbed up the rope and sped off over the heather to the cliff side. Down the narrow path he went, and jumped down into the cove.

Meanwhile, the others had sat down in the tunnel, to wait patiently for any noise they might hear.

"It will be terribly disappointing if we don't hear anything," said Frances. They waited and waited. It seemed ages to them.

And then suddenly they heard something! It was Ben's voice, rather muffled and faint, but still quite unmistakable: "Helloooooooooo! Helloooooooooo!"

Then came the sharp noise of a spade on rock: Crack! Crack! Crack!

"Helloooooooooo!" yelled back all three children, wildly excited. "Helloooooooooo!"

"Come – and – join – me!" yelled Ben's voice. "Come – and – join – me!"

"Coming, coming, coming!" shouted Alec, Hilary and Frances, and all three scrambled back up to the entrance of the hole, swarming up the rope like monkeys.

They tore over the heather back to the cliff side and almost fell down the steep path. Down into the cove on the sand – in the big cave – up on to the ledge – up the nail-studded hole – out on the ledge in the enormous cave – down to the rocky floor – over to the passage between the two caves – up the wall – and into the blocked-up passage where Ben was impatiently waiting for them.

"You *have* been quick," he cried. "I say – I could hear your voices quite well. The blocked piece can't stretch very far. Isn't that good? Do you feel able to tackle it hard now? If so, I believe we might clear it."

"I could tackle anything!" said Alec, taking off his mac. "I could tackle the cliff itself!"

Everyone laughed. They were all pleased and excited, and felt able to do anything, no matter how hard it was.

"What's the time?" suddenly said Alec, when they had worked hard for a time, loosening the soil and filling the sacks. "Mother's expecting us in to tea, you know."

"It's quarter-past four already," said Hilary in dismay. "We must stop. But we'll come back after tea."

They sped off to their tea, and Mother had to cut another big plateful of bread and butter because they finished up every bit. Then off they went again, back to their exciting task.

"I say, I say, I say!" suddenly cried Alec, making everyone jump. "I've just thought of something marvellous."

"What?" asked everyone curiously.

"Well – if we can get this passage clear, we can come down it on Thursday night, from outside," said Alec. "We don't need to bother about the tides or anything. We can slip out at half-past eleven, go to the entrance on the moor and come down here and see what's happening!"

"Golly! I never thought of that!" cried Hilary.

Ben grinned. "That's fine," he said. "Yes – you can easily do that. You needn't disturb your mother at all. I think I'd better be here earlier, though, in case those people change their plans and come before they say. Though I don't think they will, because if they come in by motorboat, they'll need high tide to get their boat into the long cave."

The children went on working at the passage. Suddenly Ben gave a shout of joy.

"We're through! My spade went right through into nothing just then! Where's my torch?"

He shone it in front of him, and the children saw that he had spoken the truth. The light of the torch shone beyond into the other side of the passage! There was only a small heap of fallen earth to manage now.

"I think we'll finish this," said Alec, though he knew the girls were tired out. "I can't leave that little bit till tomorrow! You girls can sit down and have a rest. Ben and I can tackle this last bit. It will be easy."

It was. Before another half-hour had gone by, the passage was quite clear, and the children were able to walk up and down it from end to end. They felt pleased with themselves.

"Now we'll have to wait till Thursday," sighed Alec. "Gosh, what a long time it is – a whole day and a night and then another whole day. I simply can't wait!"

But they had to. They met Ben the next day and planned everything. They could hardly go to sleep on Wednesday night, and when Thursday dawned they were all awake as early as the sun.

CHAPTER EIGHT

THURSDAY EVENING

The day seemed very long indeed to the children – but they had a lovely surprise in the afternoon. Their father arrived, and with him he brought their Uncle Ned. Mother rushed to the gate to meet them as soon as she saw them, and the children shouted for joy.

Uncle Ned said he could stay a day or two, and Daddy said he would stay for a whole week.

"Where's Uncle Ned going to sleep?" asked Alec. "In my room?"

In the ordinary way the boy would have been very pleased at the idea of his uncle sleeping in the same room with him – but tonight a grown-up might perhaps spoil things.

"Ned will have to sleep on the sofa in the sitting room," said Mother. "I don't expect he will mind. He's had worse places to sleep in this war!"

Both Daddy and Uncle Ned were in the Army. It was lucky they had leave just when the children were on holiday. They could share a bit of it, too! All the children were delighted.

"I say – how are we going to slip out at half-past eleven tonight if Uncle Ned is sleeping in the sitting room?" said Hilary, when they were alone. "We shall have to be jolly careful not to wake him!"

"Well, there's nothing for it but to creep through to the door," said Alec. "And if he does wake, we'll have to beg him not to tell tales of us."

The night came at last. The children went to bed as usual, but not one of them could go to sleep. They lay waiting for the time to pass, and it passed so slowly that once or twice Hilary thought her watch must have stopped, but it hadn't.

At last half-past eleven came – the time when they had arranged to leave, to go to meet Ben in the passage above the caves. Very quietly the children dressed. They all wore shorts, jerseys, their smugglers' hats, sashes and rubber boots. They stole down the stairs very softly. Not a stair creaked, not a child coughed.

The door of the sitting room was a little open. Alec pushed it a little farther and put his head in. The room was dark. On the sofa Uncle Ned was lying, his regular breathing telling the children that he was asleep.

"He's asleep," whispered Alec, in a low voice. "I'll go

across first and open the door. Then you two step across quietly to me. I'll shut the door after us."

The boy went across the room to the door. He opened it softly. He had already oiled it that day, by Ben's orders, and it made no sound. A streak of moonlight came in.

Silently the three children passed out and Alec shut the door. Just as they were going through the door, their uncle woke. He opened his eyes – and to his very great amazement saw the figures of the three children going quietly out of the open door. Then it shut.

Uncle Ned sat up with a jerk. Could he be dreaming? He opened the door and looked out. No – he wasn't dreaming. There were the three figures hurrying along to the moor in the moonlight. Uncle Ned was more astonished than he had ever been in his life before.

"Now what in the world do these kids think they are doing?" he wondered. "Little monkeys slipping out like this just before midnight. What are they up to? I'll go after them and see. Maybe they'll let me join in their prank, whatever it is. Anyway, Alec oughtn't to take his two sisters out at this time of night!"

Uncle Ned pulled on a mackintosh over his pyjamas and set out down the lane after the children. They had no idea he was some way behind them. They were thrilled because they thought they had got out so easily without being heard!

They got to the hole in the heather and by the light of their torch slid down the rope. Uncle Ned was more and more amazed as he saw one child after another slide down and disappear completely. He didn't know any hole was there, of course. He found it after a time and decided to go down it himself.

Meanwhile, the children were halfway down the passage. There they met Ben, and whispered in excitement to him. "We got out without being seen – though our uncle was sleeping on the sofa near the door! Ben, have you seen or heard anything yet?"

"Not a thing," said Ben. "But they should be here soon, because it's almost midnight and the tide is full."

They all went down to the end of the passage, and jumped down to stand at the end of the long, narrow cave. This was now full of water, and the waves rushed up it continually.

"Easy enough to float any motorboat right in," said Ben. "I wonder what they're bringing."

"Listen!" said Hilary suddenly. "I'm sure I can hear something."

"It's the chug-chug of that motorboat again," whispered Alec, a shiver going down his back. He wasn't frightened, but it was all so exciting he couldn't help trembling. The girls were the same. Their knees shook a little. Only Ben was quite still and fearless.

"Now don't switch your torches on by mistake, for goodness' sake," whispered Ben, as the chugging noise came nearer. "We'll stay here till we see the boat coming into the long channel of this cave then we'll hop up into the passage and listen hard."

The motorboat came nearer and nearer. Then as it nosed gently into the long cave with its deep inlet of water, the engine was shut off.

"Now we must go," said Ben, and the four children turned. They climbed up into the passage above the caves and stood there, listening.

People got out of the motorboat, which was apparently

tied up to some rock. Torches were switched on. Ben, who was leaning over the hole from the passage, counted three people going into the big cave – two men and a woman. One of the men seemed somehow familiar to him, but he was gone too quickly for Ben to take a second look.

"Well, here we are," said a voice from the enormous cave below. "I will leave you food and drink, and you will wait here till it is safe to go inland. You have maps to show you how to go. You know what to do. Do it well. Come back here and the motorboat will fetch you a week from now."

The children listening above could not make out at all what was happening. Who were the people? And what were the two of them to do? Alec pressed hard by Ben to listen better. His foot touched a pebble and set it rolling down into the space between the caves. Before he could stop himself he gave a low cry of annoyance.

There was instant silence in the cave. Then the first voice spoke again very sharply: "What was that? Did you hear anything?"

A wave roared up the narrow cave nearby and made a great noise. Whilst the splashing was going on Ben whispered to Alec: "Move back up the passage, quick! You idiot, they heard you! They'll be looking for us in a minute!"

The children hurried back along the passage as quietly as they could, their hearts beating painfully. And half-way along it they bumped into somebody!

Hilary screamed. Frances almost fainted with fright. Then the somebody took their arms and said:

"Now what in the world are you kids doing here at this time of night?"

"Uncle Ned, oh, Uncle Ned!" said Hilary in a faint

voice. "Oh, it's marvellous to have a grown-up just at this very minute to help us! Uncle Ned, something very strange is going on. Tell him, Alec."

Alec told his astonished uncle very quickly all that had happened. He listened without a word and then spoke in a sharp, stern voice that the children had never heard before.

"They're spies! They've come over from the coast of Ireland. It's just opposite here, you know. Goodness knows what they're going to do – some dirty work, I expect. We've got to stop them. Now let me think. How can we get them? Can they get away from the caves except by motorboat?"

"Only up this passage, until the tide goes down," said Ben. "Sir – listen to me. I could slip down the hole and cast off the motorboat by myself. I know how to start it up. I believe I could do it. Then you could hold this passage, couldn't you, and send Alec and the girls back to get their father. You'd have to get somebody to keep guard outside the cave as soon as the tide goes down, in case they try to escape round the cliffs."

"Leave that to me," said Uncle Ned grimly. "Can you really get away in that motorboat? If you can, you'll take their only means of escape. Well, go and try. Good luck to you. You're a brave lad!"

Ben winked at the others, who were staring at him open-mouthed. Then he slipped along down the passage again until he came to the opening. He stood there listening before he let himself down into the space between the caves. It was plain that the people there had come to the conclusion that the noise they had heard was nothing to worry about, for they were talking together. There was the clink of glasses as the boy dropped down quietly to the floor below the passage.

"They're wishing each other good luck!" said the boy to himself, with a grin. He went to the motorboat, which was gently bobbing up and down as waves ran under it up the inlet of water in the cave. He climbed quietly in. He felt about for the rope that was tied round a rock, and slipped it loose. The next wave took the boat down with it, and as soon as he dared, Ben started up the engine to take her out of the deep channel in the cave.

He was lucky in getting the boat out fairly quickly. As soon as the engine started up, there came a shout from the cave, and Ben knew that the two men there had run to see what was happening. He ducked in case there was any shooting. He guessed that the men would be desperate when they saw their boat going.

He got the boat clear, and swung her out on the water that filled the cove. The boy knew the coast almost blindfold, and soon the little motorboat was chug-chug-chugging across the open sea towards the beach where a little jetty ran out, and where Ben could tie her up. He was filled with glee. It was marvellous to think he had beaten those men – and that woman, too, whoever she was. Spies! Well – now they knew what British boys and girls could do!

He wondered what the others were doing. He felt certain that Alec and the girls were even now speeding up the passage, climbing out through the heather and racing back home to waken their father.

And that is exactly what they *were* doing! They had left their uncle in the passage – and in his hand was his loaded revolver. No one could escape by that passage, even if they knew of it.

"Tell your father what you have told me, and tell him Ben has taken the boat away," he said. "I want men to guard the outer entrance of the caves as soon as the tide goes down. I'll remain here to guard this way of escape. Go quickly!"

CHAPTER NINE

THINGS MOVE QUICKLY

Alec and the two girls left their uncle and stumbled up the dark passage, lighting their way by their small torches. All three were trembling with excitement. It seemed suddenly a very serious thing that was happening. Spies! Who would have thought of that?

They went on up the passage. Soon they came to the place where the roof fell very low indeed, and down they went on their hands and knees to crawl through the low tunnel.

"I don't like that bit much," said Frances, when they were through it. "I shall dream about that! Come on –

we can stand upright again now. Whatever do you suppose Daddy and Mother will say?"

"I can't imagine," said Alec. "All I know is that it's a very lucky thing for us that Daddy and Uncle happened to be here now. Golly – didn't I jump when we bumped into Uncle Ned in this passage!"

"I screamed," said Hilary, rather ashamed of herself. "But honestly I simply couldn't help it. It was awful to bump into somebody strange like that in the darkness. But wasn't I glad when I heard Uncle Ned's voice!"

"Here we are at last," said Alec, as they came to where the rope hung down the hole. "I'll go up first and then give you two girls a hand. Give me a heave, Hilary."

Hilary heaved him up and he climbed the rope quickly, hand over hand, glad that he had been so good at gym at school. You never knew when things would come in useful!

He lay down on the heather and helped the girls up. They stood out on the moor in the moonlight, getting back their breath, for it wasn't easy to haul themselves up the rope.

"Now come on," said Hilary. "We haven't any time to lose. I shouldn't be surprised if those spies know about the passage and make up their minds to try it. We don't want to leave Uncle Ned too long. After all, it's three against one."

They tore over the heather, and came to the sandy lane where Sea Cottage shone in the moonlight. They went in at the open door and made their way to their parents' bedroom. Alec hammered on the door, and then went in.

His father and mother were sitting up in astonishment.

They switched on the light and stared at the three children, all fully dressed as they were.

"What's the meaning of this?" asked their father. But before he could say a word more the three children began to pour out their story. At first their parents could not make out what they were talking about, and their mother made the girls stop talking so that Alec could tell the tale.

"But this is unbelievable!" said their father, dressing as quickly as possible. "Simply unbelievable! Is Ned really down a secret passage, holding three spies at bay? And Ben has gone off with their motorboat? Am I dreaming?"

"No, Daddy, you're not," said Alec. "It's all quite true. We kept everything a secret till tonight, because secrets are such fun. We didn't know that anything serious was up till tonight, really. Are you going to get help?"

"I certainly am," said Daddy. He went to the telephone downstairs and was soon on to the nearest military camp. He spoke to a most surprised commanding officer, who listened in growing amazement.

"So you must send a few men over as quickly as possible," said Daddy. "The children say there are three men in the caves – or rather, two men and one woman – but there may be more, of course – and more may arrive. We can't tell. Hurry, won't you?"

He put down the receiver of the telephone and turned to look at the waiting children. "Now let me see," he said thoughtfully. "I shall want one of you to take me to where Ned is, and I must leave someone behind to guide the soldiers down to the cove. They must be there to guard the entrance to the caves, so that if the spies try to escape by the beach, they will find they can't. Alec, you had better come with me. Frances and Hilary, you can go with Mother and the soldiers, when they come, and show them the way down the cliff and the entrance to the caves. Come along, Alec."

The two set off. Alec talked hard all the way, for there was a great deal to tell. His father listened in growing astonishment. Really, you never knew what children were doing half the time!

"I suppose your mother thought you were playing harmless games of smugglers," he said, "and all the time you were on the track of dangerous spies! Well, well, well!"

"We didn't really know they were spies till tonight," said Alec honestly. "It was all a game at first. Look, Daddy – here's the hole. We have to slide down this rope."

"This really is a weird adventure," said his father, and down the rope he went. Alec followed him. Soon they were standing beside Uncle Ned, who was still in the passage, his revolver in his hand.

"There's been a lot of excited talking," he said in a low voice to his brother, "and I think they've been trying to find a way out. But the tide is still very high, and they daren't walk out on the sand yet. If they don't know of this passage, they won't try it, of course – but we'd better stay here in case they do. When are the soldiers coming?"

"At once," said Daddy. "I've left the two girls behind to guide them down to the cove. Then they will hide, and guard the entrance to the caves, that is as soon as the tide goes down enough."

"Do the spies know you're here, Uncle Ned?" asked Alec, in a low voice.

"No," said his uncle. "They know someone has gone off with their motorboat, but that's all they know. What about creeping down to the end of the passage to see if we can overhear anything? They might drop a few secrets!"

The three of them crept down to the end of the passage, and leaned out over the hole that led down to the space between the two caves. They could hear the waves still washing up the narrow channel in the long cave.

The two men and the woman were talking angrily. "Who could have known we were here? Someone has given the game away! No one but ourselves and the other three knew what we were planning to do."

"Is there no other way out?" said a man's impatient voice, very deep and foreign. "Rondel, you know all these caves and passages – or so you said. How did the old smugglers get their goods away? There must have been a land path they used."

"There was," said the other man. "There is a passage above this cave that leads on to the moors. But as far as I know it is completely blocked up."

"As far as you know!" said the other man, in a scornful voice. "Haven't you found out? What do you suppose you are paid for, Rondel? Aren't you paid for letting us know any well-hidden caves on this coast? Where is this passage? Do you know?"

"Yes, I know," said Rondel. "It's above this one, and the entrance to it is just between this cave and the one we used for the motorboat. We have to climb up a little way. I've never been up it myself, because I heard it was blocked up by a roof-fall years ago. But we can try it and see."

"We'd better get back up the passage a bit," whispered Alec's father. "If they come up here, we may have trouble. Get on to that bit where the big rock juts out and the passage goes round it. We can get behind that and give them a scare. They'll shoot if they see us. I don't want to shoot if I can help it, for I've a feeling they will be more useful alive than dead!"

Very silently the three went back up the passage to where a rock jutted out and the way went round it. They crouched down behind the rock and waited, their torches switched off. Alec heard their breathing and it sounded very loud. But they had to breathe! He wondered if Daddy and Uncle could hear his heart beating, because it seemed to make a very loud thump just then!

Meanwhile, the three spies were trying to find the entrance to the passage. Rondel had a powerful torch, and he soon found the hole that led to the ledge where the secret passage began.

"Here it is!" he said. "Look – we can easily get up there. I'll go first."

Alec heard a scrambling noise as the man climbed up. Then he pulled up the other two. They all switched on their torches and the dark passage was lighted up brightly.

"It seems quite clear," said the other man. "I should think we could escape this way. You go ahead, Rondel. We'll follow. I can't see any sign of it being blocked up, I must say! This is a bit of luck."

They went on up the passage, talking. They went slowly, and Alec and the others could hear their footsteps and voices coming gradually nearer. Alec's heart beat painfully and he kept swallowing something in his throat. The excitement was almost too much for him to bear.

The three spies came almost up to the jutting-out rock. And then they got the shock of their lives! Alec's father spoke in a loud stern voice that made Alec jump.

"Halt! Come another step, and we'll shoot!"

The spies halted at once in a panic. They switched off their torches.

"Who's there?" came Rondel's voice.

Nobody answered. The spies talked together in low voices and decided to go back the way they had come. They were not risking going round that rock! They didn't know how many people were there. It was plain that somebody knew of their plans and meant to capture them.

Alec heard the three making their way quietly back down the passage.

"Daddy! I expect they think the tide will soon be going down and they hope to make their escape by way of the beach," whispered Alec. "I hope the soldiers will be there in time."

"Don't you worry about that!" said his father. "As soon as the tide washes off the beach, it will be full of soldiers."

"I wish I could be there," said Alec longingly. "I don't expect the spies will come up here again."

"Well, you can go and see what's happening if you like," said Daddy. "Your uncle and I will stay here – but you can see if the soldiers have arrived and if the girls are taking them down to the cove."

Alec was delighted. More excitement for him, after all! He went up the passage and swarmed up the rope out of the entrance-hole. He sped over the moor to the cottage.

But no one was there. It was quite empty. "I suppose the soldiers have arrived and Mother and the girls have taken them to the cove," thought Alec. "Yes – there are big wheel-marks in the road – a lorry has been here. Oh – there it is, in the shade of those trees over there. I'd better hurry or I'll miss the fun!"

Off he dashed to the cliff edge, and down the narrow, steep path. Where were the others? Waiting in silence down on the beach? Alec nearly fell down the steep path trying to hurry! What an exciting night!

CHAPTER TEN

THE END OF IT ALL

Just as Alec was scrambling down the steep cliff, he heard the sound of a low voice from the top. "Is that you, Alec?"

Alec stopped. It was Ben's voice. "Ben!" he whispered in excitement. "Come on down. You're just in time. How did you get here?"

Ben scrambled down beside him. "I thought it was you," he said. "I saw you going over the edge of the cliff as I came up the lane. What's happened?"

Alec told him. Ben listened in excitement.

"So they know there's someone in the secret passage,"

he said. "They'll just have to try to escape by the beach then! Well, they'll be overpowered there, no doubt about that. I tied up the motorboat by the jetty, Alec. It's a real beauty – small but very powerful. It's got a lovely engine. Then I raced back to see if I could be in at the end."

"Well, you're just in time," said Alec. "I'm going to hop down on to the beach now and see where the others are."

"Be careful," Ben warned him. "The soldiers won't know it's you, and may take a pot shot at you."

That scared Alec. He stopped before he jumped down on to the sand.

"Well, I think maybe we'd better stay here then," he said. "We can see anything that happens from here, can't we? Look, the tide is going down nicely now. Where do you suppose the others are, Ben?"

"I should think they are somewhere on the rocks that run round the cove," said Ben, looking carefully round. "Look, Alec – there's something shining just over there – see? I guess that's a gun. We can't see the man holding it – but the moonlight just picks out a shiny bit of his gun."

"I hope the girls and Mother are safe," said Alec.

"You may be sure they are," said Ben. "I wonder what the three spies are doing now. I guess they are waiting till the tide is low enough for them to come out."

At that very moment Rondel was looking out of the big cave to see if it was safe to try and escape over the beach. He was not going to try to go up the cliff path, for he felt sure there would be someone at the top. Their only hope lay in slipping round the corner of the cove and making their way up the cliff some way off. Rondel knew the coast by heart, and if he only had the chance he felt certain he could take the others to safety.

The tide was going down rapidly. The sand was very wet and shone in the moonlight. Now and again a big wave swept up the beach, but the power behind it was gone. It could not dash anyone against the rocks now. Rondel turned to his two companions and spoke to them in a low voice.

"Now's our chance. We shall have to try the beach whilst our enemies think the tide is still high. Take hold of Gretel's hand, Otto, in case a wave comes. Follow me. Keep as close to the cliff as possible in case there is a watcher above."

The three of them came silently out of the big cave. Its entrance lay in darkness and they looked like deep black shadows as they moved quietly to the left of the cave. They made their way round the rocks, stopping as a big wave came splashing up the smooth sand. It swept round their feet, but no higher. Then it ran back down the sand again to the sea, and the three moved on once more.

Then a voice rang out in the moonlight: "We have you covered! There is no escape this way! Hands up!"

Rondel had his revolver in his hand in a moment and guns glinted in the hands of the others, too. But they did not know where their enemies were. The rocks lay in black shadows, and no one could be seen.

"There are men all round this cove," said the voice. "You cannot escape. Put your hands up and surrender. Throw your revolvers down, please."

Rondel spoke to the others in a savage voice. He was in a fierce rage, for all his plans were ruined. It seemed as if he were urging the others to fight. But they were wiser than Rondel. The other man threw his revolver down on the sand and put his hands above his head. The woman did the same. They glinted there like large silver shells.

"Hands up, you!" commanded a voice. Rondel shouted something angry in a foreign language and then threw his gun savagely at the nearest rocks. It hit them and the trigger was struck. The revolver went off with a loud explosion that echoed round and round the little cove and made everyone, Rondel as well, jump violently.

"Stand where you are," said a voice. And out from the shadow of the rocks came a soldier in the uniform of an officer. He walked up to the three spies and had a look at them. He felt them all over to see if there were any more weapons hidden about them. There were none.

He called to his men. "Come and take them."

Four men stepped out from the rocks around the cove. Alec and Ben leapt down on to the sand. Mother and the two girls came out from their hiding place in a small cave. Ben ran up to the spies. He peered into the face of one of the men.

"I know who this is!" he cried. "It's Professor Rondel, who lived in Sea Cottage. I've seen him hundreds of times! He didn't have many friends – only two or three men who came to see him sometimes."

"Oh," said the officer, staring with interest at Ben. "Well, we'll be very pleased to know who the two or three men were. You'll be very useful to us, my boy. Now then – quick march! Up the cliff we go and into the lorry! The sooner we get these three into a safe place the better."

Alec's father and uncle appeared at that moment. They had heard the sound of the shot when Rondel's revolver struck the rock and went off, and they had come to see what was happening. Alec ran to them and told them.

"Good work!" said Daddy. "Three spies caught – and maybe the others they work with, too, if Ben can point them out. Good old Smuggler Ben!"

The three spies were put into the lorry and the driver climbed up behind the wheel. The officer saluted and took his place. Then the lorry rumbled off into the moonlit night. The four children watched it go, their eyes shining.

"This is the most thrilling night I've ever had in my life," said Alec, with a sigh. "I don't suppose I'll ever have a more exciting one, however long I live. Golly, my heart did beat fast when we were hiding in the cave. It hurt me."

"Same here," said Hilary. "Oh, Daddy – you didn't guess what you were in for, did you, when you came home yesterday?"

"I certainly didn't," said Daddy, putting his arm round the two girls and pushing them towards the house. "Come along – you'll all be tired out. It must be nearly dawn!"

"Back to Professor Rondel's own house!" said Alec. "Isn't it funny! He got all his information from his books – and we found some of it there, too. We'll show you if you like, Daddy."

"Not tonight," said Daddy firmly. "Tonight – or rather this morning, for it's morning now – you are going to bed, and to sleep. No more excitement, please! You will have plenty again tomorrow, for you'll have to go over to the police and to the military camp to tell all you know."

Well, that was an exciting piece of news, too. The children went indoors, Ben with them, for Mother said he had better share Alec's room for the rest of the night.

Soon all four children were in their beds, feeling certain that they would never, never be able to go to sleep for one moment.

But it wasn't more than two minutes before they were all sound asleep, as Mother saw when she peeped into the two bedrooms. She went to join Daddy and Uncle Ned.

"Well, I'd simply no idea what the children were doing," she told them. "I was very angry with them one night when they came home late because they were caught by the tide when they were exploring those caves. They kept their secret well."

"They're good kids," said Daddy, with a yawn. "Well, let's go to sleep, too. Ned, I hope you'll be able to drop off on the sofa again."

"I could drop off on the kitchen stove, I'm so tired!" said Ned.

Soon the whole household slept soundly, and did not wake even when the sun came slanting in at the windows. They were all tired out.

They had a late breakfast, and the children chattered nineteen to the dozen as they ate porridge and bacon and eggs. It all seemed amazingly wonderful to them now that it was over. They couldn't help feeling rather proud of themselves.

"I must go," said Ben, when he had finished an enormous breakfast. "My uncle is expecting me to go out fishing with him this morning. He'll be angry because I'm late."

But before Ben could go, a messenger on a motorbike

arrived, asking for the four children to go over to the police station at once. The police wanted to know the names of the men with whom Professor Rondel had made friends. This was very important, because unless they knew the names at once, the men might hear of Rondel's capture and fly out of the country.

So off went the four children, and spent a most exciting time telling and retelling their story from the very beginning. The inspector of the police listened carefully, and when everything had been told, and notes taken, he leaned back and looked at the children, his eyes twinkling.

"Well, we have reason to be very grateful to you four smugglers," he said. "We shall probably catch the whole nest of spies operating in this part of the country. We suspected it – but we had no idea who the ringleader was. It was Rondel, of course. He was bringing men and women across from Ireland – spies, of course – and taking them about the country either to get information useful to the enemy, or to wreck valuable buildings. He was using the old smugglers' caves to hide his friends in. We shall comb the whole coast now."

"Can we help you?" asked Ben eagerly. "I know most of the caves, sir. And we can show you Rondel's books, where all the old caves are described. He's got dozens of them."

"Good!" said the inspector. "Well, that's all for today. You will hear from us later. There will be a little reward given to you for services to your country!"

The children filed out, talking excitedly. A little reward! What could it be?

"Sometimes children are given watches as a reward,"

said Alec, thinking of a newspaper report he had read. "We might get a watch each."

"I hope we don't," said Hilary, "because I've already got one – though it doesn't keep very good time."

But the reward wasn't watches. It was something much bigger than that. Can you possibly guess what it was?

It was the little motorboat belonging to the spies! When the children heard the news, they could hardly believe their ears. But it was quite true. There lay the little motorboat, tied up to the jetty, and on board was a police officer with instructions to hand it over to the four children.

"Oh – thank you!" said Alec, hardly able to speak. "Thank you very much. Oh, Ben – oh, Ben – isn't it marvellous!"

It *was* marvellous! It was a beautiful little boat with a magnificent engine. It was called *Otto*.

"That won't do," said Hilary, looking at the name. "We'll have that painted out at once. What shall we call our boat? It must be a very good name – something that will remind us of our adventure!"

"I know – I know!" yelled Alec. "We'll call it *Smuggler Ben*, of course – and good old Ben shall be the captain, and we'll be his crew."

So *Smuggler Ben* the boat was called, and everyone agreed that it was a really good name. The children have a wonderful time in it. You should see them chug-chugging over the sea at top speed, the spray flying high in the air! Aren't they lucky!